SHAKESPEARE, MEMORY AND PERFORMANCE

'Remember thee?
Ay, thou poor ghost, while memory holds a seat
In this distracted globe.'

Hamlet's lines pun on the globe as both his skull and the Globe Theatre.
But what does memory have to do with Shakespeare and performances
past and present? This is the first collection of essays to provide a meeting
between the flourishing fields of memory studies and Shakespeare
performance studies. The chapters explore a wide range of topics, from
the means by which editors of Shakespeare plays try to help their readers
remember performance to the ways actors sometimes forget Shakespeare's
lines, from the evocative memories instilled in the archives of costumes to
the photographing of props that act as memories of performances past.
The fifteen contributors are leaders in the field of Shakespeare
performance studies and their consideration of the possibilities of the
subject opens up a rich new vein in Shakespeare studies.

PETER HOLLAND is McMeel Family Professor in Shakespeare Studies in
the Department of Film, Television and Theatre at the University of Notre
Dame. He was Director of the Shakespeare Institute, Stratford-upon-Avon
and Professor of Shakespeare Studies at the University of Birmingham (UK)
from 1997 to 2002, and prior to that was Judith E. Wilson Reader in Drama
and Theatre in the Faculty of English, University of Cambridge. He is Editor
of *Shakespeare Survey* (Cambridge) and General Editor of *Redefining British
Theatre History, Oxford Shakespeare Topics* (with Stanley Wells) and *Great
Shakespeareans* (with Adrian Poole). His books include *English Shakespeares*
(Cambridge, 1997) and, most recently, with Stephen Orgel, *From
Performance to Print in Shakespeare's England* (2006).

SHAKESPEARE, MEMORY AND PERFORMANCE

edited by

PETER HOLLAND

CAMBRIDGE
UNIVERSITY PRESS

CAMBRIDGE UNIVERSITY PRESS
Cambridge, New York, Melbourne, Madrid, Cape Town, Singapore, São Paulo

Cambridge University Press
The Edinburgh Building, Cambridge CB2 2RU, UK

Published in the United States of America by Cambridge University Press, New York

www.cambridge.org
Information on this title: www.cambridge.org/9780521863803

Cambridge University Press 2006

First published 2006

Printed in the United Kingdom at the University Press, Cambridge

A catalogue record for this publication is available from the British Library

ISBN-13 978-0-521-86380-3 hardback
ISBN-10 0-521-86380-5 hardback

Contents

List of illustrations

Notes on contributors

MICHAEL CORDNER is Ken Dixon Professor of Drama at the University of York and Director of the Writing and Performance programmes there. He is founding General Editor of Oxford English Drama, to which he has contributed two volumes: *Four Restoration Marriage Plays* and Richard Brinsley Sheridan's '*The School for Scandal*' *and Other Plays*. His most recent publications explore the relationships between Shakespearean editing and Shakespearean performance. He also regularly directs early modern plays – most recently, James Shirley's 1632 comedy, *Hyde Park*.

ANTHONY B. DAWSON Professor of English at University of British Columbia, has published several books, including a stage history of *Hamlet* for the Shakespeare in Performance series (1995) and *The Culture of Playgoing in Shakespeare's England* (2001, written with Paul Yachnin). He edited *Troilus and Cressida* for the New Cambridge Shakespeare (2003) and is currently at work on an edition of *Timon of Athens* (co-edited with Gretchen Minton) for the Arden 3 series.

MICHAEL DOBSON is Professor of Shakespeare Studies at Birkbeck College, University of London. He is theatre reviewer for *Shakespeare Survey*, a commentator on live Shakespeare for the BBC, and a regular contributor to the *London Review of Books*. His publications include *The Making of the National Poet* (1992), *England's Elizabeth* (with Nicola Watson, 2002), *The Oxford Companion to Shakespeare* (with Stanley Wells, 2001), the revised New Penguin *Twelfth Night* (2005), and *Performing Shakespeare's Tragedies Today* (2006). He has also edited *Wit at Several Weapons* for the *Complete Oxford Middleton*.

BARBARA HODGDON is Adjunct Professor of English at the University of Michigan. Her books include: *The Shakespeare Trade: Performances and Appropriations* (1998), *Henry IV, Part One: Texts and Contexts* (1997), *Henry IV, Part Two*, Shakespeare in Performance Series (1993), and *The End Crowns All: Closure and Contradiction in Shakespeare's History* (1991); she is the co-editor of the *Blackwell Companion to Shakespeare and Performance* (2005) and is currently editing *The Taming of the Shrew* for the Arden 3 Shakespeare series.

PETER HOLLAND is the McMeel Family Professor in Shakespeare Studies in the Department of Film, Television and Theatre at the University of Notre Dame. Among his books are *The Ornament of Action* (Cambridge University Press, 1979) and *English Shakespeares: Shakespeare on the English Stage in the 1990s* (Cambridge University Press, 1997). He is currently editing *Coriolanus* for the Arden 3 series. He is editor of *Shakespeare Survey* and general editor (with Stanley Wells) of *Oxford Shakespeare Topics* for Oxford University Press.

RUSSELL JACKSON holds the Allardyce Nicoll Chair in the Department of Drama and Theatre Arts at the University of Birmingham. His publications include (as editor) *The Cambridge Companion to Shakespeare on Film* (2000) and, with Jonathan Bate, *The Oxford Illustrated History of Shakespeare on Stage* (2nd edn, 2001). From 1993 to 2004 he reviewed Shakespeare productions at Stratford for *Shakespeare Quarterly*. His book on *Romeo and Juliet* appeared in the 'Shakespeare at Stratford' series from New Arden in 2003. He has worked as text adviser on stage, film and radio productions of Shakespeare, including all of Kenneth Branagh's Shakespeare films.

JOHN J. JOUGHIN is Professor of English Literature and Dean of Cultural, Legal and Social Studies at the University of Central Lancashire. He is editor of *Shakespeare and National Culture* (1997), *Philosophical Shakespeares* (2000) and joint editor with Simon Malpas of *The New Aestheticism* (2003).

DENNIS KENNEDY is Beckett Professor of Drama in Trinity College Dublin. His books include *The Oxford Encyclopedia of Theatre and Performance* (2003), *Looking at Shakespeare: A Visual History of Twentieth-Century Performance* (2nd edn, 2001), *Foreign Shakespeare* (1993), and *Granville Barker and the Dream of Theatre* (1985). He works internationally in the theatre, recently directing *Pericles* in Dublin and *As You Like It* in Beijing.

MARGARET JANE KIDNIE, Associate Professor of English at the University of Western Ontario, Canada, is the editor of Philip Stubbes, *The Anatomie of Abuses* and *Ben Jonson: 'The Devil is an Ass' and Other Plays*. She has co-edited *Textual Performances: The Modern Reproduction of Shakespeare's Drama*. She is currently editing *A Woman Killed with Kindness* for the Arden Early Modern Drama series, and writing a book on late-twentieth century performance and adaptation.

STEPHEN ORGEL is the Jackson Eli Reynolds Professor in the Humanities at Stanford. His most recent books are *Imagining Shakespeare* (2003), *The Authentic Shakespeare* (2002) and *Impersonations: The Performance of Gender in*

Shakespeare's England (Cambridge University Press, 1966). His many editions include *The Tempest* and *The Winter's Tale* in the Oxford Shakespeare, and *Macbeth, King Lear, Pericles, The Taming of the Shrew* and *The Sonnets* in the New Pelican Shakespeare, of which he and A. R. Braunmuller are general editors.

CAROL CHILLINGTON RUTTER, Professor of English at the University of Warwick, is the author of *Clamorous Voices: Shakespeare's Women Today* (1988) and *Enter the Body: Women and Representation on Shakespeare's Stage* (2001). General editor of the Shakespeare in Performance Series for Manchester University Press, she is co-author of *Henry VI in Performance* (forthcoming), has edited *Documents of the Rose Playhouse* (1984) for the Revels Plays Companion Library, and has written the Introduction to the Penguin *Macbeth* (2005). Her current project is *Shakespeare and Child's Play*.

ROBERT SHAUGHNESSY is Professor of Theatre at the University of Kent. His publications include *Representing Shakespeare: England, History and the RSC* (1994), *Shakespeare on Film: Contemporary Critical Essays* (1998), *Shakespeare in Performance: Contemporary Critical Essays* (2000) and *The Shakespeare Effect: A History of Twentieth-Century Performance* (2002). He is currently writing the volume on Shakespeare for the Routledge Critical Guides series and editing *The Cambridge Companion to Shakespeare and Popular Culture*.

BRUCE R. SMITH is Professor of English at the University of Southern California. Among his books are *Ancient Scripts and Modern Experience on the English Stage 1500–1700* (1988), *Homosexual Desire in Shakespeare's England* (1991), *The Acoustic World of Early Modern England* (1999) and *Shakespeare and Masculinity* (2000). His current work centres on passionate perception before Descartes.

STANLEY WELLS is General Editor of the Oxford Shakespeare and Chairman of the Shakespeare Birthplace Trust. He has published extensively on many aspects of Shakespeare and his contemporaries. Among his recent books are *Shakespeare: For All Time* (2002), *Looking for Sex in Shakespeare* (Cambridge University Press, 2004), and (with Paul Edmondson) *Shakespeare's Sonnets* (2004).

W. B. WORTHEN is Collegiate Professor of English at the University of Michigan. His books include *Shakespeare and the Force of Modern Performance*, *Shakespeare and the Authority of Performance, Modern Drama and the Rhetoric of Theater*, and *The Idea of the Actor*, as well as several edited collections, including *The Blackwell Companion to Shakespeare and Performance* (with Barbara Hodgdon), *Theorizing Practice: Redefining Theatre History* (with Peter Holland), and *Theatre History and National Identities* (with Helka Mäkinen and S. E. Wilmer).

Acknowledgements

In a volume considering memory, it seems especially important to acknowledge – and thereby remember – the help that made this possible. These chapters began as papers for a conference, 'Shakespeare: Remembering Performance', held at the University of Notre Dame in November 2004 as the Inaugural Conference for the McMeel Family Chair in Shakespeare Studies. It was an opportunity to celebrate John and Susan McMeel's generosity in endowing the chair but the speakers also remember the McMeels' stamina in attending all the papers over the two days of the event. The conference was funded by the Office of the Provost, by the Institute for Scholarship in the Liberal Arts and by the Dee and Jim Smith Endowment for Excellence in Shakespeare and Performance. The support of all three of these segments of the University is gratefully acknowledged here, together with the individuals who embodied those parts of the whole: Provost Nathan Hatch, Professor Julia Braungart-Rieker, then Director of ISLA, and Ted Smith, Chair of the Performing Arts Advisory Council and founder of the Dee and Jim Smith Endowment. I must also remember here, with great gratitude, the extraordinary and calm efficiency of Harriet Baldwin in all aspects of the organization of the event.

The inclusion of so many illustrations in this volume was made possible by a subvention from the Institute for Scholarship in the Liberal Arts, College of Arts and Letters, University of Notre Dame. My thanks to ISLA and to its Director, Gretchen Reydam-Schils. As always, working with Sarah Stanton at Cambridge University Press has been a real pleasure; she is, as so many Shakespeare scholars have had good cause to know and recall, the very best of editors, someone whose long experience and profound knowledge both of publishing and of Shakespeare studies have combined in a remarkable way to enable our work to appear better than it may at times deserve.

Finally, I remember here and thank my wife Romana Huk. At a dinner for new incumbents of endowed chairs at Notre Dame in 2002, I was so carried away when I was describing the importance of theatre during my speech of thanks that I completely forgot to say how much Romana means in my life, not least in every aspect of my work. I hope this act of remembrance here will, in a very small part, make up for that 'too much memorable shame'. She has been the sharer in every step towards the creation of this volume, a journey which began with our move to Notre Dame; as for years we have shared very nearly every experience of watching Shakespeare on stage together, my memories of Shakespeare and performance are now hers and hers mine. The sharing of memory is a recurrent theme of this volume; Romana knows, I hope, exactly how much the sharing of memory can be a sign of the deepest love.

Foreword

Stanley Wells

How, if at all, can we memorialize performance? How can we re-create for ourselves and for others the impact that great actors and productions have had upon us? To modern readers the instinct to do so seems to be a natural one, as understandable as that of a painter to preserve the memory of real or imagined visual experience. But it is of relatively recent development. Audiences of Shakespeare's time had great experiences in the theatre. A few of them wrote in generalized terms of the pleasures that they experienced.

> So have I seen, when Caesar would appear,
> And on the stage at half-sword parley were
> Brutus and Cassius; O, how the audience
> Were ravished, with what wonder went they thence,
> When some new day they would not brook a line
> Of tedious though well-laboured *Catiline*.

That is Leonard Digges in his revision of verses originally printed in the First Folio. But who among these ravished and wondering audiences felt the impulse to fix their memories with any detail or precision, either for themselves or for others, in either words or visual images? The only writer I can think of is Simon Forman, and his accounts of performances at the Globe are fragmentary and designed, it would seem, rather for his own practical purposes, to remind him to beware of rogues like Autolycus. But at least there is a hint in his account of seeing *Macbeth* of the emotional impact that an actor – was it Richard Burbage? – made upon his imagination.

> The next night, being at supper with his noblemen whom he had
> bid to a feast to the which also Banquo should have come, he began

xvii

to speak of 'noble Banquo', and to wish that he were there. And as he thus did, standing up to drink a carouse to him, the ghost of Banquo came and sat down in his chair behind him, and he turning about to sit down again saw the ghost of Banquo, which fronted him so that he fell into a great passion of fear and fury, uttering many words about his murder by which, when they heard that Banquo was murdered, they suspected Macbeth.

'A great passion of fear and fury' suggests that Forman was subliminally recalling Macbeth's description of life as 'a walking shadow' – the word was used for an actor – 'a poor player / That struts and frets his hour upon the stage, / And then is heard no more', a tale 'full of sound and fury' (5.5.23–6). And Forman's description, besides giving precise information about the staging of the scene – Banquo's ghost really did appear – suggests that Burbage or his successor in the role performed with a naturalistic simulation of true passion. This is rudimentary theatre criticism.

In painting and drawing there is even less – the *Titus Andronicus* sketch, result of who knows what impulse, and a few drawings, engravings, or paintings of actors – Richard Tarlton and Will Kemp, Richard Burbage, John Lowin and Nathan Field, for the most part formal, unrelated to performance, only the drawing of Tarlton with his pipe and tabor giving even a faint impression of what he might have looked like in action as a performer.

Things look up a bit at the Restoration but, although for example Samuel Pepys loved theatre and recorded many visits to plays, he, who was marvellously well placed to do so, made scarcely any attempt to analyse the sources of the pleasure he took in performances by his favourites, Thomas Betterton and Edward Kynaston, Nell Gwyn and Elizabeth Knepp. And pictorial illustration of Shakespeare in performance does not start until the early eighteenth century, as in the illustrations to Rowe's edition of 1709 and, a little later, in paintings by Hogarth. It is only when we arrive at the age of Garrick that writers and artists begin with any frequency to translate their pleasure in performance into artistic terms. The rise of performance criticism and of the attempt to represent stage action visually, we must deduce, is inextricably bound up with the development both of sensibility in response to the arts, and of literary and other techniques for recording and conveying these impressions. The rise of the periodical essay as a literary form, and the subsequent, partly consequent, development of newspaper criticism and of emotional biography and autobiography, provided techniques and channels for the literary exploration of the pleasure taken in performance by our earliest great writers on theatre, Charles Lamb, Leigh Hunt and William Hazlitt conspicuous among them, and so for the fact that we have far fuller impressions of the impact of performances from the late eighteenth century onwards than for those of earlier times. The performances of Sarah Siddons and John Philip Kemble, of Edmund Kean and Dora Jordan, reverberate in our imaginations because of what was written about them and, to a lesser extent, because of visual images and archival reports. But in all the verbal and visual records these performances have passed through the transfiguring power of the imaginations and intellects of those who witnessed them. This is both a weakness and a strength. It is a weakness because it removes objectivity. The lens through which we witness these performances can distort as well as record. The critics are writing for effect; they may be more interested in coining a flashy phrase than in recording objective truth. They may even be influenced by personal likes and dislikes or by mercenary motives, as Hunt, in his *Autobiography*, accused his colleagues of being: 'what the public took for a criticism on a play was a draft upon the box-office, or reminiscences of last Thursday's salmon and lobster-sauce'. And inevitably reviewers select. Hazlitt's description of Edmund Kean's death as Richard III is a literary construct just as Harlow's painting of Mrs Siddons as Lady Macbeth or Lawrence's of Kemble as Coriolanus is a subjective work of art. But their very subjectivity is in itself a strength as well as a weakness. We should gain no impression of the impact of the performances that gave rise to them if they did not at the same time tell us, or convey to us through the eloquence of their prose, or the power of their composition, something of the emotional and intellectual impact that they had upon their creators and which is the fundamental source of the value we place upon theatre.

Since the Romantic period, mechanical recording devices have transformed the historicization of performance. We can hear (if only through a horn scratchily) what Edwin Booth and Ellen Terry, Henry Irving and Beerbohm Tree sounded like – at least in the difficult conditions of the primitive recording studio. In more recent times performances by John Gielgud and Laurence Olivier, Judi Dench and Kenneth Branagh have been far more accurately caught. The coming of film, both silent and audible, added a new dimension. But it has not been all gain. Film is a medium in its own right, and one which, unlike theatre, creates an immutable text. If we think of it as a means of preserving performances of the past – and all performances belong to the past as soon as they are given – we are in danger of being deluded. Russell Jackson writes below of the 'desire on the part of audiences to be able to enjoy individual performances – Olivier's Richard III, for example – which have long since ceased to be available "live"'. I saw Olivier play Richard III on stage, and I know how that performance fed into his film made a few years later, and I can still see the film with pleasure and admiration, but it does not substitute in my memory for the performance that I saw when I was an undergraduate. As Dennis Kennedy writes in this volume, 'film and video are always partial witnesses, recording only what the camera can see or the operator has chosen to see, denying the force and atmosphere of live performance: they are transformatively false to what they appear to document'. At least Olivier's Richard III was fully translated into the film medium, unlike his Othello which I saw on stage in 1964. The filming of that performance, which took place in a studio over a period of only a few days, is more accurate as a record of the way the play was staged but it is infinitely less true to the audience's experience; a falsification because it remains a stage performance imperfectly translated to the medium of film, growing ever more dated with the passage of time. To see it with an audience of people who never saw Olivier in the theatre is acutely embarrassing.

For all the limitations of literary responses to performance, at least they record the impression created, if only on one individual, at the time the performance was given. Performance is not an objective phenomenon. It reaches out to an audience and is incomplete without the audience's reactions. It deserves to be judged by the impact it has in its own time, unaffected by changes in fashion – in styles of costume and haircuts, of vocal and gestural technique. If we are interested purely and simply in the external appurtenances of the theatrical event, then mechanical recording media may satisfy our needs. But if we want to know how it felt to be there, what it was like to be in the presence of Kean or Irving, Olivier or Edith Evans, the contribution made by the written word – assisted maybe by the visual artist – is indispensable.

Introduction

Peter Holland

Some things can be remembered rather too well. For Charles VI of France, contemplating the invasion of Henry V, the shame of the defeat at the battle of Crécy was 'too much memorable' (*Henry V* 2.4.53).[1] The adjective was one that fascinated Shakespeare in this play but only here: all four occurrences of the word 'memorable' in Shakespeare's works are in *Henry V*, as if there was something about its action, its mode of exploration of history that made the word especially, peculiarly appropriate. When, in the same scene, Exeter delivers to Charles the pedigree that marks Henry's claim to France, he names it 'this most memorable line' (88), a genealogical table that is both a full repository of the memories of the past, the processes of historiography out of which the lineage has been constructed, and something that can be remembered; it is an object that both enshrines and enables memory, a mnemonic aid that assists in the functioning of political, dynastic and imperialist memory. The paper, the sign of Henry's 'pedigree', documents, presumably accurately, what was known and what had been chosen to be remembered and recorded of the family line.

But memory can also become fallible and even oddly contingent on its own naming. After Agincourt is won, Fluellen asks Henry to think back to Crécy (just as the French King earlier had been unable to prevent himself remembering that defeat) and to the victor of the battle, his 'grandfather of famous memory', though he is misremembering this particular genealogy and should have said 'great-grandfather' (4.7.90). Fluellen creates a joint recall of the way, '[i]f your majesties is remembered of it, the Welshmen did good service in a garden where leeks did grow' (95–7). Henry wears the leek himself on St David's Day 'for a memorable honour' (102) and Gower tells Pistol later that this is 'an

[1] All quotations from Shakespeare are taken from William Shakespeare, *The Complete Works*, ed. Stanley Wells and Gary Taylor *et al.* (Oxford: The Clarendon Press, 1986).

ancient tradition, begun upon an honourable respect and worn as a
memorable trophy of predeceased valour' (5.1.67–9). But the wearing of
the leek on 1 March is usually held to commemorate a British victory over
the Saxons in 540 AD and there is no evidence whatsoever, apart from this
passage in *Henry V*, for the Welsh ever having done anything at Crécy in
a garden of leeks. The memory may have been current in Shakespeare's
time or, equally probably, it may have been invented by him, a creation
of something that we now remember within the play and beyond it, as
part of our knowledge of Shakespeare and, perhaps falsely, as some myth
of English and Welsh history. The act of commemoration, the communal
and visible remembering by a society of its own history, is here constructed on a myth that is, at the very least, fallible, a story potentially
made up in the very act of Fluellen's remembering it – and Fluellen is also
significantly the character who cannot remember Falstaff's name: 'the fat
knight with the great-belly doublet ... I have forgot his name' (4.7.46–8).
The naming of Fluellen himself is, of course, in a sense a commemorative
act, a political transformation and controlling diminution of the name
Llywelyn carried both by many kings and princes of Gwynedd (Wales),
including the last native-born Prince (Llywelyn yr Olaf), and by the
historical figure Dafydd ap Llywelyn of Brecon, the real 'Davy Gam
Esquire' (4.8.104), who died at Agincourt.[2] What is remembered and who
remembers it is a central feature of the play's activity.

   If Shakespeare's is some of the history that we remember, we do not
necessarily remember it as Shakespeare's. It has moved outside the plays
to become some popular construction of history itself. But Shakespeare is
a central part of Western cultural memory and it is difficult to think of
Shakespearean memory without also remembering performance. Sometimes, of course, the memory has come to occupy the lines themselves.
I cannot think of Fluellen, let alone read his lines, without hearing
Esmond Knight's voice from Olivier's 1944 film and seeing those
impossible, beetling eyebrows. I remember, too, how some Fluellens, in
the many productions of the play I have seen, have been memorable and
many have not; some have inscribed themselves – or, more actively, I have
consciously inscribed some – in my memory. The concerns of memory,
in other words, move from the acts of remembering within the plays to
the acts of remembering the plays themselves in performance. These

[2] On the Welsh background, see for example, Terence Hawkes, 'Bryn Glas' in Anua Loomba and
Martin Orkin, eds., *Post-Colonial Shakespeares* (London: Routledge, 1998), pp. 117–40 (pp. 133–5).

memories of performance may be as creatively inaccurate as Fluellen's may have been in turn created to be.

Beyond the performance, there may be other complex acts of cultural memory: Olivier's film, as propaganda, recalled – reminded its audience of the memory of – an invasion and a victory at a time when the summoning up of such memory was especially necessary – hence the willingness of the wartime Ministry to support its making. Its performance was itself a summoning of memory, both of Henry V and of Shakespeare, at a point when such memory might be predictive and supportive of future acts of nation. Further, to watch the film now is also to remember 1944, to see it as an anticipation of the Normandy landings, to embed it in the social memory of wartime cultural performance.

In the rapid stretching out of such ripples of acts of memory, ripples I have barely sketched here, there is an interlacing of the play with its varying cultural histories in ways that threaten to be all-consuming as if memory can be the key to unlock all the play's several mysteries. Memory has indeed become a distinctly fashionable topic in the humanities these days, moving far beyond the traditional boundaries of its concerns in departments of psychology, a set of conventional limits typified by the enormous *Oxford Handbook of Memory*.[3] There are dozens of studies that explore aspects of memory in history, sociology, narrative and all aspects of culture.[4] A number of major publishers run series specifically devoted to the topic, for example Routledge's *Studies in Memory and Narrative*. Important theorists and philosophers have made substantial pronouncements about it, as, for example, Paul Ricoeur's brilliant and complex *Memory, History, Forgetting*,[5] while Harald Weinrich's provocative study of forgetting in Western culture, *Lethe*, considers the manifestations of memory's inevitable concomitant.[6] There have been remarkable explorations of the history of memory, including investigations of medieval and early modern practices of memory, their mnemotechniques, like Mary Carruthers' groundbreaking *The Book of Memory*, Janet Coleman's

---

[3] Endel Tulving and Fergus I. M. Craik, eds., *The Oxford Handbook of Memory* (Oxford: Oxford University Press, 2000).

[4] See, for example, Richard Cándida Smith, ed., *Art and the Performance of Memory* (London: Routledge, 2002) or Susannah Radstone and Katharine Hodgkin, eds., *Regimes of Memory* (London; Routledge, 2003).

[5] (University of Chicago Press, 2004), first published in French in 2000 as *La Mémoire, l'histoire, l'oubli*.

[6] Harald Weinrich, *Lethe: The Art and Critique of Forgetting* (Ithaca: Cornell University Press, 2004), first published in German in 1997 as *Lethe: Kunst und Kritik des Vergessens*.

longer view in *Ancient and Medieval Memories* and Lina Bolzoni's fine *The Gallery of Memory*.[7]

Performance studies has, far from being immune, become a central player in the field with some of its most influential works of the last decade arising out of a profound contemplation of performance as cultural memory, for instance in Joseph Roach's powerful and wide-ranging *Cities of the Dead* or Peggy Phelan's superb and moving *Mourning Sex: Performing Public Memories*, or the complex functioning of theatre as a space of many kinds of acts of memory, for instance in Marvin Carlson's *The Haunted Stage: The Theatre as Memory Machine*.[8]

Surprisingly, Shakespeare studies and, in particular, Shakespeare performance studies have so far been (sub)disciplines which have tended to ignore the recent theorization of memory and investigation of its cultural and social practices, in spite of Shakespeare's own sustained concern with the functioning of memory. In an even more substantial way memory ought to be a matter of major concern to Shakespeare performance critics for memory is fundamental to the processes of performance, from the actors' remembering their lines, through the ways performances remember each other, to the ways in which audiences remember what they have seen – and Shakespeare performance critics are themselves members of those audiences, trying to make into memory the experience of theatre or film but encountering the crucial uncontrollability of memory and the inevitable torrent of forgetfulness.

This volume attempts to mark an inauguration of the study of memory in Shakespeare performance studies as a vital topic of debate. There has been some – and no doubt will be much more – work on Shakespeare and memory. To take only four examples, I recall John Kerrigan's elegant analysis of memory in *Hamlet*; Jonas Barish wrote, at the very end of his great career, on 'Remembering and Forgetting in Shakespeare'; the Deutsche Shakespeare Gesellschaft devoted the first Shakespeare-Tage at Weimar of the newly reunited society in 1993 to 'Shakespeare and memory'; as I write this, Garrett Sullivan's *Memory and Forgetting in English Renaissance Drama: Shakespeare, Marlowe, Webster* has just been

---

[7] Mary Carruthers, *The Book of Memory* (Cambridge: Cambridge University Press, 1990); Janet Coleman, *Ancient and Medieval Memories* (Cambridge: Cambridge University Press, 1992); Lina Bolzoni, *The Gallery of Memory* (Toronto: University of Toronto Press, 2001), first published in Italian in 1995 as *La stanza della memoria*; see also Mary Carruthers and Jan M. Ziolkowski, eds., *The Medieval Craft of Memory* (Philadelphia: University of Pennsylvania Press, 2002).

[8] Joseph Roach, *Cities of the Dead* (New York: Columbia University Press, 1996); Peggy Phelan, *Mourning Sex: Performing Public Memories* (London: Routledge, 1997); Marvin Carlson, *The Haunted Stage: The Theatre as Memory Machine* (Ann Arbor: University of Michigan Press, 2001).

published.[9] All four examples, fine in their own right, are concerned with issues of Shakespeare and memory that do not impinge directly on performance studies. To that extent, the concerns of this collection, while overlapping with such work, attempt to map out a different territory, substantially adjacent to or within the kinds of fields that such studies have investigated, a territory signalled by the three nouns in the book's title, Shakespeare *and* memory *and* performance, rather than the encounter of any two of the three.

In its quest to do so, *Shakespeare, Memory and Performance* has not sought to rein in too tightly the interests of its contributors. There will be time later, as the study of memory in Shakespeare performance develops, to establish narrower parameters for the work in subsequent studies and collections. Instead, the contributors were asked to take up the topic in whatever ways interested them. The result was remarkable both in the range of topics and in the complex interconnections, themselves oddly like memory synapses, between different chapters. The volume attempts cumulatively through its chapters, rather than initially through, say, this introduction or a brief given to the contributors, to define how the topic it studies might be defined and limited, charted and mined.

The five sections of the book are not, then, discrete and impermeable divisions in the topic but simply convenient markers for the closer connections between certain chapters. The first considers memory as a function of the playtexts' performances of their arguments and as an intersection with forms of early modern practices of memory (both physical and cultural). The second section considers how performance figures in the context of editing, the place where the Shakespeare text is now represented to be read in relation to performance. The third section considers how Shakespeare performance is remembered in the costumes and props of production and in the practice of an actor's remembering (and forgetting), while the fourth moves on to see how particular forms of Shakespeare performance (a film and a location) figure their own acts of memory (of an actor's stage performance or of a cultural meaning of classicizing status) as well as how they are able to be remembered. The final section investigates the technologies of recording seen both as means

---

[9] John Kerrigan, 'Hieronimo, Hamlet and Remembrance', *Essays in Criticism* 31 (1981), 105–26; Jonas A.Barish, 'Remembering and Forgetting in Shakespeare' in R. B. Parker and Sheldon P. Zitner, eds., *Elizabethan Theater: Essays in Honor of S. Schoenbaum* (Newark: University of Delaware Press, 1996), pp. 214–21; some of the papers from the 1993 Weimar Shakespeare-Tage were published in *Jahrbuch 1994* (= vol. 130 of *Shakespeare Jahrbuch West*); Garrett A. Sullivan, Jr, *Memory and Forgetting in English Renaissance Drama* (Cambridge: Cambridge University Press, 2005).

of structuring memory and as forms that themselves become integral parts of practices of performance that re-engage the text in reproducing its own structures of memory, looping the book's argument back to the place from which the opening essays had launched it. From the tables in which Hamlet records something he wishes to remember[10] to the fantasy of the Museum of Jurassic Technology, Shakespeare and performance intertwine in the processes of memory.

Bruce Smith is not sure what he remembers about *King Lear*. Some memories can be corroborated, some only half-remembered. Memories of performance may in some senses be verifiable: who played *King Lear* for the Royal Shakespeare Company in 1990 can be checked. Alongside the precision or imprecision of the performance details comes a sequence of feelings, feelings that define the memory of *King Lear*s seen. But the feelings the performance gave rise to cannot easily be connected with the vignettes of performance memory. The act of verification may confirm and order memory but it cannot confirm both the past and present feelings in the memory of performance, an object that will not stay still in order to be remembered. Indeed, as Smith explores the model of performance memory set out by a modern theorist of theatre like Patrice Pavis or early modern structures of memory adumbrated by Sir Philip Sidney in *The Defence of Poesie* or by Spenser in the Castle of Alma in Book Two of *The Faerie Queene*, what becomes striking is the mobility of memory. As early modern students of the brain imaged it, memory is always linked to movement, whether it is the subject who moves in the storehouses of memory or the memories that move, swimming about in 'the liquid vaporous substance' of the brain.

The movement of memory can then be traced – as Smith moves on to trace it – in the sequence that begins with Shakespeare's writing the script of the play and ends with 'the implicit claims of film and video to offer memory in an always accessible medium'. Shakespeare's writing contains and makes available certain kinds of memories of his sources, parts of *King Leir*, Shakespeare's source-play, forming, suppressed or manifest, a set of 'passions', as early modern psychologists would have termed them, things felt and then communicated, steps in a chain that existed for Shakespeare, for the actors of the King's Men and for their audiences, before Shakespeare began writing his own version of the narrative. As the

---

[10] For the mechanics of this process see Peter Stallybrass, Roger Chartier, J. Franklin Mowery and Heather Wolfe, 'Hamlet's Tables and the Technologies of Writing in Renaissance England' *Shakespeare Quarterly* 55 (2004), 379–419.

boy-actor worked with the cue-script for Cordelia, conning the part in order to remember it, he constructed a somatic experience of passions, just as passion dominates one of the play's afterlives in the ballad of King Lear, itself a kind of memory of Shakespeare's play, dating, in the earliest surviving printing, to 1620.

In print and performance *King Lear* negotiates with differing kinds of memory. Yet at the play's end, it poses a problem of speaking – and specifically of the memory of speaking and the speaking of memory – in the distinction between speaking 'what we feel' and 'what we ought to say' (*History* Q 24.319). Seeing 'ought' as something cued from external models and 'feel' as cued by subjectivity and its attendant mobile memory, Smith defines the history of *King Lear* as residing in both models of memory, in the way that the two combine to 'constitute the totality of memory'.

Over the last twenty years of critical analysis, there has been a shift of attention from the semantic to the somatic, from language to the history of the body itself, so that critics, whether historicist or materialist, have kept a fascinated attention on the ways the dead body is represented, 'the memorial aesthetics' which are the focus of John Joughin's chapter. Seeing *Hamlet* and *Richard II* as Shakespeare's 'mourning plays', Joughin studies the aestheticisation of suffering, the moments at which tragedy intersects with the performance of grief as a space in which the ritualisation of mourning connects that tragic performance with the communal practices and subjective experiences of grief as memory. Those intense feelings which for Smith were a fundamental aspect of the experience of *King Lear* are here extended into broader concerns with Shakespeare's power, a force which often resides precisely in the performative forms of grief such as Hamlet so potently describes to his mother as a distinction between seeming (as performance) and feeling, external and internal, performed and offered as true, distinctions which demand an ethical response, 'exposing us directly to what an ethical criticism, influenced by the readings of Levinas and Derrida, might term "the irreducible otherness of the other"'. The theatricalized grief which is necessarily public is set against the private which Hamlet cannot turn into open mourning. As we watch Hamlet and Richard II mourning, 'they serve to confirm that we cannot "know" what they suffer, yet they do so in a language of generality which is in some sense transcendental and with which we can all identify'.

Richard II moves in his grief beyond the position that Hamlet will later adumbrate, for Richard's vision of the commemorative practices of his memory makes him into 'the impossible object of his own grief'. The gap between the spectator and the act of memory that is grieving narrows in Richard even as it widens, dividing his subjectivity at the same time as he watches his own performativity. At the play's end, as Bolingbroke, now King Henry IV, asks us and the others on stage to mourn, to perform the collective act of memory that the state rituals of grief make manifest, even as they attempt to atone and erase the act of regicide which necessitated their very existence, we contemplate the national rites of the cult of ancestors and, in so doing, redefine the forms of memorialisation that they always seek to perform.

Anthony Dawson's chapter continues this investigation of memory, mourning, grief and performance, in its consideration of the activity of literary remembrance in Virgil's *Aeneid* as remembered and represented, performed and investigated in Marlowe's *Dido Queen of Carthage* and Shakespeare's *The Tempest*. Like Bruce Smith, he is concerned with the interconnections of memory but here the specifically literary recall of Virgil's Troy, a recall that in Marlowe's case involves direct translation. Remembering Virgil is to be aware of what epic achieves that stage representation cannot, recalling the extent to which the stage is a limited, almost impoverished space for playing out the topoi of heroism. The anxiety over the stage is an extension, though, of a broader cultural anxiety over what can be remembered and commemorated in a society almost phobic about the icons of the past. A crucial part of the distrust of the adequacy of performance as representation lies in the possibility, even probability, that representing grief diminishes its pain. It is not going too far to see in Marlowe's play a crisis in early-modern theatre (though Dawson goes no further than defining it as a dilemma) and its forms of representation of 'its remembrance of the heroic past'.

The line from Virgil to Marlowe extends towards the double remembering in *The Tempest* where both are recalled and, alongside them, the Player's account of Aeneas's tale to Dido in *Hamlet*, a memory both of Priam's death and of a mode of performance that is seen as old-fashioned, and yet (or should that be 'and therefore'?) powerfully adequate to its subject. *Hamlet* which, like Joughin, Dawson finds to be pervaded by mourning, becomes a narrative both of the loss of fathers and of the politics of the state's collapse and replacement in a way that engages with the action of the *Aeneid*, even as it mirrors it. Shakespeare's careful and intense reading of Virgil connects to his reading of Marlowe's *Dido* (more likely than his having seen the play in performance). In rewriting Marlowe rewriting Virgil, Shakespeare bound the literary to the performed in the memory of earlier modes of performance as Hamlet meditates on the affective power of performance, exactly the problem of affectivity with which Smith's chapter is so much engaged. The return that *Hamlet* marks, a return both to Marlowe and to Virgil, has a sense of belatedness embedded in it as well as a homage to the past, a sense, both melancholic and triumphant, of the theatre-space, the Globe itself, as both Troy and Rome, as that which fell and that which rose.

All three of these chapters are acts of sustained reading of the plays' memories and the modes in which they are performed. Perhaps no-one reads in such a sustainedly close way as an editor but, as the mode of Shakespeare editing in the late twentieth century shifted decisively towards requiring the editor to have an awareness of performance and its history, the sheer difficulty of presenting the materials of performance in conjunction with the text have begun to loom large. Editors now need a vast range of skills and, alongside philology, textual bibliography and a variety of other disciplines, training in performance history would seem to be a requirement. Even more problematic than the fact that not all that many editors have the experience and skills to be good theatre historians is the absence of effective guidance about how commentary notes, the editor as annotator, should engage with the forms of memory of the play in performance available to the editor, materials which, however well researched, often appear fundamentally intractable to the annotator's needs.

Concentrating on examples drawn from two recent editions of *Macbeth*, those by Nicholas Brooke and A. R. Braunmuller, Michael Cordner explores the ways in which editions as 'complex acts of cultural memory' recall performances. The risk is anecdotage and the construction of commentary which reports events from the performance record without motivating them. To note, for instance, that Irving as Macbeth left the stage slowly on his way to murder Duncan is only helpful if we are also enabled to contemplate other modes of exit, like Godfrey Tearle in 1949 running 'nimbly off to do the murder, instead of creeping from the stage as is the usual custom', as a playgoer noted. Remembering one possibility without remembering the other turns the memory into anecdote and risks a form of prescriptiveness, a denial of the fuller range of performance possibilities in the text that performance history richly documents.

Too often annotation makes assumptions about what must be happening on or with a particular line that a better recall of what actors have performed would suggest are disturbingly limited. Remembering options is often to open up the meanings that editors would often seem to prefer to close out, denying the memory of performance its function as an explorer of the text. As Cordner, for a number of crucial moments in *Macbeth*, shows what actors found and what we ought to remember as we encounter the lines, he shows too how often editors are caught by their traditional concept of their function, 'wrought with things forgotten' both by the burden of that tradition and by the challenging demands of the new imperative to remember performance. Cordner summons up a new kind of edition which 'will be confidently fashioned from a lively and questioning curiosity about all that the performance record can teach the academy', marking an intersection between performance and scholarship that would be more genuinely collaborative as acts of sharing memory and less like a series of uncertain pillaging raids.

Cordner's anxieties over the forms in which editors remember performance are shared and rethought by Margaret Jane Kidnie who starts from Claudette Sartiliot's investigations into how citation operates within the culture of modernity, where memory is preserved precisely through citation: 'To keep the memory of things ... one has to cite them, to keep them encrypted in one's discourse so that they can survive'. She pursues two tracks: editors citing performance and actors citing plays in performance, both seen as 'prompts to memory that preserve the past for a present moment through an on-going process of invention'. If we cannot share the memory of performance until it becomes fixed in a narrative that both preserves and, I would want to suggest, denies the possibility of the memory in the very act of preserving it by the transformations that narratives make, then we cannot cite fully, only seek to cite effectively. As Colley Cibber wrote in remembering Betterton,

Could how Betterton spoke be as easily known as what he spoke, then might you see the Muse of Shakespeare in her Triumph, with all her Beauties, rising into real Life, and charming the Beholder. But, since this is so far out of the reach of description, how shall I show you Betterton?

Kidnie cites this passage from Furness's New Variorum edition of *Hamlet*, a moment of a late nineteenth-century editor realizing what cannot be done to recall performance. But, as editors narrativize performance, they look forward and back, creating a body of memory by seeking to preserve them in the forms of their own narratives.

Performance, too, can find acts of memory, as when an actor playing Fool in a 1993 *King Lear* scrawled on the wall part of Hamlet's 'What a piece of work' speech. Kidnie's memories of seeing this, of being aware of it as a moment of citation, contrast with my own: she saw five words but

I saw four, 'work' missing, leaving the audience to fill in the blank as it pleased. Uncertainty or different performances, accurate or inaccurate memories, the choices pale beside the mere fact of remembering, the insistence and importance that memory gives the event. From quiz-shows to the work of the Reduced Shakespeare Company, Kidnie looks at how citation defines a form of memorializing, of definition of the narratives that Shakespeare can mean in popular culture. But citation is also a call to expansion, a metonymic form of referencing that requires expansion, that conjures up that to which it refers not only as play-text but also as cultural artifact, the artifact that the editor is also engaged in annotating.

Editors trawl libraries and archives in search of the materials for their annotations, their construction of commentary and citation. But one area which they have not searched has been the costume archives. Barbara Hodgdon looks at costumes in the Royal Shakespeare Company's costume archive, 'looks' not only in the sense of a critic's investigating, considering, analysing but also in the literal gaze of the observer, seeing the costumes, on their racks, in their boxes, as objects profoundly imbued with memories, the memories of seeing these objects being worn. The act of looking becomes an active one, the activity of making the memory, of the performance of memorizing, which, barely, inadequately but also necessarily, remains in the still photograph. When giving this chapter as a conference paper, Hodgdon used photographs that coloured the memories through the richness of the palette of the costumes. Here, constrained to black-and-white, the photographs become a kind of meta-memory, a memory of a memory.

Yet the objects survive often as partial witnesses. A fire in the archive has left the club-footed boot Ian Holm wore as Richard III in 1964 as a fragment, a loaded symbol of the archaeology of this process of finding memories in the archives. But the objects also survive through their transformation from the materiality of the costume archive into the worn object, the costume known through the art of the theatre photographer, an art barely sustained in contemporary practices of recording performance.

The acts of recall that photo and costume make, for gazers who did not see the productions to which they bear their forms of witness, can also lie potently in the system of memory that the costume becomes for the theatre company. Tracing the history of a cardigan, 'a rat-coloured long cardigan with deep pockets, an everyday sort of garment, an index of practicality – less a costume than *clothes*', Hodgdon narrates the story of the Peggy, the cardigan worn by Peggy Ashcroft as the Countess in *All's*

Well That Ends Well in 1982 and then worn again – and again – by other actors in other productions of other plays, worn by choice, perhaps seeking a numinous presence of the greatness of Ashcroft, by actresses 'in remembrance' of her. The costume became dynamic, like other borrowings, re-wearings that Hodgdon records, an act of gift-giving like the passage of Edmund Kean's Richard III sword handed on until Olivier could think no-one worthy to receive it from him.

Hodgdon ends with a lost sound, the sound of a Free-Ka, as used by the fairies in Peter Brook's *A Midsummer Night's Dream*, lost because Hodgdon's own Free-Ka is cracked and hence, so potently, enshrines the impossibility of memory, the sound of the performance no longer to be heard, the trace that draws attention to itself as trace even as it denies its own function. Carol Chillington Rutter searched in the same archives Hodgdon explored for one of a whole set of lost props, one of the handkerchiefs that successive Desdemonas have lost, Emilias found, Iagos dropped, and Cassios wanted copied. Only at the end of her quest did one appear, by post and no longer archived.

The handkerchief is an example of what happens when, as Anthony Dawson, observes, 'theatre ... invests the objects it shows', whether imbued with exoticism in Othello's twin accounts of the handkerchief's origins or as mundane as a book, 'with more than they carry in themselves'. But the meaning of the object may be private: Alan Howard as Henry VI in 1977 reading a book onstage throughout the interval of *Part 3*, a book whose title was invisible to the audience but which was actually a copy of *Coriolanus*, the part he was studying, his bribe for agreeing to Terry Hands's request to play Henry VI at all; Emrys Jones wearing a white scarf in a succession of roles, an object that seems to have had particular meaning for the actor as a performance fetish; Antony Sher moving thrillingly on metal legs as Richard III, the crutches that propelled him across the stage, making the 'bottled spider' move at breakneck speed, using the crutches as support in another sense, as a means of hiding his terror of Shakespeare's language.

These actors' mnemonics, through the intensification of meaning in performance, become focused for Rutter in the history of the handkerchief, not only the varieties of work (often women's work) that the prop signifies in performance but also the history of actors' actions with the object. As the handkerchief keeps changing hands in the play, moving from character to character, a remarkably complex sign of semiotic virtuosity in *Othello*'s exploration of the ways meanings are created, transformed and remade, so it keeps changing hands in the history of performance, most often seen in photographs of Iagos with it, each, perhaps consciously and perhaps inevitably, perhaps accidentally and perhaps because objects have their own memories, replicating a gesture of spreading it out performed by his predecessors – or at least performed by the photographs of those predecessors. But Rutter also records, remembers and re-examines other uses to which the handkerchief is put by Iagos, its temporary possessors, and ways in which the prop has become the icon for the play, the sign of *Othello* used on edition covers and theatre programmes as standing for the play, suspended in the air, floating freely, dropping slowly towards the ground.

'Memory', Joseph Roach suggests in *Cities of the Dead*, in a passage Rutter quotes, 'is a process that depends crucially on forgetting'. As Rutter and Hodgdon looked in or at the archives for signs of the lost presence of performance, so my own contribution to this volume looks at the memory of what occurs when an actor loses the text and forgets the 'right' word, when the play escapes from his/her memory. Intertwining the cultural memory of Shakespeare (in, for instance, the building of the Shakespeare Memorial Theatre as a cultural act of commemoration) with the moments of individual memory, separated out by its memory of forgetting from the collective memories of an audience or the sequence of audiences for a particular production on one night or in the course of its run, the chapter seeks in the actor's moment of forgetting the word also the meanings of the substitutions, that which is inserted in the place of memory.

My chapter examines the processes by which Shakespeare actors seek to remember as evidenced in books of actor training and specifically in the training of the Shakespeare actor, noting the processes of memory as an absence, barely found as trace in such practical manuals, as well as examining the ways in which the history of theatre as an institution is a history of how to cope with forgetting, what, in effect, to do with the necessity of the prompter. But the systems of memory by which an actor remembers a role, especially those appropriate to the conditions of work of the early modern actor, are also responsible for one traditional account of the transmission of text. The hypothesis that certain quartos were the product of 'memorial reconstruction', of actors' accurate memories of their own and hazy memories of others' lines, has been a potent concept in the editorial tradition. My investigation uses instead a modern example, the transposition of memorial reconstruction from the domain of textual bibliography to the example of a radical experiment in filmmaking in Kristian Levring's film *Dogme #4: The King is Alive* (1999), in which a group of stranded tourists rehearse *King Lear* while awaiting rescue in the African desert, the play having been remembered and reconstructed by one of the lost Westerners.

Such memory is a cultural act and the essay finally moves towards a theatre performance that was explicitly a reconstruction of the cultural meaning of Shakespeare, of Shakespeare as cultural memory, in Peter Stein's vast two-part, many hour, promenade performance *Shakespeare's Memory* (1976), a point of intersection between actors and the archives, between the performers and their own researches in the libraries, a display of the complexities of cultural memory created solely as a step along a prolonged journey towards his company's production of a Shakespeare play.

The struggles of Stein's company, the Schaubühne, to find a place where Shakespeare could be performed, are in part a product of the complex cultural history of Germany's memories of Shakespeare. Russell Jackson charts one such process in the memories of Elisabeth Bergner's stage performance as Rosalind that were recalled and transmuted in the transfer from German-speaking stage performance to an English-language film, Paul Czinner's version of *As You Like It* (1936), the first talking-picture film of the play that Peter Stein would be preparing to direct, once again in German, in the aftermath of *Shakespeare's Memory* forty years later.

Czinner's film, only the second feature film of a Shakespeare play with synchronized sound to be made, stands at a point of anxiety, an anxiety never fully resolved in the history of the cultural response to Shakespeare on film, over whether Shakespeare plays could be filmed, even with the new technologies of sound recording. Viewed now, it is the energy and sexiness of Olivier's Orlando that is most exciting and Bergner's performance that most glaringly marks her linguistic otherness, her voice never other than awkwardly non-anglophone, a sign of one of the great cultural movements of Western art in the twentieth century, the emigration of so many German artists (actors, painters, directors and composers) as a response to Nazism. Bergner herself had left Germany before 1933 but she sought in the film – indeed, the film as a whole sought, in its especial emphasis on her performance – to recapitulate, to remember, to have audiences remember her spectacular success as Rosalind from 1923 to 1936. Like Hodgdon, Jackson places part of the memory of performance in the material of costume, Bergner's 'russet tunic resembling a gym-slip, worn over a soft-collared shirt, tights of the same colour with very short shorts worn over them, and dainty lace-up ankle boots'. If the costume suggests Peter Pan, it serves as a reminder of J. M. Barrie's involvement in the film.

But what was caught on film could not mirror what theatre audiences saw. The enchanting performance – the adjective often used by those who saw the stage performance – had a freshness and spontaneity, an 'uninhibited physical expressiveness' that exhilarated playgoers. Film critics found her nervous and restless, overemphatic and querulous. And the film itself is a reminder of the frequent lack of success of Shakespeare films at the box-office, like the Reinhardt-Dieterle 1935 *A Midsummer Night's Dream* of which Warner Brothers had such high hopes and the 1936 *Romeo and Juliet* now so strange with its middle-aged stars. But, screened in Germany in 2002, Bergner's performance in Czinner's film could still remind those movie-goers with long memories of the stage performance they had witnessed so long before.

Michael Dobson is concerned with a different kind of cultural memory of performance in productions of *As You Like It*, not a single actor but an entire culture, as the history of the rediscovery of out-door Shakespeare production emerged from the attempts in English public schools to perform Greek tragedies in appropriately Grecian outdoor amphitheatres. Dobson is throughout trying to answer a question that signals one of the more self-evident eccentricities of English culture: 'Why, in the English climate, long after the invention of the comfortable, roofed proper theatre, would anyone choose to stage Shakespeare's plays in the open air?' The ideological need that this supremely uncomfortable, risky, damp, cold, inadequate mode of production seeks to fill is part of the complex cultural work that Shakespeare does throughout England, not only outdoors in what passes for the summer. In its striking rejection of the boundary between amateur and professional, as well as between mainstream, academic and fringe theatre, English open-air productions claim a curious naturalness, a closeness to the Englishness of landscape, the sense that the right way of suggesting the Forest of Arden or a wood somewhere near Athens is to play on a lawn close to a wood.

Dobson traces the history of two of the most famous examples of this phenomenon: the Open-Air Theatre in Regent's Park in London and Rowena Cade's Minack Theatre in Cornwall, close to Land's End, the rocky, rural antithesis to the urban parkland of London. A surprising by-product of the Aesthetic Movement, open-air Shakespeare begins again with the Pastoral Players in 1884 but the gospel was spread by Ben Greet whose Woodland Players copied the Wildean original and toured their own *As You Like It*. Greet's work stretched to America where he performed in front of President Roosevelt in 1908 but he found his true home in Regent's Park when Robert Atkins established a permanent summer venue there in 1932, exactly the same year in which Rowena Cade put on her first production in Cornwall, *The Tempest* backed with a real sea.

Powerfully nostalgic in their search for Shakespeare's Merrie England, seen as surviving only in the English natural world and denied by the history of urbanization and modernity, the progenitors of open-air Shakespeare – and their hundreds of contemporary successors in the productions that are to be found across the entire country every summer – may seem, as Dobson proposes, 'twee and even philistine' but they also create Shakespeare's England, that 'mutually reinforcing' duality, a dyad to be seen among the dryads so frequently placed to be glimpsed in the open-air performances.

Reconstructing theatre performances from the 1930s, whether Bergner in Germany or Cade's work in Cornwall, is an action of conventional theatre historiography. But the digital age redefines the activities of recording, recovering and remembering. Even the obsessive desire for film memory that underscores the concept of cinephilia has become revised, using new technologies while nostalgically remembering the outdated formats overridden and overwritten by contemporary possibilities.[11] W. B. Worthen is fascinated by a toy camera, a Fisher-Price PXL 2000 Pixelvision, briefly sold in the late 1980s and then withdrawn, the camera Hamlet is seen using to record Claudius's first speech in Michael Almereyda's *Hamlet* film (2000), a technology that has also intrigued some contemporary film-makers and video artists. Given that in the aftermath of his encounter with the ghost, Shakespeare's Hamlet turns to one technology of recording, his writing tables, Worthen asks 'how contemporary Shakespeare dramatizes the impact of the new technologies on the performance of "humanity" ... it may bring into view'. Though Harold Bloom made us wonder only for a brief while whether Shakespeare invented the concept of the human, digital technology repeatedly demands that we rethink the frameworks in which our humanity is defined.

Packed in almost every scene with the devices of recording (photographs and security cameras, computer monitors and Hamlet's toy camera), Almereyda's *Hamlet* searches for the cybercultural representation of technologies of reproduction that become the contemporary versions of 'fond records', the devices that are themselves the methods of modern memory, the ways we are enabled to recall and remember. Almereyda adds to this systematizing of the means of memory the fact that the

---

[11] See Marijke de Valck and Malte Hagener, eds., *Cinephilia: Movies, Love and Memory* (Amsterdam: Amsterdam University Press, 2005).

processing of the information is his Hamlet's means of reflection. Editing is at the core of this Hamlet's practice of film- and video-making, seen as the practice both of rendering disjunct and of finding modes of connection between the fragments of informational materials that constitute the postmodern cultural matter and the individual's access to the means of knowing. Montage, which for so long was at the post-Eisenstein core of film's means of making meaning, is now 'finally absorbed to the narcotic aesthetics not of the conventional stage but of the invisible rhetoric of the digital screen'. But Worthen recognizes too that the digital technology that so fascinates and defines Almereyda's Hamlet is 'a technology of *transformation*' and, as a result, editing, the manipulation of digital data, becomes 'a creative and critical practice, where the subject frames and encounters his own reflection', a reflection that is (re)defined and repeatedly remade in the fabric of memory that the digital and digitized information represents.

If Almereyda's fascination with technologies includes barely a trace of theatre (most marked in the brief glimpse of John Gielgud as Hamlet taken not from stage but from a film), theatre has become enmired in the possibilities of its own uses of recording, of constructing a particular kind of memory of Shakespeare and of memory in Shakespeare through the engagement with the apparatus of media record. Robert Shaughnessy tracks ways in which theatre is mediatised and mediated as a cultural project, from the screening on BBC Four in 2003 of a live broadcast from Shakespeare's Globe of its production of *Richard II* to the use of tv screens in Simon McBurney's production of *Measure for Measure* staged at the Royal National Theatre in London in 2004. Less concerned with the recording of theatre performance than with the presence of recording within theatre practice, Shaughnessy traces the history of the presence of media culture in live theatre as a concept of the Shakespeare play as film-like, as cinematic and as screenplay – a recurrent trope in the rhetoric of theatre directors such as Peter Brook. But he is also concerned with the incorporation of media technology as visible presences on stage in, for instance, RSC productions of *Julius Caesar* in 1983 and 2004 or Peter Sellars's Goodman Theatre production of *The Merchant of Venice* in 1994. In such cases, mediatization is seen as a sign of a production's definition 'as a self-consciously "public" political discourse'.

But theatre has on occasion also seen in mediatized forms of transmission within its performance a possibility of the representation of dream and fantasy, of non-mimetic forms which question the material evidence that it purports to record, turning the hard fact of film into something questionable and vulnerable precisely as memory – as in the images of both Hamlets, father and son, playing in the snow in the 'grainy, silent monochrome images' that flickered behind Alex Jennings's Hamlet (RSC, 1997) as he poured his father's ashes from an urn. Film and theatre meet here, as in McBurney's *Measure*, 'as a means of exploring, in complex, provocative, and richly-imaged ways, the relations . . . between the spaces of representation, imagination and desire'. In those spaces, desire is so often figured as the space between the mediatised form as the material fact of memory, individualized or collectivized, and the liveness that theatre claims as peculiarly its own.

As Dennis Kennedy knows well, performance 'is one of memory's greatest tests . . . because it decays before our eyes, and thus in the moment of its accomplishment escapes into memory'. Culturally, performance, not only but strikingly often Shakespeare performance, is defined as a memorial practice, be it at the Shakespeare Memorial Theatre or in the emergence of festivals, especially post-1945, where Shakespeare functioned as a reassuring sign of the continuities of culture, defined as high art, in the aftermath of the kinds of social discontinuities that the war had thrown up. Since, Kennedy argues, the 'attempt to codify the memory of performance', which is the central project of theatre historiography, 'necessarily exists outside the cognition of the spectators' so that the task of performance history 'is to understand and give meaning to the event through social and aesthetic analysis, not to be the sum of the audience's experiences', his chapter turns to the space where collective cultural memory is most emphatically located and tested, in the idea and practice of the museum.

The memory of performance becomes, from this perspective, a practice that conceptually shares space with the cultural functions of the museum in the cataloguing, comparative process in which performances are remembered through alignment with other performances. But Kennedy also analyses the memory of performance as both subjectivised and inaccurate (in proportion to the degree of excitement it provoked), independent of the event and, in its replaying, a type of dream performance. Performance memory is thus a space of sustained forgetting, something particularly explored in a group of *Hamlet* performances which foregrounded the impossibility of not forgetting, like Lyubimov's Taganka production of 1971 where a great curtain swept the stage clear of bodies or Heiner Müller's East Berlin version in 1990 that staged the only response possible to the collapse of the East German state during rehearsals in its performance of cultural forgetting.

It is appropriate then that Kennedy's chapter should end with an exploration of the Museum of Jurassic Technology in Los Angeles and its exhibition of the work of Geoffrey Sonnabend, the memory researcher whose masterpiece, *Obliscence*, studied theories of forgetting – except that Sonnabend and his book are the invention of the Museum's creator and its exhibition a fabrication that acts as a questioning of the entire project of cultural memory. As the explorations throughout this volume – but most especially in the final section – repeatedly emphasize, the memories of Shakespeare and performance and their intersections are least reliable, most vulnerable, at exactly the points at which they appear most secure. Stephen Orgel's memories of theatre as the space of desire in his Afterword are exactly that process of self-construction through the activity (never the passivity) of memory. Whatever the ghost asks of Hamlet and us in demanding that he and we 'remember me', it is the fragile nature of that memory that is most hauntingly and sustainedly present, known only as that which cannot be known, remembered only as that which memory is no longer able to remember.

PART I

Shakespeare's performances of memory

CHAPTER I

Speaking what we feel about King Lear

Bruce R. Smith

Just what do you remember about *King Lear*? Say it. Put it into words. When I pose that question to myself, I find any number of things that I, as a Shakespeare scholar, probably ought to say: 'an existential probing of the very bases of meaning', 'Shakespeare's greatest tragedy', 'a play that to some critics exceeds the possibilities of stage performance'. On a more visceral level I could say, 'I remember Lear's raving on the heath', 'I remember Cornwall's plucking out Gloucester's eyes and calling them "vile jelly"', 'I remember the wait for Cordelia's breath to stir the feather that Lear holds before her mouth.' When I speak these memories, I don't just remember certain events: I remember what they feel like to me. 'Moments of affective intensity' is John J. Joughin's phrase for such experiences, and he demonstrates in '*Lear*'s Afterlife' how the image of Lear holding the dead Cordelia in his arms has taken on an 'ob-scene' life of its own in the play's critical history.[1] Curiously, that image is not what I personally remember about *King Lear*. Where do my memories come from? Where do they reside? How do I get in touch with them? What connects the events that I remember to the feelings I have about them? About such questions I find it hard to say anything that feels authentic.

On occasion I give myself a lesson in humility by taking out the tattered Signet edition of *King Lear* that I used in freshman English at Tulane University in autumn 1964 and going back over my marginalia. It was my first encounter with the play – indeed, it was only the third Shakespeare play I had ever read, after those two fixtures of the high-school curriculum, *Julius Caesar* and *Macbeth*, two plays that made up in brevity what they lacked in appeal to the life-experiences of fifteen- and seventeen-year-olds. I have to report that most of my markings in the Signet *Lear* are reminders, notes to help me remember which character is

---

[1] John J. Joughin, '*Lear*'s Afterlife', *Shakespeare Survey* 55 (Cambridge: Cambridge University Press, 2002), pp. 67–81.

which and what is going on in the plot. Several jottings are concerned with keeping those two 'Ed–' characters straight.

Many years later, in 1990, I happened to be in England just at the right moment to catch three productions of *King Lear* within the space of a single week: Deborah Warner's at the National, Nicholas Hytner's at the RSC in Stratford, and Kenneth Branagh's somewhere in the West End, just back from a world tour. What do I remember about these four encounters with *King Lear*? In the case of my freshman year, I have hard evidence – embarrassing as it is – in the form of those markings in the margins. Over all, I remember feeling that I didn't understand what all the fuss was about. The instructor, Alexander Lamar Stevens, told us that *King Lear* was Shakespeare's supreme masterpiece. Noted. In the case of the three 1990 productions, what I remember are certain moments: Lear's entry in a wheelchair festooned with birthday balloons in the Warner production, Claire Higgins's nervous hands in the same production as she turned Regan into the ever-anxious middle sister called upon to match her older sibling Goneril in the 'how-much-do-I-love-thee?' contest, the huge open cube that revolved in the Hytner production to indicate the formlessness and directionlessness of the heath scene (even though Peter Holland in his 1992 *Shakespeare Survey* review tells me I ought *not* to remember a production gimmick that 'failed to suggest substantive disorder'),[2] Emma Thompson's Fool in the Branagh production (black-clad, in white face with big red nose and red-circled eyes, like the figure of Death in a Dance of Death), John Wood's offstage 'howl, howl, howl, howl, howl' in the Hytner production. Or at least I *think* it was Wood in the Hytner production. It could have been Richard Briers in the Branagh production or Brian Cox in the Warner production. What I remember, in effect, is a series of isolated moments that, at this distance, have fused these three productions inextricably in my mind. Plato would approve: I've taken a series of discrete sense impressions and moved inductively beyond them to arrive at The Idea of *King Lear*. But that Platonic induction doesn't feel quite right.

To write this paragraph, to specify which production took place where and who played what, I had to rummage through a disorganized box of souvenir programs, go to the library and check out three stage history books on *Lear*, order three others on interlibrary loan, click my way through twenty or so screens on the internet, locate a copy of *The*

---

[2] Peter Holland, 'Shakespeare Performances in England, 1989–90', *Shakespeare Survey 44* (Cambridge: Cambridge University Press, 1992), pp. 178–86.

Cambridge King Lear CD-ROM, insert the CD in a reader, learn to navigate the program, and move back and forth, up and down, into and out of the CD's three sectors. As a result of these actions, I've reordered my memories. They're tidier now, but they still don't compose a coherent whole. And I still don't know who howled offstage. What I'm left with are two different sorts of phenomena: (1) a series of visual and aural vignettes and (2) a sense of how I felt – no, how I *feel* – about them. There is, to put it mildly, a serious subject–object problem here. What's missing is connective tissue – the segue from one vignette to another, the sinews that connect vignettes to feelings. Attempting to make those connections constitutes my project in these pages.

The problem I face when I try to remember productions of *King Lear* is merely a personal version of the larger problem of remembering productions that Patrice Pavis analyses in *Languages of the Stage*. Any stage performance occupies its own space-time. How can that space-time be rendered in another medium? Any reconstruction of a performance text must, according to Pavis, provide information about five elements: (1) speech, (2) 'figuration of stage space', (3) relationships between actors and audience, (4) connections between 'dramaturgical analysis' and 'the concrete appearance of character and action', and (5) 'framing devices' that divide the continuum into meaningful ensembles.[3] In trying to codify this information directors and theatre historians have resorted to one or another set of Cartesian coordinates. Pavis mentions Ivanov's 'theatrical semiography' with its horizontal lines for areas of the stage and musical notes for duration and direction, Brecht's *Modelbuch* with its photographic record of up to 1,500 separate stills for a given play, and various attempts at 'thick description' with highly precise stage descriptions, dramaturgical text analyses, and outlines of the changing mise-en-scène, as well as the more familiar notation system of videotape, which imposes its own version of Cartesian coordinates and leaves out the actor–audience interaction entirely. The fundamental problem is that performances constitute moving targets. They resist being fixed, however finely graded the coordinates we may attempt to impose on them. Memory, like the performances themselves, is a species of movement.

Two distinct models of memory are put forward by early modern writers. Both of them involve movement, but in radically different forms. The more familiar model conceptualizes memory as a room or chamber

---

[3] Patrice Pavis, *Languages of the Stage: Essays on the Semiology of the Theatre* (New York: Performing Arts Journal Publications, 1982), p. 128.

in which records are kept. In *The Defence of Poesie* Sir Philip Sidney praises verse for exceeding prose 'in the knitting up of the memory'. Experts in memory, Sidney says, have likened that human faculty to a room in which each idea or element finds a place: 'they that have taught the Art of memory have shewed nothing so apt for it as a certaine roome divided into many places well and throughly knowne. Now, that hath the verse in effect perfectly, every word having his naturall seate, which seate must needes make the words remembred.'[4] This model, which has its origins in classical rhetoric, has been studied *in extenso* by Frances Yates, who has even proposed that paintings under the canopy over the stage of the Globe were designed to turn the stage itself into a 'house of memory'.[5]

It was easy enough to commend this mnemonic model when the faculty of memory itself was imagined to be located in a specific 'chamber' of the brain. It's at the back of the brain that memory is situated by Pierre de La Primaudaye, whose massive tome *The French Academy* functioned in translation, despite its name, as the closest thing late sixteenth, and early seventeenth-century English readers had to *The Encyclopaedia Britannica*.[6] La Primaudaye's word for the brain's ventricles, at least in English translation, is 'bellies'. Compared with the rest of the brain, the belly dedicated to memory is 'less moist, and most solid and firme'. There are two reasons why. First, because this part of the brain communicates directly with the marrow in the backbone, the tissue has to be capable of transmitting strong motions to the rest of the body.

Secondly, forasmuch as the memory is as it were the Register & *Chancery Court* of all the other senses, the images of all things brought and committed vnto it by them, are to be imprinted therein, as the image and signe of a ring or seale is imprinted and set in the waxe that is sealed. Therefore it is needefull that the matter of the instrument of Memory should be so well tempered, that it be neither too soft nor to hard.[7]

---

[4] Sir Philip Sidney, *Sidney's the Defence of Poesy and Selected Renaissance Literary Criticism*, ed. Gavin Alexander (London: Penguin, 2004), pp. 109–10.

[5] Frances Yates has developed this spatial model of memory in three works: *The Art of Memory* (London: Routledge and Kegan Paul, 1966), 'New Light on the Globe Theatre', *New York Review of Books* 6.9 (26 May 1966), and *Theatre of the World* (London: Routledge and Kegan Paul, 1969). Other spatial models of memory have been set in place by Mary Carruthers, *The Book of Memory: A Study of Memory in Medieval Culture* (Cambridge: Cambridge University Press, 1990), pp. 122–55. See also the graphic schemes illustrated in Lina Bolzoni, *The Gallery of Memory: Literary and Iconic Models in the Age of the Printing Press* (Toronto: University of Toronto Press, 2001).

[6] Anne Prescott, 'Pierre de La Primaudaye's *French Academy*: Growing Encyclopedic', in *The Renaissance Computer*, ed. Neil Rhodes and Jonathan Sawday (London: Routledge, 2000), pp. 157–69.

[7] Pierre de La Primaudaye, *The French Academie*, trans. Thomas Bowes, Richard Dolman, and William Phillip (London: Thomas Adams, 1618), p. 417.

In his discussion of the brain in *Microcosmographia* (1615) Helkiah Crooke traces the origins of this conceit to Arabic philosophy, specifically to Avicenna and Averroes. For his part, Crooke can describe memory as 'a faithfull Recorder or Maister of the Rolles', even as he follows Galen in denying that sensation, common sense, imagination, reason and memory occupy specific locations in the brain.[8] According to La Primaudaye's model, all my sense experiences of Warner's production, Hytner's and Branagh's ought to be stored away as impressions in the semi-hard tissue of my memory's belly. So why can't I find those impressions? Why can't I remember which actor howled offstage?

My own experience of memory comes closer to what Sir Kenelm Digby describes in his 1644 treatise *On the Nature of Bodies*. Citing Democritus, Hippocrates and Galen, Digby thinks of memories, not as impressions on semi-hard tissue, but as atoms that swim about in a fluid until fantasy summons them up and arrests their movement. 'The medium which these bodies move in', according to Digby, '... is a liquid vaporous substance, in which they floate and swimme at liberty'.[9] He pictures 'the litle similitudes, which are in the caues of the braine wheeling and swimming about (almost in such sort, as you see in the washing of currantes or of rise, by the winding about and circular turning of the cookes hand)'.[10] The more numerous objects, the kind we see everyday, swim into view more often; rarer objects, less often. Needless to say, my memories of Brian Cox, John Wood and Richard Briers belong to the rarer sort. They are swimming around in a very remote cave in my brain. Or, if Digby is correct, I should say that Brian Cox, John Wood and Richard Briers *themselves* are swimming around in a very remote cave in my brain. Digby believes that actual physical particles of things seen and heard enter the body of the perceiver through the eyes and ears. I wonder what Cox, Wood and Briers have found to say to each other all this time. And I wonder what *they* think about Alan Howard's Lear, particles of which joined them in the liquid vaporous substance of my brain seven years later.

As different as these two models of memory may be, they do have one thing in common: motion. In the house-of-memory model it's the memories that remain stationary and the thinker who does the moving, as he moves from place to place about the chamber of memory, noting one

---

[8] Helkiah Crooke, *Microcosmographia: A Description of the Body of Man* (London, 1615), pp. 502, 208.

[9] Sir Kenelm Digby, *Two Treatises, in the one of which, the nature of bodies; in the other, the nature of mans soule; is looked into: in way of discovery, of the immortality of reasonable soules* (Paris, 1644), p. 286.

[10] Digby, *Two Treatises*, p. 285.

memory here and another there. In the vaporous liquid model it's the memories that do the moving and the thinker who remains stationary. In either case, memory does not happen unless there is motion. The two models are superimposed in Spenser's Castle of Alma in Book Two of *The Faerie Queene*. Every detail of the castle – its main entrance guarded by sixteen warders, its stately hall presided over by the steward Diet, its centrally located ovens where Concoction and Digestion supervise the distribution of food to the entire castle, the postern gate where waste is 'auoided quite, and throwne out priuily' – figures as an image of the human body.[11] The castle's high turret is constructed according to early modern ideas about the brain. Memory is 'th'hindmost roome of three', behind the chamber of phantasy in the front and the chamber of understanding in the middle (2.9.54.9). 'Ruinous and old' (2.9.55.1), the chamber of memory is 'hangd about with rolles, / And old records from auncient times deriu'd' (2.9.57.6–7) and is presided over by 'an oldman, halfe blind,/ And all decrepit in his feeble corse' (2.9.55.5–6). Though weak in body, the man's mind is full of 'liuely vigour' (2.9.55.7). Restless activity characterizes the room full of rolls and old records:

> Amidst them all he in a chaire was set,
>   Tossing and turning them withouten end;
> But for he was vnhable them to fet,
> A litle boy did on him still attend,
> To reach, when euer he for ought did send;
> And oft when things were lost, or lain amis,
> That boy them sought, and vnto him did lend.
> Therefore he *Anamnestes* cleped is,
> And that old man *Eumnestes*, by their propertis.
>   (2.9.58.1–9)

Despite its vital activity, there is an unsettled and unsettling disorder to Spenser's chamber of memory that contrasts sharply with the clear and pristine images of 'gestes' of wise men and 'picturals' of social institutions that cover the chamber of understanding's walls (2.9.53.3–4).

With respect to those *King Lear*s past, it would be nice to station myself in Spenser's chamber of understanding, where everything is clear. In more ways than one, I'm beyond that now. If I want to connect one vignette to another, and each of those vignettes to a feeling, and each of these feelings to a larger coherent whole, I need an Anamnestes to act as a

---

[11] Edmund Spenser, *The Faerie Queene* 2.9.32.9 in Spenser, *The Faerie Queene*, ed. Thomas P. Roche Jr (London: Penguin, 1978), p. 320. Further quotations are cited in the text by book, canto, stanza and line numbers.

runner. I propose to look for him in a series of six discrete moments in the performance history of *King Lear* – a series that (1) begins with Shakespeare's writing of the script, (2) passes through the play's original stage performance, (3) considers the various forms in which the script came into print, (4) examines the play's afterlife in the form of 'A Lamentable Song of the death of King Leare and his three Davghters', (5) considers what theatre historians have said about problems of writing the play's performance history, and (6) concludes by scrutinizing the implicit claims of film and video to offer memory in an always accessible medium.

THE WRITING OF THE SCRIPT

My favourite fun fact about Shakespeare (admittedly there aren't that many to choose from) is not that he left his wife his second-best bed or that a Catholic tract was found in the roof of his birthplace more than a hundred years after his death but that his ineffable masterpiece *King Lear* is a remake of an earlier play by somebody else. For Shakespeare, certainly, and for some of the actors and audience members, probably, the *King Lear* that hit the boards in 1605 or 1606 was not the first link in a chain of memory but a new link in an already established chain. To use the metaphors of memory we have just been talking about, Shakespeare, the King's Men players, and at least some members of the audience walked into a room that was already built or they stirred up a vaporous liquid that was already full of current and currants. Shakespeare's primary source, *The True Chronicle History of King Leir and His Three Daughters* had just been printed. How did Shakespeare the scriptwriter negotiate those memories? The most obvious answer, if a twentieth-century metaphor is permissible, is that he *suppressed* them. *The True Chronicle History* begins, not with the rhetorical love-test in front of all the court, but with a series of private scenes in which the reasons for Gonorill and Ragan's duplicitous rants and for Cordella's reticent answer are fully established. Take, for example, what Gonorill says to Ragan moments before the love-test:

> I maruell, *Ragan*, how you can indure
> To see that proud pert Pear, our youngest sister,
> So slightly to account of vs, her elders,
> As if we were no better then her selfe!
> We cannot haue a quaynt deuice so soone,
> Or new made fashion, of our choyce inuention;
> But if she like it, she will haue the same,

Or study newer to exceed vs both.
Besides, she is so nice and so demure;
So sober, courteous, modest, and precise,
That all the Court hath worke ynough to do,
To talke howe she exceedeth me and you.[12]

In place of their predecessors' thoroughly dramatized jealousy, Shakespeare's Gonoril and Regan have only cryptic comments to make – and
that after the fact. 'Sister', says Gonoril at the end of the first scene, 'it is
not a little I have to say of what most nearly appertains to us both'.[13] In
the event, she mentions two things briefly: 'You see how full of changes
his age is' (1.279) and 'He always loved our sister most' (1.281). For her
part, Cordelia is even more cryptic – and again after the fact: 'what I well
intend, / I'll do't before I speak' (1.217–18).

What happens to the suppressed memories of *Leir*? They become, in
early modern terminology, 'passions', passions of the heart that are *felt*
but not *said*. Joseph Roach has given us a model of how these passions
were imagined to work in Shakespeare's theatre. An actor conceives a
passion, not just in his head, but in his whole body, by wilfully changing
his body chemistry. He communicates that passion to the spectator/
listeners through body movement, through the beams of light radiating
from his eyes, through the penetrating power of his voice. If the actor is
successful, the spectator/listeners take on that passion.[14] And as a result,
they remember the play, not just in their heads, but in their nerves and
muscles. Claire Higgins in Deborah Warner's production offers a modern
analogue: she managed to suggest what it felt like to be the neglected and
emotionally abused middle sister, and what I remember about her performance is not what she said but how she used her hands.

THE ORIGINAL STAGE PERFORMANCE

Memory of a different sort was engaged when Shakespeare's fellows
received their parts for *King Lear* and began to work up the play's first

---

[12] *The True Chronicle History of King Leir, and His Three Daughters* (London, 1605), sig. A3r.
[13] *M. William Shak-speare: His True Chronicle Historie of the life and death of King Lear and his three Daughters* (London, 1608), sig. B4v, edited as *The History of King Lear* in Shakespeare, *The Complete Works*, ed. Stanley Wells and Gary Taylor (Oxford: Clarendon Press, 1986), 1.274, p. 913. Further quotations from the original printing are cited in the text by signature number; further quotations from the edited text are cited by scene and line numbers.
[14] Joseph Roach, *The Player's Passion: Studies in the Science of Acting* (Newark: University of Delaware Press, 1985), pp. 24–7.

performance. As we know, each of these fellows received, not a copy of
the entire script, but only his own lines, just as a bassoon-player would
in a symphony orchestra today. A roll of papers gave the actor his role.
The best known surviving exemplar of these player's parts, later known
as an actor's 'side', is Edward Alleyn's lines for the title role in Robert
Greene's *Orlando Furioso*.[15] In this manuscript a horizontal line separates one speech from another and gives the actor his cue. Let me
reconstruct what Cordelia's part would have looked like for scene one of
*M. William Shak-speare: His True Chronicle Historie of the life and death
of King Lear, and his three Daughters*, the text that was printed in quarto
in 1608:

_____so much I love you.
[1] What shall Cordelia doe, loue and be silent.
_____your deere highnes loue.
[2] Then poore Cord. and yet not so, since I am sure
My loues more richer then my tongue.
_____Then your sisters.
[3] Nothing my Lord.
_____speake againe.
[4] Vnhappie that I am, I cannot heaue my heart into my mouth, I
loue your Maiestie according to my bond, nor more nor lesse.
_____mar your fortunes.
[5] Good my Lord,
You haue begot me, bred me, loued me,
I returne those duties backe as are right fit,
Obey you, loue you, and most honour you,
Why haue my sisters husbands if they say they loue you all,
Happely when I shall wed, that Lord whose hand
Must take my plight, shall cary halfe my loue with him,
Halfe my care and duty, sure, I shall never
Mary like my sisters, to loue my father all.
_____with thy heart?
[6] I good my Lord.
_____So yong and so vntender.
[7] So yong my Lord and true.
_____Could never plant in me.

---

[15] Two leaves are reproduced as figure 17 in Andrew Gurr, *The Shakespearean Stage 1574–1642*, 3rd
edn. (Cambridge: Cambridge University Press, 1992), pp. 108–9.

[8] I yet beseech your Maiestie,
     If for I want that glib and oyly Art,
     To speake and purpose not, since what I well entend
     Ile do't before I speake, that you may know
     It is no vicious blot, murder or foulnes,
     No vncleane action or dishonored step
     That hath depriu'd me of your grace and favour,
     But euen for want of that, for which I am rich,
     A still soliciting eye, and such a tongue
     As I am glad I haue not, though not to haue it,
     Hath lost me in your liking.
     _____must loose a husband.

[9] Peace be with Burgundie, since that respects
     Of fortune are his loue, I shall not be his wife.
     _____to your sisters.

[10] The iewels of our father,
     With washe eyes Cordelia leaues you, I knowe you what you are,
     And like a sister am most loath to call your faults
     As they are named, vse well our Father,
     To your professed bosoms I commit him,
     But yet alas stood I within his grace,
     I would preferre him to a better place:
     So farewell to you both?
     _____that you haue wanted

[11] Time shal vnfould what pleated cunning hides,
     Who couers faults, at last shame them derides:
     Well may you prosper.[16]

For the actor learning the part, each of these horizontal lines indicates a
gap that has to be filled in by memory. It's not just the verbal lines that
the actor has to memorize; it's the *lines*, the strokes of the pen that
indicate everything that comes in between. A modern method actor
would connect the dots by constructing a 'journey' for the character, by
drawing on her own experiences of what it feels like to be a child under a
parent's command, to be a sister who is the object of sibling jealousy, to
be a bride who is suddenly spurned by her suitor, to be the object of
another suitor's unexpected tenderness. An early modern actor would
have found in those strokes of the pen the space and time for a passion to
build. Seeing Cordelia's lines in isolation does, to me, suggest a passionate
presence, a gradual build to her two long speeches, that is not always

---

[16] Text transcribed from Shakespeare, *True Chronicle Historie*, sigs. B1v–B4v.

realized in modern productions. The biggest gap of all is indicated by the seventh horizontal line, which separates Cordelia's final exchange with Lear after the love-test ('So young, my lord, and true') from the long speech 115 lines later when she pleads with Lear to reconsider his judgement ('I yet beseech your majesty ... '). What the actor playing Cordelia, in 1608 or 2008, must remember in this gap is a sequence of somatic experiences: moving over there, standing thus, hearing that, hearing the next thing and the next and the next, reacting so, moving away, moving toward, perhaps kneeling, and only *then* speaking again: 'I yet beseech your majesty ... '. What those horizontal lines tell an actor to memorize are feelings – feelings of two sorts: what it feels like to be possessed by a certain passion (1608) or a certain emotion (2008) and what it feels like to move one's body in certain ways.

THE PASSAGE FROM STAGE TO PAGE

The title-page to *M. William Shak-speare: His True Chronicle Historie of the life and death of King Lear* claims to present the text 'As it was plaid before the Kings Maiesty at White-Hall, vppon S. Stephens night, in Christmas hollidaies. By his Maiesties Seruants playing vsually at the Gloabe on the Bancke-side.' Such descriptions, increasingly common on the title-pages of printed plays during the 1590s and after, speak to a variety of motives on the part of buyers as well as printers. Laying down sixpence for the quarto *Lear*, for example, allows the purchaser to connect with a royal occasion. But the title-page also associates the play with the Globe on the Bankside. The printed script offers itself as a mnemonic device for purchasers who may have actually seen and heard the play in performance there. The words on the page become a way of returning, in memory, to that experience. In terms of speech-act theory, the printed words are not just *signs* of semantic meaning; they are *indices* of bodily experiences, reminders of what the speakers looked like, what their words sounded like, and what the vision/sound *felt* like.

There were two schemes of punctuation current in Shakespeare's time: an older body-based scheme that used commas, colons and full stops to indicate varying lengths of pauses for breath and a newer grammar-based scheme that used these marks to indicate logical divisions of thought. One hesitates to make too much of the evidence in the 1608 quarto. Only in *The Boke of Sir Thomas More* do we have a possible example of which scheme of punctuation Shakespeare himself preferred. The pages attributed to Shakespeare use very few marks of punctuation, and those few in

a thoroughly body-based way.[17] Copyists and type-setters could inter-
polate their own ideas, but it is worth noting that Cordelia's speeches in
the 1608 quarto seem to be marked with cues to somatic memory, not
cerebral logic. Not a single one of Cordelia's speeches in Scene 1 contains
a full stop until the end. What comes in between are commas, cues for
momentary pauses for breath. The penultimate speech she makes to her
sisters (that's number 10 on the transcript) demonstrates body-based
punctuation particularly well. The colon in the next to last line calls for a
longer pause than a comma, but yet not a full stop. The question mark at
the end has the force of an exclamation point:

> The iewels of our father,
> With washe eyes *Cordelia* leaues you, I knowe you what you are,
> And like a sister am most loath to call your faults
> As they are named, vse well our Father,
> To your professed bosoms I commit him,
> But yet alas stood I within his grace,
> I would preferre him to a better place:
> So farewell to you both? (sig. B4v)

The Quarto *History of King Lear* enhances the mnemonic effect by presenting the entire script as one continuous action, without act and scene
divisions. The Folio text of 1623, although it probably represents a version
trimmed down for the two hours' traffic of the stage, nonetheless breaks
up the text with precise act and scene numbers. In the context of the
volume's monumental size and the gallery of commendatory verses like
Jonson's 'To the memory of my beloved, The Author, Master William
Shakespeare, and what he hath left us', the effect of this editorial paraphernalia is to shift the focus of memory from the performance of *King
Lear* to the place of *King Lear* in Shakespeare's collected achievement.

RESIDUALS

Every time the bookseller Nathaniel Butter sold a copy of the Quarto
Lear he collected what modern show-business knows as a 'residual', a
royalty for a repeat performance, often in a different medium. Actors in
films collect residuals when those films are shown on television or get
sold as DVDs. In the case of *The History of King Lear*, the transfer in
media was from live performance to print. Ballads likewise functioned as

---

[17] I study this document and the larger phenomenon of body-based punctuation in my essay 'Prickly
Characters' in *Reading and Writing in Shakespeare*, ed. David M. Bergeron (Newark: University of
Delaware Press, 1996), pp. 25–44.

residuals, but in a more fundamental way than just royalty payments. The core idea of *residual* is, after all, *residuum*, something left over or left behind. Ballads like 'A Lamentable Song of the death of King Leare and his three Davghters' let us know just what it was that versifiers, singers and listeners found worthy of remembering and keeping alive.[18] Although Samuel Johnson desperately wanted the ballad to be a source for the play, the first surviving printing dates to no earlier than 1620. Like Shakespeare's play, the ballad defies the historical sources in the matter of Lear's and Cordelia's deaths. *The True Chronicle History of King Leir* ends with Leir regaining his kingdom, but the ballad preserves from Shakespeare's play the monstrous injustice of Cordelia's death and Lear's despair over her body:

> But when he heard *Cordela* dead,
>   who dyed indeed for loue
> Of her deare father, in whose cause
>   she did this battell mooue
> He swounding fell vpon her brest,
>   from whence he neuer parted,
> But on her bosome left his life,
>   that was so truely hearted.[19]

To judge from the ballad, the play's chief residual was passion. The ballad of King Lear distils from Shakespeare's play the subjectivity of the sufferer and locates that suffering in certain parts of the body: rent hair, stained cheeks, above all the daughter's breast on which the father expires. As visual as those details might seem, the residuals of Lear's story happen through sound, though the singer's taking on Lear's personhood and giving it voice. Memory resides in lungs, throat, mouth and ears.

PROBLEMS OF WRITING PERFORMANCE HISTORY

Reading the books I checked out on the production history of *King Lear* and navigating my way around *The Cambridge King Lear CD-ROM*, I was relieved to learn that my own problems with remembering *King Lear* were hardly unique. I took special comfort in Alexander Leggatt's confession near the start of his volume on *Lear* in Manchester University

---

[18] This notion of 'residuals' is developed more fully in my essay 'Shakespeare's Residuals' in *Shakespeare and Elizabethan Popular Culture*, ed. Neil Rhodes (Thompson, 2005), forthcoming.

[19] Anonymous, 'A Lamentable Song of the death of King Leare and his three Daughters', in Richard Johnson, *The Golden Garland of Princely Pleasures and Delicate Delights* (London: A.M. for Thomas Langley, 1620), sig. A5v.

Press's Shakespeare in Performance series: 'Memory cheats: I have seen all the productions described in the following chapters except those involving Gielgud, and in researching this book I have been astonished by how often my memory is at odds with the evidence – much of which depends on other people's memories'.[20]

Every theatre historian faces a problem of selectivity – or rather *three* problems of selectivity. The first concerns evidence, *what* gets remembered and *how* it gets remembered. The 1608 quarto lets us know that *Lear* was performed by the King's Men before James I and his court at Whitehall Palace on St Stephen's night. Except for omitting the exact year, that information is astonishingly precise. But for the purposes of performance history it's the wrong sort of information. All the ingenuity in the world about which actor is likely to have played which role, about the way written parts were handed around, about punctuation, about horizontal lines, about early modern theories of the passions is not going to tell us what we really want to know, what we really wish had been remembered. The closer we come to our own moment in time, the fuller the documentary record becomes, but we are still dependent, as Leggatt notes, on 'other people's memories'.

A second problem of selectivity concerns just which productions an historian chooses to discuss. Leggatt tries to strike a balance among landmark productions (John Gielgud's with Harley Granville-Barker at the Old Vic in 1940, Peter Brook's with Paul Scofield at the Royal Court Theatre in 1962), geographical range (Robin Phillips's with Peter Ustinov at Stratford, Ontario), in 1979, Adrian Noble's with Antony Sher as Fool at the RSC in 1982), and variety of media (Grigori Kozintsev's 1971 film, Peter Brook's 1971 film, Laurence Olivier's 1983 television performance).

A third problem is presented by the sheer length and scale of the script. How do you account for the Quarto text's 3,109 lines (as numbered in the Oxford edition) or the Folio's 2,931? Historians of *Lear* in performance have found a variety of stratagems. Let me take them up in order of publication. J. S. Bratton's volume on *Lear* in the Bristol Classical Press's 'Plays in Performance' series prints the entire script on left-hand pages, with notes on productions, engravings, and production stills on right-hand pages, all cued to the text by scene numbers and line numbers. This arrangement allows Bratton to highlight 'scenes and aspects of the play which each generation has chosen to make the central focus of its version

---

[20] Alexander Leggatt, *Shakespeare in Performance: King Lear* (Manchester: Manchester University Press, 1988), p. 15.

of *King Lear*', primarily through cuts, restorations, and rearrangements in the sequence of scenes.[21] Production choices within particular scenes are the focus of James P. Lusardi and June Schlueter's *Reading Shakespeare in Performance: 'King Lear'*. Lusardi and Schlueter have isolated and given nonce names to six key scenes – 'Cordelia's Plight' (1.1), 'The Wicked Sisters' (1.4 and 2.4), 'The Mock Trial' (3.6), 'Dover Cliff' (4.6), 'The Anonymous Captain' (5.3), and 'The Promised End' (5.3) – and have compared how two videotaped productions (Jonathan Miller with Michael Horden for the BBC in 1982 and Michael Elliott with Laurence Olivier for Granada Television in 1983) capitalize on one or another possibility.[22] Grace Ioppolo in *A Routledge Literary Sourcebook on William Shakespeare's 'King Lear'* (2003) has thrown up her hands in despair. Part of the design of the 'Sourcebook' series is a selection of so-called 'key passages'. In the case of *Lear* one sympathizes with Ioppolo's predicament:

> *King Lear* is now considered to be Shakespeare's greatest play, and indeed each and any passage of it can be, and has been, considered 'key', as evidenced by the variety of passages discussed by literary and performance critics above. It is simply not possible to divide the play into a handful of scenes or passages and still represent it in any way similar to Shakespeare's rendering of it or even to make sense of its enormous impact on past, present, and future audiences.[23]

In effect, Ioppolo wants to remember it all. Her solution is to cram in as much of the text as possible and to summarize the rest in square brackets.

Part of the problem facing all these theatre historians is the relentless linearity of print as a medium. Even in the house of memory, one's progress through the room is not necessarily in a straight line. Certainly it would not have been so for an actor who was using the canopy of the Globe's stage as a reference point. Christie Carson and Jacky Bratton, co-editors of *The Cambridge King Lear CD-ROM: Text and Performance Archive* (2003), believe that the electronic medium obviates these difficulties. The database they present on *King Lear* in performance is organized into three sectors: (1) a chronological list of productions, with

---

[21] J. S. Bratton, ed., *King Lear: William Shakespeare* (Bristol: Bristol Classical Press, 1987; Plays in Performance), p. 4.

[22] James P. Lusardi and June Schlueter's *Reading Shakespeare in Performance: 'King Lear'* (Rutherford, NJ: Fairleigh Dickinson University Press, 1991). Lusardi and Schlueter explain their choices thus: 'we have been painfully selective in our choice of sequences to analyse. Yet those we have selected represent paradigms for performance-oriented study, and collectively our analyses amount to a substantial exploration of the play' (p. 18).

[23] Grace Ioppolo, *A Routledge Literary Sourcebook on William Shakespeare's 'King Lear'* (London: Routledge, 2003), p. 96.

directors, casts, etc., (2) a pictorial archive of engravings, set designs and photographic production stills organized chronologically by production, and (3) a compendium of information organized by act and scene. All of this data can be cross-referenced with the script itself. As with Bratton's 'Plays in Performance' edition, they have set out to demonstrate 'the fluidity of the text over time'. They think of themselves as providing a map to a territory, but they refrain from telling the user what to think about that territory or how to proceed in exploring it: 'This CD allows the user to choose one preferred version and work with that as their central text, but also, or instead, to move freely between many versions. Nothing about the disk is final or in any way aims for a definitive reading. Every attempt has been made to allow for as many uses as possible.' Here, in an abundance matched nowhere else, are the materials of memory.[24] What is *not* here – and how could it be? – is any sense that the link between one piece of information and another could be somatic (beyond the tapping fingers) or emotional.

THE CLAIMS OF FILM AND VIDEO

We all know the syndrome. We hear about a book that we think we should read. We buy the book. We don't read it. But we feel somehow that we possess the ideas in it because the book resides on our shelves. Film and video productions of *King Lear*, it seems to me, encourage the same dubious claim to knowledge. I've got in my hands the plastic box that contains the videotape of Laurence Olivier's performance of 1983; therefore I've got complete knowledge of the production. I can hold the memory in my hands. But whose memory is it? Leggatt catches my sentiments exactly when he compares the elusiveness of stage history with the artifactuality of film and video: 'The film and television versions are more fixed, but only in that the sounds and images do not change. (Even when a film exists in different cuts, each cut is fixed within itself.) What changes, continually, is the impression they make not only on different viewers but also on subsequent encounters by the same viewer.'[25] My primary memory of Olivier's Lear is watching its United States television premiere with my friend and colleague Elias Mengel in the upstairs study

---

[24] Christie Carson and Jacky Bratton, eds., *The Cambridge King Lear CD-ROM: Text and Performance Archive* (Cambridge: Cambridge University Press, 2000), 'Introduction and User's Guide'.

[25] Leggatt, *Shakespeare in Performance*, p. 15.

of his house on 29th Street in Georgetown in Washington, DC. It was a cold night. Having been lucky enough to see and hear Olivier onstage several times, I found the sight and sound of him inside a plastic box disappointing. And Elias later met an end as bleak as Lear's. That's what I feel about Olivier's Lear, not what I ought to say.

The writing of the script, the original stage performance, the passage from stage to page, residuals, problems of writing performance history, the claims of film and video: these six moments in the history of *King Lear* all involve memories that are (1) non-linear, (2) not reducible to an argument, and (3) more like liquid and vapour than impressions on stone. They are, in the literal sense of the word, *discursive*. They are movements between one point and another.[26] As a species of movement, discourse needs to embrace 'feel' as well as 'ought'.

Differences between those two modes of remembering *King Lear* became especially clear to me in connection with Alan Howard's Lear under Peter Hall's direction, particles of which entered the vaporous liquid of my memory in 1997. I went to the performance at the Old Vic with my friend Patricia Tatspaugh, who happened to be a friend of Jenny Quayle, who played Regan. My disappointment with Olivier's miniature Lear on TV was nothing compared to my disappointment with this production. Having decided to become a Shakespeare professor in part because I'd thrilled to the work of Hall and Howard during the RSC's glory days in the late 1960s and early 1970s – and fully conscious that the Old Vic had been the venue for the John Gielgud and Harley Granville-Barker production in 1940 – I came to the performance with huge expectations. But 1997 wasn't 1977. For me, the effect of Hall's vocal coaching and Howard's mannered delivery was absolutely stultifying. Sitting through that performance was like hearing a technically perfect rendition of the notes in a late Beethoven quartet that lacked any emotional presence whatsoever. Alas, my friend Patricia had already arranged that we would go backstage afterward and visit with Jenny Quayle. If ever there were a time to speak what we ought to say, not what we feel, this was it. In the event, I spoke what we ought to say.

The problem I have been confronting here, the problem of how to *speak* memory, is actually anticipated in the last scripted speech in *King Lear*. No sooner have the horrific events of the final scene become

---

[26] 'Discourse', etymology, in *The Oxford English Dictionary*, 2nd edn. (Oxford: Oxford University Press, 1989), accessed electronically 26 June 2005. Further references to the *OED* are cited in the text.

memories than the speaker offers the play's listeners two ways of putting
into words what they have just witnessed:

> The weight of this sad time we must obey,
> Speak what we feel, not what we ought to say.
> The oldest have borne most. We that are young
> Shall never see so much, nor live so long.
> (*History* 24.318–21)

The perennial complaint about this final speech is that it is woefully
inadequate as a summary of the play. The Quarto's assigning of the speech to
Albany might make more sense than the Folio's assigning it to Edgar, since
Albany is constantly trying to fix the implications of the action in some neat
bit of verbiage. He's at it even in the moment Lear is preparing to die:

> All friends shall taste
> The wages of their virtue, and all foes
> The cup of their deservings.–O see, see!
> (*History* 24.297–8)

Whether spoken by Edgar or Albany, the final speech stands as a *sententia* or
'sentence': a command to 'remember this'. It's the verbal equivalent of
those pointing fingers drawn in the margins of early modern books, perhaps with a vertical line to set off the speech or a series of quotation marks
before each of the lines that the reader wants to remember.[27]

A few minutes, or a few centuries, after the play's catastrophic events,
our cue to speak remains the same. We are given two possible positions:
'feel' or 'ought'. If forced to choose, I'll take 'feel'. There is a dynamic,
tactile basis to 'feel'. The word's earliest meaning in the *OED* is 'to examine
or explore by touch' (feel, v. 1), whence the more abstract meaning 'to
perceive, be conscious' (11). In *Lear*, as elsewhere, Shakespeare puns again
and again on 'feel' as 'perceive' and 'feel' as 'experience by touch'. Lear's
curse on Gonoril – his wish that she may give birth to a 'child of spleen'
like herself, 'that she may feel – / That she may feel / How sharper than a
serpent's tooth it is / To have a thankless child' (*History* 4.280–3) – comes
back to him full circle on the heath: 'Take physic, pomp, / Expose thyself
to feel what wretches feel' (*History* 10.30–1). The most painful of these
puns occurs during the mad Lear's encounter with the blinded Gloucester. 'You see how this world goes', Lear taunts the blind man. 'I see it

---

[27] Margreta de Grazia, 'Shakespeare in Quotation Marks', in *The Appropriation of Shakespeare: Post-Renaissance Reconstructions of the Works and the Myth*, ed. Jean Marsden (New York: St Martins, 1991), pp. 57–71.

feelingly' is Gloucester's reply (*History* 20.142–4). The contrast here between seeing and feeling points up the quasi-passive quality of 'feel', a quality that is registered in the *OED*'s third meaning ('To be felt as having a specified quality; to produce a certain impression on the senses [*esp.* that of touch] or the sensibilities; to seem') but is implicit in the other two senses as well. Feeling is an experience that the subject receives from without but knows from within. Contrast this exquisitely perceived in-between state with the total passivity of 'ought', an imposition from without. 'Ought' is the past tense of 'owe', a conjugation of 'owe' that may have begun in the past but exerts continuing force in the present and the future. 'The *weight* of this sad time': the first of the two nouns in this phrase can be felt ('relative heaviness', *OED* weight, n.^{1}, 1.3. a) as well as paid due attention ('importance, moment, claim to consideration', III.15.a).

'Ought' and 'feel' shape up as two quite distinct modes of memory. 'Ought' takes its cue from outside, from external models for the ordering of memory. The house of memory is most accommodating to fixed ideas. As such, it forms the perfect repository for the verbal formulations of academic criticism. 'Feel', by contrast, takes its cue from subjectivity, from internal experiences of sensation and movement. Movement disorders the house of memory, but it stirs up the vaporous liquid of the caves in a most provocative way. If Juan Huarte Navarro can be believed, understanding and memory stand in a reciprocal relationship to one another. In *The Examination of Mens Wits*, translated into English in 1594, Navarro enlists Aristotle in support of his observation that

vnderstanding and memorie, are powers opposit and contrary, in sort, that the man who hath a great memorie, shall find a defect in his vnderstanding, and he who hath a great vnderstanding cannot enioy a good memorie: for it is impossible that the braine should of his owne nature, be at one selfe time drie and moist.[28]

The whole truth, surely, is to be found in both places, in the solidities of the house of memory and in those moist, vaporous caves. We draw on both models as we remember *King Lear*. I can't unthink what Alexander Lamar Stevens said to that freshman class in 1964, anymore than I can unthink what I've read, heard, reflected upon, and taught concerning *King Lear* across the forty years since then. But I can recognize that these

---

[28] Juan Huarte Navarro, *The Examination of Mens Wits*, trans. Richard Carew (London, 1594), p. 63.

formulations do not, by themselves, constitute the totality of memory. Rather, memory consists in movement between two very different ways of knowing. Speak what we feel? Or speak what we ought to say? The *true* chronicle history of *King Lear* consists in doing both.

CHAPTER 2

Shakespeare's memorial aesthetics

John J. Joughin

MEMORIAL AESTHETICS?

Historicist and materialist critics alike have remained fascinated with the hermeneutic yield provided by the representation of dead bodies, re-enacting a type of 'memorial aesthetics' which has centred on the allegorization of the body *in extremis*, or on images of its dismemberment. This trend actually locates a paradigm-shift within the wider currents of cultural criticism itself of course, as, during the eighties and the nineties, we witnessed a shift from the 'semantic to the somatic' – confirming, in some part, a 'reaction formation' against various brands of critical formalism that had hitherto prevailed, in order to confront what Keir Elam refers to as the 'irreducible and unrationalizable materiality' of 'sheer untidy, asyntactic, pre-semantic bodiliness'.[1] At its best this work has illuminated the complex ways in which the history of modernity was itself compliant in the erasure, repression and supplementation of the body; and yet there are ways too, in which the recent affirmative corporeal 'turn' of cultural criticism has also served to elide the political significance of a recovery of the importance of body, so that, as Terry Eagleton observes, while

few literary texts are likely to make it nowadays into the new historicist canon unless they contain at least one mutilated body ... At the same time, it is difficult to read the later Roland Barthes, or even the later Michel Foucault, without feeling that a certain style of meditation on the body, on pleasures and surfaces, zones and techniques, has acted among other things as a convenient displacement of a less immediately corporeal politics, and acted also as an ersatz kind of ethics. There is a privileged, privatised hedonism about such discourse,

---

[1] Cf. Keir Elam, '"In what chapter of his bosom?": Reading Shakespeare's Bodies', in *Alternative Shakespeares: Vol 2*, ed. T. Hawkes (London: Routledge, 1996), pp. 140–63 (p. 143), and also cf. Maurizio Calbi, *Approximate Bodies: Aspects of the Figuration of Masculinity, Power and the Uncanny in Early Modern Drama and Anatomy* (Salerno: Oedipus, 2001), pp. 13–14.

emerging as it does at just the historical point where certain less exotic forms of politics found themselves suffering a setback.[2]

Certainly, within recent variants of new historicism, suffering bodies regularly 'staged history' and by doing so they become the alibi for a Foucauldian inspired 'poetics of (Elizabethan) power' – in the process there is often an occlusion of the political and ethical implications of theatrical performance itself. Instead, we are offered a 'flattening out' of the ontological distinctions between theatre and society, as well as an oversimplification of the complex ways in which aesthetic and lived practices are inter-implicated in the process of informing our relation with others, both inside and outside the theatre.[3] In confronting the aestheticization of suffering within new historicism and in developing a new aestheticist approach to performance, much remains to be said about our 'interpretation' of the moments of affective intensity to which Eagleton alludes and, if in its interrogation of history Renaissance studies has for some years occupied what Blanchot would term 'the near side' of suffering, this also secretes a type of spectatorship which needs to be interrogated more closely. In the absent present of a play's afterlife the glorious cruelties of Jacobean drama serve to remind us of that which we have chosen in our finite world to forget: precisely the constraints of finitude. In this chapter I want to interrogate the ethical and political implications of this hermeneutic encounter in relation to Shakespeare's 'mourning plays' *Hamlet* and *Richard II*.

THE EMBASSY OF DEATH

In fact, a predilection for suffering, often almost lyrical in its extreme, is actually a fairly constant feature of Shakespearean studies past and present; and for humanist critics too, the Shakespearean uncanny has long evoked a form of remembering where pain and pleasure are inextricably entwined – and which, at times, conveys a performative intensity that is almost purgatorial in its extreme. For Harold Bloom, for example, insofar as Shakespeare's 'power' is in some sense exemplary it is because it teaches us

that pain is the authentic origin of human memory [and thereby in some sense what makes drama historical] and since Shakespeare [Bloom reasons] is the most memorable of writers, there may be a valid sense in which the pain Shakespeare

---

[2] Terence Eagleton, *The Ideology of the Aesthetic* (Oxford: Blackwell, 1990), p. 7.
[3] For an analogous argument developed at greater length see Francis Barker, *The Culture of Violence* (Manchester: Manchester University Press, 1993), esp. pp. 161–5.

affords us is as significant as the pleasure ... primal ambivalence ... remains central to Shakespeare ... memorable pain, or memory engendered through pain, ensues from an ambivalence both cognitive and affective, an ambivalence that we associate most readily with Hamlet.[4]

Confronted with this scale of unthinkable affectivity, Bloom habitually opts for a humanist solution that would reconcile us to suffering:

Shakespeare will not make us better, and he will not make us worse but he may teach us how to overhear ourselves when we talk to ourselves. Subsequently, he may teach us how to accept change, in ourselves as in others, and perhaps even the final form of change. Hamlet is death's ambassador to us.[5]

It is evident that Bloom confuses remembering Hamlet with monumentalizing him. And ironically of course, humanism's inability to witness suffering via the wishful act of self-identification which will eventually eliminate suffering all together is itself symptomatic of its failure to confront its own finitude, even if, somewhat paradoxically, that means securing its own self-preservation in death and immortality. Yet, even for Bloom, the ambivalence of suffering, its 'painful pleasure', is that even as it remains incomprehensible, it affects an encounter with the unexpected, the alien, or the *unheimlich* – an effect he characterizes elsewhere, as Shakespeare's 'weirdness'.[6]

Hamlet of course functions for Bloom (and for others) as the exemplification of, and for, the modern human subject. What interests me though are the terms by which (for humanist and non-humanist alike) this instantiation of finitude is inextricably bound up with an isolated act of witness or, more precisely, an attempt to come to terms with the 'performance of grief'. In these terms one is never far from the figure of the scapegoat who suffers alone and, although once 'excoriated' by their contemporaries, latterly becomes 'the founding figure of community' – a 'sacred other' whose original plight and exile is now remembered long after, as being forgotten in their own time.[7] In the political memory of a culture, the scapegoat figure locates a crossing point where the political and the singular conjoin powerfully as a community negotiates its sense

---

[4] See Harold, Bloom, *Shakespeare: The Invention of the Human* (London: Fourth Estate, 1999), p. 11.

[5] Again compare Bloom in *The Western Canon* (New York: Harcourt Brace and Company, 1994), p. 31, also cited by Catharine Belsey 'English Studies in the Postmodern Condition: Towards a Place for the Signifier', in Martin McQuillan *et al.*, eds., *Post-Theory: New Directions in Criticism* (Edinburgh: Edinburgh University Press, 1999), pp. 123–38.

[6] See Belsey, 'English Studies'.

[7] See Richard Kearney, 'Aliens and Others: Between Girard and Derrida', *Cultural Values* 3:3 (1999), 251–62.

of collective identity according to its original exclusion of the other and its ability to make reconciliation in the political present.

Critics are customarily drawn to Hamlet in terms which evoke the paradoxical logic of 'exemplary' suffering, as a figure who is invoked as unprecedented and singular and yet one whose fate can simultaneously be formalised into a law concerning the generally applicable significance of such isolation. Here, for example, is how G. Wilson Knight commences his well-known essay on 'The Embassy of Death: An Essay on Hamlet' (a title to which Bloom also evidently alludes):

> My purpose will therefore be first limited strictly to a discussion, not of the play as a whole, nor even of Hamlet's mind as a whole, but of this central reality of pain, which, though it be necessarily related, either as effect or cause, to the events of the plot and to the other persons, is itself ultimate, and should be the primary object of our search.
>
> Our attention is early drawn to the figure of Hamlet. Alone in the gay glitter of the court, silhouetted against brilliance, robustness, health, and happiness is the pale, black-robed Hamlet ... When we first meet him, his words point the essential inwardness of his suffering ... [8]

In searching for the 'primary object' of his criticism the scene to which Wilson Knight is irresistibly drawn is itself of course a scene of mourning:

> QUEEN. Good Hamlet, cast thy nightly colour off,
>   And let thine eye look like a friend on Denmark.
>   Do not for ever with thy vailèd lids
>   Seek for thy noble father in the dust.
>   Thy know'st 'tis common – all that lives must die,
>   Passing through nature to eternity.
> HAMLET. Ay, madam, it is common.
> QUEEN.   If it be
>   Why seems it so particular with thee?
> HAMLET. Seems, madam? Nay, it *is*. I know not 'seems'.
>   'Tis not alone my inky cloak, good-mother,
>   Nor customary suits of solemn black,
>   Nor windy suspiration of forced breath,
>   No, nor the fruitful river of the eye,
>   Nor the dejected haviour of the visage,
>   Together with all forms, moods, shapes of grief,

---

[8] See G. Wilson Knight, *The Wheel of Fire* (London: Methuen and Co Ltd, 1930), p. 17.

That can denote me truly. These indeed 'seem',
For they are actions that a man might play;
But I have that within which passeth show –
These but the trappings and the suits of woe.

(1.2.68–86)

This exchange has, of course, attracted its share of attention from materialist critics as well, most notably from Francis Barker who returns to it during what turns out to be a seminal account of the inauguration of modern subjectivity in Renaissance criticism, though Barker construes the 'essential interiority' that Wilson Knight identifies with such confidence, as premature and merely 'gestural':

Hamlet asserts against the devices of the world an essential interiority. If the 'forms, modes, shapes' [of grief] fail to denote him truly it is because in him a separation has already opened up between the inner reality of the subject, living itself, as 'that within which passes show', and an inauthentic exterior: and in that opening there begins to insist, however prematurely, the figure that is to dominate and organise bourgeois culture .... But this interiority remains, in Hamlet, gestural.[9]

Again, for Barker, our own inability to conceive of Hamlet and its body politic otherwise is already a mark of a considerable bourgeois forgetting, yet it also serves to witness a related affinity, as, despite its latter-day erasure and its present remove, the insistent materiality of the Jacobean corpus of Shakespeare and his contemporaries nevertheless retains its potential to light the poetic touch-paper:

The Jacobean body – the object, certainly, of terrible pressures – is distributed irreducibly through a theatre whose political and cultural centrality can only be measured against the marginality of the theatre today; and beyond the theatre it exists in the world whose most subtle inner organization is so different from that of our own not least because of the part played by the body in it. In the fullest sense of which it is now possible to conceive, from the other side of our own carnal guilt, it is a corporeal body, which, if it is already touched by the metaphysics of its later erasure, still contains a charge which, set off by the violent hands laid on it, will illuminate the scene, incite difference, and ignite poetry. This spectacular visible body is the proper gauge of what the bourgeoisie had to forget.[10]

---

[9] See Francis Barker, *The Tremulous Private Body* (London: Methuen and Co Ltd, 1984), pp. 35–6.
[10] Barker, *The Tremulous Private Body*, p. 25.

In the performance of suffering, as Barker insinuates, there is a poetics, a pathos or 'charge' that will repay further interrogation. Set off for Barker in this instance by violent hands (of interpretation no doubt) which will 'illuminate the scene, incite difference, and ignite poetry' such moments clearly activate an interpersonal notion of 'readerly responsibility' in exposing us directly to what an ethical criticism, influenced by the readings of Levinas and Derrida, might term the 'irreducible otherness of the other' even as it is distributed as Barker himself puts it 'irreducibly throughout a theatre whose political and cultural centrality can only be measured against the marginality of the theatre today'.[11] Beyond its savage reappropriation, beyond its appropriation of savagery itself, in the process of its recuperation as 'our tradition', Jacobean poetry nonetheless ignites an ethical impulse which cannot be grounded by criticism or much less located by its retrospective justification(s), but rather instead evokes a sense of unrelinquished belatedness: the felt need to bear a 'last witness', an ' "inspiring" insomnia', which haunts liberal humanists and historicists alike.[12]

THE PERFORMANCE OF GRIEF

In situ of course, Hamlet's own performance of grief (which he carefully insists is not a matter of show) already remains wilfully misunderstood by those who witness it, so that his uncle reprimands him for his 'obstinate condolement'(1.2.93). Indeed, as Graham Holderness comments, Hamlet's grief introduces

[an] unwelcome discontinuity as he continues to 'seek for [his] noble father in the dust' (1.2.71), staring downwards at the earth, not upwards towards the king; looking to death, not life, the past, not the future. In clinging to an unappeasable wounded 'memory', Hamlet nurtures a destabilising and oppositional historical consciousness.[13]

This is surely right. Yet more accurately still we might say that what Hamlet grieves for here is to be deprived of mourning itself, a fate he feels bitterly and which surfaces as a recurrent preoccupation in the play as Hamlet is increasingly insistent in drawing a distinction between the mere

---

[11] Barker, *The Tremulous Private Body*, p. 25.
[12] On 'inspiring insomnia' see Maurice Blanchot, *The Writing of the Disaster*, trans. Ann Smock (Lincoln: University of Nebraska Press, 1995), p. 101.
[13] Graham Holderness, *Shakespeare: The Histories* (Basingstoke: Macmillan, 2000), p. 65.

theatricalization of grief and his own inability to mourn openly, so that, as he later complains of the player,

> Is it not monstrous that this player here,
> But in a fiction, in a dream of passion,
> Could force his soul so to his whole conceit
> That from her working all his visage wanned,
> Tears in his eyes, distraction in 's aspect,
> A broken voice, and his whole function suiting
> With forms to his conceit? And all for nothing.
> For Hecuba!
> What's Hecuba to him, or he to Hecuba,
> That he should weep for her? What would he do
> Had he the motive and the cue for passion
> That I have?
>
> (2.2.553–64)

Here, as elsewhere when he himself is cast as a spectator of grief, Hamlet 'weeps at not weeping' ('O what a rogue and peasant slave am I', etc.) and as such, the 'authentication' of his position as a mourner is curiously tantamount to a form of dispossession – 'a mourning not allowed ... a mourning without tears, a mourning deprived of weeping'.[14] Again, Hamlet's experience of alienation and its relation to the figure of the scapegoat are never far away here and directly reminiscent of course of the generational legacy of Oedipus or Christ as, 'officially' at least, the late king his father is forgotten. Indeed, it is as if Hamlet's father ('Remember me') already died elsewhere and as such Hamlet remains a hostage or a foreigner in his own land as there is no 'determinable resting place' for his indeterminable mourning, no official commemorative monument for Hamlet Senior. The former King, is as Jacques Derrida puts it, 'without monument without a localisable and circumscribed place of mourning'.[15] In place of the stately procession of monumental grief we are offered instead the undue haste of 'funeral baked meats' unceremoniously reprocessed for the marriage table (1.2.179–80).

In *Hamlet* (as in most of the histories and the tragedies) this time and space of mourning is joined explicitly with the state of the nation. In one sense this is clearly because the suffering of sovereigns and princes constitutes the very 'borderline condition' which constitutes the nation and which thereby also opens up 'a certain play of difference' within the idealization of

---

[14] I owe this reflection on 'mourning without tears' to Jacques Derrida; see his *Of Hospitality*, trans. Rachel Bowlby (Stanford: Stanford University Press, 2000), p. 111.

[15] Jacques Derrida, *Of Hospitality*, p. 111.

national identity itself – in short, the performance of grief plays the troubling other to a 'commemorative' historicism. Indeed, for a monumental historicism committed to orderly succession, the danger of such figures of and for mourning is that they are sited simultaneously inside and outside the official archive where the sedimented memory of their sacrifice resides as an indeterminable countersignature for future national determination.[16] Here, 'for once', as Holderness observes of Shakespeare's *Richard II*,

> history is not written by the victors, but unforgettably formulated by the dispossessed, in a poignant poetry of defeat and inconsolable loss ... [so that] the myth of the deposed king will live far longer than the practical achievements of his enemies ...[17]

Beyond the crude propagandizing of nationalism then we could say that characters like Hamlet and Richard articulate the exemplary in another register and in doing so they offer a more radical legacy for the future allegorization of a political present. The attraction of these figures might be said to lie in the fact that they manifest a form of nameless intimacy (particular yet common) so much so that, at one juncture, Richard desires the fate of the unknown soldier – often itself of course at times of emergency paradoxically a powerful signifier of nationalism – offering to swap his kingdom 'for a little grave, / A little, little grave, an obscure grave' (3.3. 152–3). Ironically, in historical terms at least, the question of Richard's actual burial place which was never certain has returned, even relatively recently, to haunt historians.[18] By the end of the play, like Old Hamlet, Richard is still in some sense without a tomb. Yet, as Benedict Anderson reminds us, the question of national identity is less a case of forensic evidence and more a matter of what he terms 'ghostly national imaginings',[19] and in this respect, in what we might term the crypt of nationalism, we find nothing more or less than the sense of

---

[16] So that, as John Brannigan reminds us, insofar as 'death exists outside the borders of the nation', then it also constitutes the threshold space of and for future national determination: 'As the end of "people living" death marks the end of nation, and thereby constitutes the space of the nation in its very otherness to that space ... the nation *is*. It lives. And yet only becomes apparent at the border, when the difference against which the nation is constituted is waiting "on the other side" ... Death is the other nation, what lies outside the border, "the undiscovr'd bourn" consciousness of "ourselves" as "people living" is made possible only by a certain movement or step at the border, a movement at the threshold.' See 'Writing DeTermiNation: Reading Death in (to) Irish National Identity', in J. Brannigan, R. Robbins and J. Wolfreys, eds., *Applying: To Derrida* (Basingstoke: Macmillan, 1996), pp. 55–70 (p. 56).

[17] See Holderness, *Shakespeare: The Histories*, p. 196.

[18] See for example *The Times*, 28 January 2002, 'Building site grave could solve mystery of Richard II.'

[19] See Benedict Anderson, *Imagined Communities: Reflections on the Origin and Spread of Nationalism* (London: Verso, 1983), p. 9.

dispossession that lies at the heart of another tradition, 'the forgotten dead'. This spectre is raised insistently in *Richard II* as for Richard again, persistently, it is 'matter out of place' rather than the official narrative of monumental history that preoccupies him, often quite literally the recitation of a history from below, as Richard, like Hamlet, spends his time with his eyes downcast seeking the past which has turned to dust:

> Let's talk of graves, of worms and epitaphs,
> Make dust our paper, and with rainy eyes
> Write sorrow on the bosom of the earth.
>
> (3.2. 141–3)

To summarize then, Hamlet and Richard remain haunting yet exemplary figures, each uncommon yet somehow typical insofar as each is cast in 'a supposedly singular situation by bearing witness to it in terms which go beyond it'.[20] Rather like the unknown soldier, they serve to confirm that we cannot 'know' what they suffer, yet they do so in a language of generality which is in some sense transcendental and with which we can all identify. What goes for me they seem to say goes for everybody, it's enough to hear me, 'I am the universal sacrificial victim'[21]:

> . . . you have but mistook me all this while.
> I live with bread, like you; feel want,
> Taste grief, need friends. Subjected thus,
> How can you say to me, I am a king?
>
> (*Richard II*, 3.2. 170–3)

In short 'tis common, but then why seems it so particular with them? In the case of Hamlet, as Francis Barker remarks, it is almost as if history itself is hypostatized as individual grief. Hamlet is historical then because inconsolable and this again in turn points us to the problem of the political, as Hamlet's petition to justice (and indeed Richard's) remain in some sense unfulfillable – we can't 'set things right'. Grief introduces a disruptive continuum which will continue to haunt us partly because as Freud reminds us for humans pain and memory are clearly linked: it is not so much that history makes us suffer, we suffer (Hamlet insinuates) because we are historical. Yet having introduced this relation which hints at a being in common Hamlet then still insists that this grief is particular only to him and thus simultaneously defies our comprehension. His

---

[20] See Jacques Derrida, *Monolingualism of the Other; Or, The Prosthesis of Origin*, trans. P. Mensah (Stanford: Stanford University Press, 1998), *passim*, and Geoffrey Bennington, 'Double Tonguing: Derrida's Monolingualism', http://www.usc.edu/dept/comp-lit/tympannum/4/bennington.html, p. 5
[21] Derrida, *Monolingualism of the Other*, pp. 19–20.

father's death then like history manifests itself as an otherness which both attracts and defies our understanding, presenting us with unimaginable horrors which we nevertheless share an affinity.

In speaking of history in these terms one is immediately drawn to Walter Benjamin's inconsolable 'Angel of history'. Like Hamlet and Richard his gaze too is directed downwards at the dust, this after all (as Benjamin reminds us) is how one pictures the angel of history:

His face is turned toward the past ... The angel would like to stay, awaken the dead, and make whole what has been smashed. But a storm is blowing from Paradise; it has got caught in his wings with such violence that the angel can no longer close them. This storm irresistibly propels him into the future to which his back is turned, while the pile of debris before him grows skyward.[22]

This storm (Benjamin adds) is 'what we call progress'. Again told from the point of view of the spectator, history is a matter of perspective; where monumental historicism perceives an orderly succession or 'a chain of events', the angel of history 'sees one single catastrophe which keeps piling wreckage upon wreckage and hurls it in front of his feet' – a disruptive continuum indeed. Interestingly, of course, Benjamin suggests here that history is an analogue of the sublime and part of the lure of the sublime of course is that it too can be construed as a category that simultaneously opens and limits manifesting a form of otherness which both attracts and defies our comprehension in presenting us with a form of history that both will and will not be recovered and, unsurprisingly of course, it follows that as a spectator of history the Angel is left entranced and appalled in almost equal measure, 'looking as though he is about to move away from something he is fixedly contemplating. His eyes are staring, his mouth is open, his wings are spread.'

It is clear as Jacques Lacan remarks in speaking of Saint Teresa and others like her 'that the essential testimony of the mystics is that they are experiencing [*jouissance*] but know nothing about it'.[23] The angel's vacant gaze and open mouth could be construed at one level as a moment of dumbfound rapture. Yet as Homi Bhabha observes: 'If the testimony of rapture consists of a type of breach between experience and knowledge,

[22] Walter Benjamin, 'Theses on the Philosophy of History', in *Illuminations*, trans. H. Zohn, ed. and introd. H. Arendt (London: Fontana, 1968), pp. 245–55 (p. 249).

[23] Jacques Lacan, 'God and the *Jouissance* of the Woman', in Juliet Mitchell and Jacqueline Rose, eds., *Feminine Sexuality: Jacques Lacan and the école freudienne* (New York: W. W. Norton, 1982), pp. 137–48 (p. 147) as cited in Homi Bhabha, 'Aura and Agora: on Negotiating Rapture and Speaking Between' in Richard Francis, ed., *Negotiating Rapture: The Power of Art to Transform Lives* (Chicago: Museum of Contemporary Art, 1996), pp. 8–17 (p. 8).

then what account can it give of itself?' or, to put it another way: 'who speaks for rapture? Can it be witnessed or represented?'[24] It is as if the spectator experiences an untimely pause in both time and knowledge, a relation beyond relation insofar as it insinuates an 'absolutely asymmetrical relation with the wholly other'.[25] To return to the context of theatrical performance, I would want to argue that there is a link to be established here between Aristotle's doctrine of tragedy and the aesthetics of the sublime – again of course (and Harold Bloom would be reassured by this) for the spectator at least each manifests a contradictory mix of pleasure and pain. There has been a tendency to psychologise tragedy, yet, if the 'tragic effect' condenses around the notion of the sublime it is in no small part because, as Philippe Lacoue Labarthe reminds us, the tragic effect is a 'political effect':

when Aristotle talks about a tragic effect, I think one would have to begin to analyse this as a *political* effect. 'Terror' and 'pity' are essentially political notions. They are absolutely not psychological. Pity refers to what the modern age, under the name of compassion thinks of, as the origin of the social bond (in Rousseau and Burke, for example): terror refers to the risk of the dissolution of the social bond, and the pre-eminent place of that first social bond which is the relation with the other.[26]

The sublime then clearly comes close to the aesthetic register of indeterminate alterity we have traced so far, and certainly insofar as it touches on the risk of the political. Yet how then can we historicize and politicize this relation with that which is indeterminably other? In attempting to overcome the dissolution of the social bond that the image of the Angel so clearly evokes as a mixture of terror and speechless compassion, can tragedy and history ever be reconciled? How are we to eventually come to terms with, or remember, the forgotten dead if their history is fated only to be construed as the figure of and for inconsolable loss? Is it possible to construct a politics for this poetry of defeat or is it fated to remain, for all its poignancy, unreconciled and unreconcilable? Can the inconsolable be consoled? When will the angel of history close his wings and rest? How are we to embrace the nameless undead?

<hr />

[24] See Bhabha, 'Aura and Agora', p. 8.
[25] Bhabha, 'Aura', and also see Jacques Derrida, *Specters of Marx: The State of the Debt, the Work of Mourning, and the New International*, trans. P. Kamuf (London: Routledge, 1994) and Derrida, *The Gift of Death*, trans. D. Wills (Chicago: University of Chicago Press, 1995), p. 91.
[26] See Philippe Lacoue-Labarthe, 'On the Sublime', in *ICA Documents 4: Postmodernism* (London: ICA, 1986), pp. 11–18 (p. 17).

PASSION PLAY

In construing this relationship otherwise I want to close by exploring the dramatisation of sacrificial victimage in more direct relation to Shakespeare's *Richard II* where, in his insistent apprehension of bereavement, Richard eventually settles for casting himself in terms of those future commemorative practices that will canonize his memory and by which his anonymity will simultaneously guarantee his legacy – as the impossible object of his own grief. In short, Shakespeare's 'lamentable tragedy', *Richard II*, is situated as a Passion play, where the legacy of an incomprehensible grief and the aporetic configuration of its interiority is entwined with the homilectic *exemplum* – we are confronted with the sublime alterity of our own being configured as the 'inward beholding' of an external truth in which we now may acknowledge a share. As such, Richard's lyricism dramatises a process self-iconisation where Christological metaphors and allusions to sacrifice and martyrdom are painfully embodied in the act of performance itself:

> I'll give my jewels for a set of beads,
> My gorgeous palace for a hermitage,
> My gay apparel for an almsman's gown,
> My figured goblets for a dish of wood,
> My sceptre for a palmer's walking staff,
> My subjects for a pair of carved saints,
> And my little kingdom for a little grave
> (3.3.146–52)[27]

Yet the risk is that Richard's hyperbole will be taken literally, or rather as merely theatrical. And of course it is precisely in these terms that Richard is often accused by his latter-day critics of waxing too lyrical, his overt theatricalisation of grief drawing the accusation of improbability, the tears of a 'player king' re-enacting the terms of what Freud would term a 'hysterical' mourning – interminably immersed in sad events that 'occurred long ago'. Yet if the denial of Richard's grief by others only consolidates the process by which he is cast as irretrievable, it also offers an audience a position from which to redeem themselves. In short, the extent of Richard's over-dramatic isolation will in time also itself prove a

---

[27] Here as elsewhere Richard bears a striking resemblance to Walter Benjamin's description of the German *Trauerspiel* or Mourning Play, where again, as George Steiner remarks, 'It is not the tragic hero who occupies the centre of the stage, but the Janus-faced composite of tyrant and martyr of the Sovereign who incarnates the mystery of absolute will and of its victim (so often himself)'. Steiner in his 'Introduction' to Walter Benjamin, *The Origin of German Tragic Drama*, trans. John Osborne (London: Verso, 1992), p. 16.

measure or gauge of an audience's willingness to overcome their scepticism and to commit to the very rites of pilgrimage he envisages.

In *Richard II* the visual turn of anamorphism surfaces as the most persistent register of, and for, this asymmetrical relationship between the spectator and the performance of grief:

> BUSHY. Each substance of a grief hath twenty shadows
> Which shows like grief itself, but is not so.
> For sorrow's eye, glazed with blinding tears,
> Divides one thing entire to many objects –
> Like perspectives, which, rightly gazed upon,
> Show nothing but confusion; eyed awry,
> Distinguish form. So your sweet majesty,
> Looking awry upon your lord's departure,
> Find shapes of grief more than himself to wail,
> Which, looked on as it is, is naught but shadows
> Of what it is not. Then, thrice-gracious Queen,
> More than your lord's departure weep not: more is not seen,
> Or if it be, 'tis with false sorrow's eye,
> Which for things true, weeps things imaginary
>
> (2.2.14–27)

Here, as Howard Caygill observes, in the course of refuting the Queen's 'apprehension of nothing', Bushy's argument could be cast as classically philosophical, in that it is unable to conceive a reality that would not partake of being. In the face of Isabella's grief Bushy's response is to make a reductive distinction between being and nothing and to refuse the 'equivocal character of nothing and the sadness it can provoke'.[28] With the benefit of hindsight Bushy argues that the Queen will see the error of her ways and for the time being 'rightly gazed upon' she should look instead to the 'substance' (rather than the shadow) of her grief 'which is indeed the king's departure'.[29] Yet, of course, Queen Isabella's tears repeat the chronotope of leave taking that we have already rehearsed in some detail above, as, from the outset of the scene, she is preoccupied with the unsettling anticipation of a future anterior, so that her first farewell might well be her last, or at least is already cast in anticipation of a future to come – as such she is already a hostage and a host to a grief that is tangible even as it is unpremeditated:

---

[28] See Howard Caygill, 'Shakespeare's Monster of Nothing', in John J. Joughin, ed., *Philosophical Shakespeares* (London: Routledge, 2000), pp. 105–14 (pp. 107–11).
[29] Caygill, 'Shakespeare's Monster', p. 111.

> Yet I know no cause
> Why I should welcome such a guest as grief,
> Save bidding farewell to so sweet a guest
> As my sweet Richard. Yet again, methinks
> Some unborn sorrow, ripe in Fortune's womb,
> Is coming towards me; and my inward soul
> At nothing trembles. With something it grieves
> More than with parting from my lord the King.
> . . .
> For nothing has begot my something grief –
> Or something hath the nothing that I grieve –
> 'Tis in reversion that I do possess –
> But what it is that is not yet known what,
> I cannot name: 'tis nameless woe, I wot.
>
> (2.2.6–13; 36–40)

Isabella's untimely dislocation is sited here in the abyssal relation to an interminable mourning that has 'the uncanny quality of being experienced without being an object of experience; it has the effect of an object without being an object',[30] as Caygill argues Isabella's 'heavy nothing' is not subsumed within the classical opposition between nothing or something, but it is still a nothing that is not nothing. In short this too is a type of nativity, but as yet it is only stillborn (cf. 2.2.62–6).

Here, as elsewhere in the play, the sublime links us to the 'temporal location of the spectator, the reader, the witness',[31] yet the option of 'knowing the sublime' is refused. More particularly of course the conceit of anamorphism already anticipates the sublime apprehension of 'death-in-life' that pervades *Richard II* and again Shakespeare knowingly stages a carefully orchestrated hermeneutic dilemma here by invoking the asymmetrical figure of the distorted *momento mori* most famously prefigured in Holbein's *The Ambassadors*, where, as Catherine Belsey reminds us, the anamorphic skull acts in an analogous fashion to 'an uncanny phrase or figure' which in disrupting 'our seamless mastery of the text, takes it in an unprecedented direction, or leaves us undecided between possible interpretations'.[32]

Interestingly enough, in the critical afterlife of the play it is precisely this anamorphic or indirect view of an unprecedented history witnessed from the sidelines that gains prominence, most evidently in the post-deposition report of Richard's entrance into London (5.2) which, as

---

[30] Caygill, 'Shakespeare's Monster'.   [31] See Bhabha, 'Aura and Agora', p. 10.
[32] See Catharine Belsey, 'English Studies in the Postmodern Condition', pp. 123–38.

Nicolas Brooke notes, is endlessly rehearsed by eighteenth- and nineteenth-century commentators and rapidly becomes the single most anthologised speech of the whole play:[33]

> YORK. As in a theatre, the eyes of men,
> After a well-graced actor leaves the stage,
> Are idly bent on him that enters next,
> Thinking his prattle to be tedious,
> Even so, or with much more contempt, men's eyes
> Did scowl on Richard. No man cried 'God save him!'
> No joyful tongue gave him his welcome home;
> But dust was thrown upon his sacred head,
> Which with such gentle sorrow he shook off,
> His face still combating with tears and smiles,
> The badges of his grief and patience,
> That had not God for some strong purpose steeled
> The hearts of men, they must perforce have melted,
> And barbarism itself have pitied him.
>
> (5.2.23–36)

Strikingly of course, York's 'elegy' evokes nothing more or less than Richard's progress to Calvary, as 'wearing the badges of his grief' the former King is now firmly cast as the ambivalent witness of his own fate, 'his face' contorted in pleasure and pain 'still combating with tears and smiles'. Intriguingly an analogy to the theatre is also close by, as we learn of the 'contempt' of those who refuse to acknowledge Richard or who avert their gaze or worse still 'scowl' on him. The audience is offered a Cavellian-like exposure of the failure of others to acknowledge alterity and invited to chose complicity or to place themselves in the open presence of Richard's isolation, in order to make Richard's present 'his' and 'theirs'. As the poet Dryden remarks in his recitation of the scene, 'Refrain from pity if you can . . .'[34] By the time Hazlitt considers the play, the aesthetic implications of the speech are so evident as to be superfluous:

There is only one passage more, the description of his [Richard's] entrance into London with Bolingbroke, which we should like to quote here, if it had not been so used and worn out, so thumbed and got by rote, so praised and painted, but its beauty surmounts all these considerations . . .[35]

---

[33] Cf. Nicholas Brooke, ed., *Shakespeare: Richard II* (Basingstoke: Macmillan, 1973).

[34] See John Dryden, '"The Grounds of Criticism in Tragedy", Preface to *Troilus and Cressida* (1679)', in Nicholas Brooke, p. 19.

[35] See W. C. Hazlitt, 'The Character of Richard II (1817)', in Nicholas Brooke, p. 40.

For Coleridge too, the exemplification of Richard's grief rests simultaneously on its singularity and on its pathos, observing that Shakespeare 'has represented this character in a very peculiar manner ... relying on Richard's disproportionate sufferings and gradually emergent good qualities for our sympathy'.[36]

Yet, of course, in advance of York's retrospective account of Richard's grief we already witness the entrance to London during 5.1, where it is presented 'at first hand' as an encounter between Richard and his Queen:

> QUEEN. This way the King will come. This is the way ...
> But soft, but see – or rather do not see –
> My fair rose wither. Yet look up, behold,
> That you in pity may dissolve to dew,
> And wash him fresh again with true-love tears. –
> Ah, thou the model where old Troy did stand!
> Thou map of honour, thou King Richard's tomb,
> And not King Richard! Thou most beauteous inn,
> Why should hard-favoured grief be lodged in thee,
> When triumph is become an alehouse guest?
>
> (5.1.1, 7–15)

Again, several of the lyrical antecedents to suffering that we have already rehearsed above resurface here: 'but see, or rather do not see'; 'thou King Richard's tomb, / And not King Richard' confirms the trope of anamorphism as the visual cue for Richard's outlaw status – the scapegoat who is held hostage but also now a belated host to Bolingbroke, whose act of usurpation is as undeserving 'alehouse guest' to Richard's 'beauteous inn'. In its entirety the first fifty lines of 5.1 double as a sonnet sequence rehearsed between Richard and his Queen 'in the name of the rose' – the religious connotations of which are self-evident and where, as usurping sorrow and pitying love combat 'hard-favoured grief', the thornful act of love's sacrifice is refreshed with the embalming 'true love tears' of love's pilgrimage. In the sonnets, as Lisa Freinkel recently reminds us, the withered or cankered '*Rose*' is one of the key tropes in this, Shakespeare's 'theology of figure', insofar as it secures its own form of singular exemplarity in perpetuity, as it awakens our desire for a lost love that will ever be, and yet will never be:

Given that any particular *Rose* of beauty will surely die, we desire increase that thereby the general rose of beauty might live. The individual may be lost, but that which we envisioned through him, the universal that inspirited his particular

---

[36] See S. T. Coleridge, 'Marginalia and Notebooks', in Nicholas Brooke, p. 30.

flesh, the rose that animated the *Rose*, this will live on in others. The *Rose* who enfigured beauty – who was the *Rose*, the paradigm of beauty, in fact – this *Rose* will live on in later *Roses* who carry his name and copy his example.[37]

In response, if, for Isabella, Richard's wounded memory remains in some sense unappeasable the former monarch's momentary advice to his former Queen is at once to look to the present:

> RICHARD. Join not with grief, fair woman, do not so,
> To make my end too sudden. Learn, good soul,
> To think our former state a happy dream,
> From which awaked, the truth of what we are
> Shows us but this. I am sworn brother, sweet,
> To grim necessity, and he and I
> Will keep a league till death.
> Hie thee to France,
> And cloister thee in some religious house.
> Our holy lives must win a new world's crown
> Which our profane hours here have stricken down.
>
> (5.1.16–25)

Here, at last, Richard offers a place out of joint ('Join not') from which not to merely 'join' with grief ('do not so, / To make my end too sudden') but to learn to read it too. We might say that Richard enjoins his Queen to read from another position and, in doing so, he draws attention to the subject as precisely *positioned*, 'making sense from a specific and limited place'.[38] In inviting his Queen to see 'the truth of what we are' (repositioned now by what Richard terms 'grim necessity') he locates a site for grief which is sited 'in history, in culture, in this moment as opposed to that' – and dislocated, *unheimlich*, 'other than it is, beside itself' – outside of the comfortable command of hindsight or the 'imaginary mastery' from which he reminds Isabella she must now awake: 'Learn, good soul to think our former state a happy dream.'[39]

Although characteristically, Richard equivocates to the last and quickly replaces an opening yet to be determined, with an abrupt form of idealised closure, directing his Queen to remain cloistered in religious seclusion from worldly concerns, 'Hie thee to France / And cloister thee

---

[37] Lisa Freinkel, *Reading Shakespeare's Will: The Theology of Figure from Augustine to the Sonnets* (New York: Columbia University Press, 2002), p. 196.

[38] Cf. Belsey, 'English Studies in the Postmodern Condition'.

[39] Again I'm grateful to Belsey for illuminating the fuller implications of the sited dislocation of anamorphism.

in some religious house, yet read in 'a league till death' the grim necessity of Richard's closing injunction also turns against itself, as he urges his Queen to practise a form of devotion that will build a new world of caring out of grieving and embrace a lyrical union (an impossible unity of the sublime) as the share of the gift of a divine love, thus winning a future sacred out of the profane temporal:

> Our holy lives must win a new world's crown
> Which our profane hours here have stricken down.
>
> (5.1.24–5)

LAST WORDS

For its part of course, the drama of *Richard II* itself closes with the monumental overkill of Bolingbroke's general invitation to participate in the official rites of collective mourning:

> Come mourn with me for what I do lament,
> And put on sullen black incontinent.
> I'll make a voyage to the Holy Land,
> To wash this blood off from my guilty hand.
> March sadly after. Grace my mournings here
> In weeping after this untimely bier.
>
> (5.6.47–52)

Here then, Richard's death is crudely salvaged as a strategic manoeuvre by a regime for whom grief and unrest at home are displaced on to a form of religious conflict that is now sited outside the realm. Throughout the Second Tetralogy that follows we are left where we started, negotiating the public implications of Richard's singularity, for, as Bolingbroke himself realizes, the stain of generations is not so easily washed away. Now it is Exton's turn (made a scapegoat for creating a scapegoat) to carry the mark of Cain and suffer the infamy of the outlaw:

> Exton, I thank thee not, for thou has wrought
> A deed of slander with thy fatal hand
> Upon my head and all this famous land.
> ... Though I did wish him dead,
> I hate the murderer, love him murdered.
> The guilt of conscience take thou for thy labour,
> But neither my good word nor princely favour.
> With Cain go wander through the shades of night,
> And never show thy head by day nor light.
>
> (5. 6. 34–6; 39–44)

However cynical the status of Bolingbroke's closing disavowal he seems aware that what Hazlitt terms the 'force' of Richard's 'passiveness'[40] will linger on interminably – in its close association with the shades of an endless night.

There is, Derrida reminds us, 'no culture without a cult of ancestors, a ritualization of mourning and sacrifice'[41] and the history of a national culture is nothing more or less than the history of death to which he refers us. More recently of course the psycho-drama of mourning and melancholia which links 'sacrificial' national figures to the narration of national and communal identities has become more commonplace, especially in the wake of the death of Princess Diana as a place where certain ' "outlawed" emotions – of expressivity, compassion and caring' located a type of affinity or share in dislocation and exclusion.[42] Ironically though, the revival of Richard's fortune within Romanticism as the 'player King' was to be all too brief, so that while he seems confident in predicting the endurance of his 'lamentable tale', his over-loquacious rhetorical excess is often viewed by traditionalist critics as an act of dereliction and the 'literary' legacy he seems certain will survive him is not so easily assimilated. Literary critical history labels the player King a problematic heir, especially at times of national crisis when the 'integrity' of the state is threatened and when, in the course of securing a masculinist warmongering centre, a more heroic form of individualism prevails – so that we prefer our Shakespeare productions to engender a 'sense of individual character and "personality" '.[43] Along with Hamlet and Lear, Richard's literariness and the prevaricating non-referential surplus of his speech acts remain an approximation of nationalism's other, so that it is to Harry rather than Richard that the propagandist turns – a political rather than a literary Shakespeare. By the end of the nineteenth century Gaunt's valedictory speech has already replaced York's elegy as the most frequently anthologised extract from the play. Yet actually, the choice between Gaunt and Richard is perhaps less straightforward than it seems and neither could be said to legitimate nationalism, not, at least, in any conventional sense as, in confirming the trajectory we have traced above, each exemplifies a form of lyrical victimage that stakes its claim in a future anterior. Richard and Gaunt remain haunting figures precisely

[40] W. C. Hazlitt, 'Mr Kean's Richard II (1815)', in Nicholas Brooke, p. 36.
[41] Derrida, *Aporias*, p. 43.
[42] See Adrian Kear and Deborah Steinberg, eds., *Mourning Diana: Nation, Culture and the Performance of Grief* (London: Routledge, 1999), p. 60 and *passim*.
[43] See Terence Hawkes, *Meaning by Shakespeare* (London: Routledge, 1992), p. 131.

insofar as each attests in different ways to the proverbial truth that a man is never a prophet in his own land and that breathing native breath and the language of inspiration associated with it is always a last gasp affair . . . .

Finally, it is precisely because death, lyricism and grief are bound together in unsettling and complex ways that they remain culturally and poetically marginal yet politically and symbolically central. Richard, Gaunt, Hamlet and indeed Diana (England's Rose?), each in some sense proves a thorn in the side of the monumental history and each to some extent remains in exile without a monument, yet their exemplary/singular status also locates the ways in which 'the transparent fragility' of our 'being-apart-together' are often quickly recycled by a regime keen to secure a more directly decisive or onto-political sense of reducing the other to the 'One'.

In the absent present of the play's afterlife, it is as if the unendurable excess of bodies *in extremis* retain a sense of witness, for the audience that views them. As we have seen, in *Richard II* the determining moment of death stages numerous and indeterminate figures of, and from which to choose, 'otherness' and in the process offers its audience the opportunity to shape a new politics of communal identity, in the course of positioning themselves in asymmetrical relation to the nation as a form of futural or imagined identity – or as a form of writing the 'nation which has not yet come into being'.[44] In this instance though, the exposure of the self to a form of non-justification (which is also of course the excessive demand of justice itself), might be said to be still more pressing, in that it presents us with these problems whilst also confronting us with somehow being presently involved (albeit at a distance) with these very same dilemmas. In this respect, there can be no doubt that the lyrical current of nationalism conveys an undeniable utopic impulse and thereby also shelters a 'potentially destablising' and endlessly inventive historical conscious-ness.[45] The challenge for a new aestheticism will rest in finding a way of offering a political repositioning of viewer and victim in relation to these and other rituals of national mourning without merely sentimentalizing them.

[44] See Brannigan, 'Writing DeTermiNation', *passim*.
[45] Again see Holderness, *Shakespeare: The Histories*, p. 65.

CHAPTER 3

Priamus is dead: memorial repetition in Marlowe and Shakespeare

Anthony B. Dawson

Early in Marlowe's *Dido Queen of Carthage*, Aeneas stands before the walls of the African city and bemoans his cruel fate: 'Methinks that town there should be Troy, yon Ida's hill, / There Xanthus' streams, because here is Priamus; / And when I know it is not, then I die.' (2.1.7–9).[1] His companions share his memorial fantasy ('And in this humour is Achates too', line 10) but also worry about Aeneas's submersion in it:

> AENEAS. Achates, see, King Priam wags his hand;
> He is alive, Troy is not overcome!
> ACHATES. Thy mind, Aeneas, that would have it so
> Deludes thy eyesight: Priamus is dead.
>
> (2.1.29–32)

Despite the relatively crude dramaturgy, this, I want to argue, is a highly suggestive moment of complex memorial repetition, one that will serve to introduce the theme I want to trace in this paper – how Marlowe and Shakespeare grapple with the links among literary remembrance, performance, loss and grief. The short sequence quoted above is a mere trace in Marlowe's play of a much longer and more striking passage in the first book of *The Aeneid*, in which the wandering, shipwrecked hero is led into Carthage and observes a frieze adorning a temple being built in Juno's honour. Thereon is carved, as a mark of 'Carthaginian promise' (617),[2] the story of the Trojan war, now brought powerfully back to

---

[1] References are to H. J. Oliver's Revels edition of *Dido Queen of Carthage and The Massacre at Paris* (Cambridge, MA: Harvard University Press, 1968).

[2] 'quae fortuna sit urbi' (1.454). I quote throughout from Robert Fitzgerald's translation (New York: Vintage, 1985), citing his line numbers; Latin text and line numbers are cited from the Loeb edition by H. Rushton Fairclough (Cambridge, MA: Loeb Classical Library, 1966). Fitzgerald's 'Carthaginian promise' interprets 'fortuna ... urbi' in a way that moves it away from 'fortune' in the sense of luck, to an ironic hint at greatness never quite achieved, but it is an entirely justifiable reading in the context of the scene, which depicts the rising but still uncompleted temple and introduces the beautiful, fated Dido as she presses on the work of her 'kingdom in the making' ('instans operi regnisque futuris', 504).

Aeneas's memory. 'What region of the earth, Achates, / Is not full of the story of our sorrow' (625–6),[3] he asks, struck by the fame that has travelled across the Mediterranean to be immortalized on foreign shores: 'Look, here is Priam', he exclaims, heaving a sigh at seeing the old man 'all unarmed, / Stretching his arms out' (627, 663–4).[4] Indeed, he concludes, the fame of these events and their having been so enshrined 'Insures some kind of refuge' (630–1)[5] for himself and his men.

Marlowe's version directly recalls Virgil's, even translates bits of it, but the ground has shifted. One sign of this is in the single word 'wags' – Marlowe's Aeneas has Priam wagging his hand, a distinctly undignified move as contrasted with stretching out his hands in supplication. Irony creeps into the act of remembering, and part of my aim here is to wonder why that should be. In general, besides shortening the Virgilian passage, Marlowe has psychologized it, and in a way trivialized it. His Aeneas seems to be hallucinating, Priam being a mere figment, a shadow on the blank wall of the theatre/city. There is no external, visible record of the past traumatic events, no frieze, only an elusive mental image, one that tells the story not so much of a defeated Troy but of a deracinated individual. There is no sense of 'Carthaginian promise', no assurance of refuge. All this derives first from the fact that Aeneas is grief-stricken and focused on his own feelings:

> Theban Niobe,
> Who for her sons' death wept out life and breath
> And, dry with grief, was turn'd into a stone,
> Had not such passions in her head as I.
>
> (2.1.3–6)

This completely reframes what happens in *Aeneid* where Aeneas, when he enters the temple grove and sees the frieze, finds cause for hope 'for the first time' (611–12) and tells his companions to 'throw off [their] fear' (630) – the word *primum* occurs twice, in successive lines (450–1 in the Latin text), indicating the onset of hope. It is precisely the memory of Troy and its destruction, experienced in grief but leading to Aeneas's mission, that produces the salutary effect, whereas the same memory stops Marlowe's Aeneas in his tracks, leading him into hallucination and possible despair. Though he is accompanied by a couple of companions,

---

[3] 'quae regio in terris nostri non plena laboris?' (460).
[4] 'en Priamus!... tendentemque manus Priamum conspexit inermis' (461, 487).
[5] 'feret haec aliquam tibi fama salutem' (463).

there is none of the Virgilian context of eventual achievement. He is merely alone and a man.

Dramaturgically, Marlowe here (well before Shakespeare made it a trope in *Henry V*) highlights his awareness of theatrical poverty – the problem of representing on stage the grand images of past heroism and defeat. Performance is a form of remembering just as remembering is a form of repetition; both hark back to a past that is originary and yet inaccessible. What remains for those who are left in the after-time is somehow lesser, only a shadow. There are two aspects to this: first, the theatre itself impoverishes its heroic subjects – a point made all the more vivid by the fact that children are playing the parts of the most famous of ancient heroes and lovers (the play was written for and performed by one of the boys' companies that flourished during the 1580s).[6] That is, the theatre's modes of representation of past grandeur, even at their boldest and most successful, are always belated; they inevitably fall short and require the kind of apology that Shakespeare puts centre stage in the chorus speeches of *Henry V*. And second, representation itself is suspect insofar as image-making always misrepresents actuality. This is a particularly salient problem in the context of sixteenth-century England, which witnessed a long conflict about the place and role of visual images in religious devotion and memory. Distrust of images interfered with rituals of remembrance just as the elimination of purgatory did. Death took a turn in the sixteenth century, at least for the living: lines of connection were broken and a wider gap between the dead and the living was the result.[7] Memorial, no longer institutionalized, i.e. no longer a communal ritual that connected living members of the church to those who had come before, became a largely private matter. In my previous foray into this cultural territory, I suggested that struggles over 'iconophobia' and communal rituals more generally could be read as a national trauma to which the theatre's makers and consumers of narrative kept returning; and further that this return was consequently marked by an ambivalence about the charge and the meaning of spectacle.[8]

---

[6] The title page of the earliest edition (1594) states that the play was 'Played by the Children of her Maiesties Chappell' – boys who were trained as choristers and actors to provide courtly entertainment.

[7] This is an issue that has been sensitively treated by, for example, Eamon Duffy, *The Stripping of the Altars* (New Haven: Yale University Press, 1992); Michael Neill, *Issues of Death* (Oxford: Clarendon Press, 1997); and Huston Diehl, *Reforming the Stage, Staging Reform* (Ithaca: Cornell University Press, 1997).

[8] Anthony Dawson and Paul Yachnin, *The Culture of Playgoing in Shakespeare's England* (Cambridge: Cambridge University Press, 2001), pp. 131–7, 179–80.

This ambivalence affects also the theatre's remembrance of classical heroic figures. For writers such as Marlowe and Shakespeare, the sense of distance from the classical past that was one legacy of humanism was, I would say, exaggerated by the cultural uncertainties surrounding acts of remembrance. Widespread distrust of images blends with the actual limitations of stage representation – such as the near impossibility of reproducing on stage a realistic frieze for Aeneas to contemplate – to create a kind of uneasy awareness of what is missing when the theatre remembers. For Marlowe, Priam's memory lacks solidity; it lives not in stone effigy as it does in *Aeneid*, but only in the wandering mind of Aeneas. At the same time, simply remembering and seeking to embody that heroic past is a kind of assertion of continuity, an implicit claim about the value of theatrical re-enactment. So, I would argue, acts of *literary* remembrance, specifically the ways in which Marlowe is remembering Virgil and, to anticipate slightly, Shakespeare is remembering each of his predecessors, are responding to both the limitations and the possibilities of performance as well as to the cultural forms of grief. That is, literary remembrance of the kind we get in the early scenes of *Dido* seeks to expand the scope of memorial beyond the personal in the face of its curtailment in the religious sphere, while at the same time registering an awareness of the obstacles facing any such attempt. To put this another way, feelings of loss and belatedness are interwoven with a sense of continuity and renewal.

When it comes to dramatizing forms of grief we encounter a problem: do the actual limitations of stage representation not *reduce* pain, isolating it as something merely performed and hence deeply equivocal in a climate where rituals of remembrance are themselves suspect? There's no doubt that turning to the *Aeneid* allows Marlowe, in Viola's phrase, to 'smile [sardonically] at grief'; the young playwright is a bit like the derisive figure of Death in Richard's portrayal, 'scoffing [the] state and grinning at [the] pomp' of ancient greatness. Even if putting memorial on the stage is a kind of extension into public life of forms not available any more in the religious sphere, performing grief, just because it is a performance, tends to diminish the power of the feeling even as it invokes it. Marlowe's perspective on performance seems to cut two ways, at once representing the deracinated individual and calling on the larger literary past as a kind of antidote to the isolation implied by the concentration on the merely personal.

Grief, of course, *is* always personal and in some ways always private. But it inevitably has a public dimension as well. And performance plays a necessary role in making memory public. In the scene I have been discussing, two kinds of memory, two kinds of loss are on view: there is first Aeneas's grief at the destruction of his homeland, his king, his father; in that this is part of an inheritance from the literary past, we might think of it as 'literary' grief, and note that in Marlowe's play it is more mediated and the grounds of that mediation are more evident than in the original. Indeed the 'literary' as a concept might include, along with inheritance, an element of self-referentiality.[9] But there is another kind of grief in play as well – a loss of authenticity, if you will, a failure of feeling signalled by the undercutting irony. This second we might usefully think of as performative in that the loss of authenticity is tied up with the diminishment associated with performances, which, like those of Richard II, put grief self-consciously on view. Part of my purpose in suggesting this is to undermine the wall between the literary and the performed, as it has been invoked recently by Lukas Erne as well as by the performance critics he challenges.[10] In contrast to Erne, I want to insist on the inextricable linkage between the literary and performative in writers such as Marlowe, Shakespeare and Jonson. Literary remembrance is deeply embedded in performance and the memories it makes.

Freud, in *Beyond the Pleasure Principle*, points out that we return obsessively, if unconsciously, to sites of trauma, quoting his own earlier dictum that 'hysterics suffer mainly from reminiscences';[11] and he links such repetition-compulsion to the death instincts. But Cathy Caruth and others, developing Freud's own discussion of the child's '*fort ... da*' game, which is used as a means of gaining mastery over loss, have taken Freud's point in a somewhat different direction by suggesting that traumatic narrative, as a form of repetition, can be a strategy for dealing with the 'enigma of survival'.[12] That this is one of the patterns of *The Aeneid* seems clear. Virgil revisits and rewrites both *Odyssey* and *Iliad* as part of his project of establishing his imperial vision; and within the poem, one of the main functions of repeating the story of the fall of Troy is simultaneously to stir and assuage Aeneas's grief, impelling him to

---

[9] As Howard Felperin suggests, built into the very concept of the literary is an idea of a struggle with origins – origins are foundational but also recessive or recursive. See *Shakespearean Representation* (Princeton: Princeton University Press, 1977).

[10] Lukas Erne, *Shakespeare as Literary Dramatist* (Cambridge, Cambridge University Press, 2003), *passim*, especially pp. 1–27.

[11] *Beyond the Pleasure Principle*, trans. James Strachey (New York: Liveright, 1961), p. 7.

[12] In this sense, repetition, or return to the traumatic event, may be seen as a potentially productive way of trying 'to claim one's own survival'; see Cathy Caruth, *Unclaimed Experience* (Baltimore: Johns Hopkins University Press, 1996), pp. 57–72, quotations taken from pp. 58 and 64.

confront the pain of his own survival as the first stage in the long preparation for his imperial task. (And we might observe in passing that his
sadness is always there with him, never absent, even when, especially
when, he triumphs over Turnus at the end of the poem.)[13] The scene with
the frieze in Book I is used as a prelude to his meeting with Dido and the
ensuing temptations of Carthaginian *fortuna*, and is a kind of preview of
the moving tale he goes on to tell in Book 2 of the ravaging of Troy, the
killing of Priam, the loss of Creusa and his own eventual escape. All of
this is used to set up the embedded love-tragedy of Dido, with its deep
and pervasive ambivalences, which in turn makes it possible for Aeneas to
forget his traumatic past or, more properly, to reconfigure his memory
through his visit to the underworld in Book 6, where he is greeted by
visions of what for Virgil is the past but for him is the future.

Marlowe, for his part, seems to have had an ambivalent relation to
classical writing: while he was drawn to it by personal and cultural predilection, one can also sense his desire to get out from under the weight of
it.[14] So he returns to Virgil's portrayal of grief in a lighter vein, partially
undermining the literary past on which he depends. The play begins with
a saucy representation of Jupiter 'dandling Ganymede upon his knee';
instead of attending to business, Jupiter plays erotically with Ganymede
while Mercury, the messenger who should be busy working for the divine
boss, sleeps. Ironically, the slightly salacious game with Ganymede is
accompanied by the heroic rhetoric of promise that later became
Marlowe's specialty:

> From Juno's bird I'll pluck her spotted pride,
> To make thee fans wherewith to cool thy face,
> And Venus' swans shall shed their silver down
> To sweeten out the slumbers of thy bed..
>
>   (1.1.34–7)

Such language combined with such action helps mark out the spectrum of
ambivalence.

---

[13] This aspect of his sensibility is nicely evoked by W. R. Johnson who links it to Aeneas's relative
speechlessness, his characteristic incapacity to express what he deeply feels; see 'The Figure of
Laertes: reflections on the character of Aeneas', in *Vergil at 2000: Commemorative essays on the poet
and his influence*, ed. John D. Bernard (New York: AMS Press, 1986), pp. 85–106.

[14] David Riggs relates this ambivalence to Marlowe's life as a scholarship boy, at King's School and
then at Cambridge, where classical know-how and compositional skill were a ticket to academic
success but also a sign of inescapable social inferiority – the rich, after all, did not have to work so
hard to claim a sense of privilege; see *The World of Christopher Marlowe* (London: Faber and Faber,
2004), chs. 3–5, esp. pp. 52–61.

Barbara Bono suggests that Marlowe's re-framing of Virgil, through such scenes as Jupiter's dandling of Ganymede and, later in the play, the old nurse's wounding by Cupid and her ensuing erotic daydreams (4.5), 'corrupts the defining values' of *The Aeneid*, but I think she overstates the case.[15] There's no doubt that it is a precarious perch that Marlowe occupies, whittling the branch on which he sits. But he doesn't entirely succumb to his own playful ironies and undergraduate cynicism; they are conjoined with other notes, such as the restive idealism contained in Jupiter's promises to Ganymede and, significantly, a kind of unexpected sympathy for some of the hapless victims of divine trickery. The pathetic nurse, for example, entranced by Cupid disguised as Ascanius, is more than simply a disdainful caricature on the part of a young man of an older woman's erotic fantasies, though she is that. She begins the scene in the manner of the passionate shepherd,[16] by cajoling Cupid to go with her:

> I have an orchard that hath store of plums,
> Brown almonds, services, ripe figs, and dates...
> A garden where are bee-hives full of honey,
> Musk-roses, and a thousand sort of flowers...
>
> (4.5.4–8)[17]

and moves on to fantasize the delights of taking 'a husband, or else a lover'. Though Cupid mocks ('A husband and no teeth?'), she holds her ground, shifting back and forth between fanciful self-indulgence and realistic self-appraisal:

> Foolish is love, a toy. O sacred love,
> If there be any heaven in earth, 'tis love,
> Especially in women of your years.
> Blush, blush, for shame, why shouldst thou think of love?
> A grave and not a lover fits thy age.
> A grave? Why? I may live a hundred years:
> Fourscore is but a girl's age; love is sweet.
>
> (4.5.26–32)

Despite the (once again) crude dramaturgy, one can easily discern the effort to register inner conflict and uncertainty. Aware of her own folly but helpless in the face of it, the nurse both satirizes herself and (in a surprisingly modern twist) wistfully hopes for a reprieve from age and grief. Her final lines in the scene, referring apparently to some lover of the

---

[15] Barbara J. Bono, *Literary Transvaluation* (Berkeley: University of California Press, 1984), p. 130.

[16] Riggs proposes that Marlowe's famous pastoral lyric was written early, before *Dido* (p. 107).

[17] The lines bring to mind Oberon's evocation of the bank where wild thyme blows, written around the time *Dido* was published in 1594.

past whom she now regrets having rejected, anchor the pathos: 'Well, if he come a-wooing, he shall speed: / O how unwise was I to say him nay!' Missed opportunities, regrets about lost love – the very centre of the play's theme, and of the Virgilian episodes on which it is based – make the scene more than simply a corruption of ancient values. They translate those values into different terms, more suitable to early modern performance, where a double attitude is part of the way performance is structured (in this case made even more pronounced because of the boys' company). It is an attitude, a complex stance, in which reminiscence can play a central role – what memory, we are led to wonder, stirs in the nurse's mind? We don't of course know, and we may not much care either, since the pathos is certainly susceptible to comic treatment. But it links to the more potent scenes of remembrance in the play, which themselves flow out of Marlowe's memory of Virgil, such as Aeneas's memory of Priam and the defeat of Troy, and climactically Dido's of Aeneas, as she readies herself for the flames in which she destroys herself and the various mementos Aeneas has left behind. Interestingly, among those mementos there are 'letters, lines, and perjur'd papers', written texts pointedly absent from *Aeneid* but here evoking a record of what has gone before. One is tempted to see in them a reminiscence of Marlowe's literary inheritance, a sign from within the story of the storied quality of what is coming to pass. Dido's final gesture is of course also a memory of performance – that of Virgil's Dido, who stabs herself with Aeneas's sword; but, given both the context and the exigencies of performance, it comes off as a diminished one. This is marked by a change in the method of death – she throws herself on the flames, a gesture that must have been almost impossible to realize effectively onstage.[18] Following this comes the anti-climactic, almost casual and certainly inconsequential suicide of Iarbus, Aeneas's rival (a plot twist added by Marlowe), to which is added, in an almost absurd gesture of mourning lost love, the suicide of Anna, Dido's sister whose unrequited love for Iarbus has been a glancing sub-plot throughout. Thus the ending seems to turn an ironic gaze on the very processes by which the Elizabethan theatre gets its effects, sur-rounding the heroic and tragic death of the woman whose story stood as emblem for grief and loss with elements that make it hard to take that loss entirely seriously. To some extent, the young author is simply not in

---

[18] The Revels editor, H. J. Oliver comments: 'The staging may also have presented some difficulties; Dido could perhaps have leapt "through" flames towards the rear of the stage' or 'may have descended' through a trap door (88).

control of his dramaturgy – the ironies too heavy-handed, the romance too rarefied; but the way that he is not in control, the bumpy blend of pathos and satirical comedy, tells us something important about the performance of literary memory.

I want to turn now to a different instance of restive idealism in the play – and that is the emphasis on city-building, the very end and purpose of Aeneas's quest in Virgil, and a preoccupation of the Carthaginians as well as the proto-Romans. Marlowe adds a twist. Although in 4.3, at the instigation of a dream of Hermes, Aeneas determines to sail away from the imperious Dido, he unaccountably changes his mind; in 5.1, he reappears as happy architect and builder of a new Troy/Carthage, an envisioned city built over and around Carthage to be called (after his father) Anchisaeon. In the *Aeneid* he is, as in 5.1, scolded by Hermes for attending to Carthage's buildings rather than his mission, but once he determines to leave he never wavers, despite the emotional conflict he suffers. Marlowe's character is weaker and more distracted. But his quite un-Virgilian vacillation is combined with a romantic vision expressed with typical Marlovian sweep and multi-cultural inclusiveness:

> Here will Aeneas build a statelier Troy
> Than that which grim Atrides overthrew;
> Carthage shall vaunt her petty walls no more,
> For I will grace them with a fairer frame ...
> From golden India Ganges will I fetch
> Whose wealthy streams may wait upon her towers...
> The sun from Egypt shall rich odours bring...
>
> (5.1.2–11)

Such a fancy seems almost parodic, or at least compensatory, the fruit of hesitation and a sign of failure as much as success. Soon after, Hermes appears, more like a buddy than a god, and convinces him to go, though Aeneas is petulant and tends to whine: 'How should I put into the raging deep / Who have no sails nor tackling for my ships?' (55–6). Marlowe reverses the order of Hermes's two visits in *Aeneid*, this second one translating part of his first visit in the original, while there the second is restricted to the dream designed to hasten Aeneas's departure because of the threat posed by Dido – there's no hint that Aeneas might have changed his mind between visits. Curiously, but tellingly, Marlowe does not provide any visionary language in the service of Aeneas's ultimate destiny; indeed his hero slinks off without a word after Dido's long lament. The poetic idealism is thus tied up with an impossible or falsely directed vision, a hope for what can never be; implicit in it is the fact of non-achievement, of incipient loss. I think this subtly mirrors the dilemma of the theatre in its remembrance of the heroic past.

The motif of city-building, derived from *Aeneid* but in *Dido* linked to an unfulfilled dream, reappears in an oddly transformed way in *The Tempest* where the mockery of Gonzalo's 'widow Dido', much repeated, is linked to the raising of new walls. As we are reminded by Gonzalo's musings and the reaction of his fellows, the lost courtiers are returning from an Italian/North African marriage, exactly what does *not* occur in the Dido/Aeneas story:

ADRIAN. Tunis was never graced before with such a paragon to their queen.
GONZALO. Not since widow Dido's time.
ANTONIO. Widow? A pox o'that! How came that 'widow' in? Widow
    Dido! . . . .
ADRIAN. 'Widow Dido', said you? . . . she was of Carthage, not of Tunis.
GONZALO. This Tunis, sir, was Carthage.
ADRIAN. Carthage?
GONZALO. I assure you, Carthage.
ANTONIO. His word is more than the miraculous harp.
SEBASTIAN. He hath raised the wall, and houses too.

$$(2.1.79-83, 86-93)^{19}$$

This puzzling sequence allows for only a vexed continuity between ancient and modern – Dido's city is and is not Claribel's; the moment thus troubles the process of literary reminiscence that it depends upon. Stephen Orgel reminds us that there were two traditions regarding Dido, both in play in the *Tempest* passage: Gonzalo's reminiscence of the heroic chastity of the undefeated widow is countered by Antonio's and Sebastian's cynical recall of the motif of the fallen woman (first introduced by Virgil into the older tradition).[20] Gonzalo, shortly to launch into his dream of the ideal commonwealth, here imagines an unvexed past that the recall of the *Aeneid* quickly undoes. He has raised walls, but they are fanciful, unreal, fraught with 'Carthaginian promise' perhaps, but ultimately only a dream, like Aeneas's imagined apprehension of Priamus at the outset of Marlowe's play.

Within Shakespeare's own *oeuvre*, the sequence from *The Tempest* also troubles the smooth flow of literary or performative reminiscence, by both echoing and ironically inverting his earlier foray into the Virgil/Marlowe nexus – Aeneas's tale to Dido as re-enacted by the Player in

---

[19] I have omitted the Oxford editions' stage directions for this passage, since they are overly restrictive in specifying to whom various speeches are addressed.
[20] Stephen Orgel, ed., *The Tempest* (London: Oxford University Press, 1987), pp. 40–2.

Hamlet. For there, of course, it's falling, not rising, walls that mark the decisive moment when the revenging Pyrrhus, furious about *his* father's death, confronts the ur-father, Priam; the collapse momentarily deflects Pyrrhus's murderous intent, but 'senseless Ilium' has already 'stoop[ed] to his base . . . with a hideous crash' and the paternal symbol of its glory soon follows the fate of his city. While Marlowe concentrates gleefully on the torture of Priam ('Father of fifty sons', 2.1.234), whose hands Pyrrhus cuts off while his soldiers swing Hecuba through the air like a cat, Shakespeare adds Pyrrhus's hesitation and the connection to the collapse of the city walls ('For lo, his sword . . .', 2.2.480ff.) as well as the passage about the grief of Hecuba, whose ultimate fate is ignored in both Virgil and Marlowe. But Shakespeare also portrays all this as part of a repetition of Hamlet's, and perhaps his own, memory of a performance and a play that are deliberately old-fashioned, even outmoded. This has the effect of multiply framing and distancing the expression of grief and implies that the mourning that pervades the scene and the play, while real and affecting, is not fully adequate or authentic. The speech and its setting thus suggest a break in the continuity on which the effect of the scene depends.

At the same time, the added elements connect the mourning over Troy and Priam to the pervasive mourning in the rest of the play. Shakespeare here moves decisively inside the motif, drawing out the links between loss of fathers and the collapse/renewal of cities that are embedded in Virgil's epic. In Book 6 of *The Aeneid* Aeneas visits the underworld and meets his dead father, whom, in an act that epitomized for the Romans and the Renaissance, his *pietas*,[21] he has carried successfully out of senseless Ilium as it collapsed around them. Anchises shows his son the glorious future, conjuring Romulus under whose auspices Rome will 'enclose her seven hills with one great city wall',[22] but he ends on an elegiac note, invoking, in a syntactically strained sentence that expresses both hope and a rupture of continuity, the loss of the young Marcellus (adopted son and heir presumptive to Augustus, who died at age twenty): 'si qua fata aspera rumpas, / tu Marcellus eris' (882–3).[23] The triumph of Rome is linked to

---

[21] A point that has been frequently made – see Robert S. Miola, 'Vergil in Shakespeare: From Allusion to Imitation', in *Vergil at 2000: Commemorative Essays on the Poet and his Influence*, ed. John D. Bernard (New York: AMS Press, 1986), pp. 241–58.

[22] 'septemque una sibi muro circumdabit arces' (6.783).

[23] Fitzgerald breaks it into two sentences: 'child of our mourning, if only in some way / You could break through your bitter fate. For you / Will be Marcellus' (1197–9). As the Loeb editor remarks, noting the mixing of the conditional 'si' clause with the future 'eris': 'even as [Anchises] utters the thought he realizes its hopelessness' (p. 569).

the fragile relations between father and son and hedged by the bitterness of fate. The same motif also marks Anchises's death (and Aeneas's consequent sense of loss), beautifully evoked at the end of Book 3: 'Here I, alas, who have been driven by so many tempests, lose my father [note the present tense – "amitto" in the Latin], Anchises, solace of every care and chance.' So Aeneas ends his grand tale of loss ('this,' he says 'was my final sorrow' [*labor extremus*]), and the narrator concludes: 'Thus father Aeneas...at last ceased and, making an end here, was still'.[24] In a meaningful shift, Aeneas himself, in these final lines of Book 3, gains the epithet 'pater', though the dominant tone is deeply mournful.

These passages seem to have deeply infiltrated Shakespeare's imagination when he was writing *Hamlet*, not just because of the obvious concern with the death of fathers (Old Hamlet, Old Fortinbras, Polonius, Priam), but also with the linkage between such loss and the ambiguous triumph of story-telling: 'Father' Aeneas loses his father and completes his narrative at the same moment. This insistence on memory, on tales of remembrance, is epitomized in the player's speech, but is highlighted throughout the play – in the ghost's tale of his own journey into death, in the play within the play, in Ophelia's madness and her compulsion to repeat her story ('There's rosemary, that's for remembrance. Pray, love, remember'), in Gertrude's lament over Ophelia's death, and in the untold story that Horatio promises to 'Truly deliver' (a story, of course, that the play itself tells). I've made the point elsewhere that the play is rife with remembered performances that signal a concern with national loss – 'the scars of Tudor cultural conflicts';[25] here I want to emphasize a further kind of memory at work, a specifically literary/performative one, but connected also to those cultural scars. It's the memory involved in story-telling and, specifically, the memory that propels Aeneas to tell his story, remembered and rehearsed by the player and by Hamlet who later insists on his own. No wonder that the play that was caviar to the general should have appealed so much to the melancholy prince – even before death entered the palace and his life. As a reader of Virgil, like his author, he knows that loss and narrative go hand in hand.[26]

---

[24] 'hic pelagi tot tempestatibus actus / heu! genitorem, omnis curae casusque levamen, / amitto Anchisen... / ... Sic pater Aeneas ...conticuit tandem factoque hic fine quievit' (708–18). In this instance I follow, with minor adjustments, the Loeb translation, Fitzgerald's being rather too loose.

[25] *Culture of Playgoing*, pp. 179–80.

[26] This stress on the importance of story combined with the sense that the story-teller is always behindhand may indeed be a feature of literary origins, no matter in what context; or so Felperin

And not only loss and narrative, but loss and a sense of destiny. Herein, I think, lies the connection in the drama between the classical heritage which I have been probing and the cultural struggles over the change from Catholicism to Protestantism, from icons to iconoclasm. For in that historical shift we can discern a similar pattern: the growing sense in the Elizabethan period of England's global, Protestant destiny, combined with the nagging feelings of loss associated with the demise of Catholicism, the erasure of images, the disappearance of embodied comforts before the mastery of a more rigorously austere religious aesthetic.[27] Thus Virgil's sense of the inevitable mixture of triumph and loss, the personal cost of destiny and city-building, strikes a chord and accrues a meaning for Shakespeare and some of his fellows at this historical moment.

Virgil's proclivity for building his theme around the loss of fathers and sons, thereby highlighting the problem of continuity, provided a resonant way for Shakespeare to dramatize analogous conflicts. Indeed, in several of the middle plays, Shakespeare, as he does in *Hamlet*, probes the question of continuity through paternal loss, and in so doing he succeeds in inhabiting Virgil and remaking him from within. Virgil is for him what Robert Miola calls a 'deep source'.[28] In *Julius Caesar*, for example, the emotional resonance of the assassination turns on the filial relationship of Brutus to Caesar, and no doubt Brutus's grief, which dominates the latter part of the play, derives partly from that sense of a father betrayed and lost. In *2 Henry IV*, Hal famously seems to hurry his father's impending death so that he can deal in a businesslike way with mourning and move forward; his tales are all of the future, which is why he refuses to remember Falstaff ('I know thee not'). At the same time, a profoundly elegiac mood marks the play, so full as it is of reminiscences: Shallow's 'Jesus, the days that we have seen' (3.2.215–16), Silence's repeated 'Dead', Falstaff's 'Old, old, Master Shallow' (3.2.203), Doll's 'I have known thee these twenty-nine years come peascod-time, but an honester and truer-hearted man – well, fare thee well' (2.4.386–8), and even the King's 'God knows, my son, / By what bypaths and indirect crook'd ways / I met this crown' (4.3.312–14). The play begins with a father mourning a lost son,

---

(see n. 8) argues in discussing the role of the blind bard Demodocus in Book 8 of *The Odyssey* (pp. 29–33).

[27] These latter feelings might also have included a sense of belatedness in relation to Catholicism, in that Protestantism defined itself partly as a return to the religious forms of early Christianity, one effect of which was to deny belatedness.

[28] 'Vergil in Shakespeare', p. 251.

and ends with a son mourning a dead father (and exiling another, live one), while also of course setting out in triumph. The past is a powerful presence, but in this play, pointing (albeit wanly) toward *Henry V*, there is also 'promise': Hal, a bit like Aeneas, is destined to 'bear our civil swords and native fire / As far as France' (5.4.104–5) – as the final lines of the play proper remind us. While, unlike Aeneas, he doesn't seem to suffer for it, both *2 Henry IV* and *Henry V* limn the cost of destiny, the inevitable mix of triumph and loss. Biographical critics would no doubt see in such motifs the shadow of Shakespeare's son's death in 1596, and perhaps his Catholic father's illness and imminent death; while John Shakespeare did not die till September 1601, too late to directly colour any of these plays, his apparent Catholicism might be another element in the complex genesis of his son's remembrances and repetitions.[29]

Without discounting such possibilities I look instead to literary parentage and note that the kinds of ambivalence represented in *2 Henry IV*, the hovering sense of loss inflecting and tempering the triumphalism, is Virgil's specialty. Over and over again in *The Aeneid* come the painful reminders, though I have time here to examine only one, particularly complex, example. As Aeneas fights his way to ultimate triumph, his story is interwoven with that of the loss of his young companion Pallas, the son of the Arcadian king Evander (traced through Books 8–11). It is Pallas's cruel death that Aeneas revenges in the final lines of the poem, as he sinks his sword into the chest of Turnus. Evander's pain at the death of his son is experienced proleptically in Book 8 when he bids farewell to Pallas and prays that no bitter message of loss will ever wound his paternal ears; his vain hope for his son is recalled later when Aeneas, mourning the dead boy, thinks of Evander's hopeful ignorance of the painful message that will soon be delivered: 'Even at this hour, / Prey to false hopes, he may be making vows / And heaping altars with his gifts, while here / We gather with a soldier young and dead' (11.66–8).[30] Such extraordinary sympathy with human bafflement is a hallmark of Virgil's art; even the villainous Mezentius, whose son Lausus saves him from death but is killed in the process, is allowed his elegiac moment: 'Am I your father, / Saved by your wounds, by your death do I live?' (10.1187–8).[31] Climactically, in the final

[29] Stephen Greenblatt, in *Will in the World* (New York: Norton, 2004), speculates that 'the death of his son and the impending death of his father' would have 'constitute[d] a psychic disturbance that may help to explain the explosive power and inwardness of Hamlet' (p. 318) and lays great emphasis on John Shakespeare's Catholicism. See pp. 311–12, 317–18, 320–1.
[30] 'et nunc ille quidem spe multum captus inani / fors et vota facit cumulatque altaria donis; / nos iuvenem exanimum ... comitamur' (11.49–51).
[31] 'tuane haec genitor per volnera servor, / mote tua vivens?' (10.848–9).

moments of the poem, when Aeneas defeats Turnus, the doomed man calls upon him to honour his corpse: 'If you can feel a father's grief – and you, too, / Had such a father in Anchises – then / Let me bespeak your mercy for old age / In Daunus, and return me, or my body, / Stripped if you will of life, to my own kin.' (12.1268–72);[32] Aeneas seems ready to relent but then notices the sword-belt that Turnus has stripped from Pallas and delivers the final blow in Pallas's name; we cannot but recall that earlier scene, when Turnus seizes the belt and the poet comments:

> The minds of men are ignorant of fate...
> For Turnus there will come a time
> When he would give the world to see again
> An untouched Pallas, and will hate this day,
> Hate that belt taken.
>
> (10.701–7)[33]

Turnus may be the enemy of Roman destiny, but the very human limitations of his awareness call forth a characteristic sympathy.

I pause over these examples, even though they take me away temporarily from the Elizabethan theatre, because my theme has to do with reading *Aeneid*, as I believe Shakespeare did attentively and thoroughly.[34] Of course Virgil himself looked backward to Homer, and that paradigmatic scene of parental mourning, Priam's mission to Achilles in the final book of the *Iliad*. In *Troilus and Cressida*, Shakespeare seems to be remembering both. In 5.3 of that play, in a moment that doesn't get much critical attention, Priam is brought in by his daughter and daughter-in-law to persuade Hector not to fight. Surrounded by prophecies of doom, Priam entreats his son: 'I myself / Am like a prophet suddenly enrapt / To tell thee that this day is ominous' (5.3.64–6);[35] but his repeated pleas for Hector to 'not go', to 'come back', are fruitless. He can only stand by in silence, while Hector sends Andromache away and Cassandra shrieks; 'amazed' by Cassandra's warnings, Priam nevertheless reluctantly capitulates to Hector's need for approval and blessing: 'Farewell,

---

[32] 'miseri te si qua parentis / tangere cura potest, oro (fuit et tibi talis / Anchises genitor), Dauni miserere senectae / et me, seu corpus spoliatum lumine mavis, redde meis' (12.932–6). No doubt too we are meant to recall at this moment Aeneas's farewell to his own son earlier in the same book, so tender and yet so constrained and tenuous. See Johnson, 'The Figure of Laertes,' (n. 12).

[33] 'nescia mens hominum fati ...Turno tempus erit, magno cum optaverit emptum / intactum Pallanta, et cum spolia ista diemque / oderit' (10.501–5).

[34] Robert Miola made this point in 1983 in *Shakespeare's Rome* (Cambridge: Cambridge University Press), and a few others, such as Barbara Bono, have followed suit, but in general it seems to have been ignored or forgotten.

[35] Quotations from *Troilus* are taken from my own edition (New Cambridge Shakespeare, 2003).

the gods with safety stand about thee' (94). But of course it is the Myrmidons, not the gods, who will 'stand about' Hector–Achilles's murder of his rival being more savage than just about anything else in this savage play.

Perhaps in keeping with the overall ironic tone, Shakespeare chooses not to dramatize the sad episode which brings the *Iliad* to conclusion, but he does remember it in those brief lines in 5.3, and he does so through Virgil, whose Evander, like Priam, knows and yet hopes he does not know that his son is doomed. Reading *Troilus and Cressida* beside *The Iliad* and *The Aeneid* yields a complex picture of the waste and shattered hopes of war, where loss and yearning go briefly hand in hand, where the need to tell the story links up with the hope of reconciliation. *The Iliad* ends with pyre and feast and remembrance; *The Aeneid* with a similar sense of the loss of the heroic enemy and a reminder of the grief of fathers; Shakespeare's play ends doubly with reminiscence of the dead Hector ('Hector is gone: / Who shall tell Priam so, or Hecuba?', 5.11.14–15) and Pandarus's poisoned rhyme:

> Till then I'll sweat and seek about for eases,
> And at that time bequeath you my diseases.
>
> (53–4)

Pandarus forces upon us a certain memory of performance, a jaundiced, deeply ironic one, which is juxtaposed with the sense of heroic loss. As in *Dido Queen of Carthage*, only much more so, the sense prevails that the evocation of the heroic past requires both performative irony and a celebration of continuity between past and future.

It's doubtful that Shakespeare ever saw a performance of *Dido*, though he must have read it after it was published in 1594. So when he came to rewrite part of Marlowe's rewriting in *Hamlet*, Shakespeare wasn't exactly remembering performance but, as he did so often, he was binding the literary to the performed, and in doing so highlighting the complexity of repetition. He even provides a meditation on the topic, spoken famously by Hamlet, as he wonders about the emotional value of repeating in performance what has been heartily felt before by *real* people like himself:

> Is it not monstrous that this player here,
> But in a fiction, in a dream of passion,
> Could force his soul so to his whole conceit
> That from her working all his visage wanned ...
> > And all for nothing.
> For Hecuba ...
>
> (2.2.553–6, 559–60)

This forgets, momentarily, the value of Hecuba's grief, because Hamlet is so narcissistically wrapped up in his own feelings. But it poses an age-old question about the quality of feeling required of acting – how repetition (which is, we recall, the French word for rehearsal) falsifies feeling, turns it to fiction or dream. Actors don't feel, they just repeat and in so doing seem to feel – or if they do feel, it is a second-hand kind of thing. Performance is in this account the opposite of mourning, even though mourning is itself a form of repetition. In one sense performing grief is an oxymoron – grief can't be performed since once performance enters in, the pain of grief dissipates, turning it into performative élan. In another sense, though, performance is all there is. Grief, as Hamlet sees it, can't be anything other than performance: 'What would he do / Had he the motive and the cue for passion / That I have?' (562–4). Hamlet's dilemma – his awareness that real feeling, while it 'passes show', cannot escape 'show' if it is to be made manifest and real in the world – extends analogically, I want to suggest, to Shakespeare himself in relation to the classical past he inhabits and tries to exceed. In formulating the issue as Hamlet's response to an actor evoking Priam and Hecuba, Shakespeare thus questions whether his own repetitions are themselves substantial or merely reproductive.

The problem of coming later, of building on the work of the ancients, was a staple of humanist thought and pedagogy. And just as Shakespeare was beginning to write *Hamlet* it found expression in Chapman's praise of the 'divine' Homer: '*Homers* poems were writ from a free furie, an absolute & full soule: *Virgils* out of a courtly, laborious, and altogether imitatorie spirit.'[36] (Note how similar this is to the kinds of things later said about Ben Jonson in relation to Shakespeare, most famously by Dryden who compares the latter to Homer, the former to Virgil.) To imitate is to lack 'free furie', it is to labour not to sing. But I don't want to suggest that Hamlet's feelings precisely match those of his creator. Rather, Shakespeare expresses through Hamlet something of the uncertainty that he might indeed feel, but he does so to exorcise and manage it. Thus, while Hamlet's rumination on the player's imitative emotions in some way registers the sense of Shakespeare's own belatedness, his repeating the motifs of classical loss without genuinely feeling them, it also creates a new space; in a sense Shakespeare is both Hamlet, upset because of the lack of feeling he struggles to muster, and also the player/playwright who

[36] Cited in T. W. Baldwin, *Shakespeare's small Latine and lesse Greeke* (Urbana: University of Illinois Press, 1944), vol. 2, p. 458.

repeats but also remakes as part of his métier. No doubt the feeling of loss extends to a sense, like Hamlet's, of inauthenticity, of lagging behind, and thus being unable to have direct access to the sorts of passions and themes available to his own father, not to mention the ancients. The player's speech and Hamlet's meditation on it is, I venture, a kind of allegory of the whole process, a wonderfully evocative and powerful dramatic sequence whose theatrical contrivance both makes access to the literary past possible and at the same time keeps its essence somehow estranged. And yet in that estrangement lies something of the value as well as the vicissitudes of repetition. Hamlet, of course, is both plagued and fascinated by repetition, most especially in the form of performance, and the question of his mastery of it remains moot even at the end when he instructs Horatio to repeat his story to the unsatisfied. It looks like the sheer difficulty of making repetition meaningful might be what, in the widest sense, is at stake.

Repetition, in this literary-performative context, is inescapable, but also in one sense impossible. It is inescapable because it is the imperative of mourning and of story-telling, just because the cultural forms that mourning and story telling take must involve ritual and narrative repetition. But it is also impossible, since the kind of triumphant continuity implied, for example, by the return to *Aeneid* is unavailable. Such continuity is always vexed: even as it is asserted a gap inevitably opens up between past and present. Perhaps, indeed, as Kierkegaard (like Hamlet, a philosophical, melancholy and witty Dane) rather whimsically suggests in his book called *Repetition*, there is no possibility of 'repetition', period. Difference, time, always intrudes: 'Are not all orators, both the religious and the secular, both sea captains and undertakers ... are they not all in agreement that life is a stream? How then can one get so foolish an idea as that of repetition, and, still more foolishly, erect it into a principle?'[37]

But Kierkegaard does erect it into a principle later in his book, when he moves beyond the ethical phase into a religious apprehension of what he still calls repetition though it now takes on quite a different penumbra. Becoming a figure for transcendence, repetition breaks from recollection, with which it was originally connected. The love of recollection, Kierkegaard says early on, is the 'only happy love'. To be in love with recollection is to be in love with loss, in which recollection begins. Religious repetition, by contrast, is constituted by a leap, a transcendent

---

[37] Søren Kierkegaard, *Repetition: an Essay in Experimental Psychology*, trans. Walter Lowrie (New York: Harper and Row, 1964), p. 80.

break, a kind of escape into liberated subjectivity. Kierkegaard of course has his own agenda and I don't want to pursue his dialectical thinking too far since to do so would lead me off-track. But we might be able to take what he says and think *Hamlet* through it. For it isn't continuity that the play celebrates, it is precisely the loss of continuity and Hamlet's happy recollection of that loss – Gertrude is not Hecuba, Hamlet himself is not Pyrrhus. Furthermore, in the gaps between re-writings of the lost past, in the play's astringent awareness of those gaps, there lies the possibility of subjective freedom, not perhaps exactly in Kierkegaard's sense but comparable to it. The result is not a new religious order, a way out of an ethical log-jam as it might be for Kierkegaard, but a way of acknowledging belatedness, both for Shakespeare as a writer and for Hamlet as a son and heir. If, for Kierkegaard, repetition underpins the move out of the ethical into the irrational dimension of faith, for Shakespeare it has quite a different valence. It both makes performance possible and condemns it to being a mere shadow, a sign of loss, while at the same time transforming that loss into a source of continuity.

The re-framing that takes place when Shakespeare recollects Marlowe recalling Virgil establishes in the first instance a relation based on loss, an emptiness that must be both acknowledged and outstripped. For both author and hero, that is, leaping between frames is a hard necessity – the only available way to assert individuality. For Shakespeare to leap between frames means recollecting and bringing together the motifs he draws from the literary and theatrical past. For Hamlet, it means moving between his own situation and those that mirror his: first of these latter would be the echoes he recognizes in Virgil and makes part of a command performance; but there are also those that he recognizes in his life as it unfolds, especially the parallel situations of Laertes and Fortinbras (which themselves, I'd say, derive from the closely knit parallels in the final books of *Aeneid*).[38] Hamlet remarks on the resemblances, most pointedly when he apologizes for 'forgetting himself' in his behaviour toward Laertes: 'For by the image of my cause I see / The portraiture of his' (5.2.78–9). He here recollects a kind of literary parallel, couched in the image of portrait painting, the very same image that had animated his memory of his father and Claudius (that mildewed ear) when he tried in vain to force that memory on his mother. The phrase about Laertes thus recalls his own earlier performance with his mother and his awareness of

[38] Johnson (n. 12) links the 'foil' relationship between Aeneas and Turnus to that between Hamlet and Laertes.

the value of foils (King Hamlet in relation to Claudius, Fortinbras and Pyrrhus, as well as Laertes, in relation to himself). Furthermore, Hamlet's memory, his recording of the parallels between himself and the others who have lost fathers (why else would Fortinbras earn his 'dying voice'?) links more broadly, I would suggest, to Shakespeare's own awareness of *his* analogical relationships to Marlowe, Virgil *et al.* That is, Shakespeare puts into his play of remembering a sampling of mirrored representations, involving his hero in the recognition of them as a way of signalling his own sense of being invested in a literary nexus. While this might be construed as a version of the 'anxiety of influence', I don't see it in the light of Harold Bloom's psychoanalytic model;[39] I don't see Shakespeare wrestling with Virgil but rather inhabiting him, finding sustenance not in the conflicts of the family romance but in the process of remembering.[40]

To sum up some of what I have been saying: we have a repeated motif of falling and rising city walls, linked hesitantly to triumph and steadily to grief and loss, especially for fathers and/or sons: in *The Aeneid*, Aeneas, grieving for both Priam and Anchises, helps, briefly, to put the finishing touches on the walls of Carthage before being drawn away to his destiny and more decisive city-building, which itself originates in multiple mourning. In Marlowe, those Carthaginian walls are the screen on which Aeneas projects a memorial fantasy of the living Priam, only to have it transform into a blank sign of bereavement; later, they become the site of Aeneas's failure and Dido's self-immolation. In *Hamlet* they signal the crash of defeat and the repeated mourning that follows from that primal loss; while in *The Tempest*, a text that in many ways reverses *Hamlet*, they suggest, not without irony, the possibility of a new beginning that will re-write the bitter memorial legacy of the past.

What does all this repetition, taken together, mean? First, I want to suggest, the theatre is responding to the sense of belatedness that accompanied a return to the classics, especially Virgil; but this sense of coming later, while it acknowledges loss and diminishment, also expresses

[39] Harold Bloom, *The Anxiety of Influence* (New York: Oxford University Press, 1975).

[40] I would thus connect my position more with that of Howard Felperin (see notes 8 and 24), who argues that the matter of repetition and belatedness is contained within the literary – it is part of what literature is about (thus Homer is not an absolute source but is himself aware of the problem and introduces the blind bard in Book 8 of *Odyssey* as a figure for what he, Homer, must come to terms with). Felperin, writing before the historicist turn in literary studies, sees the struggle not as one of psychology or even history, but as purely literary. I think that's wrong – it is historical, and comes out of historical exigency, but it is also intrinsic, so that 'the poetic uses to which he [the poet] puts his models rather than the poetic situation he shares with his contemporaries' is what counts (p. 20).

itself in writing that proclaims a kind of continuity through repetition, and indeed, in that repetition, a sort of assurance. Second, I would claim that the uncertainty and ambivalence about remembering performance registers a widespread ambivalence about performative memorial in the culture, which in turn is connected to the profound sense of loss, along with the equally powerful hope about the building of England, that arose out of the trauma of the Reformation. (And of course, the Reformation defined itself in terms of memorial repetition, as a return to the forms of early Christianity.) Third, I'm suggesting that narrative repetition-compulsion is a kind of homage to the past, a mode of celebration as well as melancholy, which the Elizabethan theatre, with both exuberance and self-deprecation, built itself on.

The walls of the Globe, from this perspective, are those of both senseless Ilium stooping to its base and of the rising new Rome envisioned repeatedly throughout the *Aeneid*. In all of that epic, there is only one clear reference to remembered performance (and even it is disputed); coming across it in the context I have been adumbrating, I began to wonder if it in any way echoes behind the Player's story or that of Marlowe's Aeneas, and the questions about memory and achievement that those scenes raise. Once again it is Dido, whose loss is at the heart of all the motifs I have been juggling, that spawns the allusion. She is haunted by furious dreams, which the poet compares to the nightmarish visions of Greek theatre: her mind is broken like 'Pentheus gone mad' when he 'sees the oncoming Eumenides and sees / A double sun and double Thebes appear'; she is pursued, as is Orestes, when, 'hounded on the stage', he 'Runs from a mother armed with burning brands, / With serpents hellish black, / And in the doorway squat the Avenging Ones' (4.649–55).[41] In both these allusions (to Euripides's *Bacchae* and the final play in Aeschylus's *Oresteia*), there is a hint of something greater than the madness and the fear and the horror of parent killing child and child parent. The *Oresteia* ends with the appeasement of the furies and the establishment of Athenian law, a clear enough reference to city-building; but what of this 'double Thebes'? The line is a version of a line from the *Bacchae*, and no one seems to know exactly what in performance it might have referred to;[42] but I'd speculate that, at least as Virgil uses the

[41] 'Eumenidum veluti demens videt agmina Pentheus / et solem geminum et duplices se ostendere Thebas, / aut Agamemnonius scaenis agitatus Orestes / armatum facibus matrem et serpentibus atris / cum fugit, ultricesque sedent in limine Dirae' (4.469–73).
[42] One commentator presses for the use of a mirror onstage, but how that reflected the sun and especially the city is difficult to imagine; see Richard Seaford, *Euripides: Bacchae* (Warminster:

allusion, the doubleness of the city suggests something of the destruc-
tiveness and the creative power of Dionysius, which annihilates Pentheus
but alerts his city to a necessary and ultimately hopeful awareness of the
double-sidedness of things. In the *Aeneid* context, Dido's suffering is
foundational, a double sun if you will, that burns and renews. It may be a
stretch to see this as an image for the double way that the Elizabethan
theatre memorialized its performances, but, to adapt Hamlet's phrase,
'sure the bravery of [its] grief' (in both senses of 'bravery' – narcissistic
display *and* courage) might give us reason to think so.

1996, 2001), p. 223. More likely the allusion is to a psychological state, but it also seems to point to
the doubleness of Dionysius himself, who appears in this very scene as both bull and man; see
E. R. Dodds, *Euripides: Bacchae*, 2nd edn, (Oxford: Oxford University Press, 1960), p. 193. It's also
noteworthy that Virgil seems to merge this moment in the *Bacchae*, in which Pentheus is preparing
to join the Dionysian rites, with the off-stage attack on the part of the bacchantes that results in his
death. I am indebted to C. W. Marshall for these references.

PART II

Editing Shakespeare and the performance of memory

CHAPTER 4

'Wrought with things forgotten': memory and performance in editing Macbeth

Michael Cordner

Readers of the notes in modern Shakespeare editions sometimes learn the oddest and most unexpected things. Did you know, for example, that the British Eighth Army, during the invasion of Italy in 1943, found itself seriously inconvenienced by outbreaks of digestive disorders among its soldiers, as a result of the latter's too eager conviction that passion-fruit are a potent aphrodisiac?

I owe this memorable, if unshakespearean, titbit to the note, in the Arden 2 *Troilus and Cressida*, on Thersites's evocation of lechery with his 'potato finger' (5.2.56).[1] The Arden 2 editor, Kenneth Palmer, tantalizingly provides no further information about the incident and therefore leaves many urgent questions unanswered. His phrasing, for instance, implies the involvement of significant numbers of troops, but should we be counting in tens, in hundreds, or – perish the thought – in thousands? And how many passion-fruit must individuals have been greedily devouring in order to produce these undesired effects? Meagre with circumstantial detail, Palmer is also uncommunicative about his source, prompting speculation as to whether we are dealing with, say, a tale recollected from some confessional military memoir or, perhaps, rueful personal reminiscence on the part of our editor himself.

By a strict definition of an annotator's duties, this part of the Arden 2 note is a pure act of supererogation. The indispensable business here is to reassure uninitiated readers that early modern opinion did indeed credit potatoes with aphrodisiac properties. To add – as Palmer proceeds to do – that similar beliefs have attached themselves to other (to our eyes, equally unlikely) vegetables and fruit might be considered interesting,

For their many invaluable comments on earlier versions of this paper, I am deeply grateful to Anne Barton, Jacques Berthoud, David Bevington, Judith Buchanan, Niccy Cordner, Barbara Hodgdon, Peter Holland, John Kerrigan, M. J. Kidnie, Mary Luckhurst, Richard Rowland, Carol Chillington Rutter, Robert Shaughnessy and William Sherman.

[1] William Shakespeare, *Troilus and Cressida*, ed. Kenneth Palmer (London: Methuen, 1982), p. 272.

though it is the kind of embellishment general editors, worried about volume length, frequently target for cutting. But Palmer's further excursion into Second World War anecdotage is openly playful and self-indulgent, as is reflected in its being, literally, bracketed off at the end of the note. It also appears fated to remain a one-off. Certainly neither David Bevington in his 1998 Arden 3 *Troilus and Cressida* nor Anthony B. Dawson in his 2003 New Cambridge Shakespeare one has chosen to imitate their predecessor's interest in passion-fruit. Palmer appears to have produced a piece of annotation perfectly contrived to leave no imprint on the work of his successors.

If we are not to anticipate stories from the 1940s about military experiments with aphrodisiacs, what kinds of information can we expect to find in the notes to a modern Shakespeare edition? One answer unanimously given by the three major single-play series currently in process – and one which sharply distinguishes them from earlier generations of editions – is that the annotation they provide will display a novel alertness to the texts' theatrical histories and performance potentialities. The New Cambridge Shakespeare's cover blurb, for example, promises 'attention to the theatrical qualities of each play and its stage history', while the Oxford Shakespeare's equivalent headlines include the boast that the commentary will explain 'meaning, *staging*, language, and allusions' (my emphasis). The Arden 3's publicity similarly highlights the ways in which its 'illustrated introductions' will map 'the play's historical, cultural and *performance* contexts', and its General Editors' Preface insists that this latest re-editing is built 'upon the rich history of scholarly and *theatrical* activity that has long shaped our understanding of the texts of Shakespeare's plays' (my emphases).[2] These are claims alien to the priorities of its Arden 2 predecessor, many of whose volumes appeared to believe that the inclusion of a blank recital of selected performance dates and castings across the centuries satisfactorily absolved them from paying further attention to matters theatrical.

Reviewers of the current series often take such publicity at face value and celebrate the transformation which, they presume, has been effected in editorial practice as a consequence. This praise for two 1990s editions of *Titus Andronicus* sounds a characteristic note: 'Each editor's critical

[2] These quotations are derived, respectively, from the following paperback editions: the Oxford Shakespeare *Henry VI Part Two*, ed. Roger Warren (London: Oxford University Press, 2003), the New Cambridge Shakespeare *Troilus and Cressida*, ed. Anthony B. Dawson (Cambridge: Cambridge University Press, 2003), the Arden 3 *Henry IV Part I*, ed. David Scott Kastan (London: Thomson Learning, 2002).

approach to the play', we are told, 'is deeply informed by consciousness of its stage history and its qualities in performance'.[3] Accordingly, Lukas Erne was building on the testimony of many other voices when he recently observed that Shakespeare editions 'have been giving ample space to the theatrical dimension as evidenced not only in copious stage histories but, increasingly, throughout the introduction and the annotations'.[4] Erne is inclined to think of this as a now-accomplished act of revisionism. I hold the opposite view and believe that, in this field, words have too often been taken for deeds.

The devil, as always, is in the detail. There has been almost no systematic published exploration of what the application of these new principles to the line-by-line design of a commentary might, or should, entail. As a consequence, editions within the same series frequently interpret this mission statement in radically divergent ways, and many appear to experience major difficulties in carrying it out.[5] The goals espoused in this respect by the current series seem to me wholly admirable in principle; but the declaration of scholarly aims and the successful execution of those aims are two decisively different things.

The present chapter seeks to investigate some of the problems which have arisen via a case-study of the two most recent major editions of *Macbeth* – Nicholas Brooke's 1990 Oxford Shakespeare text and A. R. Braunmuller's 1997 New Cambridge Shakespeare one.[6] Both represent

---

[3] Macdonald P. Jackson, reviewing the 1994 New Cambridge Shakespeare edition, ed. Alan Hughes, and the 1995 Arden 3 edition, ed. Jonathan Bate, of *Titus Andronicus*, *Modern Language Review*, 92 (1997), p. 947. I have laid out my reasons for thinking that Jackson's celebration is premature with respect to *Titus* in 'Are We Being Theatrical Yet?: Actors, Editors, and the Possibilities of Dialogue', in Barbara Hodgdon and W. B. Worthen, eds., *A Companion to Shakespeare in Performance* (Oxford: Basil Blackwell, 2005), pp. 399–414.

[4] Lukas Erne, *Shakespeare as Literary Dramatist* (Cambridge: Cambridge University Press, 2003), p. 20.

[5] I have explored related aspects of this problem in three previous articles: 'Annotation and Performance in Shakespeare', *Essays in Criticism*, 46 (1996), 289–301; 'Actors, Editors, and the Annotation of Shakespearian Playscripts', *Shakespeare Survey 55* (Cambridge: Cambridge University Press, 2002), pp. 181–98; ' "To Show Our Simple Skill": Scripts and Performances in Shakespearian Comedy', *Shakespeare Survey 56* (Cambridge: Cambridge University Press, 2003), pp. 167–83. An interesting indication of wide divergencies of view on this subject among the current generation of Arden editors can now be found in Ann Thompson and Gordon McMullan, eds., *In Arden: Editing Shakespeare – Essays in Honour of Richard Proudfoot* (London: Thomson Learning, 2003). The distance, for instance, between the relatively conservative views of Helen Wilcox and the radical ones of Lynette Hunter and Peter Lichtenfels, as evidenced by their respective essays here, is substantial. It is a welcome sign that differences within the Arden family are now being debated publicly in this way.

[6] William Shakespeare, *The Tragedy of Macbeth*, ed. Nicholas Brooke (Oxford: Clarendon Press, 1990); William Shakespeare, *Macbeth*, ed. A. R. Braunmuller (Cambridge: Cambridge University Press, 1997).

significant advances in the play's editorial history; and Braunmuller's, in particular, amply deserves the praise it has received from reviewers for its many invaluable innovations. Neither edition, however, is at its happiest in its handling of performance issues. My particular focus will be on how they respectively use – or, indeed, often fail to use to best advantage – relevant testimony from the play's rich theatre history.

Major Shakespeare editions are complex acts of cultural memory. Scholars who today undertake yet another re-editing of *Macbeth* confront an inordinately rich inheritance of exegesis and analysis, the product of four centuries' close, often contentious engagement with this canonical text. Drawing open-mindedly, but discriminatingly, upon this vast database, while aiming to design a lucid, economical and focused line-by-line commentary, poses severe intellectual and technical challenges. This situation has now been further aggravated by the current series' injunction that editors must extend this work of information retrieval by paying ambitious 'attention to the theatrical qualities of each play and its stage history'. That instruction potentially confronts the new generation of editors with an overwhelming plenitude of fresh material. As a result, many are likely to fear being lured into anecdotage and anxious about ever being able to rise above it.

Tempting and amusing stories solicit their attention on every side. *Macbeth* is notoriously the most accident-prone of Shakespeare's plays in performance, to illustrate which an editor might, for instance, cite such stories as Philip Hope-Wallace's recollection of hearing Charles Laughton, in a hushed and crowded Old Vic in the early 1930s, calmly contrive the immortal transposition, 'How full of scorpions is my wife dear mind.'[7] It is also a script which onstage has often seemed to court bathos – a tendency re-enforced by some of its adaptors, as, for instance, in the 1877 operatic version, where an underemployed chorus, during the letter-reading scene, was required by their (mischievous?) librettist to sing plaintively, 'If we only had a letter / We might ponder o'er it too.'[8]

If I were ever to edit *Macbeth*, I would be tempted to find a place somewhere in the volume for these two stories, but not, I hope, in the notes to the play-text. To invoke them in the annotation would be to use incidents from the stage history merely decoratively and waste precious space. The challenge in researching the commentary for a major

[7] Philip Hope-Wallace, 'An Age of Smartness', *Plays and Players*, 8, no. 2 (November 1960), p. 5.
[8] Winton Dean, 'Shakespeare and Opera', in Phyllis Hartnoll, ed., *Shakespeare in Music: A Collection of Essays* (London: Macmillan, 1966), p. 161.

Shakespeare edition today has to be how to deploy the play's performance record in ways which genuinely illuminate issues of interpretative difficulty. To achieve that end, I would argue, editors need to perceive that an open-minded exploration of the stage history can *both* redefine which areas of the text require an annotator's attention *and* re-invigorate the explication of numerous other passages on which a great deal of scholarly ink has already been expended. At the same time, however, it must be admitted that an inadequately motivated reporting of this or that story from the performance record can serve no useful purpose. Current practice, to judge by our two *Macbeth* editions, has some way to go in maximising the opportunities now opening up and avoiding the dangers which accompany them.

Let us begin our explorations with the closing passage of 3.2, words spoken by Macbeth to Lady Macbeth:

> Thou maruell'st at my words: but hold thee still,
> Things bad begun, make strong themselues by ill:
> So prythee goe with me.
>
> (TLN 1213–15)[9]

I wish to concentrate for the moment on those three spare monosyllables: 'hold thee still'. Seventeenth-century usage authorises an intriguing line-up of possible meanings for them. If we interpret 'still' as an adverb carrying its common early modern sense of 'constantly, always, continuously', one plausible paraphrase is: 'always, and in all circumstances, keep yourself under tight control'; while an equally credible option, deploying the same adverbial meaning for 'still', would be: 'stay loyal to the same mode of conduct – and the same firm resolve – as you have shown throughout our attempt on the crown'. If, however, we invoke the adjectival meanings for 'still' available to Shakespeare, further possibilities open up. For instance, 'still' could mean, then as now, 'motionless', which could here generate 'stand still', but also, by extension, 'don't let your physical control lapse'. 'Still' could also signify 'silent, taciturn', and from that might be educed: 'stay tight-lipped, be careful to say nothing to betray us'. Another current sense was 'soft, subdued, not loud', which might suggest: 'keep your behaviour normal, unemphatic'. And, finally, it could mean 'secret', which might lead to: 'take care you remain unreadable', thus generating a provocative – and (depending on the

---

[9] Quotations from *Macbeth* throughout this essay are taken from *The Norton Facsimile of The First Folio of Shakespeare: Based on Folios in the Folger Shakespeare Library Collection*, 2nd edn (New York: W. W. Norton & Company, 1996), prepared by Charlton Hinman, with a new introduction by Peter W. M. Blayney. The line numberings for quotations are derived from this text.

actor's choice of intonation) possibly barbed – echo of Lady Macbeth's earlier criticism that his face 'is as a Booke, where men / May reade strange matters' (1.5; TLN 417–18).[10] For the sake of clarity, I have laid out the various paraphrases for 'hold thee still' sequentially here; but, in particular renderings of this moment, it is easy to imagine a Macbeth bringing several of them into play simultaneously.

When Shakespeare penned these lines, he presumably had in mind a clear idea of how he intended them to be inflected. Despite the pressured rehearsal circumstances under which Jacobean actors worked, he may have carved out time to instruct Richard Burbage in those intentions and secured the latter's agreement so to perform them. But no evidence of these preferences survives in the bare words printed upon the relevant page of the First Folio, which is all we have to work from. Consequently, modern readers and actors, while remaining strictly faithful to early modern usage, can construct a rich array of interpretative possibilities from this brief phrase. This is not a situation, it would appear, where commentators can justly legislate in favour of one of these readings as indisputably possessing an authenticity superior to its rivals.

What do our recent editors have to say about these three words? As in too many such cases, Brooke passes by in silence, providing no guidance. Braunmuller sees the need for a note – the phrase is, after all, being used in ways no longer current – but all he offers is a single paraphrase, which registers only one of the alternatives we have identified: 'continue steadfast as you have been'. He does not, therefore, inform his readers accurately about the range of meanings, and performance options, in play here.

The traditional remit for annotation in major Shakespeare editions has always prioritized questions of linguistic explication. *Macbeth* is a frequently re-edited text; yet no edition of it which I have consulted does better than Braunmuller here, and many, like Brooke, perceive no reason to act at all. So, the scholarly tradition has not in this instance lived up to one of its core commitments – the elucidation of all passages where alterations in the language may confuse modern readers or conceal from them important interpretative possibilities.

The inadequacy of the existing annotation of these words implies a second failure. Modern editors of *Macbeth*, charged with deploying a new responsiveness to performance issues, are fortunate in having to hand substantive research on the play by theatre historians. In addition to lively

---

[10] The meanings for the adjectival uses of 'still' invoked in this paragraph are derived from the first three entries for the adjective in the *OED*.

short studies by Gordon Williams and Bernice Kliman[11] and numerous enlightening accounts of particular stage and screen versions, there are also available two major monographs – Dennis Bartholomeusz's *Macbeth and the Players* and, especially, Marvin Rosenberg's gargantuan but resplendent *The Masks of Macbeth*.[12] Brooke and Braunmuller cite the latter tomes; but in what ways has the scholarship such studies offer influenced in practice the way they discharge their editorial responsibilities?

In notating how the stage has handled this moment, Rosenberg, for instance, lists some of the same readings of those three words which I have deduced from the purely linguistic evidence. He poses these as questions about how the phrase might be voiced and the physical relationship between the two characters enacted – 'Asking her to remain loyal? To be calm? Is she physically restless, ready to flee from him?' His researches into the different ways in which actors across the centuries have interpreted this moment have alerted Rosenberg to these possibilities.[13] The performance-alert agendas the current series advertise are sometimes articulated as if, *in addition to* explaining verbal complexities, the notes will *also* address performance matters, representing these as two sharply differentiated kinds of activity. The example before us demonstrates the misguidedness of so conceiving them. Braunmuller would in this case have produced more helpful annotation – simultaneously more attuned to the words' multiple meanings *and* to the performance choices they present – if he had attended more carefully to what the stage history can in many such cases reveal about the dialogue's inherent properties.

At other points, our two editors of *Macbeth* do invoke material from the performance history, but in ways which prove problematic. In 1.5, for instance, Lady Macbeth welcomes Macbeth's return:

> Great Glamys, worthy Cawdor,
> Greater then both, by the all-haile hereafter,
> Thy Letters have transported me beyond
> This ignorant present, and I feele now
> The future in the instant.
>
>   (TLN 406–10)

---

[11] Gordon Williams, *'Macbeth': Text and Performance* (Basingstoke: Macmillan, 1985); Bernice W. Kliman, *Shakespeare in Performance: 'Macbeth'* (Manchester: Manchester University Press, 1992).
[12] Dennis Bartholomeusz, *Macbeth and the Players* (Cambridge: Cambridge University Press, 1969); Marvin Rosenberg, *The Masks of Macbeth* (Newark: University of Delaware Press, 1978).
[13] Rosenberg, *Masks of Macbeth*, pp. 422–3.

Editors have traditionally commented here on such matters as the resonances of her use of 'all-haile', and Braunmuller duly follows tradition on
that. But he is also interested in how husband and wife might physically
greet one another:

Rowe added *Embracing him* after 'Cawdor', which presumably reflects a
Restoration stage-practice that certainly appeared in mid-eighteenth-century
Pritchard-Garrick performances and has since become a defining moment for
the actors' relationship.

What is the point of such a note? Actors preparing this scene clearly need
to make decisions which may have major consequences for the subsequent development of the play's central relationship. The same, however, is true of a host of other moments when Braunmuller offers no
comment. In addition, invoking the possibility of an embrace here gives a
questionable prominence to what is, in the end, only one of the
numerous solutions performers of the roles have devised. Some Lady
Macbeths have, for example, taken 'Greater then all, by the all-haile
hereafter' as a cue for her to enact 'The future in the instant' and, treating
him as already her monarch, prostrate herself before him.[14]
    Similar queries arise elsewhere in the New Cambridge text. As Macbeth
exits to Duncan's chamber in 2.1, Braunmuller observes:

Henry Irving made an actor's 'point' of his exit when he hesitated an unusually
long time before leaving the stage very slowly; see Sprague, p. 241.

Many of his readers will be unfamiliar with the technical meaning of
'point' in nineteenth-century theatre, but Braunmuller's note leaves the
term unglossed. It also offers only a sketchy impression of a celebrated
moment. Rosenberg, in contrast, provides us with a richly detailed
examination of it. In his account, Irving's Macbeth suffered under 'a
double fearfulness'. He was 'keenly sensitive to the physical danger of an
attempt to murder the king' and also 'oppressed by his inward apprehension'. This inspired some vividly imagined performance detail. For

---

[14] For an example of a Lady Macbeth who knelt at this point, see J. C. Trewin, *Going to Shakespeare*
(London: George Allen and Unwin, 1978), pp. 213–14. For a helpful discussion of the multiple
performance possibilities potentially in play here, see Anthony B. Dawson, *Watching Shakespeare:
A Playgoers' Companion* (Basingstoke: Macmillan Press, 1988), pp. 198–9. Cambridge University
Press's Shakespeare in Production series commits itself to documenting this kind of performance
diversity. Unfortunately, the volume devoted to *Macbeth* – John Wilders, ed., *Shakespeare in
Production: 'Macbeth'* (Cambridge: Cambridge University Press, 2004) – is one of the least
energetic of the series to date and at this point (p. 101), for example, gives little sense of the
historical diversity of players' responses to the Macbeths' meeting. Rosenberg, pp. 227–34, offers
much richer documentation.

instance, as he moved toward the stairway on 'hear not my steps', 'one observer thought he staggered, another that his feet seemed to be feeling for purchase, as if he was advancing a step at a time on a reeling deck'. A further witness noted the following invention:

As Irving pushed open the door at the bottom of the stair, a draft blew it back and the hinges creaked; he started as if someone were coming down to defend Duncan.[15]

Beside such reports, Braunmuller's account looks unhelpfully generalised. Does it succeed in telling the reader anything of substance about this chapter in the play's Victorian stage history?

But, even if it did succeed in doing so, would it warrant its place in the notes? Nothing in the text dictates that Macbeth must leave the stage slowly here. As an extreme alternative, one might cite Godfrey Tearle, at Stratford-upon-Avon in 1949, who 'ran nimbly off to do the murder, instead of creeping from the stage as is the usual custom'.[16] Without going that far, other actors have rediscovered in Macbeth at this moment a man whose trade is killing, and who, having screwed his 'courage' to the 'sticking place' (1.7; TLN 541), finally leaves the stage with firm, soldierly resolve – an interpretation which creates the opportunity for an eloquent contrast with the man who re-enters traumatised, in the aftermath of the regicide, only a few lines later.

Highlighting Irving's interpretation in this way seems in the end merely anecdotal. If Irving is to be invoked, why not also tell us about the handling of this exit by David Garrick and by Laurence Olivier, by Ian McKellen and by Edmund Kean, and so on, until, at the very least, a representative sampling of different staging options had been laid before the reader? But what would be the expository purpose of a note which offered such a survey? What problem in the text, likely to cause readers difficulty, would it be designed to unknot? That Macbeth is intended to leave the stage after his soliloquy seems indisputable. How he might leave it is best left to readers – and to actors – to surmise.

Braunmuller intervenes a number of times to identify actions he believes necessary. The simplest form this takes is when he identifies what he dubs 'implicit' stage directions. One of these allegedly occurs in the passage at the end of 3.2 we have already explored. There Braunmuller labels Macbeth's 'Thou maruell'st at my words' an 'implicit SD to

---

[15] Rosenberg, *Masks of Macbeth*, p. 313.
[16] Gordon Crosse, *Shakespearean Playgoing 1890–1952* (London: A. R. Mowbray and Co. Limited, 1953), p. 88.

Lady Macbeth' – a note which, on the face of it, looks redundant, since it appears merely to reiterate what the text already states. On closer inspection, it is also arguably misleading, since the fact that Macbeth so interprets her expression does not mean that he reads it correctly. Henry Irving, in his production notes, comments here: 'and she *does* [i.e. marvel] – *no knowledge of his scheme*', and reinforces the point with the further observation that 'She doesn't understand & goes off abruptly.'[17] The firmness of his insistence reflects Irving's awareness that others have read this exchange differently.

That alternative performance tradition was recently sustained in Gregory Doran's 1999 Royal Shakespeare Company production, in which Harriet Walter's Lady Macbeth was instead appalled by what Antony Sher's Macbeth had now become. In Walter's own account, 'the husband she thought she knew would not kill his closest friend; at least not without her courage to sustain him'. 'Not being privy to his motives', therefore, 'she is all the more dismayed by the thought of what's to be done'. Accordingly, Macbeth's interpretation of 'her demeanour as astonishment' is, in this version, wide of the mark, and may be deliberately so, since to respond to the truth of her expression would engage him in a dialogue he wishes to evade.[18]

Braunmuller's response to Macbeth's words therefore misrepresents the complexity of the choices performers – and armchair readers – face at this moment. Here a more alert responsiveness to the performance record would have recommended caution. The annotation in a New Cambridge edition clearly cannot itemise the full range of the plausible interpretations actors and directors have generated from this moment; but attention to what the stage history tells us could have prevented the composition of a note which simplifies in this way the nature of the challenge posed by this passage to readers and players alike.

In 1.4, Duncan welcomes and praises his victorious generals – first Macbeth, then Banquo:

> Noble *Banquo*,
> That hast no lesse deseru'd, nor must be knowne
> No lesse to haue done so: Let me enfold thee,
> And hold thee to my Heart.
>
> (TLN 314–17)

[17] Bertram Shuttleworth, 'Irving's Macbeth', *Theatre Notebook*, 5 (1951), p. 30.
[18] Harriet Walter, *Actors on Shakespeare: 'Macbeth'* (London: Faber and Faber, 2002), p. 47.

On Duncan's use of 'enfold', Braunmuller observes: 'embrace (an implicit direction to the actor)'. Glossing the word is useful, but, as with 'Thou maruell'st at my words', noting the 'implicit direction' looks redundant, since the gloss, by clarifying the verb's meaning, renders the need for an accompanying action sufficiently evident.

But more may be at stake in this case. Some critics and actors have detected a greater warmth in the tribute paid to Banquo than the one Macbeth receives. Rosenberg is once again suggestive:

> The language again emphasizes degree, with its comparatives: 'That hast no less deserv'd, nor must be known / No less to have done so:' ... but his gesture suggests *more*, a personal affection: 'Let me enfold thee, / And hold thee to my heart.'[19]

Duncan's compliments to Macbeth certainly contain no equivalent to 'Let me enfold thee'. So, a literal interpretation of the dialogue might suggest that, as Shakespeare imagined the scene, Duncan was to embrace Banquo, but not Macbeth. This was, for example, how the encounter was played in Dominic Cooke's 2004 Royal Shakespeare Company production.

When such a distinction between the two welcomes is brought into play in performance or in reading, a possible parallel opens up with another exchange, later in the scene, when Macbeth is indisputably, as his subsequent soliloquy makes clear, in the position of watching as another receives from Duncan a prize he covets: the bestowing of the title of Prince of Cumberland, and heir apparent, upon Malcolm. This is a moment which productions often gently underline, as when, in 1947, Michael Redgrave's Macbeth was 'just a second late in drawing his sword' to acclaim Malcolm's elevation along with the other thanes.[20] Similarly, as Duncan moves to 'enfold' Banquo, some actors draw the spectators' eyes towards Macbeth's reaction. In Rosenberg's account, Macbeth

> may show some jealousy, as did Sothern's Macbeth. This may take the form, as with Scofield, of the slightest of unguarded reactions, instantly controlled, but in that instant revealing the terrible pressure within; or, at the other extreme, of Salvini's shuddering with an overt jealousy he could not for the moment master.[21]

The implications of Braunmuller's 'implicit direction' are therefore, once again, more intricate than his note recognises. As with the previous

---

[19] Rosenberg, *Masks of Macbeth*, p. 151.
[20] Alan Strachan, *Secret Dreams: The Biography of Michael Redgrave* (London: Weidenfeld and Nicolson, 2004), pp. 249–50.
[21] Rosenberg, *Masks of Macbeth*, p. 151.

example, my invoking relevant information from the performance record is not intended to imply that all this detail should have been rehearsed in the New Cambridge note. But absorbing this readily available material might have inspired a concise note about the interpretative implications of the different styles of welcome Duncan bestows on his two triumphant generals.

In 1.3 Macbeth apologizes to Banquo, Ross and Angus for his rude self-absorption: 'My dull Braine was wrought with things forgotten' (266). Here Braunmuller provides a gloss for 'wrought' and makes the following observation about this section of the speech as a whole: 'Macbeth excuses his preoccupation.' Kenneth Muir, in the Arden 2 *Macbeth*, also commented on 'things forgotten', but with a heavier interpretative spin: 'i.e. which he is trying to recall. He is lying.'[22] Brooke's note at this point takes its lead from Muir: 'an excuse, the opposite of the truth'. So, as Muir and Brooke interpret this moment, the words Macbeth speaks misrepresent the reality of the situation and should, presumably, be enacted accordingly. But why assume that he must be 'lying'? Macbeth is often a master of equivocation and could well be exercising that skill here. He might, for example, expect Ross and Angus to hear the sense Muir offers, but his private meaning – one to which, in some performances, Banquo may also be attuned – could be that his mind has before been exercised by ideas of regicide which he thought he had consigned to oblivion, but which changed circumstances and the witches' prophecy have now reawakened. As Rosenberg remarks, 'When Macbeth disguises truth, he sometimes speaks truth.'[23]

Rosenberg also notes, among other stage realisations of this moment, Paul Scofield's deft variation:

He masks again – this man who has been thinking of murder – as he works out his apology. Scofield's pause told the slow recovery of Macbeth's mind to the now ...

The phrasing Scofield favoured is notated by Rosenberg as follows:

> Give me your favour:
> My dull brain was wrought ... with things forgotten.[24]

Here too, differing inflections will tell the audience different stories. One possibility is to play 'with things forgotten' as the convenient evasive formula Macbeth needs a moment's pause in order to invent; while

---

[22] Kenneth Muir's Arden 2 edition was originally published in 1951. I quote from it – both here and throughout this essay – from the final, revised edition (London: Methuen and Co., 1982).
[23] Rosenberg, *Masks of Macbeth*, p. 142.   [24] Rosenberg, *Masks of Macbeth*, p. 142.

another is for him to voice it, after the pause, as, on one level, an instruction to himself that he must – for the present at least – drive these thoughts of murder from his brain. Brooke's exegesis reifies the line into a single formation, while the performance history documents numerous other rich possibilities which can be conjured from it.

In 2.3, while Macduff discovers Duncan's body offstage, Lennox catalogues the bewildering, 'vnruly' phenomena of the night just past in a speech which ends:

> Some say, the Earth was feuerous,
> And did shake.
>   *Macb.* 'Twas a rough Night.
>   *Lenox.* My young remembrance cannot paralell
> A fellow to it.
>
>   (TLN 810–14)

Neither Muir nor Brooke comments on Macbeth's line here, but Braunmuller ventures this brief note:

rough stormy. Macbeth is laconic

This gloss builds on *OED*'s entry for a relevant meaning, late medieval in origin – 'Of the sea or weather: stormy, turbulent, violent' – and is, on balance, probably helpful. But what about Braunmuller's further comment? Does it not state the obvious? In one sense, it clearly does. Lennox's anxious, and extended, itemising of the bizarre occurrences he has witnessed or heard reported finds an obvious foil in Macbeth's emphatic brevity of utterance – a brevity which can be convincingly rendered in performance as deliberately anti-climactic and dismissively unresponsive to the young man's ingenuous fearfulness.

But this is not the only option here. In a classic description Sir Walter Scott celebrated what he judged to be John Philip Kemble's brilliance at this point:

When Macbeth felt himself obliged to turn towards Lennox and reply to what he had been saying, you saw him, like a man awaking from a fit of absence, endeavour to recollect at least the general tenor of what had been said, and it was some time ere he could bring out the general reply, ''Twas a rough night.' Those who have had the good fortune to see Kemble and Mrs. Siddons in Macbeth and his lady, may be satisfied they have witnessed the highest perfection of the dramatic art . . .[25]

---

[25] Stanley Wells, ed., *Shakespeare in the Theatre: An Anthology of Criticism* (Oxford: Clarendon Press, 1997), pp. 33–4.

Olivier, too, prolonged this moment:

Olivier had the ghost of a Scots accent which he used with superb judgment of tone and effect ... One notable example of its use was in the phrase "Twas a rough night' ... He spoke it side-stage right – as far away from Duncan's death chamber as he could get and from which any moment the appalled Macduff would emerge. If there had been a pillar, one felt that Olivier would have leant against it in utter fatigue. As it was, he stood listening to Lennox's alarmed accounts of the wild weather of the preceding night with his head shaking up and down in silent confirmation. When Lennox stopped speaking there was a very short but awful pause: Olivier's head stopped shaking, he looked towards Duncan's chamber and with slight elongation of the vowel in "Twas' and a rasp on the -r-, he spoke the line as if it were a curse.[26]

Braunmuller's 'laconic' does not begin to match the experiences such performances communicate. These Macbeths must struggle fiercely to articulate even these four short words, and Olivier's thane inflects the phrase with the bitterest of self-knowledge. I remain unsure why Braunmuller felt his comment to be necessary; but his note simultaneously declares what is, in effect, self-evident and obscures the real interpretative choices.

At other moments both recent editors covertly legislate in favour of narratives they wish to promote in situations where the script can be construed, as the performance history testifies, in a variety of different ways. One example of this arises earlier in the Macbeth/Lady Macbeth encounter in 3.2:

> *Lady.* Come on:
> Gentle my Lord, sleeke o'er your rugged Lookes,
> Be bright and Ioviall among your Guests to Night.
> *Macb.* So shall I Loue, and so I pray be you:
> Let your remembrance apply to *Banquo*,
> Present him Eminence, both with Eye and Tongue:
> Vnsafe the while, that wee must laue
> Our Honors in these flattering streames,
> And make our Faces Vizards to our Hearts,
> Disguising what they are.
> *Lady.* You must leaue this.
>
> (TLN 1183–92)

Muir's Arden 2 note on 'Present him Eminence' simply states: 'i.e. assign to him the highest rank'. Brooke feels the need to go further:

The primary sense is 'pay attention to Banquo above the other guests', but Macbeth has already organised the murder and is directing her attention to

---

[26] Gareth Lloyd Evans, '*Macbeth*: 1946–80 at Stratford-upon-Avon', in John Russell Brown, ed., *Focus on 'Macbeth'* (London: Routledge and Kegan Paul, 1982), p. 98.

Banquo as their greatest danger in the hope of securing her complicity – hence the elaboration of their danger in lines 35–7.

This seems damagingly prescriptive to me. Braunmuller's note at this point suggests that he too is uneasy about Brooke's rigidity:

Since Macbeth has just arranged Banquo's murder, this advice presumably means to misdirect Lady Macbeth (Macbeth is now acting independently; compare 1.5. and 1.7), or (as Brooke suggests) it is an attempt to win Lady Macbeth's complicity by stressing Banquo's dangerousness.

But this still confines readers to a reductive either/or choice, which fails to reflect the diversity of the possible readings Shakespeare's writing can happily accommodate.

Emrys Jones, for instance, detects here a foreshadowing of what he terms 'the "schizophrenia" of the banquet scene – Macbeth's genuine desire for Banquo to be present coupled with his fear lest he should'. In Jones's interpretation of the 3.2 passage, Macbeth can commission Banquo's murder and immediately afterwards enjoin Lady Macbeth 'to be especially courteous to' him 'as if he really expected him to be there'.[27] This is a version which does not seek to explain away the apparent strangeness, as Brooke instinctively does, but which instead locates part of the scene's force in that very phenomenon.

Harriet Walter and Antony Sher settled on yet another rendering, which included elements of the first of Braunmuller's two options, but with crucial variations his formulation does not allow for. Sher's Macbeth 'suddenly broke off when he reached 'Eye and Tongue', which he inflected as a bitter, if muted, recollection of her instruction to him in 1.5: 'bear welcome in your eye, / Your hand, your tongue'. In Walter's description,

Macbeth knows that Banquo won't be at the feast and he can't go on with the lie to his wife. Tony delivered the remaining – 'Unsafe the while, that we / Must . . . make our faces vizards to our hearts, / Disguising what they are' – with a sad perusal of my face as if to say, 'And here am I, disguising my true self even from *you*'.[28]

The Sher/Walter production postdated Braunmuller's edition, and annotators cannot reasonably be required to be prophets. The inherent problem with his note's phrasing, however, is that he is too eager to be legislative about the range of possible interpretations which can be derived from the words he explicates and thus appears to rule out, in

[27] Emrys Jones, *Scenic Form in Shakespeare* (Oxford: Clarendon Press, 1985), corrected edition, p. 214.
[28] Walter, *Actors*, pp. 45–6.

advance, this subtle and lucid reading. This could have been avoided if his comments had been phrased less absolutely – as an exploration of possibilities, which did not implicitly claim to cover all the legitimate options. One of the best lessons a study of the performance history of a major play can teach editors may indeed be the advisability of this kind of restraint.

Similar miscalculations are repeated in Brooke's handling of the next speeches in this duologue:

> *Macb.* O, full of Scorpions is my Minde, deare Wife:
> Thou know'st, that *Banquo* and his *Fleans* liues.
> *Lady.* But in them, Natures Coppie's not eterne.
> *Macb.* There's comfort yet, they are assaileable,
> Then be thou iocund: ere the Bat hath flowne
> His Cloyster'd flight, ere to black Hecats summons
> The shard-borne Beetle, with his drowsie hums,
> Hath rung Nights yawning Peale,
> There shall be done a deed of dreadfull note.
> *Lady.* What's to be done?
> *Macb.* Be innocent of the knowledge, dearest Chuck,
> Till thou applaud the deed: Come, seeling Night, ...
>
> (TLN 1193–1205)

Brooke instructs his readers how this passage should be read. For 'in them, Natures Coppie's not eterne', for instance, he provides two paraphrases, followed by a statement about the two characters' differing understanding of the line's sense:

1. their descendants won't go on for ever; 2. they are not immortal. Macbeth picks up the second sense, while she retreats into the first.

No evidence is advanced why we should agree with the latter assertion, and I cannot see how it could be. Lady Macbeth's next speech – 'What's to be done?' – scarcely offers the necessary proof. In addition, it is eminently possible to conceive of a Lady Macbeth who does here confidently intend Brooke's second meaning, and a Macbeth whose response fully acknowledges that fact. This was how, for example, Isabella Glyn played the moment in 1850, when it represented the last point in the play when she could fight off her despair and briefly imagine a deed which might finally secure them;[29] while, in 1982, Sara Kestelman's Stratford-upon-Avon Lady Macbeth spoke the line chidingly and then roared with laughter.[30]

---

[29] Bartholomeusz, *Macbeth and the Players*, p. 189.
[30] Edward L. Leiter, ed., *Shakespeare Around the Globe: A Guide to Notable Postwar Revivals* (New York: Greenwood Press, 1986), p. 388.

That the scene can also be interpreted in the fashion Brooke decrees does not mean that it must be so interpreted. In addition, so interpreting it means supplying, in readerly imagination or in an actual performance, a precise range of inflections for particular lines, and appropriate body language for the characters, which are nowhere specified in the surviving text. This is, of course, the work actors normally undertake in drawing a performance from a Shakespearean script. Brooke here indulges in an exactly parallel activity; but where the actors' incarnation is by definition offered as only one version of what performance can make of the play, Brooke's interventions consistently claim for themselves a command of the text's 'true' meanings.[31] In some hypothetical continuous present, this note proclaims, Macbeth forever 'picks up the second sense, while she retreats into the first'. Such tactics seem to me misguided.

Brooke is similarly confident about how Lady Macbeth's 'What's to be done?' must be understood:

That she blinds herself to the obvious only confirms Macbeth's awareness of her withdrawal. He has begun his apostrophe to Night in l.43 which, though clearly delivered in her hearing, is effectively soliloquy ...

Again, one particular way of translating the dialogue into an imagined action is treated as if it were incontrovertibly and uniquely authoritative. In this case, his note also takes the line, as it were, at face value – i.e. someone who asks 'What's to be done?' is assumed to be acting as if in complete (though perhaps, in this case, willed) ignorance of her interlocutor's plans. But this reading is predicated on too simple a notion of how lines in a play are realised, by readers and by actors, as speech-acts. An apparently simple English sentence can, in practice, be inflected so as to yield a rich array of different effects, and, in the absence of clear direction from the author, legislating in favour of one against another – as long as the contenders make contextual sense and are congruent with early modern language use – is a forlorn mission.

Thus, 'What's to be done?' can, despite Brooke's implicit denial, be convincingly voiced as the utterance of someone who knows only too well what is to be done, but wishes to hear her husband confess that her surmise is accurate. This was how Harriet Walter played it, and her Lady

---

[31] For important commentary on the parallels between the work of the critic/scholar and of the actor in this respect, see Barbara Hodgdon, 'Parallel Practices, or the Un-Necessary Difference', *Kenyon Review*, NS, 7 (1985), pp. 57–65.

Macbeth's consequent failure to achieve what she sought had devastating consequences for her:

> when she probes further with: 'What's to be done?', the former 'partner of greatness' is fobbed off with a patronizing: 'Be innocent of the knowledge, dearest chuck, / Till thou applaud the deed.' The Lady Macbeth of earlier scenes would have protested, would have wrung an explanation out of him; but she says nothing for the rest of the scene.[32]

This became, therefore, a moment when their relationship was irretrievably transformed. In my view, it has to be problematic for an annotator to prescribe – effectively, via an *ex cathedra* declaration, since Brooke marshals no supporting evidence – that a cogent and eloquent reading of this kind is untruthful to Shakespeare's 'intentions', as this editor, by some mysterious process undivulged to us, has come to conceive of the latter.

The final puzzle here is why Brooke embroiled himself in these difficulties when the passage in question did not demand that he do so. 'What's to be done?' poses no linguistic difficulties and is not an obvious candidate for an annotator's attention. 'Natures Coppie's not eterne' does invite explication, and the alternative meanings Brooke provides address that challenge adequately. But why then say more? What territorial imperative requires an editor to insist that only one way of imagining the encounter is authentic? This type of colonization of the text is too frequent a phenomenon in modern Shakespeare editing.

The preceding instances illustrate editors aspiring to circumscribe, in what seems to me to be a highly questionable manner, the meanings performance can aptly generate from specific sequences of text. In the process, they fail to absorb into their editions' memory-system the relevant evidence afforded by the play's stage history. In my next examples both our *Macbeth* editors take yet more emphatic steps in this direction, venturing to prescribe what they take to be the precise styles of performance required by particular passages.

Macbeth begins his 3.1 soliloquy with the words: 'To be thus, is nothing, but to be safely thus: ... ' (TLN 1038). Experts disagree about the meaning of 'but to be' here. Brooke offers 'without being'; Braunmuller adopts an earlier editor's paraphrase: 'To be king is nothing unless to be safely one.' Both, therefore, assume that they are dealing with a single main clause and make no mention of the alternative tradition of commentary, which instead identifies two parallel main clauses here. This

---

[32] Walter, *Actors*, p. 46.

is how Kenneth Muir, for instance, understood it: 'to be a king in name is
nothing, but to reign in safety is the thing'. A variant of this reading
would construe 'but to be safely thus' as effectively a rhetorical question,
on the lines of 'but what would it be like to enjoy kingship in absolute
security?' Many actors have judged the two main-clause interpretation
attractive, and Jacobean syntactical usage renders both this version and its
rival possible. So I can see no justification for our recent editors' failure to
record the version they happen not to favour.

Braunmuller extends his note on this passage to include directorial
instructions: 'The repeated "thus" urges the actor to some gesture (e.g.
indicating the royal trappings, or the throne if there is one).' This begs
a large number of questions. It assumes, for instance, the most ele-
mentary kind of co-ordination between language and gesture – to the
point, it might seem, of tautology – and reduces the latter's function to
the delivery of the simplest effects of illustration and emphasis.
Modern actors would be unlikely to employ gesture in this way. What
evidence can Braunmuller provide that early modern players did so? It
is as if our imagining of their developing practice has to be restricted
to the most literal-minded interpretation of Hamlet's instruction to
his players to 'Suit the action to the word, the word to the action'
(3.2.17–18).

Braunmuller's intervention also treats acting as essentially transhis-
torical – i.e. in all times and places this line, it is implied, solicits actors
to acknowledge such an obligation. What instances of leading modern
actors obeying this supposed imperative can he invoke? If he cannot, is
he convicting contemporary performers of a violation of the script's
requirements? Re-viewing Ian McKellen's performance of the role.[33]
would provide him with an example of a living performer of the first
rank who negotiates the speech with supreme vividness, but without
indulging in any such gestures. Is McKellen somehow to be judged
defective in this key respect? Notes of this kind seem to me best
avoided.

Another passage which tempts Braunmuller into legislating about
performance occurs at the beginning of Macbeth's 1.7 soliloquy:

> *Macb.* If it were done, when 'tis done, then 'twer well,
> It were done quickly: if th'Assassination

---

[33] The Thames Television recording of Trevor Nunn's celebrated Royal Shakespeare Company
production of the play, with McKellen and Judi Dench in the leading roles, is currently available
on DVD from FremantleMedia (see www.fremantlehomeentertainment.com).

> Could trammell vp the Consequence, and catch
> With his surcease, Successe: that but this blow
> Might be the be all, and the end all. Heere,
> But heere, vpon this Banke and Schoole of time,
> Wee'ld iumpe the life to come.
>
> (TLN 475–81)

He comments: 'These tongue-twisting lines (compare 1.5.16–23) force the actor either to gabble or to speak very slowly.' Again I can only dissent. The speech contains strong alliterative effects which may defeat the academic would-be actor's attempts to articulate them, as he paces his study, imagining himself on the Globe stage. But clarity of enunciation under extreme pressure is one of the indispensable resources for professional actors who aspire to undertake Shakespearean leads. This is a skill Burbage must certainly have possessed. Alexander Leggatt has indeed recently proposed that 'the quick-cutting of Macbeth, some of whose speeches are like verbal equivalents of a rock video', is tailored to exploit Burbage's outstanding vocal expertise.[34]

The twentieth-century performance record also invalidates Braunmuller's confidence. Derek Jacobi has written, for instance, of Macbeth as 'thinking at the speed of light as he begins' this soliloquy, and so he chose to perform it.[35] Godfrey Tearle attacked it with such momentum that it 'was over almost before it had begun'. T. C. Worsley, who reports Tearle's alacrity, regretted it for other reasons, but did not record that it resulted in gabbling.[36] McKellen too adopted a fast tempo for the opening of this solo – a fact recorded by Roger Warren in his *Shakespeare Survey* review[37] – and here the television recording of his performance allows us direct proof of the intellectual and technical command with which McKellen outbids the speech's challenges and potential treacheries.

---

[34] Alexander Leggatt, 'Richard Burbage: A Dangerous Actor', in Jane Milling and Martin Banham, eds., *Extraordinary Actors: Studies in Honour of Peter Thomson* (Exeter: University of Exeter Press, 2004), p. 13. See Michael Pennington's recent comment: 'All great Shakespearians are quick – look at Gielgud: mind and tongue simultaneous' ('A Lass Unparallel'd', in John Miller, ed., *Darling Judi: A Celebration of Judi Dench* (London: Weidenfeld and Nicolson, 2004), p. 60).

[35] Derek Jacobi, 'Macbeth', in Robert Smallwood, ed., *Players of Shakespeare 4: Further Essays in Shakespearian Performance by Players with the Royal Shakespeare Company* (Cambridge: Cambridge University Press, 1998), p. 200.

[36] T. C. Worsley, *The Fugitive Art: Dramatic Commentaries 1947–1951* (London: John Lehmann, 1951), p. 75.

[37] Wells, *Shakespeare in the Theatre*, p. 284.

Brooke too is happy to legislate about what actors can or cannot manage to do, as, for instance, in this speech of the Bloody Sergeant's from 1.2:

> *Cap.* As whence the Sunne 'gins his reflection,
> Shipwracking Stormes, and direfull Thunders:
> So from that Spring, whence comfort seem'd to come,
> Discomfort swells: . . .
>
> (TLN 44–7)

Many modern editions read, in the second line above, 'direful thunders break', following the precedent of Alexander Pope's variation of the Second Folio reading at this point, i.e. 'Thunders breaking'. In his 1967 New Penguin Shakespeare edition, G. K. Hunter stayed loyal to the First Folio and defended this with the argument that 'both rhythm and syntax work by suspension; the discord is not resolved till we reach *come* in the following line'.[38] Such suspensions are common in early-modern dramatic verse, and seventeenth-century actors must have been extremely practised in coping with them. In addition, *Macbeth* contains so many incomplete or irregular verse-lines that the missing syllable here may not be a reason to suspect the omission of a word. So, a case can be made for Hunter's preferred reading.

Brooke, however, like many of his predecessors, favours emendation. He quotes Hunter's self-defence for retaining the First Folio version, but counters: 'I find it impossible to deliver, and so accept Pope's variation on F2.' Once again, the image of the academic actor testing out line readings in the solitude of his study is conjured up; and the unfortunate, if unintended, implication seems to be that what Brooke cannot contrive to pull off, professionals – even, say, Olivier or Scofield – will also find beyond their powers. Braunmuller leaves the First Folio reading standing, though he offers no explanation of his decision. Naxos Audiobooks are currently recording the complete canon, employing the New Cambridge Shakespeare texts; and, as a result, their version of *Macbeth* performs the First Folio reading of this line, which Brooke pronounces undeliverable. A competent, if unremarkable, actor handles it confidently and clearly.[39] In matters of performance, it is probably advisable for editors never to say 'Never'.

---

[38] William Shakespeare, *Macbeth*, ed. G. K. Hunter (Harmondsworth: Penguin Books, Ltd, 1967), p. 140.

[39] The recording is directed by Fiona Shaw, who also plays Lady Macbeth, with Stephen Dillane as Macbeth, and is available on three CDS (ISBN 0521 62539 4). David Timson plays the Sergeant.

A brief exchange in 1.7 prompts a puzzling response from Braunmuller:

> *Macb. Hath he ask'd for me?*
> *Lady.* Know you not, he ha's?
> (TLN 505–6)

Braunmuller comments on Lady Macbeth's response:

Lady Macbeth assumes Macbeth has deliberately withdrawn to avoid Duncan's attention. Capell (*Notes*, p. 10) conjectured 'Know you not? he has.', and his punctuation is more easily spoken.

Despite this judgement, Braunmuller's own text puzzlingly reads: 'Know you not, he has?', in imitation of the First Folio punctuation. Muir did the same, without speculating on its implications or on alternative readings. Brooke, like Hunter and many others, prefers the following modernisation: 'Know you not he has?' Much can be said for and against these various options; but my present concern is Braunmuller's claim that Capell's 'punctuation is more easily spoken'. This neglects a substantial weight of theatrical evidence, which documents performers fluently voicing the phrase as Brooke punctuates it. Sarah Siddons, perhaps the most distinguished of all Lady Macbeths, for instance, according to one contemporary observer, inflected it as follows: '*Know* you not he has?'[40] – a reading which conveys perfectly the outrageousness of Macbeth's breach of his responsibilities as host and subject. This Lady Macbeth scornfully rebukes her husband's disingenuousness via a question which implies: 'You know perfectly well that he will have done so.' Braunmuller's 'more easily spoken' formula dwindles here into a rhetorical ruse to boost support for a reading to which he is attracted, but for which he has failed to assemble more convincing evidence.

In 2.2, Macbeth and Lady Macbeth share a passage which faces modernizing editors with painful choices:

> *Macb*. Methought I heard a voyce cry, Sleep no more:
> *Macbeth* does murther Sleepe, the innocent Sleepe,
> Sleepe that knits vp the rauel'd Sleeue of Care,
> The death of each dayes Life, sore Labors Bath,
> Balme of hurt Mindes, great Natures second Course,
> Chief nourisher in Life's Feast.
> *Lady*. What doe you meane?
> *Macb*. Still it cry'd, Sleepe no more to all the House:
> Glamis hath murther'd Sleepe, and therefore *Cawdor*

---

[40] Professor G. J. Bell's notation of Sarah Siddons as Lady Macbeth, *c.* 1809, reprinted in Fleeming Jenkin, *Papers, Literary, Scientific, &c.* (London: Longmans, Green, and Co., 1887), vol. I, p. 55.

> Shall sleepe no more: *Macbeth* shall sleepe no more.
>
>   (TLN 691–700)

Seventeenth-century punctuation did not normally use quotation-marks in such contexts as this, but modern convention makes editors of *Macbeth* feel that their introduction here is mandatory. The problem is where to deploy them. The First Folio version leaves uncharted which parts of Macbeth's speeches are direct reportage of words he claims actually to have heard, and which, if any, are his own commentary on what he says he heard. Muir offers the following comment on the problem and then rests content with the arrangement he has inherited from an editorial tradition reaching back two centuries:

It cannot be determined from the Folio where the voice is supposed to end, but Johnson's arrangement has been followed by nearly all subsequent editors. 'the innocent . . . feast' 'is a comment made by Macbeth upon the words he imagined he heard'. (Clarendon)

Under this disposition, therefore, only 'Sleep no more: / *Macbeth* does murther Sleepe', the second 'Sleepe no more', and the concluding couplet are separated out as direct speech. Muir's phrasing confesses, however, that certainty about Shakespeare's original intention is impossible to achieve. So, the solution accepted is offered only as a reasonable compromise, given that modernization imposes the need to make decisions.

Brooke, in his turn, treats the whole of Macbeth's first speech from 'Sleep no more' onwards as what the 'voyce' cried and observes:

F uses no inverted commas, and editors vary in their placing; the whole passage is a formal apostrophe to Sleep, in the mode of Sidney's and Daniel's well-known sonnets (*Astrophel and Stella* 39; *Delia* 54) and so is only vaguely associated with the illusion of an actual voice; it cannot be divided sensibly in delivery.

The vagueness in this case seems to me to be Brooke's. He provides no analysis of either sonnet to establish precise grounds of comparison. The Sidney is a direct invocation of Sleep, pleading for its protection from 'those fierce darts, dispaire at me doth throw', and promising, as an inducement, that Sleep will 'in me, / Livelier then else-where, *Stella's* image see'.[41] The relevant Daniel sonnet – number 45, and not (as Brooke states) number 54 – similarly invokes the balm of 'Care-charmer sleepe' and envisions a slumber so absolute that the speaker will 'neuer wake, to feele the dayes disdayne'.[42] The contrast with Macbeth's speeches is

---

[41] Sir Philip Sidney, *Poems*, ed. William A. Ringler, Jr (Oxford: Clarendon Press, 1962), p. 184.

[42] Samuel Daniel, *'Poems' and 'A Defence of Ryme'*, ed. Arthur Colby Sprague (Chicago: University of Chicago Press, 1965), p. 33.

emphatic. In place of an afflicted lover wishing for the safe oblivion of sleep, Shakespeare confronts us with a murderer obsessed with hearing, in the immediate aftermath of his crime, an unidentified voice prophesying from the darkness that he will never sleep again because of what he has done. One of the influences working in Shakespeare's mind as he created this sequence may well have been such non-dramatic celebrations of sleep's healing properties as Brooke cites; but Shakespeare's response to that memory was to create something decisively different. While the sonnets indeed take the form of 'a formal apostrophe to Sleep', Macbeth's speeches report his own mesmerized responses as well as ventriloquizing the terrifying voice which, instead of apostrophizing Sleep, instructs the inmates of the castle that they must 'sleep no more' because of the horror that has been perpetrated while they have been unconscious. Accordingly, the claim that, *because* 'the whole passage is a formal apostrophe to Sleep' in the mode of the two sonnets, it is, *therefore*, 'only vaguely associated with the illusion of an actual voice' cannot withstand scrutiny.

Braunmuller reverts to the punctuation Muir favoured for Macbeth's first speech, but in his second diverges from Muir and Brooke by marking only 'Sleepe no more' and '*Glamis* hath murther'd Sleepe' as direct speech. His note reads:

There is no way of telling how much of this passage (or of 44–6) is quoted speech, and an audience is unlikely to hear fine discriminations ...

But if there is 'no way of telling', why then behave as if there were by repunctuating the text? Why not simply accept that modernization here exacts too high a price, and explain to the reader why it may be better to leave these speeches unpoliced by quotation-marks?

Braunmuller construes the problem with performance as a question of what an audience is likely to discern; Brooke sees it as a matter of the speech's resistance to an actor's attempt to divide it in ways that make sense. Both commit themselves, therefore, to simultaneously claiming that they can, via punctuation, divide the lines perfectly coherently between reported speech and Macbeth's own perfervid improvisations, *and* asserting that the distinctions they thus propose as an interpretative hypothesis could never be conveyed to an audience by even the most talented of actors. This is clearly unsustainable. A McKellen or a Sher would have no problem in lucidly enacting the differing punctuations Brooke and Braunmuller introduce into the text.

Numerous further examples of this kind could be provided. I will rest content with just one more – Lady Macbeth's faint in 2.3, on 'Helpe me hence, hoa' (884). Brooke responds in the manner we by now expect:

It is ambiguous whether Lady Macbeth is pretending, or does actually faint – and will inevitably be so in performance, despite the many editors who have pronounced one way or the other.

This note confuses two different issues. It is indeed unclear from the text whether Shakespeare intended the faint to be performed as tactical or genuine, or perhaps as an event impossible for the spectator to parse either way. But it is certainly untrue that it 'will inevitably be' ambiguous 'in performance'. To assert this, Brooke must ignore the plentiful evidence to the contrary from the stage history – a solecism of which he is repeatedly guilty. Gordon Williams, for instance, recorded the brilliance of 'Judi Dench's diplomatic faint', which he judged 'especially successful as Macbeth both caught her and gained respite by carrying her off'.[43] In 1951 Audrey Williamson described the vividness with which Margaret Rawlings conveyed her 'disquiet at Macbeth's overplaying of the scene after the murder', and that, consequently, 'her "faint" was patently ... manufactured to distract attention from him'.[44] In the opposite camp was Tyrone Guthrie's 1930s Old Vic production, where care was taken 'that there could be no doubt about the genuineness of Lady Macbeth's collapse'.[45] And so on and on.

Braunmuller offers his own variation on Brooke here:

Traditionally, Lady Macbeth faints here, and critics have long debated ... whether her collapse is read or feigned (Rowe's SD is *Seeming to faint*). A feigned faint would be hard to convey, though Adelaide Ristori apparently did so 'after what must have been an extraordinary piece of silent acting' (Sprague, p. 247), and obvious deceit risks inappropriate laughter ...

Well, yes, perhaps, if one is prepared to restrict arbitrarily one's conception of what an outstanding performer might be able to achieve; but if it is, for instance, an actress of Judi Dench's calibre you have in mind, then the case is altered. Among the relevant evidence consigned to oblivion here is Gordon Williams's celebration of the vivid clarity of Dench's 'diplomatic faint' at this moment, which I quoted in the preceding paragraph. Without a sympathetic, ambitious, and historically

---

[43] Williams, '*Macbeth*', p. 43.
[44] Audrey Williamson, *Theatre of Two Decades* (London: Rockliff, 1951), pp. 273–274.
[45] Bartholomeusz, *Macbeth and the Players*, p. 241.

informed sense of the potentialities of exceptional performance, the annotation of Shakespeare's scripts can become, like Macbeth in the later stages of the play, 'cabin'd, crib'd, confin'd' (3.4: TLN 1283) – and risk consigning its readers to similar fates.

If imagining the resources at the command of great Shakespearean actors today often proves troublesome for these editors, their attempts to conceive of the play in its circumstances of first performance can also be markedly tentative. A striking example of this occurs in 2.2, as Lady Macbeth awaits her husband's return from Duncan's chamber:

> He is about it, the Doores are open:
> And the surfeted Groomes do mock their charge
> With Snores. I have drugg'd their Possets,
> That Death and Nature doe contend about them,
> Whether they liue, or dye.
>
> *Enter Macbeth.*
>   *Macb.* Who's there? what hoa?
>   *Lady.* Alack, I am afraid they have awak'd,
> And 'tis not done: th'attempt, and not the deed,
> Confounds vs: hearke: I lay'd their Daggers ready,
> He could not misse 'em. Had he not resembled
> My Father as he slept, I had don't.
> My Husband?
>   *Macb.* I haue done the deed.
>
>   (TLN 652–65)

Muir echoes many earlier editors by treating 'Who's there? what hoa?' as to be spoken offstage and reassigns Macbeth's entry to just after 'My Husband?'. He justifies this with these observations:

Macbeth loses control over himself, and breaks out into an exclamation, fancying he hears a noise (see line 14). The SD [i.e. *Within*] was added by Steevens in place of the Folio 'Enter'. Chambers makes Macbeth enter above, for a moment; and Booth thinks the line was spoken by one of the drunken grooms. Wilson is doubtless right when he says that the Folio SD merely means that the player is to speak, and that it is far more effective for Macbeth to be unseen here than seen.

To Muir, the First Folio positioning of the entrance is so self-evidently mistaken that he feels no need to justify that view. His claim that an offstage cry is 'far more effective' begs the question of what effect is being sought. Presumably he judges it to be more frightening and ominous. Issues of plausibility implicitly influence Muir's thinking here, as they

also influence the lengthy editorial tradition to which he is indebted.[46]
That Macbeth can linger on the main stage close to Lady Macbeth, and
she not recognise him or acknowledge his presence, in this view, strains
credibility. So the action is better if re-sorted into a sequence which
avoids this illogicality, either by having him speak offstage on his first line
and only reappear near her as she addresses him, or by having him appear
on the upper stage for the cry, then immediately exit, and, again, reappear
on the main stage in time for her 'My Husband?'.

Brooke breaks with convention here and leaves Macbeth's entry as the
First Folio positions it. His defence of his decision, however, does not
sound especially confident:

> The delay in Lady Macbeth's recognition of her husband has been much dis-
> cussed; it may indicate that he speaks line 9 offstage, or possibly 'above' (line 17)
> and enters the main stage in line 14; but it may be part of enacting darkness on a
> daylight stage.

So, the options his predecessors favoured are left strongly in play, while
the best he can muster in defence of following the First Folio is that 'it
may be part of enacting darkness on a daylight stage', almost as if the
latter were an arcane ritual in which the original players of *Macbeth*
perforce indulged. His phrasing does not make it sound like a dramatically purposeful activity.

Braunmuller follows Brooke's precedent and does not move the
entrance, while his note circles around the same issues:

> Dorothea Tieck's German translation of *Macbeth* has Macbeth enter *oben*
> (*above*) to deliver this line, exit, and enter again to speak 14 ... Other editors
> have instructed Macbeth to speak 8 *within* (i.e. off-stage). All seek to explain
> Lady Macbeth's apparent ignorance that it is her husband who speaks line 8 (see
> 9–10 n.). One effective staging (accepted here and compatible with F's
> directions) construes her puzzlement as the consequence of the stage's
> (imaginary) darkness: two anguished actors, uncertain of each other's identity
> but in full view of the audience, deepen the scene's terror. Dessen, 'Problems',
> pp. 154–6, usefully discusses F's staging here, although it is also possible that F
> prints the sD too early.

Though largely in accord with Brooke here, Braunmuller manages a more
positive account of an original staging in which actors, in full daylight on
the Globe stage, moved in a fictional world of pitch darkness. He does
not, however, confront directly the arguments of those who find the First

---

[46] Cp. Alan C. Dessen, *Recovering Shakespeare's Theatrical Vocabulary* (Cambridge: Cambridge
University Press, 1995), p. 103.

Folio arrangement of the action unsustainable. Even the force of the one sentence in which he defends as 'effective' (that word again) the staging which can be deduced from the 1623 text is lessened by Braunmuller's concluding the note with the concessionary thought that perhaps, even so, 'F prints the SD too early.' The final impression is of an editor who cannot quite muster the arguments he needs to defend the editorial decision he remains set on carrying out.

What if we started from a different point? Why should we concede any credence to the claim that there is a problem in the First Folio version of this sequence? An edition of *Macbeth*, which seeks to be truly performance-friendly, needs to have as one of its prime objectives a systematic reconsideration, from first principles, of the play as a script tailored to the specific constraints and opportunities provided by an open air amphitheatre in the first decade of the seventeenth century. One of the few indisputable facts we possess is that this play, containing so many scenes set in darkness, was composed to be performed in daylight. We may therefore reasonably deduce that Shakespeare was confident that his actors could instantly establish, by their movement and by their handling of the stage-space, which scenes took place in an environment where the characters could see each other clearly, and which did not. In the *commedia dell'arte*, the '*lazzo* of nightfall' entailed darkness descending in an instant on the fictional world of its characters and the audience being cued to that fact by the immediate alteration in the performers' actions and interactions.[47] A script like *Macbeth* depends on its original actors being expert in a graver variation on the same skill. Otherwise, Shakespeare would have been ill-advised to design a script like this for performance at the Globe.

At the play's first performances, accordingly, it will have been no problem for Macbeth and Lady Macbeth to be simultaneously on stage together *and* accepted by the spectators as being blanketed in darkness and, therefore, totally invisible to one other.[48] This fact enables us to develop further Braunmuller's thought that, in such an enactment, the sight of 'two anguished actors, uncertain of each other's identity but in full view of the audience', would have deepened 'the scene's terror'. That

---

[47] Herschel Garfein and Mel Gordon, 'The Adriani Lazzi of the Commedia Dell'Arte', *Drama Review* 22 (1978), 5–6.

[48] As Braunmuller's note indicates, Alan C. Dessen has led the way in querying the traditional editorial adjustment of this passage. In his latest comments on the subject, Dessen, however, still visualizes the incident being 'staged with the two figures facing in opposite directions' (p. 104); but the day-for-night convention renders such residual subterfuge redundant.

sight will also generate a telling counterpoint between Lady Macbeth's precipitate (and, in some readings, disdainful) assumption that 'th'attempt, and not the deed, / Confounds us' and the transfixing testimony to the contrary of Macbeth's stunned figure, with the blood-stained daggers in his hands, of which she remains, as yet, oblivious. That diptych forcefully ironises the terms in which Lady Macbeth expresses her despair. It will be the (already accomplished) performance of the deed, and not a failed 'attempt' to carry it out, which in the end 'Confounds' them. The die is already irretrievably cast, and this vivid stage image epitomizes that 'future in the instant', as well as predicting the gulf in perception which will from now on haunt the dealings of these two co-conspirators. Moving or adjusting the First Folio stage direction obliterates all these possibilities.[49]

Editions truly geared to rendering *Macbeth*'s 'theatrical qualities' accessible and palpable would have as one of their primary goals the recovery of such moments of eloquent visual invention – effects specific to the performance circumstances for which the play was originally crafted. By retaining the First Folio positioning of the entrance, Brooke and Braunmuller hover on the brink of doing so here. But neither summons the confidence to defend that textual decision with the requisite conviction. The recollection of all those past scholarly voices which have construed the situation differently weighs too heavily on them; and so, instead, Braunmuller's note begins with a recording of what was done long ago in Tieck's translation and ends by a concession to others' views which threatens to cut the ground from beneath his own handling of the text.

The gap between the performance-friendly aims promised by the current series' publicity and the achievements of our two *Macbeth* editors, therefore, remains substantial. A tougher independence of judgement in scrutinizing and challenging editorial precedent is certainly indispensable to the successful delivery of these new goals. But of equally critical importance is a willingness to think positively and ambitiously about the potential eloquence of performance, as well as an open-minded eagerness to learn bolder lessons from the theatre history of the play they are re-editing. A deep immersion in the performance history seems to me

---

[49] An interesting, parallel point has recently been made about the dramatic advantage that can accrue from Macbeth's being onstage, as in the First Folio arrangement, to overhear his wife's 'I am afraid they have awak'd, / And 'tis not done', which he could then deliberately cap with his 'I haue done the deed.' See James P. Lusardi and June Schlueter, ' "I have done the deed"; *Macbeth* 2.2.', in Frank Occhiogrosso, ed., *Shakespeare in Performance: A Collection of Essays* (University of Delaware Press: Newark, 2003), pp. 76–7.

to be indispensable to the preparation of a major Shakespeare edition today; but equally indispensable is a keen alertness in discerning exactly when citation of this or that piece of information from this history will truly assist in the disentangling of a genuine interpretative problem. Use of such material should always be designed to explicate something which a reader is unlikely to be able to decode for her/himself. It should also be deployed in an open-ended way. Attending properly to all that the multifarious stage history can tell us about the line-by-line intricacies of potential signification in a play like *Macbeth* will often enable us to refine and question inherited assumptions about what its dialogue must mean. In addition, it will invaluably warn us against premature judgements about what may or may not be interpretatively impossible or inevitable.

Both Brooke and Braunmuller, as we have seen, frequently behave as if they themselves were 'wrought with things forgotten' in two interlinked senses – i.e. as if unable to liberate themselves sufficiently from the burden of the past, and, also, as if perturbed by, and uncertain how to respond to, the general editorial imperative which decrees that they put to effective use the abundance of information and ideas which theatre history places at their disposal, but to which the editorial tradition has, until very recently, been largely indifferent. The editions of Shakespeare we now urgently need will be 'wrought with things forgotten' in another sense, in that they will be confidently fashioned from a lively and questioning curiosity about all that the performance record can teach the academy about masterpieces which were, after all, originally created as working documents within a process of playhouse production. The debate as to how that can best be achieved has still some way to go.

CHAPTER 5

Citing Shakespeare

Margaret Jane Kidnie

One of my favourite books is called *My Last Breath* by the Spanish film-maker Luis Buñuel ... At the beginning, he tells a little story about how his memory plays tricks on him. He recalls finding a photograph from a friend's wedding in the Twenties, and is surprised to see someone in the picture whom he didn't expect to have attended the event. He telephones the bridegroom to ask about the presence of the guest, to be told that he himself was the one who didn't attend the wedding. This amazes him, as he can remember a lot of things about it even though it transpired he wasn't actually there. He must have heard so many stories from his friends who were there that his mind had appropriated the experience (Hugh Cornwell)[1]

To keep the memory of things ... one has to cite them, to keep them encrypted in one's discourse so that they can survive (Claudette Sartiliot)[2]

Performance, whether it takes the form of a wedding, or – the specific concern of this chapter – Shakespearean theatre, is ephemeral. Whether one participates in it as actor or spectator, the experience of a moment is thereafter relived as memory, and it can only be communicated to others through forms of story-telling. 'Let me show you the video recording'; 'Look at our pictures'; 'Here is the cast list/guest book' ... let me find words and means to describe to you what happened. And when the participants who once told their stories are no longer around, the many or few, and often curiously random, physical remnants of performance – a newspaper article, a dress, a photograph – provide the clues that allow still others, long after the event, to continue to formulate and tell stories about it. Until and unless memories of performance are transformed into

---

[1] Hugh Cornwell, *A Multitude of Sins: The Autobiography* (London: HarperCollins, 2005), p. xiv.
[2] Claudette Sartiliot, *Citation and Modernity* (Norman and London: University of Oklahoma Press, 1993), p. 154.

narrative, their scope is constrained to the individual life, and the speechless artifacts of the archive.

But in the form of stories, memory of performance can be shared and learned. Buñuel's experience of a tricksy memory, as related by Cornwell, is commonplace. One hears so many accounts, sees so many pictures, has been animated so often by the story of a particular event, that it becomes possible, even easy, to find a place for oneself in the story, to take ownership of the memories-as-narrative. The learned performance is internalized to the extent that one's memories of the stories come to seem indistinguishable from memories of the experience itself, an experience lost at its moment of realization, and relived now only through the stories told of it: Warner's *Titus*, Bogdanov's *Shrew*, Brook's *Dream*. One learns the stories of the memories of performance well enough to tell them oneself to friends, to students, to readers. Indeed, when the last surviving participant dies, this sort of second-hand reportage is the vehicle on which continued memory of the event relies: Garrick's Hamlet, Macready's Macbeth, Terry's Imogen. By citing the stories, one enables others to remember, if not performance, then at least the narrativized memories of performance; the uncited performance, by contrast, slides into an oblivion of forgetfulness.

This is an essay about how, in Sartiliot's words, it is possible to 'keep the memory of things' through forms of citation. Specifically, it explores editorial citation of Shakespearean performance and actorly citation of Shakespeare's plays in performance as peculiar, but related, prompts to memory that preserve the past for a present moment through an on-going process of invention. Positioned as the absent but remembering guest, one comes to know the plays anew through efforts of recreation.

To begin then with the editors and a citation. H. Howard Furness, writing in a previous century, had cause to regret that performance occupied so 'meagre' a space in his landmark two-volume variorum edition of *Hamlet*.[3] He explains his scant account of stage interpretation by remembering Cibber remembering Betterton:

Pity it is that ... the animated Graces of the Player can live no longer than the instant Breath and Motion that presents them, or at best, can but faintly glimmer through the Memory or imperfect Attestation of a few surviving Spectators. Could how Betterton spoke be as easily known as what he spoke, then might you see the Muse of Shakespeare in her Triumph, with all her

[3] Horace Howard Furness, *A New Variorum Edition of Shakespeare: Hamlet*, 2 vols. (Philadelphia: J. B. Lippincott Company, 1877), vol. 1, p. ix.

Beauties, rising into real Life, and charming the Beholder. But, since this is so far out of the reach of description, how shall I show you Betterton?[4]

An acknowledgement of the evidently unique power of performance to give life to the plays is caught up in the impossibility of translating into print, the more durable medium, the 'instant Breath and Motion' of the actor. This is the problem of memory that continues to confront the performance-oriented editor of Shakespeare: how shall I show you the performances, or moments of performances, I want you to remember?

No editor, as Furness recognized, can give his or her reader Betterton. But not to cite the performances, or at least the 'imperfect Attestation' of the memories of performance, is to risk marginalizing to the point of forgetting altogether interpretative insights and traditions found through the stage and, latterly, film. The scholarly turn in recent decades to the theatre has encouraged editors to include in their introductions accounts of the drama's life on the stage, and notes on performance, analysed elsewhere in this collection by Michael Cordner, have increasingly become a feature of modern commentary.[5] This shift in explanatory emphasis in the editorial reproduction of Shakespeare's plays has been recently given new impetus by the Shakespeare in Production series published by Cambridge University Press. These books, priced and marketed to appeal to a wide readership, are devoted to issues of performance history. Their coverage is deliberately broad, with the editor of each volume seeking to distil from the wealth of potential evidence available in theatre archives located around the world the most significant moments in the production history of one of Shakespeare's plays. Histories of production, of course, have long been a staple form of Shakespearean research.[6] What marks the Shakespeare in Production series as

---

[4] Furness, ed., *Hamlet*, vol. i, p. ix.

[5] Other useful discussions of the integration of performance into modern editions of Shakespeare, with particular attention to issues of annotation, include Barbara Hodgdon, 'New Collaborations with Old Plays: The (Textual) Politics of Performance Commentary', in *Textual Performances: The Modern Reproduction of Shakespeare's Drama*, ed. Lukas Erne and Margaret Jane Kidnie (Cambridge: Cambridge University Press, 2004), pp. 210–23, and three essays by Michael Cordner, '"To Show Our Simple Skill": Scripts and Performances in Shakespearian Comedy', *Shakespeare Survey 56* (Cambridge: Cambridge University Press, 2003), pp. 167–83, 'Actors, Editors, and the Annotation of Shakespearean Playscripts', *Shakespeare Survey 55* (Cambridge: Cambridge University Press, 2002), pp. 181–98, and 'Annotation and Performance in Shakespeare', *Essays in Criticism* 46 (1996), pp. 289–301.

[6] Stage and film histories of the plays are numerous, but see, in particular, the Shakespeare in Performance series published by Manchester University Press, Macmillan's Text and Performance series, and Arden's Shakespeare at Stratford series.

something strikingly different is the way it resists the monograph form – a narration of the material as a sequence of interlinked chapters – to embrace instead the conventions of a scholarly editorial apparatus. The production history finds its narrative logic not, for instance, in terms of chronology, geography or interpretative theme, but through the lineation of a fixed intertext, the reprint of the New Cambridge text which lies at the heart of the volume.

The value of these editions is that they make discoveries of archival research widely available to readers perhaps not able or inclined to undertake such specialist study themselves. In terms of format and page layout the design of the books is reminiscent of the New Cambridge single-volume editions; visually, these are scholarly editions specially tailored to the needs of the performance-oriented consumer. And yet if one looks beyond the CUP catalogue, the goal of the Shakespeare in Production series to gather in one place an historically significant range of original production choices, keyed to specific lines of text, finds an even more apt point of comparison in the variorum tradition. A variorum edition or, more fully, *editio cum notis variorum* – 'edition with the notes of various' – conventionally collects in relation to a play or poem the best and most reliable interpretative opinions of editors and commentators ever published. Its purpose is to refresh scholarly memory through citation in order to keep the past 'encrypted' in modern discourse. The Shakespeare in Production series adapts the principle of the variorum to accommodate in compendium form the choices, rather than notes, of 'various' actors and directors. This potentially all-inclusive yet ultimately discriminating effort to tell, and so remember, the stories of performance shapes for each of Shakespeare's plays a particular perception of traditions and innovations of production.

The virtues of the variorum approach are many. Its exhaustive citations not only save from oblivion noteworthy analysis, but allow scholars to avoid rediscovering that which has already been found. The variorum Shakespeare has been an essential research tool for more than a century because it seeks to recover and save everything of value, enabling memory by predetermining for its readers what can be safely forgotten. As Richard Knowles, one of the current general editors of the New Variorum Shakespeare, explains, a crucial function of any variorum editor is to judge and evaluate:

A search for all interpretations of a word or passage or whatever in all the editions and commentaries and critical studies of *Hamlet* would yield an overwhelming mass of material, much of it erroneous or loony, a great deal of it flatly contradictory, and at the best, most of it endlessly, uselessly redundant. Such a search needs to be made only once, as it is by a variorum editor, who selects whatever is usable once and for all and ignores the remaining enormous mass of the useless and the continually repeated. For most purposes, no researcher will prefer hundreds or thousands of pages of undigested data to a syncretic statement – selected, assimilated, digested, organized, when necessary evaluative – by a competent authority.[7]

The benefits of the variorum, as Knowles's frank account of the 'loony', 'contradictory' and 'redundant' implies, are also its limitations. It is by definition partial, in both senses of the word, the editor assembling 'once and for all' a comprehensive, yet critically discriminating, abridged commentary. This commentary, prepared at most once in a lifetime and a labour only rarely completed within a single editor's lifetime, is designed, ideally, to provide its readers with everything they need to know about a single word or passage. Out of the 'everything' that might be cited, are the 'somethings' bound between the covers of a book or, more recently, made available in electronic format.[8]

Similar benefits and limitations pertain to the variorum model as appropriated for performance. The Shakespeare in Production editions disseminate valuable and relatively inaccessible fragments of information in a format that implies that much one needs to know about the history of a particular play in production is contained here. In this instance, however, what is abridged is not critical–editorial insights into the drama but historical evidence of performance recovered, for the most part, out of theatre archives. Live performance archives exist as an attempt to compensate for the ephemerality of performance, a deliberate, even paradoxical, effort to save that which no longer survives. Nearly anything – except the actual performance – can, in theory, be kept. Depending on the particular company and its resources, historians of theatre look at set designs, scour promptbooks, programmes and reviews, read notes passed between directors and stage managers, study fixed-camera video-recordings of (a) performance, perhaps even handle props and items of costume once thought by somebody worth keeping. Such materials are reassuringly tangible, seeming to provide a reliable, evidentiary check to the vagaries of

---

[7] Richard Knowles, 'Variorum Commentary', *Text* 6 (1993), 35–47, pp. 46–7.
[8] *The Winter's Tale* (New York: The Modern Language Association of America, 2005) is the first volume in the New Variorum Edition of Shakespeare series accompanied by CD-ROM; the disk makes the contents of the book available in Portable Document Format (PDF). As the general editors, Richard Knowles and Paul Werstine, explain in their introduction to the electronic version, this is 'a first step'. The MLA is currently encoding the volume in XML (eXtensible Mark-up Language) to the TEI (Text Encoding Initiative) standard.

memory, promising through their very presence, direct access to an absent past.

As archive theory has made us aware, however, such collections bring with them their own sorts of distortions.[9] In the case of unrecorded changes to a production made during previews, after press night, or over the course of a long run, the official documents can lend authority to moments and memories shared by few, if any, audience members. Archives, moreover, like the variorum editions they enable, are both limited and partial. Decisions are made about which theatrical events are valuable enough to document, a subjective process of selection further restricted by choices about which few documents will serve as the traces, or legacy, of each individual lost event selected for such treatment. Once a body of material is gathered, there emerge related interpretative issues such as how – and once again which – items will be catalogued. Into this series of parts which constitutes the archival whole enter trained specialists who patiently seek, reassemble and formulate stories able to make sense of the evidence that seems to them worth recovering. As witnesses to the past, the materials of live performance archives come to seem in such ways no less discursively constructed than they are precious.

While it seems unlikely either that the historian of performance would, or could, depend on the Shakespeare in Production editions to the exclusion of independent archival research, or that the project was ever conceived by either publisher or editors as comprehensive in scope or definitive in aim, the series' points of contact with the variorum, a specialist edition that contains the reliable results of a 'search [that] needs to be made only once' are provocative. As with more conventional variorum projects, the Shakespeare in Production initiative constitutes a powerful moment of canon formation. This is not simply to note that interpretations of Shakespeare, but not Middleton or Jonson, found in and through performance have been saved from oblivion. It is also to remark that implicit in this extensive effort of cataloguing and analysis lies the creation of a textualized archive of archives, a self-perpetuating meta-archive. That is, in order to communicate and so preserve the memory of lost events, editors sift through the residue of performance – the

---

[9] See, in particular, Jacques Derrida, *Archive Fever: A Freudian Impression*, trans. Eric Prenowitz (Chicago and London: Chicago University Press, 1995), Matthew Reason, 'Archive or Memory? The Detritus of Live Performance', *New Theatre Quarterly* 19 (2003), 82–9, Carolyn Steedman, *Dust: The Archive and Cultural History* (New Brunswick, New Jersey: Rutgers University Press, 2002), and the special issue of *Studies in the Literary Imagination* 32 (1999), ed. by Paul J. Voss and Marta L. Werner, especially David Greetham, '"Who's in, who's out": The Cultural Poetics of Archival Exclusion', 1–28.

stories composed through direct experience of the event, related by spectators, or formulated through investigation of the archives. Necessarily selective, and valuable precisely because it is selective, the discerning authority of the editor identifies the productions and production choices thought worth compendium treatment; that which is kept, as well as, implicitly, that which is forgotten, assumes a knowable shape, a knowledge that in turn anticipates future assumptions and expectations of research into live performance archives. Editorial annotation thus looks forward and back simultaneously, bringing into being the body of memories it seeks to preserve, remembering the narratives to which it has itself given shape.

Certain forms of performance are likewise Janus-faced, but in these cases, citation, unregulated by the authority of the editor, seems rather to invite, than deliver, the stories of memory. To take an example, my earliest memory of Hamlet's 'What a piece of work' monologue – the moment the speech became lodged in my mind as something to remember – is in fact a memory of citation. At some point in the second half of the Royal Court's staging of *King Lear* in 1993, Lear's transvestite Fool scrawled a few words of Hamlet's monologue as graffiti on the back wall. Watching the performance, I recognized the citational quality of the line, but could not immediately bring to mind a source for the words. The visual image haunted my memory even after I eventually identified its origin in *Hamlet*, probably because the performance seemed to ask a question I was unable at once to answer. The Fool's inscription marked a disjunction that in turn created a space – an opportunity that was no less a demand – for memory and annotation.

Curiously, it seems at least possible that this formative incident of personal revelation and discovery is founded in error. In my mind's eye I see the Fool painting on the wall the words, 'What a piece of work'. Peter Holland, reviewing the production for *Shakespeare Survey* in 1994, found the image no less significant. But he remembered seeing four, not five, words, going on to note that '"What a piece of – " leav[es] open the question whether the quotation is to end "rubbish" or "work is man"'.[10] Textual remnants of performance, so present and ontologically certain, easily come to replace, rather than aid, memory, and my instinct is to assume that Holland, or at least the Peter Holland who wrote about the moment in 1994, is almost certainly right. But perhaps we saw different performances and different graffiti, or perhaps he misremembered what

---

[10] Peter Holland, 'Shakespeare Performances in England, 1992–1993', *Shakespeare Survey 47* (Cambridge: Cambridge University Press, 1994), pp. 181–207, p. 187.

he saw more quickly than I. An investigation of the promptbook in the Royal Court archives could be made, but that type of record, as already noted, is vulnerable in its own ways to omissions and error: the promptbook may be lost, the Fool's business may not have been recorded, the actor playing the Fool may have chosen independently to adapt the graffiti during one or more performances.

Something was written as graffiti in that performance, but I can no longer be certain exactly what. As Niels Bohr reflects in Michael Frayn's *Copenhagen* as he tries with two others to reconstruct a past encounter, memory is a 'curious sort of diary'.[11] Holland's account of an ambiguously worded phrase has come to stand in my memory alongside, not in place of, another recollection of a slightly fuller, and so more certainly identified, citation of *Hamlet*. Like Frayn's two scientists, Gamow and Casimir, 'simultaneously alive and dead' in the memories of Bohr and Heisenberg, '[l]ike a pair of Schrödinger cats', *both* inscriptions are now painted on the wall in my memory of that Royal Court performance.[12] This doubled, impossible picture stands in place of whatever might have actually happened during the performance of *King Lear* I saw in 1993.

There is something more, however, that might be said about the Fool's inscription, which is simply that this piece of business, after all these years, is recalled at all. Out of all of the theatrical moments that might be remembered, and that have been forgotten, this one, of a Fool quoting something on the wall, perhaps *Hamlet*, remains vividly impressed on my mind. What distinguishes this moment from others is not so much the precise details of performance, but the disruptive experience of citation *within* performance, where something 'other' – another time, another text, another performance – makes itself suddenly felt. By enfolding within a performance of *King Lear* an unattributed line that might, or might not, be *Hamlet*, the Royal Court production implicitly asked audiences to remember.

This specialized kind of doubled citation (citation within live performance) which sounds, and is, out of place and time generates, *pace* Austin, not a twice 'hollow' effect, but the effect of a command: 'Remember me.'[13] And the injunction to memory becomes the work of

[11] Michael Frayn, *Copenhagen* (London: Methuen Drama, 1998), p. 6.
[12] Frayn, *Copenhagen*, p. 28.
[13] In *How to Do Things with Words*, J. L. Austin famously argues that 'a performative utterance will ... be *in a peculiar way* hollow or void if said by an actor on the stage, or if introduced in a poem, or spoken in a soliloquy' (Cambridge, Mass.: Harvard University Press, 1962), p. 22; see also 'Signature Event Context', Jacques Derrida's response to Austin, in *Margins of Philosophy*, trans. Alan Bass (Hemel Hempstead: Harvester Press, 1982, rpt. London: Prentice Hall), 307–30.

annotation. My explanation of a supposed citation – hunted-after, reflected on, documented with an asterisk in my Oxford *Complete Works* – has taken on, for me, its own authority. Like the editor of a single-volume edition whose paratextual voice crosses over, encodes, and at its most extreme marginalises the text she annotates, I have become, in effect, my own author of that lost moment.[14] For this reason, even if I accept on faith the reviewer's account of the supposed facts of the performance event, I also know that for me, now, the memory of a citation – or rather, the memory of the effort to *annotate* and so make sense of a (perhaps non-existent) citation – has taken on an independent existence quite separate from anything that might have actually happened in that Royal Court production.

As other details slip away, the story of my memory of that performance has become increasingly a story about a quest for *Hamlet*. A gap was opened in performance, a moment that was simultaneously here and not-here, that spectators were left to bridge as best they could. Citation occupies a strange space in performance. It belongs to the event, yet seems to arrive from somewhere else, bringing with it another's voice and authority. This inherent intertextual condition creates as an effect of language the certainty that quotation, here seemingly out of place, has an identifiable origin. In the case of the Fool's inscription, I recognize this home as *Hamlet*. This answer seems at first to return the citation from whence it came, bringing my quest to an end. However, as I probe further what I think I know of *Hamlet*, this proposed destination comes to seem as unstable and indeterminate as my memory of the Fool's irretrievable performance. I uncover unsettling discrepancies, not unlike Buñuel who has trouble making the artifacts of the wedding correspond to his memory of it. The problem is not the unexpected guest in the picture, but rather the picture that seems to change in its details every time I revisit it.

What is it, precisely, that the citation cites? Where has it come from? Lear's Fool cites *Hamlet*, Act 2.2 – perhaps line 303, 301, or in other editions 295 – a speech that sometimes, following the 1604–5 Quarto,

---

[14] This account of the editorial apparatus alludes to Laurent Mayali's analysis of the late twelfth-century reinvention of the annotator as author: 'Interlinear glosses and marginal commentaries are regrouped in apparatuses that begin to circulate without the annotated text. On the page, they have taken the place of the text. The margins shelter a second generation of annotations that are additions to the existing commentary. The annotator has become an author: he is a source of knowledge, his opinions are discussed. What were originally annotations are now cited as independent works' ('For a Political Economy of Annotation', *Annotation and its Texts*, ed. Stephen A. Barney (Oxford: Oxford University Press, 1991): pp. 185–91, p. 190).

reads, 'What piece of work is a man', or, if one prefers the Folio version, 'What a piece of work is a man', or else, to give the line in its best-known, editorially emended, guise, 'What a piece of work is man.'[15] The origin of the citation, a thing one believes to exist not least because citation demands it, somehow includes each of these textual variants, yet exceeds all of them. This is possible because the search for the play, as distinct from its one or many texts, always comes back to the individual spectator. One generates a pragmatic notion of the play constructed from a series of plausible memories – some textual, some theatrical and filmic – that come to stand for *Hamlet* and give shape, at least provisionally, to the 'home' to which one can finally return the citation. Spectators become not only their own annotators, but their own archivists, gathering a partly discretionary, partly inherited, and ever-changing body of memories that for each of them constitutes *Hamlet*. Citation seems troubling and problematic because it asks one to find somewhere else the home that is always right here; convinced to look elsewhere, one creates the *effect* of an external origin out of selective memories of the play's various iterations.

This search for *Hamlet* has turned me into a collector of sorts, one who gathers memories of citation in performance, many of which, not surprisingly, cluster around the 'What a piece of work' monologue. The items I keep in this pseudo-archive share with the Royal Court performance the sensation of an encounter with a borrowed *Hamlet* that speaks with an authority and from a place that is foreign to the performance in which it is enfolded. In each instance, however, the citation seems to come from a slightly different place, creating that effect, mentioned earlier, of the picture that changes in its details each time I return to it.

Withnail and I (dir. Bruce Robinson, 1986), for instance, a British comedy about two out-of-work actors living in London in the late 1960s, ends with the character known simply as 'I' (Paul McGann) moving to Manchester to play the lead role in *Journey's End*. After an awkward parting with his friend and former housemate outside the wolf enclosure at the London zoo, Withnail (Richard E. Grant), standing alone in the rain, delivers the 'What a piece of work' monologue. This speech, enfolded as a soliloquy within a film about would-be actors, cites *Hamlet*,

---

[15] These line numbers are taken, respectively, from Harold Jenkins, ed. *Hamlet* (London: Routledge, 1982), G. R. Hibbard, ed. *Hamlet* (Oxford: Oxford University Press, 1987), and Furness, ed., *Hamlet*; Jenkins follows the second Quarto, Hibbard adopts the Folio reading, and Furness emends.

not as text, but as theatrical legacy, as a play shot through with the traditions, aspirations, ambitions, and triumphs of the great stage actors who have made its leading role famous and memorable: Burbage, Betterton, Bernhardt, Gielgud, Olivier. More locally, within the film, it also remembers Withnail's Uncle Monty (Richard Griffiths), himself a failed actor, who in an earlier scene describes 'the most shattering experience of a young man's life when one morning he awakes and – quite reasonably – says to himself, "I will *never* play the Dane." ' Performing the role to the indifferent wolves, Withnail gives voice to the otherwise unspoken realization that as an actor he will never play the great classical parts. The film's citation of *Hamlet*, a speech that, typically of citation, seems both here and not-here, thus 'keep[s] the memory' of Shakespeare's play in the shape of a past and, more problematically, future canon of performance, summoning up a theatrical legacy that simultaneously includes and excludes Withnail's performance of a *Hamlet* that will (never) be.

The quest for *Hamlet*, prompted by the sense of unease that comes with the partial, often unattributed, quotation, can sometimes feel like a game into which one is drawn. The cited fragment functions as a tease to memory – no longer a demand to 'Remember me', but a taunt, '*Can* you remember me?' – where the ability successfully to meet the challenge seems to promise access to knowledge and the key to meaning. This game-like aspect of citation came to the fore in a rather unusual performance of Shakespeare that took place in North American homes on 26 April 2005. As part of the '2005 Ultimate Tournament of Champions', a week-long contest of skill and knowledge televised on NBC's *Jeopardy!*, Alex Trebek asked three contestants – David Triani, a high school administrator from Moorestown, New Jersey, Chris Miller, a retail specialist from Louisville, Kentucky, and Ryan Holznagel, a writer originally from Forest Grove, Oregon – to name 'each Shakespeare play that will be performed from start to finish by the Reduced Shakespeare Company'. Miller's request near the end of the round, 'Shakespeare $400, please', cued an audio-visual clue in which three actors wearing vaguely period costumes and carrying toy swords and a wine goblet enacted, in about eleven seconds, a play in which all the protagonists died. The full-text script of the performance is stored on-line in the 'J! Archive' (www. j-archive.com):

'Boo-oo!'
'Bl-bl-bl-bl! Mad! Ow!'
'Poison!'

'Mother! Treachery!'
'Agh-hh-hh-hh!!'
'Ugh!'

The correct annotation of this performance, of course, phrased to accord with the gameshow's conventions of response, is 'What is *Hamlet*?'.

Jeopardy! rewards with cash the speed with which contestants are able to respond to clues on the board. Part cryptic crossword, part 'Trivial Pursuit', the show's format is typically characterized by abbreviation and wordplay (another clue in the same round, under the category of 'AP Female Athletes of the Year', was '2003: This Swede Young Thing'). As performed by the Reduced Shakespeare Company (RSC), *Hamlet* is abridged to a web of interlocking verbal and visual citations. There are four words (mad, poison, mother, treachery), five characters (the Ghost, Hamlet, Laertes, Gertrude, Claudius), and a set of theatrical actions recorded in the 'J! Archive' as textualized sound effects: otherworldly behaviour ('Boo-oo!'), semblance of madness ('Bl-bl-bl-bl!'), stabbing ('Ow!'), consumption of wine at sword point ('Agh-hh-hh-hh!!'), and falling down dead ('Ugh!'). In order for this embedded citation to work, a significant proportion of the television audience must be able to annotate it successfully. As in the Royal Court example, a space which is also an opportunity has been made available to spectators. In this case, however, indeterminacy gives way to factual certainty since, according to the rules of play, there must be an original behind the citation – and only one – that can be recognized and named. Citation is thus used as a means to check memory, in the senses both of testing and constraining it.

Probably few people would answer the question 'What is *Hamlet*?' in quite the same way as the RSC: this network of clues cites neither the play as it is defined by its text(s), nor even the play as defined by key moments in its history of performance (a film clip of Olivier or Branagh holding the skull or the dagger). And yet Holznagel's correct answer and the audience's ready laughter (along with, one imagines, the responses shouted at televisions in at least some homes across Canada and the United States) attest to a widespread ability to recognize *Hamlet* in these fragments of text and performance. The play the RSC cites is Shakespeare's tragedy as it circulates popularly and informally in what might be described as an imprecise, yet for that no less powerfully formative, social archive of shared memories.[16] Yet again, the activity of remembering and

---

[16] The term 'social archive' is borrowed from Greetham, '"Who's in, who's out"', p. 4.

the thing remembered become reciprocally defining, with the work of memory serving not simply to recover an absent event, but to transform it – parodic and farcical though condensed Shakespeare may seem, the inevitable conclusion one draws from Holznagel's reply is that '*This* is *Hamlet*.'

RSC productions, of course, are premised on citation and the operation of memory. Whether performing the Bible, American history or Shakespeare, the company depends on their audiences remembering, and so correctly annotating, the event, scene or play they perform in abbreviated form. Although inspired by Tom Stoppard's *15-Minute Hamlet*, and despite an ambitious claim in the opening moments to 'capture, in a single theatrical experience, the magic, the genius, the towering grandeur' of Shakespeare's entire literary output, *The Compleat Works of Wllm Shkspr (abridged)* is not accurately described as even a radically cut performance of the canon. Rather, it is a play that self-consciously comments on the modern-day institutional, theatrical and educational production of Shakespeare, a narrative punctuated by a series of sometimes extended, but always heavily condensed, passages from the drama. The comedy rests in the effect of wrenching a quotation from one (high culture) context to insert it into a (low culture) vaudeville performance, so creating the perception of a rupture between what one remembers or has heard of Shakespeare, and what one hears and sees enacted on stage.

The RSC's long-lived popularity rests in the fact that the comedy works for non-specialists who have read or seen on stage relatively little of the canon.[17] Partly this is due to a fast-paced, high-energy delivery style that relies heavily on audience interaction and farcical slapstick. Another important factor, however, is the overt citational quality of the performance. All the parts are played by just three actors, and tone of voice, histrionic posturing and fluid shifts in and out of character create the effect in performance of invisible quotation marks around the Shakespearean language (the published play-text uses quotation marks deliberately to distinguish Shakespeare's words from the rest of the script, visually marking the former as citation within a larger drama).[18] The

---

[17] A one-hour version of the *Compleat Works* was first performed at the Edinburgh Festival in 1987, and versions of the production have since toured the United States, Canada, and Britain. The *Compleat Works* played at the Lillian Bayliss Theatre (London, England) in December, 1991, and for an eleven-month engagement in 1992 at the Arts Theatre, London. The RSC opened the show at the Criterion Theatre, London, on 7 March 1996, where it was in continuous repertory until 2005.

[18] Jess Borgeson, Adam Long, and Daniel Singer, The Reduced Shakespeare Company's *The Compleat Works of William Shakespeare (abridged)*, ed. Professor J. M. Winfield (New York:

actors also offer verbal notes to their own performances, providing the
parodic annotative paratext ostensibly designed to help the audience
interpret what they are watching as they watch it: the play begins with a
badly researched biography of Shakespeare, a free interpretation of *Titus
Andronicus* as a cooking show is justified as concept theatre, the conventions of the comedies are dismissed as formulaic and self-plagiarizing,
and an actor's collapse onstage during Hamlet's 'To be or not to be'
soliloquy is explained by an analysis of the speech as 'heavy' and 'emotional'. This authoritative control of the meaning of Shakespeare and his
plays is replicated and embellished further in print through the display of
a pseudo-scholarly editorial apparatus. That these annotations may seem
to some spectators and readers partial, unreliable or discriminating in
peculiar ways is part of the point: cultural reception of Shakespeare's plays
is shaped by those who archive, research and narrate it. Memory of the
Shakespearean original is in such ways fabricated for the audience,
arriving ready-made, as it were, in the theatrical–textual performance of
its abridged other. The RSC's performance of the complete works is thus
an extended citation, less of the canon, than of Shakespeare's canonical
status within modern culture.

Nowhere is this effect more evident than during the 'What a piece of
work' speech. Jess has just failed to deliver the 'To be or not to be'
soliloquy, and Adam, insisting that talk of suicide merely weakens
Hamlet's character, suggests they should simply 'move on to a later point
in the play':

DANIEL   Shall we skip to the play-within-a-play sequence?

ADAM   Yeah. We'll just skip ahead, so you really don't miss anything –

DANIEL   Wait a minute, there's that one other speech of Hamlet's. I
         don't know if we should cut it.

ADAM   Oh, the 'What a piece of work is man' speech?

DANIEL   Yeah.

ADAM   Right. Well, there's this one speech that goes: 'I have of late,
         but wherefore I know not, lost all my mirth, forgone all
         custom of exercise; and indeed it goes so heavy with my
         disposition that this goodly frame, the earth, seems to me a
         sterile promontory; this most excellent canopy, the air, look
         you; this brave o'erhanging firmament, this majestic roof

Applause Books, 1994); see also the DVD/video recording, starring Adam Long, Reed Martin and
Austin Tichenor, directed by Paul Kafno (Acorn Media, 2001).

fretted with golden fire, why it appears to me no more than a
foul and pestilent congregation of vapours. What a piece of
work is man; how noble in reason, how infinite in faculty, in
form and moving how express and admirable; in action how
like an angel; in apprehension how like a god. The beauty of
the world, the paragon of animals; and yet to me, what is this
quintessence of dust? Man delights not me.'

DANIEL   So we'll skip that speech and go right to the killing.

The treatment of this, the longest Shakespearean speech included as part
of the performance of the *Compleat Works*, is curious. The placement of
the prose monologue establishes it as explicitly *not* the supposedly profound 'To be or not to be' verse soliloquy which was intended as part of,
but then unexpectedly elided from, the show; it is delivered in a direct
and understated manner, unembellished by comic gags, by the actor who
plays, not Hamlet, but the female parts; it is introduced as paraphrase
('there's this one speech that goes'); and it is cited in order immediately to
be disallowed ('So we'll skip that speech').

The speech is thus thrown away – performed in its entirety, but
bracketed off as a seemingly cursory footnote to the main body of
the production. And yet this performance that presents itself as a non-
performance removes, for the only time in the play, the audible quotation
marks that otherwise surround Shakespeare's words. The 'What a piece of
work' speech is clearly signalled both theatrically and textually as citation
but, unlike every other passage of Shakespearean drama in the *Compleat
Works*, the metatheatrical distance in performance between actor and
character is momentarily collapsed. The effect is to create a sudden
onstage stillness that generates the illusion of presence. This 'other'
suddenly and unexpectedly enfolded in the performance is unremarked
upon from the stage, with spectators left to consider for themselves the
speech that is not there, that the actors have chosen to 'skip'. This self-
contained non-event, the citation that is at once present and absent,
frames the space of memory where *Hamlet*-as-origin takes shape in and
for a present moment through an ongoing and dynamic process of
recognition and naming.

One cites to keep the memory of things, but whether this effort is
designed to recover or preserve, the process of citation transforms the
object, or body of objects, that is remembered. When it comes to
remembering performance, where the unique event is inevitably con-
sumed at its moment of realization and relived thereafter by means of

narratives constructed either out of personal memory or the physical detritus of theatrical production, citation, especially as it is authorized by textual annotation, gives shape to institutional memory. The process of recovering certain stories of memory from the past, in other words, becomes itself formative of a canon of theatrical production. Assuming that the theatrical turn in editorial production of Shakespeare is here to stay, this issue, perhaps at heart the archival problem of 'who's in, who's out', becomes as significant as the issue, identified by Cibber, Furness and others since, of how to write about, and so remember, a now lost event that once found existence in a medium inimical to print.

However, and as the citation of Shakespeare in performance illustrates, the influence of editors and theatre historians is never absolute. The disruptive intertextual effect of citation enfolded within performance can summon up for individual spectators independent and unpredictable memories of past performances and past texts – a performance of *King Lear*, for example, can seem to remember *Hamlet*, causing *Hamlet* thereafter forever to stand as a reminder of *King Lear*. More often, though, embedded citation does not, or does not only, summon to memory something from the past, but rather functions itself as a summons or call to the work of annotation. In a manner analogous to the way editorial annotation has the ability simultaneously to recover and to create, the origin one 'remembers' in such instances is generated in a present moment. Suddenly granted the authority of the annotator, one returns the citation to oneself, to a dynamic, ever-changing idea of the play as cultural artifact.[19]

---

[19] This chapter is indebted to generous and astute comments provided by James Purkis on an early draft.

PART III

Performance memory: costumes and bodies

CHAPTER 6

Shopping in the archives: material memories

Barbara Hodgdon

Whenever I go to Boston's Museum of Fine Arts, I revisit John Singer Sargent's *The Daughters of Edward Darley Boit* (figure 1).[1] Brilliantly mirroring the transformation from childhood to adulthood, Sargent's painting invites theatrical absorption, stages a scene of becoming.[2] Here, four-year-old Julia, brightly lit, sits on the floor in the foreground holding her doll, looking out; her eight-year-old sister Mary Louise stands apart on the left, hands folded behind her. At the edge of a shadowed background recess, the eldest daughters, Jane and Florence, twelve and fourteen, stand near a tall Japanese vase: one turns outward, the other, in profile, seems about to enter an opaque, mysterious realm where her child-self becomes another. On one occasion that persists in memory, another Sargent painting – of a young child in a pink dress – hangs at right of the *Boit Daughters*. It is less a portrait of the child than a painting of the dress, which clouds around her, radiating like an open peony blossom, rendered so that it treads an edge between realistic portraiture and impressionism. As I try to explain what I see in these paintings to a friend, another Sargent-admirer, introducing himself as a curator, tells us a story. When speaking about the painting of the child in the peony dress to a group of visitors, he noticed that an older woman in a wheelchair was unusually attentive. Several days later, he discovered a box on his office desk. Inside was the dress that appeared in the painting – and a note from the woman in the wheelchair. Since he so admired the painting she had posed for as a child, she wanted him to have the dress itself: keep this, she wrote, in remembrance of me. Currently, another Sargent portrait of a

---

[1] Painted in 1882, its composition is reminiscent of Velásquez's *Las Meninas* (1651), which Sargent had copied in Madrid; the four daughters gave the painting to the Museum of Fine Arts in 1919, in memory of their father. See *John Singer Sargent*, ed. Elaine Kilmurray and Richard Ormond (Washington, DC: National Gallery of Art, 1999), p. 98.

[2] On theatrical absorption, see Michael Fried, *Absorption and Theatricality: Painting and Beholder in the Age of Diderot* (Berkeley: University of California Press, 1980).

1. John Singer Sargent, *The Daughters of Edward Darley Boit*, 1882.

child – *Helen Sears* (1895) – has replaced this one; curiously enough, neither I nor the present MFA curator can identify, from exhibit catalogues or listings, what I once saw and about which I once had listened to another's story of a memorable encounter.

In catching up disappearance, replacement, repetition and story-telling – one way in which theatre talks *of* itself *to* itself – this narrative of the painting that has gone missing and the survival of the peony dress trope the conditions that pervade remembering the absent, irrecoverable performance (and performer) through a (literally) material trace. Perhaps the only way to confront memory, especially performance memory, heavy with betrayals and forgetting, is to begin with its loss – the after-effect of which, as Peggy Phelan writes, is the experience of subjectivity itself.[3] Indeed, the transformative powers of memory imply a decisive shift towards the psychological: for Henri Bergson, memories form a chain, apparently capricious yet all-pervasive, and human intuition (by which he means compassionate thinking) also is memory, the actual synthesis of all our past states[4] – something, perhaps, like an ideal archive. Certainly ever since Foucault raised the 'question of the archive' in the early 1960s, historians have desired to view the archive as a metaphor for memory – as a site capable of restoring, 'as if by magic, what is lacking in every gaze'. Yet an archive does not resemble human memory or the unconscious: it takes in heterogeneous stuff, then orders, classifies and catalogues it. So reordered and remade, this stuff remains mute until someone uses it, turns it into narrative – or performance.[5]

Just as I began with a story that situates looking as a means of speaking memory and as a performative expression, the memories I evoke here are prompted by visiting the Royal Shakespeare Company's costume archive – a place of dreams, of longing for performances past, for what has gone missing. There, as costumes work to re-member, if not to restore the bodies that inhabited them, memory aligns with theatrical subjectivity and its fabric-ation, telling stories that have less to do with Freud's primal scene or Proust's *petite Madeleine* – those two intimate and universal sites of memory – than with Proust's haunting by the design of the Fortuny cloak and by Albertine within it.[6] To rephrase Herbert Blau, where memory is, performance is;[7] or, more accurately, something other than a performance but *like* a performance, a 'second-order performance' which reintegrates surviving fragments into a narrative that links crafting the theatrical past in memory with archaeology – that branch of history

---

[3] Peggy Phelan, *Unmarked: The Politics of Performance* (London: Routledge, 1993), p. 148. See also Andreas Huyssen, *Present Pasts: Urban Palimpsests and the Politics of Memory* (Stanford: Stanford University Press, 2003), p. 4.

[4] Henri Bergson, *Matter and Memory*, trans. N. M. Paul and W. S. Palmer (New York: Zone Books, 1991), pp. 145–6.

[5] I draw on Carolyn Steedman, *Dust: The Archive and Cultural History* (New Brunswick, NJ: Rutgers University Press, 2001), pp. 2–13, 68. See also Michel Foucault, 'Archive Fever: A Freudian Impression', trans. Eric Prenowitz, *Diacritics* 25.2 (Summer 1995), pp. 9–63; and Peter Crier, 'Places, Politics and the Archiving of Contemporary Memory', in *Memory and Methodology*, ed. Susannah Radstone (Oxford and New York: Berg, 2000), pp. 37–58.

[6] I draw on Pierre Nora, 'Between Memory and History: Les Lieux de Mémoire', *Representations* 26 (Spring 1989), p. 15.

[7] Herbert Blau, *The Audience* (Baltimore: Johns Hopkins University Press, 1990), p. 382. Blau's term is 'theatre', not performance.

which most closely resembles shopping.[8] Taking costume as an interface between theatre and archaeology, I ad-dress performances past through a material mnemonics.

My focus, similar to that of Roland Barthes's *Camera Lucida*,[9] is not on the archive's entire corpus – some 1,600 costumes and costume parts as well as properties and design materials reaching back to the 1940s and beyond, even including some costumes worn by Henry Irving and Ellen Terry and others from Frank Benson's early twentieth-century performances at the Shakespeare Memorial Theatre[10] – but only on some and what my memory, supplemented by that of others, knows of them – a kind of communal epistemology in which looking functions as a form of discourse. Like the collection itself, my stories are products of archival politics and individual preference,[11] a recontextualization from surviving

[8] According to Irwin, the up-to-date supply-teacher in Alan Bennett's *The History Boys* (London: Nick Hern, 2004), p. 63. 'Second-order performance' is Mike Pearson's term; see Mike Pearson and Michael Shanks, *Theatre/Archaeology* (London and New York: Routledge, 2001), p. 10.

[9] Roland Barthes, *Camera Lucida: Reflections on Photography*, trans. Richard Howard (New York: Hill and Wang, 1981).

[10] A large collection of Irving material and Benson costumes (which Irving had supplied after the Bensons lost their wardrobe in a theatre fire) were given to the Memorial Theatre in the late 1920s when it seemed likely that a big new museum space would be part of the rebuilt theatre. Since that did not happen, the collection was put on long-term deposit at the Museum of London. Some items, however, have been loaned back to the RSC and can be seen in the Benson room in the Gallery display space on Waterside above the Swan Theatre. David Howells, private communication, 6 September 2004. An exhibition, 'First Knight: Henry Irving 1838–1905' was mounted at the RSC Collection from 30 June to 5 November 2005. Images of some of Irving's, Terry's and the Bensons' costumes can be found in M. R. Holmes, *Stage Costumes and Accessories in the London Museum* (London: Her Majesty's Stationery Office, 1968).

[11] The RSC Collection represents a mixture of various collecting styles. When the Memorial Theatre Picture Gallery was conceived, a general appeal invited gifts or loans of Shakespeare- and theatre-related materials; monies were raised for purchasing additional material. Only in the late 1940s did the collection of costuming begin. At this stage, those collected were perceived as 'star' costumes – those worn by famous actors in important roles, and even when 'stars' were less a feature of the Stratford stage once the RSC was formed in the early 1960s, that practice continued. At times, nothing at all was collected; at others, only costumes worn by minor characters and less-well-known actors survive; in part, such choices depended on who was in charge of the collection and whether access to costumes was allowed; moreover, at times limited storage space inhibited the collection process (presently the collection is housed at a building in Mason Road, Stratford). Currently, costumes are collected by agreement between the Associate Designer, the Head of Wardrobe and David Howells, the collection's Curator, who together attempt to collect two to three costumes per Shakespeare production as well as costumes from others, depending on the production's importance and its design quality. Little if anything comes directly from actors, though if they offer something they personally own that is relevant to a production, it is considered. Most material, however, is RSC property, though questions of moral rights pertain to items such as directors' notes. Indeed, acquisition of design material is the only area where intellectual property right (IP) is retained by the individual; here, the collection depends on individual gifts. Additional costumes are stored in the RSC's Hire Wardrobe. David Howells, private communication 4 August 2004. See also *Designing Shakespeare: an audio visual archive* http://www.pads.ahds.ac.uk.

remains: training close attention on a few costumes, I explore these through a layered reading. In the archive, where it hangs, naked, on a padded hanger – a trace of performance torn away from performance, no longer quite life yet not death,[12] registering simultaneously the decay of performance and its evocative afterlife – what reading attitude does the costume promote? What is the ontological status of a frame without a body that still evokes the performer who once occupied it? No meaning without the body? Surely not. Shopping tells us otherwise: examining racked-up garments, one thinks: 'That will look well on me; I might wear that – but never *that.*' Whether in Barney's, the theatre or the archive, costume insists on the body and its desires. Costume *is* subject, a material mode of praxis that defines and annotates role: remarks Paola Dionisotti, costume is 'a frame to hang a performance on; it's like a cage, you can tie bits on to it'.[13]

Since memory is not inventory but an *act* – call it a performance? – of memorizing, which is also the work of photography (or of archaeology), I turn from the costume to the still photograph. Because the photograph preserves a moment of performance time and prevents it being effaced by the supersession of further moments, photographs can be compared to images stored in memory. Yet, as John Berger writes, 'there is a funda-mental difference, for whereas remembered images are the *residue* of continuous experience or consciousness, a photograph isolates the appearances of a disconnected instant'.[14] Working somewhat like the classical means of remembering by placing a thought or image within a fictive (theatrical) architecture,[15] the still, evidence of a worn theatrical world, re-frames costume back to performance, effects its contextual re-animation. Braiding mode of production technology with mode of performance thematizes a hyperframe, a master code for re-dreaming performance. How do these operate as a resonant memory bank, mobi-lizing the vagaries of curiosity and desire, spinning out particular tales of travel from closet to stage, providing an array of sensory and intellectual pleasures, a repository of erotic knowledge?

The costume archive resembles expandable library shelving or, more pertinently, oversized garment bags, like those in which my mother would store one season's clothes, carefully cleaned, pressed and hung on

---

[12] Nora, 'Between Memory and History', p. 12.
[13] Paola Dionisotti, quoted in Carol Rutter, *Clamorous Voices: Shakespeare's Women Today* (London: Women's Press, 1988), p. xxii.
[14] John Berger, *Another Way of Telling* (New York: Vintage International, 1995), p. 89.
[15] See Frances A. Yates, *The Art of Memory* (Chicago: University of Chicago Press, 1966).

satin hangers; spring and summer in one bag, fall and winter in another.
A fantasy closet or theatrical reliquary where costumes, 'shelved' by play,
each with a label identifying the actor who once wore it, track authorial,
individual and institutional identities and memories. Yet if storage speaks
an order of things, there is no particular order to performance memory:
capricious, driven by a roving eye, it resembles window shopping – or
(again) archaeology. On first looking into this archive, I recalled Howard
Carter peering into Tutankhamen's tomb for the first time: 'What do you
see?' asked Lord Carnarvon; replied Carter, 'Wonderful things.'[16] Here,
for instance, was Antony Sher's 'bottled spider' black body suit for
Richard III (1984); John Gielgud's robes for Prospero (1957), those of the
exiled humanist magus, designed when postcolonial *Tempest*s were just
over the horizon; a silly, curled and frizzle-frazzled auburn wig for
Laurence Olivier's Malvolio (1955); Janet Suzman's golden breastplate for
Cleopatra (1972), looking like a relic unearthed from a Pharoanic tomb;
Juliet Stevenson's bowler hat for Rosalind (1985), the sign of what Lesley
Ferris has called her 'Cocky Ros';[17] Peggy Ashcroft's bronze lurex gown
for Queen Margaret (1964), glittering like jewelled armour: a wardrobe of
signs, styles and fashions, some marking signature performances. Indeed,
shopping in the archive involves 'just looking' – which, Freud claims, is a
natural extension of touching. And certainly one of the pleasures of the
archive is the thrill of touching a costume's fabric, feeling its weight and
drape in one's hand. Some of these clothes whisper, some sing or shout;
seeing them is like talking softly with someone – an emotional, even
erotic encounter – almost a private scene of love.

Because I remember them as a sign of the 1970s, I began with the
boots. Ankle boots, buckled boots, crushed boots, over-the-knee boots,
tight, shiny and high: I wanted them all. In *This So-Called Disaster: Sam
Shepard Directs Henry Moss*, Michael Almereyda's 2003 documentary of
the rehearsals for Sam Shepard's *The Late Henry Moss*, Sean Penn recalls
coveting a pair of zipper boots: if he had 'actor boots', he imagined, he
too could be an actor. Perhaps I thought so too, though I think what I
was after had more to do with sex than performing (which, to be sure,
sometimes resemble one another). And after all, as Andy Warhol writes,
'Sex is nostalgia for sex' – what Peggy Phelan imagines Freud meant to
say in *The Interpretation of Dreams*. Whereas the dresses, robes, trousers

---

[16] Thomas Hoving, *Tutankhamun: The Untold Story* (New York: Simon and Schuster, 1978).
[17] Lesley Anne Soule, 'Subverting Rosalind: Cocky Ros in the Forest of Arden', *New Theatre Quarterly* 26 (1991), 126–36.

2. Boots worn by Alan Howard as Henry V. Director: Terry Hands; Designer: Farrah.
Royal Shakespeare Company, 1976.

and jackets stored here appear indeed as *prêt a porter*, ready-to-wear-again, boots carry body memory, keep their human shape in ways that clothes do not: the very emptiness of the pair worn by Alan Howard as Henry V (1976) reveals how once they were filled and animated (figure 2). So, too, with Ian Holm's club-footed boot for Richard III (1964); a material sign that, *preceding* role, defines rather than annotates or fabricates, it is indelibly imprinted with performance (figure 3); ironically and appropriately, given the play's near-apocalyptic ending, it has been damaged by fire, which, writes Alan Read, separates the past from the present so efficiently as to have been the invention of historiography itself.[18] And just as memory looks forward as well as backwards, these charred remains look ahead to the moment when Ian McKellen's Richard, in Richard Loncraine's 1995 film, would fall to his death in flames. Perhaps because Holm's boot evoked a performance I never saw

---

[18] Alan Read, *Theatre and Everyday Life: An Ethics of Performance* (London and New York: Routledge, 1993), p. 232.

3. Boot worn by Ian Holm as Richard III. Directors: Peter Hall and John Barton;
Designer: John Bury. Royal Shakespeare Company, 1963–4.

but wish that I had – the Hall-John Barton *Wars of the Roses* – it seemed
most like an object surfacing from a dig, an artifact which made that
absent performance phenomenologically real, in contrast to knowing it
only second-hand through prompt-copies, reviews and photographs. Yet
such objects from unseen performances also belong to a memory closet:
much like the clothing one finds in attic trunks, garments one has never
seen worn, their touch and feel evokes past presences.

With that in mind, it was seeing Howard's Henry V boots that took
me to another performance I know only in this second-hand manner:
Richard Burton's Prince Hal and Henry V for Stratford's Shakespeare
Memorial Theatre, marking the 1951 Festival of Britain. 'Harey the fyftes
dublet and Harye the v. vellet gowne' – listed in Philip Henslowe's
inventory as 'gone and loste'[19] – resurface here (figures 4 and 5), Motley's
choice of fabric duplicating (perhaps consciously, given the production's
historical mandate) the orange tawny associated, in Elizabethan colour

---

[19] 'Playhouse Inventories (now lost)', Entry 65 (10 March 1598), pp. 133–7 in Carol Chillington Rutter,
ed. *Documents of the Rose Playhouse* rev. edn (Manchester: Manchester University Press, 1999), p. 135.
The RSC Hire Wardrobe perhaps most closely resembles what Henslowe's accounts reveal of his trade
in second-hand clothes: there, warehoused on two jam-packed floors, organized by time period,
gender, style and fabric, anything and everything can be rented – or, on occasion, bought.

4. Doublet worn by Richard Burton as Prince Hal. Director: Anthony Quayle and John Kidd; Designer: Tanya Moiseiwitsch. Shakespeare Memorial Theatre, 1951.

symbolism, with courtiers, and with pride.[20] In the Elizabethan theatre, even the most elaborate robes did not necessarily remove performance from the aristocratic everyday but jammed stage and world together: early-modern spectators might well read Burton's doublet and gown, not as costume but as *clothes*, markers of sumptuary laws according the performing body both (prescribed) socio-economic status and shape.[21] Juxtaposing hangered doublet and gown, haunted by the absent body, to an Angus McBean photograph of Burton (figure 6) effects a curious oscillation between garment and black-and-white still in which the costume's colours bleed over, tinting, toning, re-animating the photograph. Moreover, the still itself invites another memory, a review-as-caption: wrote Kenneth Tynan, 'Burton is a still brimming pool, running disturbingly deep; at twenty-five he commands repose and can make silence garrulous. His Prince Hal is never a roaring boy; he sits hunched or sprawled, with

[20] See M[arie] Channing Linthicum, *Costume in the Drama of Shakespeare and His Contemporaries* (Oxford: Clarendon Press, 1936).
[21] Ann Rosalind Jones and Peter Stallybrass, *Renaissance Clothing and the Materials of Memory* (Cambridge: Cambridge University Press, 2000), *passim*.

5. Robe worn by Richard Burton as Henry V. Director: Anthony Quayle; Designer:
Tanya Moiseiwitsch. Shakespeare Memorial Theatre, 1951.

dark unwinking eyes; ... He brings his cathedral on with him', said one
dazed member of the company.[22]

Read historically, Motley's doublet and gown for Burton's Henry
anticipate by fifty years the 'authentic' or 'original practices' reconstructions of early-modern dress now in fashion at London's Shakespeare's
Globe. (Currently, Globe spectators observe actors 'putting on'
another identity; dressing-up for the role becomes a pre-performance in
itself, showing off the clothes in a behind-the-scenes glimpse of theatrical
labour.) Arguably (for the term is slippery), perhaps even more
'authentic' is the costume which vividly realizes a Shakespearean image or
metaphor. Does a material mnemonics always derive from – and drive
back to – Shakespeare's words? *First study the words*, writes Ellen Terry in
her memoirs (have critics been mining the wrong semantic field all along
in their persistent dichotomy of *text* and performance?), 'then say the

---

[22] Kenneth Tynan, review of *1* and *2 Henry IV* (1951), rpt. in *Curtains* (New York: Atheneum, 1961),
pp. 11–12.

6. Richard Burton as Henry V, 1951.

words in imaginary dresses ... *& get the dress-maker to work ...* '[23]
Shortly after his father's death in *2 Henry IV*, the new Henry V describes

[23] Cited in Michael Booth, 'Ellen Terry', in *Bernhardt, Terry, Duse: The Actress in Her Time*, ed. John
Stokes, Michael Booth, and Susan Bassnett (Cambridge: Cambridge University Press, 1988), p. 91.
Terry's comments come from her copy of the Irving *King Lear* text, now preserved in the library of
the Theatre Museum, Covent Garden.

7. Henry V (Alan Howard) rejects Falstaff (Brewster Mason), *2 Henry IV*, Royal
Shakespeare Company, 1975. Director: Terry Hands; Designer: Farrah.

majesty as a 'new and gorgeous garment'; in the role's trajectory through
two plays, everything leads to the acted majesty of a 'rich armour worn in
heat of day / That scalds with safety'. Writes Farrah, Terry Hands's
designer for the 1975 *Henry V*, 'I wanted people to see a Henry who was
unreachable, untouchable. Quite beyond the appeal of Falstaff and the
others.'[24] In Joe Cocks's photograph of Alan Howard's King confronting
Falstaff (figure 7), Farrah's golden body suit gives an eloquent performance in itself. Staged against a bleak white carpet, the costume looks
heavy, non-penetrable, monumental: absorbing 'Henry' into an isolated
icon of power called 'The King', it makes him totally unreadable, chillingly 'other'. Disciplining and encompassing the actor's body, costume

[24] Quoted in Sally Beauman, *The Royal Shakespeare Company's Centenary Production of Henry V*
(Oxford and New York: Pergamon Press, 1976), pp. 34–5.

(literally) masks or insulates Henry from the (potentially painful) necessity of performing rejection while simultaneously intensifying that performance to the staged world.

If, within the visual field of performance, Henry's golden mummy-case bears a world of ideological weight, on the hanger and to the touch it looks and feels light, even airy. Yet when it appears on a mannequin, readied for staging at another site – the RSC Collection, housed in the old Memorial Theatre Picture Gallery above the neo-Elizabethan Swan Theatre – where costumes of past productions of those plays currently being performed are set side-by-side in a display, costume participates in a different fiction, becomes a different kind of artifact (figure 8). Just as slippage occurs from performance to archive, here costume slips within space and time, looks backwards and forwards. Accorded a 'stuffed' pseudo-afterlife, costume is fetishized, in the Marxian sense of commodity fetish, serves as a trailer or advert for the RSC's latest season: 'This was once the look of the play: go to the theatre and see what it looks like now' – one project of theatre history. Simultaneously, minimal captioning – the names of designer, director and actor and the production's date – not only speaks confidence in the primary and sole power of the costume itself but also, by permitting memory to move, speaks another order of things, invites a genealogy of theatrical clothes, of material surrogations.

Just as the RSC costume display invites a movement from time past to time present, the sudden collision of a play such as *Titus Andronicus* with recent global memories of traumatic violence and genocidal rape invites looking back to its first twentieth-century performance, Peter Brook's 1955 production starring – the term had particular significance then – Laurence Olivier and Vivien Leigh. As with Burton's Henry V, my knowledge of Leigh's Lavinia comes from Angus McBean's black-and-white stills. What surprises, then, is her costume's palette (figure 9): an under-dress of burnished copper, soft green for the gown, white chiffon sleeves, red velvet ribbons – colours evoking holly, the holy bush of Christmas, signifying rebirth, regeneration. Seeing it on the hanger, the eye is caught by the shimmer and drape of white chiffon, the soft velvety texture of its blood-red streamers. But the eye's itinerary differs in McBean's still (figure 10), which does not, of course, represent performance 'itself'; rather, his photographic oeuvre constitutes a visionary epistemology that replaces and reframes the look of the scene – and the actor – within his own private memory theatre. In surreal portraits and studio poses, McBean's camera idolized Vivien Leigh as the 'most beautiful woman in the world': his was the key image in the portfolio she

8. Golden body 'armour' for Henry V displayed on mannequin; worn by Alan Howard in *2 Henry IV* (1975).

sent to Hollywood, winning her Scarlett O'Hara's role.[25] Here, his image of Leigh's Lavinia not only captures the costume's motion in stillness but also freezes a moment of performance in spectacular beauty. In Janet Suzman's memory, the whole audience gasped as she appeared, not because the sight was shocking but 'because she was so beautiful'. Writing about Lavinia, Jan Kott seems to be remembering or reinventing Leigh's

[25] Adrian Woodhouse, *Angus McBean* (London and New York: Quartet Books, 1982), p. 5.

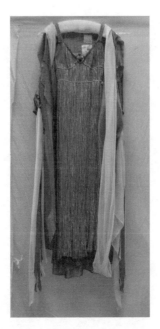

9. Costume for Lavinia, worn by Vivien Leigh in *Titus Andronicus*. Director: Peter Brook; Designer: Peter Brook with Michael Northen, Desmond Heeley and William Blezard. Shakespeare Memorial Theatre, 1955.

performance, as shot by McBean: 'What is left is just the eyes, the flutter of veiled hands, the figure, the walk. And how can she walk; how can she look! How much suffering she is able to convey just by bending her body, by hiding her face.'[26] Looking differently, others marked an aloofness in Leigh's performance which showed her disturbed, haunted mental state:[27] John Gielgud thought her 'utterly ineffective on the stage – like paper, only not so thick, no substance or power'.[28]

Although the McBean photographic world seems fully controlled, it is not: the actor-behind-the-role breaks out from it, her history made visible. Looking again, where does the gaze go? She looks away, terrified; just over her shoulder, out of shot, the memory of (theatrical) rape, her

---

[26] Suzman and Kott are cited in Pascale Aebischer, *Shakespeare's Violated Bodies: Stage and Screen Performance* (Cambridge: Cambridge University Press, 2004), pp. 39–40.

[27] Michelangelo Capua, *Vivien Leigh, a Biography* (Jefferson, NC and London: McFarland and Company, Inc, 2003), p. 135.

[28] Richard Mangan, ed., *Sir John Gielgud: A Life in Letters* (New York: Arcade Publishing, 2004), p. 188.

10. Vivien Leigh as Lavinia, 1955.

desire to hide materialized by the costume's eerie swirls. Image floods out
to infect, implicate its viewer. The entire erotic repertoire McBean
associated with Leigh is stopped dead in its tracks, countered by context
and costume. Betraying its voyeur, privy to the phantasm of rape by
proxy, the still also exposes the photographer – aptly enough, precisely

what another Shakespearean rape victim, Lucretia, addressing Tarquin, understands: 'Wilt thou be *glass* wherein it shall discern / Authority for sin, warrant for blame / To privilege dishonour in thy name?' The (photographic) gaze as violation not only informs this image but the experience of the acted Lavinia, so searchingly eyed by Marcus, a mirror of intense, intrusive looking. Yet whereas each performance disappears, McBean's image permanently fixes – and objectifies – its subject, infinitely repeating her violation.

Does costume too repeat itself, perform a self-fashioning that recalls another? Just as theatrical fashion has a flair for the topical, it also relentlessly reflects cultural ideas and ideals: what, it asks, is the meaning of your dress? As painted by Sargent (1889), Ellen Terry's shimmering blue-green gown, covered with actual beetle-wings, is an artwork in itself; and, like McBean's theatrical photographs, it is an invented pose rather than an image from performance. 'The whole thing is Rossetti – rich stained-glass effects', writes Terry in her memoirs, 'In [Sargent's] picture is all that I meant to do [as Lady Macbeth].' Ever alert to class and fashion, Oscar Wilde famously remarked: 'Lady Macbeth ... evidently patronises local industries for her husband's clothes and the servants' liveries; but she takes care to do all her own shopping in Byzantium.'[29] Questions of power and pleasure converge here: a devastating allure wars with authority and desire. Transferring the emerald-green of Terry's dress to body-clinging silk and its glitter to an encasing cloak, laced by similar golden strappings, Vivien Leigh's Lady tangibly echoes Terry's – but with a difference (figure 11). Did McBean choose a seated rather than standing pose, showing the Lady already crowned, to avoid duplicating Terry's image or imprinting Leigh's over it? And direct her steadfast gaze outwards, towards the camera, not, as with Terry, focused on an out-of-reach regal dream, the crown forever poised, forever not hers?

Some twenty years later, the Lady has gone shopping at the RSC's Hire Wardrobe (and with some necessity, given an overall production budget of £250),[30] a warehouse bulging with past theatrical dreams. She now wears, not a costume, but clothes – a rehearsal dress, a garment seemingly on the way to performance, a scarf wrapping her head (figure 12). Even when disembodied or on a mannequin, the dress evokes precisely the

[29] Edith Craig and Christopher St John, comp., *Ellen Terry's Memoirs* (New York: G. P. Putnam's Sons, 1932), pp. 233–4, 248. Terry's costume for her 1888 performance is displayed at Smallhythe, her home; Sir Joseph Duveen presented Sargent's portrait to the Tate Collection in 1906.

[30] As compared, say, to £67,000 for costumes alone for Michael Boyd's *This England* (2000–1), comprising eight history plays.

11. Vivien Leigh as Lady Macbeth. Director: Glen Byam Shaw; Designer: Roger Furse.
Shakespeare Memorial Theatre, 1955.

form and pressure of Judi Dench's 1977 performance. Material and
weight imprint themselves on performance possibility: whereas Terry's or
Leigh's elaborated elegance evince statuesque, even static, performance
styles, Dench's minimalist attire, weighing just under two pounds in

12. Costume for Lady Macbeth displayed on mannequin, worn by Judi Dench. Director: Trevor Nunn; Designer: John Napier (costumes pulled from stock), Royal Shakespeare Company, 1977.

contrast to Leigh's twelve, enables her to assert a remarkable physical performance (figure 13). I see her now, as she is captured on film (performance as mnemonic), suddenly disappearing from the circle she has drawn to invoke the spirits that tend on mortal thoughts, stabbed with the terror of having made contact, then reappearing, face and body transformed, half-fascinated, half-terrified by the pit she has entered and taking spectators with her. At the first preview, Bob Peck (Macduff) was close by when Dench needed zipping up at the last minute; once that had been established, she needed him to do it every night – a ritual staving off of the bad luck associated with both role and play. Nightly, too, she recognized the same priest, Neville Boundy, sitting in the front row holding up his crucifix to protect the actors, because he said the sense of evil was so overpowering he feared for their safety.[31]

---

[31] John Miller, *Judi Dench: With a Crack in Her Voice* (London: Orion Press, 2002), pp. 147, 149. Dench made Roger Rees (Malcolm) a birthday cake representing the set, with little icing figures on top, sitting in a circle of licorice; Rees kept the figures and had them mounted in a glass frame as his memento of the performance.

13. Judi Dench as Lady Macbeth, 1977.

As with Lady Macbeth, so with Cleopatra, though here memory chains a long history embracing 'real' rather than theatrical archaeology, stretching backwards from Carter's opening of King Tut's tomb in 1922 to Renaissance masques and forward to contemporary stages. Although theatre has its preferences, some kind of ideological bio-feedback operates with Cleopatras: what 'should' she look like? What is the precise shape or approximate image that a particular, time-bound realm of the senses ratifies as appropriate to the role's 'infinite variety'? Whatever is desired, the sense of the Cleopatra body is mediated by her clothes: theatre's Egyptian dish, she also is its fashion plate. Here, then, a cluster of Cleopatra costumes (figure 14): one of them, on the right, not hers, but worn by Richard Johnson's Antony in 1972, its stir and drape trailing ghosts of Egyptian cross-dressing over his Herculean identity. At left, two costumes from Peggy Ashcroft's 1953 performance. Thought unsuitable for the part (too nice, too middle class), she would need, so speculation ran, to be supported in every way possible by clothes and make-up – even to wearing false eyelashes for the first time in her career – Liz Taylor's influence on the 1950s. As though conforming to the myth

14. Costumes for *Antony and Cleopatra*. At left, two worn by Peggy Ashcroft (Designer: Motley, 1953); third from left, robe worn by Glenda Jackson (Designer: Sally Jacobs, 1978); right, overdrape worn by Richard Johnson as Antony (Designer: Christopher Morley with Gordon Sumpter, William Lockwood and Ann Curtis, 1972).

that Cleopatra's most natural advantage is her body, a David Levin interview in the *Daily Express* revealed Ashcroft's body measurements: bust, $36\frac{1}{2}$ inches; waist, 25 inches; hips $37\frac{1}{2}$ inches.[32] Disembodied, these two dresses, made of synthetic jersey and keyed more to Athens than to royal Egypt, seem to have drifted in from a modernist *Medea*. But then, Ashcroft saw Cleopatra as a Macedonian Greek: paling her face, she wore a vivid red wig (echoing Edith Evans's Cleopatra and, whether

[32] Cited in Michael Billington, *Peggy Ashcroft* (London: John Murray, 1988), p. 147. Today, actors' physical statistics are considered private property; because they contained actors' measurements, I was not allowed to see the costume bible for Michael Boyd's 2000–1 *This England*.

consciously or unconsciously, Elizabeth I).[33] In McBean's image (figure 15), her modern gown sculpts the body with Greek-ish drape into a figure dressed out of the Parthenon frieze to appropriate Cleopatra as English ideological property. To what extent were Motley's costumes responsible for reading Ashcroft's Cleopatra as 'too English'? – as Kenneth Tynan wrote, 'a nice, intense woman; such a pity she took up with the head gamekeeper'.[34] Reportedly, these dresses made women spectators, still feeling the deprivations of the Second World War, gasp: did their astonishment come, perhaps, from potentially lifting their own (presumably) English identities into Ashcroft's Cleopatra-fashions, seeing themselves in her theatrical mirror?

Look now at the caftan, second from right – Glenda Jackson's final costume for Peter Brook's 1978 *Antony and Cleopatra*. Like Ashcroft, Jackson became a fashion target: citing her 'unbecoming urchin cut and no less unbecoming Mother Hubbards', critics called her a tomboy Cleopatra, a 'mannish lady'; only Michael Billington seemed alert to the idea that sexuality is not a matter of physical beauty alone, that Cleopatra's sensuous appeal rests in her unpredictability.[35] Countering them, Jackson remarked: 'It's just impossible to say these words if you are swanning around in 53 yards of aquamarine tulle or whatever.'[36] In Joe Cocks's image (figure 16), the robe, spreading like wings, extends its power and that of the performer; together they dominate the space. Then, at her death, with the garment enveloping her body, the lights bouncing off and intensifying its burnished gold, and seated in an aura of light, Jackson's Cleopatra became something else. Transforming herself into a monument, she seemed no longer gendered – or even human: completely indifferent to looking, she produced her own still photograph, an inaccessible icon radiating a power that kept both Caesar and his soldiers onstage and spectators offstage at a distance. By contrast, in 1999, Frances de la Tour, following her death, discarded her monkish robe like a second skin and walked off, naked. When Caesar entered, all he found were the material remains of her performance – second-hand goods. In both cases, Cleopatra denied him what Shakespeare seems to afford him: the

---

[33] Garry O'Connor, *The Secret Woman: A Life of Peggy Ashcroft* (London: Weidenfeld and Nicolson, 1997), p. 113.

[34] Tynan, Review of *Antony and Cleopatra* (1953), rpt. in *Curtains*, p. 50.

[35] B. A. Young, *Financial Times* (12 October 1979); Michael Billington, 'The Heart has its Reasons', *Guardian* (10 July 1979).

[36] Jackson is cited in Mike Sparrow, 'The Brook Version', *Listener* (28 July 1979).

15. Peggy Ashcroft as Cleopatra. Director: Glen Byam Shaw. Shakespeare Memorial Theatre, 1953.

opportunity to put her body to his own political use, to write its history as his own.

But it is another Brook production, his 1970 *Midsummer Night's Dream*, that remains my most profound, consistently recurring memory

16. Glenda Jackson as Cleopatra. Director: Peter Brook. Royal Shakespeare Company, 1978.

of performance past. It begins with the thrill of seeing the dazzling squash-court set, at its centre, suspended on the thinnest of wires, a huge, brilliant-red feather – Titania's bower. A roll of drums: doors in the white wall smash open. Through them, a troupe of actors garbed like Chinese acrobats: brilliantly coloured sheaths of royal purple for Alan Howard's Theseus/Oberon, emerald green for Sara Kestelman's Hippolyta/Titania; yellow pyjamas for John Kane's Puck; Demetrius and Lysander in white satin trousers and spotted tops; Hermia and Helena in white sheaths, also paint-dappled. Of these, only the lovers' costumes survive. On hangers or, as in Cocks's image of them in Brook's slinky-inhabited wood (figure 17), costume fashions them as spotted and inconstant men – and women. Seen against the white background, they blend into it: infinitely interchangeable, they appear as head, hands, legs and feet, dappled with

17. The four lovers in *A Midsummer Night's Dream*; from left, Mary Rutherford, Ben Kingsley, Frances de la Tour, Christopher Gable. Director: Peter Brook; Designer: Sall Jacobs. Royal Shakespeare Company, 1970.

spots – blue for the men, pink for the women – figures in a whirling transformational dance. And just as performance – and transformation – lay at the centre of Brook's *Dream*, something of its aura travelled, resurfacing some twenty years later in Adrian Noble's 1994 restaging (figure 18). There, Sally Jacobs's giant red feather, re-mapped onto Titania's pink-feather costume, appropriated Brook's signature property as (re)-imagined materials of memory. Here, performance 'operates as both quotation and invention, an improvisation on borrowed themes, with claims on the future as well as the past'.[37]

In the Elizabethan age, Peter Stallybrass argues, memories were worn and carried, circulated and saved;[38] so too with theatrical costumes. Just as costume participates in the physical embodiment of one performance, that performance also begets another: a new performance is made from a previous costume, given a new identity – a form of surrogation. And just

[37] Joseph Roach, *Cities of the Dead: Circum-Atlantic Performances* (New York: Columbia University Press, 1996), p. 33.
[38] Peter Stallybrass, 'Worn Worlds: Clothing and Identity on the Renaissance Stage', in *Subject and Object in Renaissance Culture*, ed. Margreta de Grazia, Maureen Quilligan and Peter Stallybrass (Cambridge and New York: Cambridge University Press, 1996), p. 312.

18. Costume for Titania displayed on a mannequin; worn by Stella Gonet in
A Midsummer Night's Dream. Director: Adrian Noble; Designer: Anthony Ward. Royal
Shakespeare Company, 1994.

as costume tells part of the story, costumes themselves engender narrative.
Here, then, is a story of borrowed robes, another material memory
system. I am talking about a rat-coloured long cardigan with deep
pockets, an everyday sort of garment, an index of practicality – less a
costume than *clothes*. The cardigan was first worn by Peggy Ashcroft as
the Countess of Rossillion in Trevor Nunn's 1982 *All's Well That Ends
Well*, her last Shakespearean role. I can still see her take a pair of glasses
from her pocket, slowly put them on, unfold and then read Bertram's
letter, each precise gesture entailing the slightest pause, as though holding
off might effect a charm that would alter Bertram's message. Although
the cardigan may have had an interim resurrection, it next appears on
Estelle Kohler's Paulina in Greg Doran's 1999 *Winter's Tale* (figure 19);
far from being a local habit or confined to a single habitation, by that
time the cardigan had a name: The Peggy. In The Peggy's travels, does
ontogeny recapitulate phylogeny? What body memories does it carry?

19. *The Winter's Tale*; Director: Greg Doran. Royal Shakespeare Company, 1999. Cardigan worn by Estelle Kohler as Paulina, shown centre frame with Antony Sher as Leontes. Cardigan designed for Peggy Ashcroft's Countess of Roussillion in Trevor Nunn's *All's Well That Ends Well*, Royal Shakespeare Company, 1982; Designer: Lindy Hemming. The cardigan went on to appear in Greg Doran's *Taming of the Shrew*, 2003; worn by Alexandra Gilbreath as Katherina.

Does it, like Sean Penn's 'actor boots', serve a talismanic function? Stallybrass writes that clothes *are* material presences and that they *encode* other material and immaterial presences as identities are 'transferred from aristocrat to actor, actor to master, master to apprentice'; clothes as theatrical properties transgressed social boundaries.[39] How, then, might the aura of performance past transfer from one performer to another; how is the subject possessed and dispossessed, one identity merging into another, touched and haunted by the materials she inhabits? Wear this in remembrance of me.

Because Alexandra Gilbreath played Hermione in Doran's *Winter's Tale*, she knew the cardigan and its history; when she played Katherina in Doran's 2003 *Taming of the Shrew*, she asked to wear it – perhaps with the

---

[39] Stallybrass, 'Worn Worlds', pp. 312–13; See also Jonathan Gil Harris and Natasha Korda, ed. *Staged Properties in Early Modern English Drama* (Cambridge and New York: Cambridge University Press, 2002).

memory of Ashcroft's 1960 Kate, her flame-coloured dress and auburn curls a match for her fiery rampaging behaviour, in mind (figure 20).[40] Now *Shrew* is a play that makes a major investment in wardrobe: second-hand clothes, so to speak, constitute its stock in theatrical trade; they perform and support their own suppose-ings. In *Shrew*'s Induction, Bartholomew, the Lord's Page, dresses in suits like a lady; in performances where he appears, Christopher Sly often gets re-dressed like a lord; Lucentio and Tranio exchange clothes and identities; Petruchio shows up at his wedding outrageously apparelled, baits Katherina with fashionable attire that he (often) rips apart; much fuss is made over his servants' liveries; the false Vincentio dresses as the true – and so on. The play even makes an in-joke about it: when, about to set out for Padua, Petruchio instructs Grumio, 'bring our horses unto Long-lane end', the play suddenly swerves from fictive Italy to the Elizabethan London locale where brokers and second-hand clothes dealers hawked their wares.[41]

Tapping actors' memories, Carol Rutter records the responses of Fiona Shaw's Kate (1987) to her dress – 'too elegant'; 'I don't think Kate should be in any way glamorous. She's beginning to appear the way people look at her. I couldn't work out the story of my costume. Did Kate choose that material or did someone else? ... I wore my costume with a distaste for it: Kate doesn't fit it. It's not her dress.' – and Sinead Cusack (1983) to hers – 'exquisite, but Kate wouldn't wear it: her father may have bought it for her, but she wouldn't please him by wearing it'. Cusack remembers how she and the designer, Bob Crowley, slashed her pink silk dress with scissors; she wore boots under it.[42] And just as Kate-dressing gives actors metaphysical-material headaches, it also raises practical problems for dressers. Barbara Stone, a former RSC head dresser, remembers the split-second timing necessary to strip Josie Lawrence's Kate (1995) of her travelling dress, petticoat, coat and shoes and re-clothe her in the tradi-tional 'Big Dress'[43] – theatre's reward to *Shrew*'s 'final girl' for putting up with psychological (and physical) abuse: clothes-shopping as restorative therapy.

---

[40] Ashcroft's dress for Kate has a somewhat similar silhouette as that for Constance Benson's Kate in 1901, though its palette is considerably toned down from Lady Benson's Art Nouveau creation of dark red velvet hand-painted with old-gold tulips, full sleeves caught in at the elbow and forearm and fitted with short muslin fore-sleeves, and a bodice with scalloped lower edge and lace stomacher. See M. R. Holmes, *Stage Costume*, pp. 56, 74.

[41] Jones and Stallybrass, *Renaissance Clothing*, pp. 192–3. See John Stow, *A Survey of London*, ed. Charles Kingsford (Oxford: Clarendon Press, 1908), vol. 2, p. 28.

[42] Reported in Rutter, *Clamorous Voices*, pp. 12, xxiii.

[43] My thanks to Barbara Stone for granting me an interview, June 2004.

20. Costume for Katherina displayed on mannequin; worn by Peggy Ashcroft in *Taming of the Shrew*, Shakespeare Memorial Theatre. Director: John Barton; Designer: Alix Stone.

Doran's *Shrew*, however, made a distinctive intervention in this usual order of material things. Gilbreath wore pants and droopy petticoats; her wedding dress parodied that in a portrait (which appears, uncaptioned, in the costume bible); bedecked with too many ribbons of unfortunate colours and the wrong shoes, she was a fashion victim. She first wore the cardigan at what early editors call 'Petruchio's country house': had she brought it with her or been given it here, its Griselda-grey a charm to prompt wifely behaviours? It keeps her warm when she is refused food and taunted with the tailor's creations; she wears it on the road to Padua (under an equally shapeless grey coat) and – breaking theatrical and mnemonic codes – in her final scene. Choosing *not* to dress up, not to see herself or be seen as a re-materialized girl, she remained everyday 'Kate' to the last, central to a performance that jostled *Shrew* loose from past memories. Not, however, for some: leaving the theatre after the performance, I heard a woman behind me murmur, 'Oh, dear, I had so hoped they would give her a pretty frock.' Although I know better, I would like to imagine The Peggy as a material memory system that drove Gilbreath's performance, and the play, in a new direction. Whatever the case, any significance one might assume it to carry derives from the differential relation of its present wearing to its known past: in this serialization, does costume have semiotic boundaries? Is it a different sweater each time? Clothes are so intimate – and yet not so, at least not in a simple way: each successive actor wears Peggy Ashcroft's performance even as she tries to embody her own.[44] Radically unstable, infinitely iterable, The Peggy is a 'costume in motion', obedient less to Newtonian than to a kind of quantum theatrical physics.

When a costume or property moves through successive performances, it figures in a system of give-and-take that resembles gift-giving; touching points in a circle of exchange, the original gift is transformed in reception and gives increase, carries new meanings, a new dynamic.[45] The Peggy's passage is not an isolated incident: in Greg Doran's 2003 *All's Well That Ends Well* in which Judi Dench played the Countess, Claudie Blakley wore Judi Dench's Lady Macbeth costume as Helena in her disguise as a pilgrim.[46] Actors giving gifts to each other has an equally long tradition: in a note thanking Ellen Terry for 'your lovely red feathers', Ada Rehan writes, 'How I shall prize those feathers – Henry Irving's, presented . . . to me for my Rosalind Cap. I shall wear them once and then put them by as treasures.'[47] Still other passages and rememorations abound. Perhaps the first such, though purely conjectural, rests on the assumption that Robert Armin played the First Gravedigger in *Hamlet*. Taking that together with knowing that he was popularly supposed to have been Richard Tarlton's choice as his successor, Muriel Bradbrook imagines a moment from *Hamlet*'s first performances where, at Ophelia's graveside, Armin and Richard Burbage stand, each with a hand on Tarlton's skull – the present leading players remembering, and touching upon, their heritage.[48] And in the 1970s, the RSC's *The Hollow Crown*, a compilation from the history

[44] With thanks to Peggy Phelan, private communication, 15 November 2004.

[45] Lewis Hyde, *The Gift: Imagination and the Erotic Life of Property* (New York: Random House, 1983), p. 4. See also P. A. Skantze, 'Taking Spoils: Shakespeare's Theory of Abundance, Scarcity, and Gift', unpublished paper, Shakespeare Association of America, 2005.

[46] Gregory Doran, 'Dench-olatry', in *Darling Judi: A Celebration of Judi Dench*, ed. John Miller (London: Weidenfeld and Nicolson, 2004), p. 176.

[47] Ellen Terry, *Memoirs*, p. 225. In 'Circling like a Plane', Tim Pigott-Smith tells of what remains an on-going series of exchanges, the passing-on of a black glove between him and Judi Dench, the one finding ingenious ways of 'gloving' the other. See Miller, *Darling Judi*, pp. 123–6.

[48] Bradbrook is cited in Peter Thomson, *Shakespeare's Theatre* (London: Routledge and Kegan Paul, 1983), p. 111.

plays, used the same crown for each successive king as well as a stunning gold lamé coronation robe, worn by each in turn. Similarly, in Michael Boyd's *This England*, the crown worn by Sam West as Richard II, wrested from him by David Troughton's Bolingbroke, travels down the lineage of kings through all eight plays until coming to rest on Richmond, played by Sam Troughton, David Troughton's son.[49]

But perhaps the most famous legend of continuity and subjectivity involves the sword Edmund Kean carried as Richard III, which his son Charles Kean gave to Henry Irving, who passed it to the Terry family; Kate Terry Gielgud presented it to John Gielgud who, with its blade newly engraved with an inscription – 'This sword, given him by his mother, Kate Terry Gielgud, 1938, is given to Laurence Olivier by his friend John Gielgud in appreciation of his performance of Richard III at the New Theatre, 1944'[50] – handed it on to Laurence Olivier. As in Theatre de Complicité's *Mnemonic*, a performance built around the trope of memory living in blood and bone, memory burrs onto an object, chaining one theatrical generation to the next. Asked to whom he would give it, Olivier replied, 'No one. It's mine' – sealing off memory's transmission as though, like the Egyptian pharaohs, courting immortality through material things. When last seen, Frank Finlay, Iago to Olivier's Othello, carried it up Westminster Abbey's aisle at Olivier's memorial service (20 October 1989, exactly eighty-four years later than the day when Henry Irving was buried in the Abbey), where it was placed on the high altar, the most significant relic in a pseudo-saintly ceremony called, by Marjorie Garber, Shakespeare's surrogated burial and, by Joseph Roach, only one in a chain of such surrogations (never for the first time).[51] Near the end of that service, Olivier's disembodied voice, speaking Henry V's St Crispin's Day speech, echoes through the Abbey space. Shifting from a wide view down the Abbey to the altar, from which the voice seems to emanate, as from on high, the camera focuses on Ian McKellen, listening: ' . . . Yet all shall be forgot . . . Then shall our names . . . Be . . . freshly remembered . . . This story shall the good man teach his son . . . '. As though prompted by the words, McKellen – in a somewhat Artaudian move – shakes his head, closes his eyes. Repeating the words to himself, his

[49] Jonathan Holmes, *Merely Players? Actors' Accounts of Performing Shakespeare* (London and New York: Routledge, 2004), pp. 134–5.

[50] Quoted in Jonathan Croall, *Gielgud: A Theatrical Life* (London: Methuen, 2000), p. 322.

[51] See Marjorie Garber, *Vested Interests: Cross-Dressing and Cultural Anxiety* (New York: Routledge, 1992), p. 33; Roach, *Cities of the Dead*, p. 83.

physical ventriloquy seems to wipe away one performance, reflecting – and replacing – it (silently) with his own.[52]

Speaking back to Olivier, McKellen's self-reflective memory evokes Hamlet's trope of the mirror. So too, with Judi Dench: 'I need', she says, 'somebody to reflect me back, or to give me their reflection.'[53] And that takes me to another memorial site, New York's Museum of Natural History's 1994 installation of the American Indian, where, at the end of the circuit, there is a mirror. Located next to the exit door, it reflects the exiting viewer but nothing of the installation. Mieke Bal claims that its effect is to isolate visitors from the cultural objects they have seen and so to diminish any feeling of solidarity or hybridic identity, yet surely it also, by confronting memory's loss, engenders the after-effect of which Phelan speaks: the experience of subjectivity itself.[54] I want to imagine a mirror positioned at the end of the RSC's costume display, theatre's material remains. What might it reflect to the exiting viewer? Might it, unlike the one in the Museum, hold a mirror up to theatrical natures, their material accoutrements, inducing memories of past performances? Might this mirror, like McKellen's acutely tuned re-performance, also work as a device for speaking back?

Let me once again evoke one of my most deeply embedded performance memories. Even for those who never witnessed Peter Brook's *Midsummer Night's Dream*, it belongs to an imagined community of performances past. Vibrating in imagination, located between history and myth, Brook's white-walled space acted as a sounding board for Shakespeare's words: bouncing off walls, echoing in memory. My story ends with a material trace of that performance from my own archive; ends, too, with my own re-performance (or memory of what was once spoken and now has become writing). Not an end but an ending, one which invites the performance that has disappeared to come into view, to speak – and look – back. My mnemonic, an early 1970s fad called a Free-Ka, was appropriated by Brook as sound, symbol – and mirror. Waving in the air, at first disembodied, then seen held by the fairies, Free-Kas made 'fairy music'. The fairies tied Puck up in them, teasing him; joined to make circles, they became spy-glasses for observing Oberon's and Titania's

[52] Writing on Artaud, Derrida pursues the image of breath as inspiration, the restoration of the body and a metaphysics of the flesh. See Jacques Derrida, *Writing and Difference*, trans. Alan Bass (Chicago: University of Chicago Press, 1978), pp. 179–80.

[53] John Lahr, 'The Player Queen: Why Judi Dench Rules the Stage and Screen', *New Yorker* 77.44 (21 January 2002), 58–69.

[54] Mieke Bal, *Double Exposures: The Subject of Cultural Analysis* (New York and London: Routledge, 1996), p. 55, n. 19.

midnight meeting (in brightest light) from a distance; last of all, one became a mirror for Bottom to look at and look through. Repeating these gestures – surrogating them, Roach would say – my body remembers: the performance has vanished but I am there, once again, Brook-*Dream*ing. Yet because my Free-Ka – bought off a street vendor, a pseudo-trace, not the 'real thing' – has a crack, it no longer makes the exact sound of Brook's fairy music. Like the absent sound of Alan Howard's and Sara Kestelman's voices, there is only a faint whirr. Can you hear an echo? Now, if I hold it just so, it becomes Bottom's 'mirror', inviting theatrical – and subjective – absorption. What do you see? A few – we happy few – may remember – with advantages. Brook's *Dream* will never come back, but the play has – and will – in other guises, come again. Looking through memory's mirror, can you re-dream yet another performance, your own scene of becoming?

CHAPTER 7

'Her first remembrance from the Moor': actors and the materials of memory

Carol Chillington Rutter

KING PANDION Do you know this play, Tereus?
TEREUS No.
KING PANDION I find plays help me think.
                    (Timberlake Wertenbaker, *The Love of the Nightingale*, 1989)

An act of memory and an act of creation, performance
recalls and transforms the past in the form of the present.
       (W. B. Worthen, *Shakespeare and the Force of Modern Performance*, 2003)

'Living backward!' Alice repeated in great astonishment. ' I never
heard of such a thing!'
'—but there's one great advantage in it, that one's memory works
both ways.'
'I'm sure *mine* only works one way,' Alice remarked. 'I can't
remember things before they happen.'
'It's a poor sort of memory that only works backward,' the Queen
remarked.
                                 (Lewis Carroll, *Through the Looking Glass*, 1872)

What are we doing, 'remembering performance'? In Richard Eyre's
crushing opinion, something quixotic, or rather doomed, for performance that needs to be remembered is, by definition, lost art, unreco-
verable, vanished without trace into the 'never, never'. 'When the
theatre's there', writes the former Artistic Director of Britain's National
Theatre, 'it's there, when it's gone it's gone, and you'll never be able to
describe a memorable moment in theatre accurately, because the essential
element of context – real time and real space – will never be there in the
description.'[1] Declan Donnellan, Cheek by Jowl's Artistic Director,
thinks differently, his idea of performance extending far beyond the

[1] Richard Eyre and Nicholas Wright, *Changing Stages: A View of British Theatre in the Twentieth
Century* (London: Bloomsbury, 2000), p. 11.

theatrical event. Yes, he says, 'Theatre exists for now.' But it also 'exists in memory – as something else that nevertheless *belongs* to theatre'. He goes on: 'Let us say that a spectator sees, really *sees*, one tiny moment in the theatre. Like an epiphany, that moment of visitation that sears into the mind lasts and lives inside you. The retained part, what you take away, what you *own in memory*, is what remains of performance', doubly constitutive, for if 'how we remember is part of us', 'it's also part of theatre'. For Donnellan, remembering performance is not an archival project – it's not about accuracy or 'the record'. 'Remembering right, remembering wrong, remembering exactly, mis-remembering: that's not the point. "Wrong" memory, too, is part of theatre.' For him, the practice of remembering is more generous – and *generative* (and takes us close to Worthen's theoretical position on performance as both an act of memory and an act creation): 'To remember well, you need two things: the thing itself and you that sees it. And the third thing that emerges is a kind of baby that happens between the spectator and art. That's what memory is.' He warns us, though, not to manhandle the 'baby': 'You mustn't undo memory.'[2]

So how do we *deliver* the baby? Neither midwife nor obstetrician, Joseph Roach nevertheless adopts a language of medical intervention when he writes about remembering performance: 'The status of the evidence required to reconstruct performance depends on the success of two necessarily problematic procedures.' Fortunately for me, what I find alarming in Roach's reference to 'problematic [reconstructive] proce-dures' vanishes as soon as he tells me what they are: 'spectating and tattling'.[3] For that's what I do when I'm remembering performance, spectating, tattling – and gossiping, performing, on the model of the early modern gossip, a kind of midwifery on the 'thing that emerges', in Donnellan's metaphor, from the intercourse between spectator and theatre. 'Often', writes Roach, 'the best hedge against amnesia is gossip.'[4]

This chapter is an essay in gossip, its material culled from my own memories going back twenty-five years of Shakespeare in performance set in conversation with a number of Shakespeare performers-remembering-performance. (From the outset, I gratefully acknowledge my co-authors: King Lear, Macbeth, Coriolanus, Iago, the Ghost of Old Hamlet,

[2] Personal communication, October 2004.
[3] Joseph Roach, *Cities of the Dead: Circum-Atlantic Performance* (New York: Columbia University Press, 1996), p. 30.
[4] Roach, *Cities*, p. 30.

Richard III, Duke Vincentio, and Emilia.)[5] But I'm not, to begin with, brooding upon spectatorly memory. Rather, I want to think about *actors*, to ask how they, who clearly have a professional investment in the matter, remember performance, how they remember Shakespeare, how they remember what Alice can't, 'things before they happen'. To start, I offer three production images – tropes of memory – informed by Anthony Dawson's observation on theatrical properties, that 'The theatre routinely invests the objects it shows with more than they carry in themselves.'[6] Each of my images frames a role whose performance in the moment is caught in the process of remembering; each character, that is, is remembering something or other. But each image likewise shows the actor inside the role doing memory differently – that is, he's simultaneously remembering *something else*.

First, I offer a man with a book (figure 21): Alan Howard, playing King Henry in the *Henry VI* trilogy at the Royal Shakespeare Company in 1977. Across the interval in *Part Three*, spectators who didn't go out for a drink or a smoke watched Howard sit cross-legged and motionless on stage in the near dark, like a yoga master turned to stone in the lotus position, reading a little book. Even when the houselights dimmed and the action resumed on stage, he didn't look up, so absorbed was he in his study. (There's no photographic record of the inter-act performance I'm remembering, for of course, when the play was run for the photo call, the interval didn't happen.) My figure 21, then, is a proxy, a stand-in for the shot that's not been taken but that I nevertheless hold in my mental archive of this production, what Barbara Hodgdon calls 'a mnemonic trace that triggers a "flashbulb memory" – that mixture of personal circumstance and public event held in memory, termed by cognitive theory the "Now Print" mechanism'.[7] In figure 21, Alan Howard's Henry is some minutes into the scene, talking to the audience, telling them how, deposed and bundled under arrest into Scotland, he has escaped and, 'even of pure love', 'stolen' home to England (3.1.13). He's wrecked, filthy, hollow-eyed with grief. His book – bound in blue – is all he has left of possessions. Its appearance is heavy with investment, certainly a saturated sign. For one thing, it is evidence to condemn him, showing

[5] Corin Redgrave (Lear), Antony Sher (Macbeth, Iago), Greg Hicks (Coriolanus, Ghost), David Troughton (Richard, Duke), Maureen Beattie (Emilia).
[6] Anthony B. Dawson and Paul Yachnin, *The Culture of Playgoing in Shakespeare's England: A Collaborative Debate* (Cambridge, Cambridge University Press, 2001), p. 138.
[7] Barbara Hodgdon, 'Photography, Theater, Mnemonics, or, Thirteen Ways of Looking at a Still', in W. B. Worthen with Peter Holland, eds., *Theorizing Practice: Redefining Theatre History* (Palgrave, 2003), p. 97.

21. Alan Howard, King Henry in *Henry VI Pt 3* (1978).

him caught in the act as the book remembers the accusation that has dogged him, the pacifist son of a warrior king, since the beginning, that his 'bookish rule' has 'pulled fair England down' (*Part Two* 1.1.258): England's fathers and sons would not now be slaughtering each other if the 'effeminate' prince had been a dragon, like his dad (whom Howard was also playing that season), instead of a 'schoolboy' (*Part One* 1.1.35, 36).

But the book likewise resists such harsh remembering, coding Henry's own radical personal politics, an idea – perhaps idiotic in the bear-pit he inhabits – that the Word should prevail over the Sword. The book, and his still study of it across the interval, remembers his deep longing for the life contemplative, a shepherd's life – a trope that offers him as the sacrificial lamb ripped up by Gloucester-the-boar. Thus, it remembers forward: reading this book will be what Henry is doing when crook-backed Dickie finds him – 'What, at your book so hard?' – in the Tower (5.6.1).

Can we name this book that 'remembers' so much? The Folio tells readers it is 'a Prayer booke' (TLN 1470), and a prayer book may be what Henry is reading – but not Alan Howard. Howard is holding the New Shakespeare edition of *Coriolanus* – the text he spends the twenty minutes of every interval studying. Why? Because the title role in *Coriolanus* later that season is the out-and-out bribe the director, Terry Hands, has used to arm-twist Howard into agreeing to play the weak-kneed king in Shakespeare's unknown, nine-hour-long *Henry VI* trilogy first. 'I don't "do" weakness', Howard growls during the courtship ritual that finally sees him cast in the part, Hands chirpily assuring him that Coriolanus will restore his stage cred.[8] Henry's blue book gathers up this extra-narrative grudge and grumble: a record of the deal the deeply suspicious actor won't let the director forget, a knowing on-stage masquerade that niggles, that quite deliberately wounds the surface of theatrical representation. The book remembers backward – and forward: Howard will play Henry, but, says the book, he'll be learning Caius Martius' lines. And something more. The book reminds us how much more is always going on on stage than the play.

Figure 22 shows a man in a scarf: Emrys James, York in the RSC's *Henry VI* (1977), recently restored to his dukedom, his father's attainture wiped off; here, having hunted her to ground, triumphing over Joan of Arc. Earlier, during the period of the disgrace, he wore the white silk scarf that hangs so ostentatiously about his neck (proleptic of York's white rose, visible on his shoulder) as a memento, to remember his stripped title – I know this, because Emrys James told me so. And I wasn't being awkward when, some years later, I wanted to know why his Cassius (figure 23) wore a look-alike white silk scarf at Phillipi in the RSC's 1983 *Julius Caesar*. It was his little bit of luxury, James told me, that remembered Cassius's status as a patrician, even in the mud and muck of

---

[8] I am indebted to Michael Poulton for this anecdote.

22. Emrys James, York in *Henry VI Pt 1* (1978).

23. Emrys James, Cassius in *Julius Caesar* (1983).

battle. But consider two more images (among dozens I could have chosen): Jaques in Trevor Nunn's 1978 *As You Like It* (figure 24) where the white scarf is translated into a white collar; De Flores in Terry Hands's 1978 *The Changeling* (figure 25) where the white scarf is red – and put them against a rehearsal photograph (figure 26) of James, bandana knotted around his neck, studying the script of *Caesar*. It may be true that for York and the rest the scarf remembered untold histories tied extra-textually into the part; but for the actor, it reveals itself as a mnemonic that ties him to the book, both fetish and prophylaxis: it's how he remembers his lines how he wards off forgetting.

Figure 27 shows a man on crutches, Antony Sher as the RSC's *Richard III* (1984), propelling himself to stardom on metal legs. Critics and spectators were staggered by the sheer physical commitment of this actor and thrilled by the danger he built into the body of his performance. Richard's prosthesis sensationally – and self-consciously – remembered Shakespeare's text, this Richard the 'bottled spider' of Margaret's curse (1.3.240). But it also remembered another performer and performance, establishing Sher as the most suicidally physical actor since Laurence Olivier (and his true heir, capable of stunts every bit as gut-wrenching as Olivier's death as Coriolanus – when he fell headlong off a balcony platform, and hung there, caught by the ankles, upside down, swinging). Was it co-incidental – or ironic – that Sher's physicality in his earliest Shakespeare parts habitually represented itself in the role of the cripple? His Fool in *King Lear* two years earlier had been a desperately hyper-active little clown who, between urgent bouts of tacky patter routines conducted, pigeon-toed, in over-sized boots evidently ordered from an orthopaedic catalogue, sat scrunched up like a ventriloquist's dummy, his twisted legs dangling. A fellow actor dubbed Sher the 'Body Busy', and Sher himself admits his Olivier-like addiction to 'The casual dress of flesh' – to acting as physical disguise, physical excess – rather than acting as revelation, the discovery before spectators of something finer, rarer, 'The visible soul'.[9] The epithet Sher traded with his fellow actor as mock insult is revealing: if Sher was the 'Body Busy', his fellow was the 'Voice Beautiful'.[10] Body v. Voice. It turns out – and Sher has only recently been able to talk about this – that the crutches mobilizing the hunch-backed Richard were an exhibitionist's cover-up, paradoxically the giveaway

[9] These phrases, borrowed from Anthony Burgess's translation of *Cyrano de Bergerac* (a part Sher played in 1997), are ones the actor used in conversation (and in print) to distinguish two kinds of acting. See Antony Sher, *Beside Myself* (London: Arrow Books, 2002), pp. 110, 305.
[10] Sher, *Beside Myself*, p. 176.

24. Emrys James, Jaques in *As You Like It* (1978).

exposing the secret that Antony-the-actor wanted to forget: his terror of Shakespeare's words. Sher sees himself as a cripple all right, but it's not Richard's legs that are the problem, for the ghost that haunts him is not Olivier's but Gielgud's, who threatens to discover that Sher is 'trespassing'

25. Emrys James, De Flores in *The Changeling* (1978).

on the 'preserve of honey-voiced English actors', territory that certainly doesn't belong to 'little Yiddish poofters from Sea Point' who've arrived off the boat with a speech impediment – a South African accent – and a cultural bank account deep in the red.[11] In 1984, Sher *knows* that he's an impostor, that Shakespeare is the birthright, in the blood, of every English actor – and that a South African will need a blood transfusion and a voice-box implant to make it on the English stage. Richard's crutches are, then, the visible extension of Antony's yearning: 'If only', he says of his textual disability, 'you could do with the *text* what you can do with the body.'[12] The mind-blowing physicality that we see remembered in figure 27 is a subterfuge, a vast over-compensation. One of the things this image is doing is remembering absence.

Moving on from these images, I want to extrapolate from them a different mnemonic of my own, to propose that the book, the scarf and the crutches offer us suggestive tropes for understanding what actors say

[11] Sher, *Beside Myself*, p. 266.   [12] In conversation, September 2004.

26. Emrys James, Cassius in *Julius Caesar* (1983). Rehearsal photograph.

they're doing when they're remembering Shakespeare today. First off, they're remembering text, the *book* of the play, their part, the lines, all of which trace performance back to writing – and the effort of memory is to get the writing *right*: like Peter Quince insisting on 'Ninus' tomb, man!' (*A Midsummer Night's Dream* 3.1.92) and Hamlet correcting himself, ' "The rugged Pyrrhus, like th'Hyrcanian beast" – / It is not so: – it begins with Pyrrhus: / "The rugged Pyrrhus, he whose sable arms." ' (2.2.452–4). One actor I've talked to describes his memory-text as a map; another as a Book of Hours: the first says he studies signposts, the other, that he turns pages, sequencing words as pictures. Paradoxically, 'Body Busy' Tony Sher denies the physical in learning the book. He rather connects with textual memory via the materials of other inscriptions: he sets up the script he's learning on the draughtsman's table he uses – he's a formidably talented artist – to do his drawing. Corin Redgrave sets up mental tables: he 'sees the shape of lines on a page', and the process of remembering is about 'arranging those shapes in order', which also, for him, is a process of rhetorical remembering. That is, he retrieves the conversation the poetry is conducting in the lines, the questions and answers, examples and further examples, the turns and repetitions,

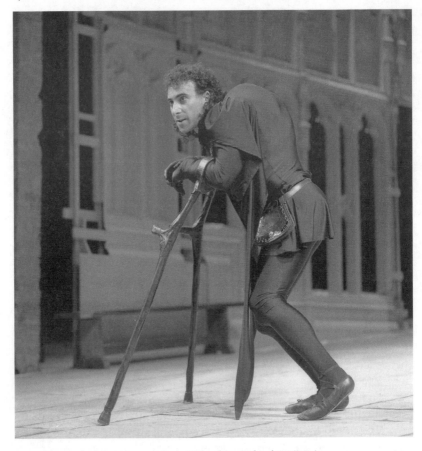

27. Antony Sher, Richard in *Richard III* (1984).

conclusion and final conclusion. Remembering rhetorically, Redgrave remembers the way Elizabethan schoolboys were taught to remember.[13]

But to say that actors remember *writing* isn't quite right – or enough. And anyway, to put it like that might be construed as playing into the hands of those 'literary scholars' who 'see the acts of the stage as lapsed reading', a kind of delinquency from the 'proper meanings prescribed by "the text"'. For, as W. B. Worthen continues, textual memory is only a piece of the action, since 'the text' – my 'writing' – 'cannot govern the

---

[13] See Carol Chillington Rutter, 'Learning Thisby's Part – or – What's Hecuba to Him?' in *Shakespeare Bulletin* 22:3 (Fall 2004), 5–30.

force of its performance'. 'The text,' he argues, becomes 'significant only as embodied in the changing conventions of its performance.'[14] He's undoubtedly right – since, as I take him to mean, he's thinking about real bodies, too, and counting actors' bodies among those 'changing conventions' he cites. Actors don't separate 'text' and 'performance' the way literary scholars (and even some writers on performance) do. Indeed, for actors, their 'lines', which we bookish people associate through metaphor to print culture, are invariably tied in to the physical. They're in-bodied: so Redgrave, describing how he remembers, first says that he 'sees the shape of lines on a page', but then immediately re-figures those lines as 'strips of fallow field', and likens the effort of learning to 'ploughing'.

This immediacy of actorly experience – the way what's thought is done – is something of what the player prince, Hamlet, is demonstrating when he greets the tragedians of the city, newly arrived at Elsinore, and, with delighted anticipation, urges them, 'Come, give us a taste of your quality' – that is, your skill as actors. What he commands is 'a speech straight', 'a passionate speech' (2.2.432–4). There's no – or little – residual performance memory of this 'excellent play', for 'it was never acted, or if it was, not above once' (436–7). Neither, for Hamlet, does this play exist as a written text: the speech he remembers he ' *heard* ... *once*'; it lives only in memory (436, my italics). When the Player's own memory needs prompting – 'What speech, my good lord?' (435) – and Hamlet starts remembering – ''twas Aeneas' tale to Dido – and thereabout of it especially when he speaks of Priam's slaughter' (448–9) – he remembers by reciting speech, his 'act of memory', to borrow (once again) Worthen's elegant formulation, 'an act of creation that recalls and transforms the past in the form of the present'. And one of the things it transforms is Hamlet: for as he 'does' Aeneas 'doing' Pyrrhus what he's bodying forth is something that is him but not him: speech that lives in his memory; speech that produces the Prince as a palimpsest, sedimented with stories of sons and their paternal relations, models – perhaps? – of filial obligation and action; and speech lifted from one of humanism's core texts, a book in which a story of the past is produced as speech.

What Hamlet is showing is that theatre speech is something other than text or performance, other than literacy or orality: it's both. Speeches are what Shakespeare writes, what early modern players hear as their first experience of the play at the company read-through when they learn the

---

[14] W. B. Worthen, *Shakespeare and the Force of Modern Performance* (Cambridge: Cambridge University Press, 2003), p. 4 and jacket.

play by listening to it read (as Philip Henslowe's *Diary* records the Admiral's Men doing, hearing *The Famous Wars of Henry the First and the Prince of Wales* at the Sun in Fish Street on 13 March 1598).[15] Speeches are what players hold as their acting parts, copied out on strips and pasted together in a roll; what lives in their memories; what they produce on stage, both their quality and their activity – and their 'mystery'. Speeches, too, are what early modern audiences hear and remember. Theatre speech, then, is never 'mere speech'; its force, as Worthen would have it, goes well beyond that, 'subjecting writing to the body, to labor, to the work of production'.[16] Speech collapses the discrepancy between writing and body. Academics may observe a discrepancy – but actors certainly don't. Actors talk about the book and the body in the same breath (evoking the metaphoric allusiveness of Emrys James's scarf, tying speaking mouth to working body at the neck). 'Like fingers remembering music', says Corin Redgrave, 'the body remembers Shakespeare.' He calls it 'muscle memory', a term, coincidentally, developed by the choreographer and dancer Jeff Friedman.[17] Greg Hicks talks about 'Thinking through the body, weaving a whole physical world that is constantly alive', a process of learning 'that is not cerebral but locked in the muscles', Shakespeare's words becoming 'chewing gum in the body'. By contrast, David Troughton talks about the actor 'locked out' of a part – as he was, he says, playing the Duke in *Measure for Measure* at the National Theatre (2004). He couldn't remember the lines – they 'wouldn't stay in' – because he couldn't find a physical point of entry into the part: 'There was no latch key. All the doors were locked.' And this wasn't a matter of the difficulty of the writing, the fact that speech, for *Measure*'s Duke, is nothing like chewing gum. In this production, production decisions disabled the actor. As the disguised Duke, he was face-less, set inside a deep cowl that blocked contact with others on stage. 'Inside the cowl',

---

[15] R. A. Foakes and R. T. Rickert, *Henslowe's Diary* (Cambridge: Cambridge University Press, 1968), p. 88. Entries on f.45 record: 'lent vnto the company to paye drayton & dyckers & chetell ther full payment for the boocke called the famos wares of henry the first & the prynce of walles the some of iiij li v s'; 'lent at that tyme vnto the company for to spend at the Readynge of that boocke at the sonne in new fyshstreate v s'. That this was ordinary practice seems confirmed by entries further down that page: 'layd owt for the company to bye a boocke of mr drayton & mr dickers mr chettell & mr willsone wch is called goodwine & iij sones fower powndes in pte of paymet the 25 of marche 1598 in Redy mony I saye iiij li', an entry followed by this one: 'layd owt the same tyme at the tavarne in fyshstreate for good cheare the some of v s'. And see Peter Holland, 'Reading to the Company' in Hanna Scolnicov and Peter Holland, eds., *Reading Plays* (Cambridge: Cambridge University Press, 1991), pp. 8–29, esp. pp. 12–13.

[16] *Shakespeare and the Force of Modern Performance*, p. 9.

[17] Jeff Friedman, 'Muscle Memory: Performing Embodied Knowledge' in Richard Cándida Smith, ed., *Art and the Performance of Memory* (London and New York: Routledge, 2002), pp. 156–80.

says Troughton, 'I was inside the prison' – a sensation intensified by the director's decision that the Duke would observe Vienna not moving among the flesh but standing still, looking upstage at video monitors. 'To remember', says Troughton, 'you have to connect.' Denied connection, his paralysis took a terrifying turn for an actor – aphasia.

Figuring actorly remembering, my mnemonic has had constant recourse to objects – the book, the scarf – as though the interiorised function of muscle memory needed the citational function of material memory to code its physical practices in metonyms. Actors share the stage with objects; they depend on objects – Sher's titanium crutches serve also as a metaphor for this dependency. For objects, says Corin Redgrave, 'are the scaffolding of performance': actors 'remember through things' as well as through bodies. But as I'm trying to tease out how theatre remembers, and what we're doing when we're remembering performance, I want to argue that on Shakespeare's stage, if actors remember through objects, objects remember *beyond* actors.

Like Peter Quince and Philip Henslowe, we call these objects 'properties' because they belong to performance: they're the part's own 'stuff'. The inventory Henslowe wrote out 'of all the properties for my Lord Admeralles men' in March 1598 suggests as much, attaching things by name to plays and players: 'j frame for the heading in black Jone', 'j dragon in fostes', 'Tamberlyne brydell', 'Kentes woden leage'.[18] Ever since Clytemnestra in Aeschylus' *Oresteia* rolled out the red carpet to welcome Agamemnon home from Troy theatre has used objects to remember in ways that exceed actorly remembering, for objects put in play on stage remember more and remember differently than characters do, their power not principally, as Paul Yachnin would have it, to prompt 'theatrical wonder', a centrifugal reaction that glances off performance, but rather to absorb attention, to 'become weighty with meaning and charged with emotion' – the phrase is Tony Dawson's, who sees objects on stage as 'charged' signs.[19] But where does the 'charge' come from? I'd say, from story – and from what follows from story, ways of knowing.

To inform these claims, I want to borrow from the anthropologist, Arjun Appadurai, who writes that 'things ..., like persons, have social lives'; that, circulating 'in different regimes of value in space and time' and moving 'through different hands, contexts, and uses', objects

---

[18] Foakes and Rickert, *Diary*, pp. 319–21.
[19] See their paired chapters, 'Magical Properties' (Yachnin) and 'Props, Pleasure, and Idolatry' (Dawson), in *The Culture of Playgoing*, esp. pp. 133, 137–40.

'accumulat[e] ... biographies', 'become weighty' with life histories.[20]
Helpful, too, in offering a language applicable to understanding how things
on stage behave in performance, Appadurai observes that objects – he calls
them 'things-in-motion' – follow 'careers'. These careers, typically fraught
with evaluative, interpretative and processual difficulties, start objects off
down specific paths – life journeys – that regularly (certainly, in theatre,
inevitably) get interrupted, blocked, diverted – diversion always 'a sign of
creativity or crisis'. Thus, an object that begins life as a gift may be inherited,
sold, lost, stolen, found, sacramentalised as a relic, copied, faked, commodified, each exchange marking a shift in value, but not every act of
exchange supposing 'a complete cultural sharing of assumptions' about that
value.[21] For what is 'priceless' – that is, beyond price – in one pair of hands
may be 'priceless' – worthless – in another: as Georg Simmel (and before
him, Troilus in Shakespeare's *Troilus and Cressida*) has observed, value is
not an inherent property of objects but rather a judgement made about
them by subjects.[22] ('What's aught but as 'tis valued?' asks the Trojan
(2.2.52).) Particularly relevant to theatre, objects that culture classifies as
'luxury goods' – furred gowns in *Lear*, let's say, or Shylock's turquoise (or
the monkey Jessica trades it for) or (more controversially) Troilus's Helen of
Troy – occupy a special 'register' of consumption and exchange: operating as
'incarnated signs' whose 'principal use is rhetorical and social', they exhibit
'semiotic virtuosity', the 'capacity to signal fairly complex social messages',
that, tellingly, connect 'their consumption to body, person and personality'.[23]

How objects behave in Appadurai's 'real life' is, I want to argue,
intensified in performance where everything spectators are going to know
about the 'life histories' of 'play things' is crammed into the 'two-hours
traffic of our stage' (*Romeo and Juliet*, Prologue 12), and where the power
that objects have is to remember the histories they've accumulated, animating those life stories as they pass through characters' hands, becoming,
in the process, as lively on stage as actors are.

Take Yorick's skull. When first it emerges from the grave – certainly, a
bizarre career diversion for such an object, poised equally for creativity *or*

[20] Arjun Appadurai, 'Introduction: Commodities and the Politics of Value', in Appadurai, ed., *The Social Life of Things: Commodities in Cultural Perspective* (Cambridge: Cambridge University Press, 1986), pp. 3, 34. I am grateful to Valerie Wayne for directing me to Appadurai – and even more grateful for her wonderful essay on Innogen's bracelet, 'The woman's parts of *Cymbeline*' in Jonathan Gil Harris and Natasha Korda, ed., *Staged Properties in Early Modern English Drama* (Cambridge: Cambridge University Press, 2002), pp. 288–315.
[21] Appadurai, 'Introduction', pp. 26, 14.   [22] Quoted in Appadurai, 'Introduction', p. 3.
[23] Appadurai, 'Introduction', p. 38. Further, luxury goods are restricted to elites, are marked by complexity of acquisition, and demand specialised knowledge for their 'appropriate' consumption.

crisis – the skull is only one of a number that the gravedigger indis-
criminately 'jowls . . . to th'ground' (5.1.76) as he clears space for fresh
burial. Like the other bones, it's a sign of work, anonymous – and 'priceless' – spoil. But once it is produced as evidence of inquiry – the Prince
wanting to know 'How long will a man lie i'th'earth ere he rot?'; the
gravedigger, picking it out of the heap, handling it, re-valuing it as 'find',
answering, 'Here's a skull now. This skull has lain in the earth three and
twenty years' (159, 168–9) – the chopless skull that 'had a tongue in it, and
could sing once' (75) begins remembering story, telling biography: 'A
whoreson mad fellow's it was . . . A pestilence on him for a mad rogue – a
poured a flagon of Rhenish on my head once!' (171, 174–5). Remembering
the gag, the skull remembers the professional man who played it and
remembers his name, Yorick, the King's jester, the grotesquely irreverent
memento mori displaying the triumph of subjectivity in the object. But the
story of the flagon of Rhenish goes on to remember more story: of childhood, absence that floods momentarily, overwhelmingly into Hamlet's
present. 'I knew him, Horatio', knew him, 'I', an unbreeched boy of seven;
'I', twenty three years ago; 'I', who rode 'on his back a thousand times',
kissed lips that once hung here 'I know not how oft' (180–5). In Hamlet's
hands, spoil is recalculated as priceless treasure, memory opening up a past
literally unearthed from the grave, when the child Hamlet had another man
in his life, a proxy father of gibes and gambols – and love; a proxy king
doubling his warrior father (as Gertrude now has another man in her life, a
proxy husband). Remembering backward, Yorick's skull simultaneously
remembers forward, imagining a future career when, admitted to 'my lady's
chamber', he will carry a message about the future, 'tell her, let her paint an
inch thick, to this favour she must come' (189). And not just *her* future, but
the *common* future, when we shall all look 'o'this fashion i'th'earth' and
smell so: 'Pah!' (193, 196). To consider so is perhaps to consider too close to
the bone, and in a move typical of Hamlet whenever he comes too near to
crippling existential discovery, the Prince retreats from intimacy with the
object, first calculating the disgust value of the relic that makes him think
too much, the 'gorge' that 'rises' at the 'abhorred' 'imagination' (lines 182–3),
then degrading the material of personal memory into a prop for imper-
sonal performances. He uses Yorick's skull to 'play' Alexander, to 'play'
imperious Caesar.[24]

---

[24] Both the Arden and the Oxford editors put their interpolated stage direction – 'He throws the
skull down' – after 'Pah!', several lines too early for actors (among them, Olivier, Gibson,
Smoktunovsky, Jacobi, Branagh, Stephens, Beall and Lester).

Thus, we see how the object that carries story generates more story, open to some, closed to others; how retrospectives prompt memorial improvisations, fantasy in play with memory and future projection that traffics with real pasts – and real imaginaries. We see, too, how objects that certainly don't qualify as 'luxury goods' demonstrate 'semiotic virtuosity'; how they generate excess, becoming materials of actorly invention, literally 'play things' for their parts that, perchance, completely reorient the role. In the iconic lithograph of 1839, his fascinated, flaccid contemplation of the skull renders Delacroix's Hamlet a pallid melancholic; on film in 1990, hunkered down nose to nose with the skull, Mel Gibson's action-man Hamlet is momentarily out of action, a stunned existentialist; on stage in 2004 Toby Stephens's rhetorically acrobatic Prince has the words literally knocked out of him when the skull, flipped from the gravedigger's spade like a rugby ball, hits him in the solar plexus, but then off-loads language by transforming Yorick into a chatty ventriloquist's dummy as he mimes the skull's lower jaw with his fist and makes him talk. In all these examples, the skull fashions the Prince.

Finally, however, the power of objects in performance lapses. Their function is to be discarded. Their careers end. 'But soft, but soft,' says Hamlet snapping out of his double act with the dead. 'Here comes the King' (212). The skull is tossed aside. Something of Yorick's last star turn – the jester re-animated in the clowning-around Prince – may persist as an atmosphere lingering over what happens next, but the object itself is forgotten as the scene hands over to new rememberings sited on different objects: 'Who is that they follow?' (213).

Remembering Yorick's skull is for me a preliminary exercise, a model of practice for tracing the life history of the object in performance that chiefly intrigues me, Shakespeare's fatal diva of semiotic virtuosity, Desdemona's handkerchief. (Or is it Othello's? Already the object's story is vexed.) If Yorick's skull is an object whose brief life and rushed transactions concentrate its charge, the handkerchief spins life out, is 'extravagant', 'wheeling', a traveller. And it's worthwhile remembering just how much story – and in what order – it picks up as it goes.

On stage it begins life incognito, doing humble housework. 'Are you not well?' Desdemona asks her husband. 'I have a pain upon my forehead here', Othello answers. 'Faith', she replies, 'that's with watching' (3.3.287–9). Not suspecting that what's disturbing his rest is the pornographic cinema Iago has been unreeling to Othello's watch-full imaginary or that the pain he's feeling is the sprouting of cuckold's horns, she assures him, ''Twill away again. / Let me but bind it hard, within this hour / It will be well'. But Othello pushes away both her diagnosis and the cure: 'Your napkin is too little. / Let it alone' (lines 289–92).[25] (There are no stage directions in Folio or Quarto to direct the business of this exchange; whatever is going on here has to be recuperated from the text.) They exit.

Only when Emilia picks up Desdemona's dropped property, names it, and starts telling its story does the object begin to signify beyond its limited domestic 'regime of value' and its thwarted functionality, the cure it can't achieve because the pain is somewhere it can't reach. 'This napkin', says Emilia, 'was her first remembrance from the Moor' (lines 294–5): that is, a keepsake (something that makes her remember the past) but also a reminder (something that makes her remember *now*). As a mnemonic prompt, it says 'remember me' twice over, locating memory in the object itself but also in Desdemona, for 'he conjured her' that 'she should ever keep it' (line 298) – this gift, then, like all gifts, binds giver and taker in a network of obligations, of on-going and reciprocal indebtedness. While conjuration has here merely the force of earnest entreaty, not yet, what it will acquire later, a sense of magic force, spell, possession, still, it dredges up the past, remembers Brabantio's hysterical ravings back in Venice when only 'witchcraft', 'medicines bought of mountebanks' or 'some dram conjured to this effect' could explain his daughter's 'revolt' (1.3.64, 61, 105; 1.1.136). That said, even now there's something magical about the napkin, the story it's telling of strange operations, animations, erotic substitutions – or simply childish day-dreaming: Desdemona 'so loves the token / ... That she reserves it evermore about her / To kiss and talk to' (lines 297, 299–300).

In the space of Emilia's seven lines, Desdemona's property moves from 'napkin' to 'remembrance' to 'token'; from lost to 'found'; is a cloth, a fetish, a stand-in for the beloved, a surrogate child; something ordinary, something extraordinary; at one extreme of interpretation, it's 'work', a textile vulnerable to commodification, its embroidery design liable to be 'ta'en out', copied, reproduced; at the other, a metonym for secret 'reserves'. And it's something more: an object Emilia's 'wayward husband' has 'a hundred times / Wooed [her] to steal' (lines 296–7), potentially, then, pilfered goods. And in the space of seven lines the value of this object, its symbolic price, jumps wildly. What's it worth to 'earnest' Iago?

---

[25] To read 'it' as the handkerchief, as Harry Berger does, and to argue that husband and wife are knowingly in collusion – that they 'work closely together to lose the handkerchief and to disremember its loss' – is, I think, simply wrong. See 'Impertinent Trifling: Desdemona's Handkerchief', in *Shakespeare Quarterly* 46: 3 (Autumn 1996), pp. 235–50, esp. p. 237.

Moreover, in Emilia's hands, the 'remembrance' diverted from its original career path begins to tell another story, brokers another exchange: 'wooed' to steal it, Emilia will use it to woo, make it a present, 'give't Iago.' What will the 'wayward husband' 'do with it'? 'Heaven knows, not I'. She can't remember forward, stuck instead with what sounds like a tired old back-story: 'I nothing, but to please his fantasy' (lines 302–3). So Emilia keeps the napkin only briefly before handing it on to Iago – who's forgotten it ('What handkerchief?') but manages simultaneously to sex-ualise and degrade the 'thing' she offers, no longer exactly a gift, but barter ('What will you give me now / For . . . ?'). Not much: for 'It is a common thing' (lines 311, 309–10, 306). In this latest exchange, where the object is called a handkerchief for the first time, nothing adds up: so valuable a thing ('Poor lady, she'll run mad / When she shall lack it' (lines 322–3)) should buy Emilia much 'please[d] fantasy'. But doesn't. 'Give it me,' commands Iago. Then, 'Go, leave me' (lines 318, 324). So maybe the women are making the wrong calculation about this object, valuing in inflated symbolic terms what Iago reckons commercially: 'I have use for it' (line 324). But once Emilia's gone, Iago proposes another career diversion for the handkerchief: just found, to be lost again, and found again, 'in Cassio's lodging', a story that reassigns the handkerchief's significance, begins to fake its history, placing it in the category of 'Trifles light as air' that double as 'proofs of holy writ' (lines 325–6, 328). Just now though, it's placed in Iago's pocket.

Does it matter that this thing that's changing hands is a handkerchief? *Othello*'s Arden editor and the *OED* make 'napkin' and 'handkerchief' synonyms.[26] But that perhaps collapses distinctions early moderns would have made: among his pawns Philip Henslowe lists 'viij flaxen napkenes & ij hancherchers j Red & j blacke'.[27] Most of the napkins we see on the early modern stage are 'suddenly raised from dinner' or 'newly risen from supper', that is, they signify eating (and by extension, appetite), while the handkerchiefs mentioned in stage directions (in *Volpone*, in *The Wise Woman of Hogsdon*) are semiotically more complicated. Put into the hands of women, and those women framed in windows that invite male gazing, the handkerchiefs they hold suggestively trope women's work *and* play (one woman labours in a seamstress's shop; the other, in holiday mood, gaily responds to a mountebank's spiel). For women, of course, work and play amount to the same thing, *both* coding women's

---

[26] See Honigmann's note to 3.3.291 and *OED* napkin, *sb.* 2.   [27] *Diary*, f.135v, p. 255.

sexuality.[28] (Remember Iago's quayside quip: women 'rise to play, and go to bed to work' (2.1.118).) Using them interchangeably in *Othello* Shakespeare is perhaps absorbing the domestic into the erotic – this is, after all, a play in which all the women, wives, lovers, brides, 'baubles', 'customers', are also housewives. But he's redeploying signs he's used before (and will again). Both napkin and kerchief *cover*: the lap, the hand. As Desdemona's hand tropes her heart (3.4.45) so it tropes her chastity – or its abuse, promiscuous liberality (line 46). Covering (symbolically, practically) reserves female sexuality, and so we see the men who give women love tokens in Shakespeare attempting acts of enclosure or cover-up, transferring clothing from his body to hers: Troilus, his heraldic sleeve, Posthumus, his manacle – and Othello. We should notice that the handkerchief, the sign of love, of erotic value and exchange, enters the play the very moment love is contaminated and sex spoiled – and the very moment its proper function is travestied. Of course it's 'too little' to cure Othello's sick fantasy! We should notice as well that all the stories the handkerchief rehearses are told retrospectively, circulated like gossip, when it's been lost. In terms of biography, the handkerchief's a corpse.[29]

But each time – six times – it changes hands it acquires more story. It's in Iago's pocket for the rest of 3.3 when, having primed Othello's imagination for 'satisfaction', a sex-scene where the 'supervisor' might 'grossly gape on' to see Desdemona 'topped' (lines 406, 400, 401), Iago swaps it for voyeurism in another bedroom – a bedroom where *he's* in bed with Michael Cassio ('I lay with Cassio lately . . .' (line 418)) playing Desdemona to Cassio's dreamed-up lust: 'then . . . would he gripe and wring my hand . . . and then kiss me hard / As if he plucked up kisses by the roots / . . . lay his leg o'er my thigh . . .' (lines 425–8)). It's on the back of this monstrous story, remembering Cassio's dream activity, that Iago suddenly asks Othello to remember a handkerchief – and a story Othello doesn't know:

> Have you not sometimes seen a handkerchief
> Spotted with strawberries in your wife's hand?
> . . . such a handkerchief,

---

[28] See relevant entries in Alan C. Dessen and Leslie Thomson, *A Dictionary of Stage Directions in English Drama, 1580–1642* (Cambridge: Cambridge University Press, 1999).

[29] For a brilliant reading of the handkerchief as marriage trope, see Lynda Boose, 'Othello's Handkerchief: "The Recognizance and Pledge of Love"', *English Literary Renaissance* 5 (1975), 360–74. She writes: 'The idea of "token" seems always to have carried overtone for Shakespeare of representative sexual exchange', p. 365.

I am sure it was your wife's, did I today
See Cassio wipe his beard with.

(3.3.439–44)

From now on the handkerchief – for the first time identified by its strawberries, more retrospective 'history' – cannot be remembered uncontaminated by plucked-up kisses, a leg laid over a thigh. Yet, sensationalized, it's paradoxically recruited to science, its invented history reconstituting it as forensic evidence: 'proofs' (line 445). But not until the next scene does it acquire its *mystified* past, a story fraught with story, memory piled on memory – or perhaps, as with Iago's tale of Cassio's dream, fantasy elaborating fantasy, lie spinning lie. Objects, we know, can be faked:

> That handkerchief
> Did an Egyptian to my mother give,
> She was a charmer and could almost read
> The thoughts of people. She told her, while she kept it,
> 'Twould make her amiable and subdue my father
> Entirely to her love; but if she lost it
> Or made a gift of it, my father's eye
> Should hold her loathed and his spirits should hunt
> After new fancies. She, dying, gave it me
> And bid me, when my fate would have me wive
> To give it her. I did so, and – take heed on't!
> Make it a darling, like your precious eye! –
> To lose't or give't away were such perdition
> As nothing else could match.

Is this story credible?

> 'Tis true, there's magic in the web of it.
> A sibyl that had numbered in the world
> The sun to course two hundred compasses,
> In her prophetic fury sewed the work;
> The worms were hallowed that did breed the silk,
> And it was dyed in mummy, which the skilful
> Conserved of maidens' hearts.

(3.4.55–75)

Wheeling and traumatizing, this dizzying story of extravagant exchange, crossed histories and diverted careers, of art, occult science, labour, gift, inheritance, loss and multiple deaths (dead maidens, mummy dye) apotheosizes the handkerchief, but constructs it an unforgiving god with a death-wish, terminal perdition. And history – ''Twould make her amiable' – is irrecoverable because the object is gone.

But of course, it's not: it returns, only eighty lines later when Cassio, who's had it in *his* pocket ever since he entered at line 104, just too late to hear Othello bellow 'The handkerchief!' (line 95) before storming out leaving Desdemona reeling, produces it. But not to Desdemona. Desdemona's gone (line 165). The woman Cassio hands it to is Desdemona's double, Bianca, just entered, who, canny, reads it as sexual betrayal, 'some token from a newer friend!' (line 178), exactly the story Iago wants it to tell. Cassio protests the handkerchief has no story: 'I found it in my chamber' (line 185). For him, it's, quite literally, an alibi; it will be missed and then 'demanded'. Wanting the 'work ... copied' (lines 186, 187), however, Cassio unwittingly adopts the wrong model for, unlike in Cinthio, Shakespeare's source, where the lieutenant knows whose handkerchief he's found, Cassio doesn't recognise it or the narratives it's accrued. He doesn't see that the 'work' in this handkerchief is not inscription, the superficial strawberry patterned embroidery applied to its surface that might be copied by a scribe using a needle instead of a pen; the work 'in' the handkerchief is story, copied by retelling, by fabrication. Indeed, the object *is* story.

For Othello, gone, the handkerchief is too much present, harped upon in 4.1.1–43 (a parody of the original 'think/think' scene (3.3)) where Iago, writing pornography ('naked with her friend in bed' (line 3)) while pretending casuisty ('if I give my wife a handkerchief –' (line 10)) uses it to rub Othello's mind raw with what the Moor 'would most gladly have forgot' (line 19). Those metaphors colliding in Othello's exploding brain finally fell him, in the fit that mimics the sex act Othello is remembering under pressure of Iago's latest story: 'Lie with her? Lie on her? ... Handkerchief!' (line 34). It comes on stage one last time only a hundred lines later, when, interrupting Iago's set-up conversation with Cassio – a conversation played to Othello's audience – a spit-fire Bianca returns it, having pondered its story and decided it's incredible: 'A likely piece of work ... !' (line 148). Throwing the thing back in Cassio's face, she's reversing its career – but unwittingly creating it a prop in Iago's melodramatic sideshow. Like a theatre prop, the real thing, performing, tells a fake story – but it's one Othello will remember: 'I saw my handkerchief in's hand'; 'I saw it in his hand' (5.2.67, 222). Othello's not wrong – yet absolutely wrong.

To the end, the handkerchief retains semiotic virtuosity: 'holy writ' condemning Desdemona ('That handkerchief / Which I so loved and gave thee, thou gavest / To Cassio' (5.2.50–2)); 'ocular proof' informing Casso's overheard 'confession' ('she did gratify his amorous works / With that recognizance and pledge of love / Which I first gave her' (5.2.220–2)). In Othello's hands, a fatal contract, a broken bond; in Emilia's – 'O thou dull

Moor' – 'such a trifle' (5.2.232, 235). About its final interpretation, we fall back on Iago's totalizing inscrutability, 'What you know, you know' (5.2.309) – knowing that one of the stories this 'tragedy of a handkerchief' tells is of how we invest objects with lives, among them, our own.[30] But as for the thing itself: it's absent. It left the play mid-way through 4.1 with Cassio in pursuit of Bianca, and with as little ado as Yorick's skull dumped by Hamlet.

Tracking the handkerchief through Shakespeare's play-text I've been conscious not only of how much remembering the 'remembrance from the Moor' is set to do as an object saturated with story, a real thing that dissolves into fantasised imaginaries, ocular proof that hoodwinks. I've been aware, too, how Shakespeare scripts for the handkerchief an excruciatingly tense life on stage of hidden presence and near misses.

But the diva who fascinates is also perchance a monster to work with. When productions come to put the handkerchief on stage, what part of the story do they materialize in the object? What do costume departments literally *make* of it? Something familiar, something strange? Something recognizably European, fine, decorated with Venetian lace and embroidered with silk thread, a product of a consumer market in elite goods? Something rare, disturbingly primitive, instinct with its occulted inheritance, Egyptian, African, unique, inimitable, dark, stained the colour of dried blood? What cloth is it cut from?

If, wanting answers to these questions, you went to the wardrobe department looking, as I did, for the handkerchief used in the Royal Shakespeare Company productions of *Othello* (1979, 1985, 1989, 1999, 2004) you'd be disappointed. You'd find it's not there. There's a washing machine-sized box marked 'Handkerchiefs' that you can search to the bottom, trawling through big ones and little ones, contemporary and period, decorative and utility, silk, linen, spotted. But none embroidered with strawberries. Desdemona's handkerchief is lost property. It's gone, like performance, its trace remaining only in words.

But not quite so. You can turn to the RSC's photographic archives for images, for production photographs, documentary evidence of the absent thing – admittedly, a controversial project, but still, photographs have long been consulted as records, preserving, as Siri Hustvedt writes, 'what *was* in what *is*', 'a subject in a *real* moment in time', photographs always 'a sign of disappearance'.[31] Again, you don't find exactly what you want, a

---

[30] That notorious phrase is, of course, Thomas Rymer's in *A Short View of Tragedy*, 1693.
[31] '*Death of Photography*: Old Pictures and a New Book', *Modern Painters* (September, 2005), pp. 96–9, esp. 96, 97.

shot of the object, up close, the kind of photograph you'd turn in at a police station or attach for identification purposes to an insurance claim ('Venetian lace', 'dyed with blood'). Instead, you become aware that you're looking at the object *posed*. That is, caught in a moment of performance. (Of course. Theatre photographs are 'stills' that capture objects in the act.) So, for example, while we can scan John Bunting's image from 1989 (figure 28) for evidence of the lost object, and can just make out the strawberries embroidered on what looks like white lawn bordered in lace, what really strikes us about the photograph is that it shows the handkerchief not so much as an object as an activity, not 'is' but 'does'. What it is, what it *means*, is expressed in the story it's telling, the actorly activity it's put to. Bunting's photograph is unusual in capturing that story at the beginning, before the handkerchief has changed hands, in a family composition that takes the couple laughing, sharing the joke of the young wife's inadequate ministrations.[32] Earlier, she didn't know to put sugar in the lemonade she offered her husband. Now, her handkerchief is 'too little' to do the work of binding up her love for him. Othello's hand is about to brush it off.

Against Bunting's, put photographs by Angus McBean (1956), Joe Cocks (1979), and Malcolm Davis (2004) (figures 29, 30, 31) – which appear to quote each other.[33] Here, through what I'd call iconic accident or deliberate memorial recall (raiding these terms from Barbara Hodgdon), the handkerchief is shown striking *the same pose*, one that, it turns out, is captured in theatrical stills (in different dress) over and over in the archives, like serial mug-shots – mostly, the *only* memory productions retain of the handkerchief.[34] (Or maybe what accounts for the visual coincidence is that, as Joseph Roach proposes, roles contain 'mnemonic reserves', moves 'remembered by bodies', a repertoire of habits, almost the role's DNA, that rehearse themselves in performance after performance, constituting a 'genealogy of performance'. All Iagos, then, will strike the *same* pose – there for the photographic taking.[35]) As against Bunting's image, the handkerchief 'means' something different here. For

---

[32] Desdemona: Imogen Stubbs; Othello: Willard White; Director: Trevor Nunn; Designer: Bob Crowley.

[33] Iago: Emlyn Williams; Director: Glen Byam Shaw; Designer: Motley. Iago: Bob Peck; Director: Ronald Eyre; Designer: Pamela Howard. Iago: Antony Sher; Director: Greg Doran; Designer: Stephen Brimson Lewis.

[34] '"Here Apparent": Photography, History, and the Theatrical Unconscious', in Edward Pechter, ed., *Textual and Theatrical Shakespeare* (Iowa City: University of Iowa Press, 1996), pp. 181–209, esp. p. 197.

[35] Roach, *Cities of the Dead*, p. 26.

28. Imogen Stubbs, Desdemona; Willard White, Othello (1989).

these theatrical stills arrest its career, fix its whole history in the hands of
Iago, and tie it down to text – text that I, the viewer (all viewers?),
automatically supply in voice-over, the only text that 'fits': 'I will in
Cassio's lodging lose this napkin'; 'This may do something' (3.3.325, 328).
Here, the theatrical still privileges 'this', shows 'this' prompting

29. Emlyn Williams, Iago (1956).

(instructing?) three actors to spread the handkerchief to voyeuristic display. Here, too, the spreading (which somehow remembers bodies) rather than the display (which offers the handkerchief to view) constitutes the *real* story. (Ian McKellen's Iago performs this action on film in 1989, where his prodding of the handkerchief feels obscene, as though he's

30. Bob Peck, Iago (1979).

opening Desdemona's legs.) In the photographic records that remember these *Othellos*, then, the handkerchief is Iago's creature. It tells *his* story.

To move from these stills to Zoe Dominic's (1961) (figure 32) is to feel that the eye has moved one frame along, across a sheet of photographic proofs, to a shot that captures what Iago *does next* with the handkerchief.[36] Splayed across his laid-back face, it mimics the covering the napkin is supposed to do – but mocks it, makes it ugly, and the sexual trope, impudent. But Dominic's image does something more – which immediately strikes us as we try to caption this photograph. It arrests Iago in the split second *before* he remembers his next line, 'Trifles light as

[36] Iago: Ian Bannen; Director: Franco Zeffirelli; Costumes: Peter J. Hall.

31. Antony Sher, Iago (2004).

32. Ian Bannen, Iago (1961).

air . . . ' To speak that line, Ian Bannen's Iago will first have to *act* the line, to blow off the handkerchief, to make it 'light as air'. Zoe Dominic doesn't 'get' this next shot; but what she *does* get, her still that arrests action before it happens, uncannily, even magically, remembers forward. For it engenders a sequence of look-alikes, returns that, by iconic accident or deliberate recall, have remembered this performance moment, effectively fixing the handkerchief's story by trapping it in Iago's action – *this* action. Put simply: we see the handkerchief made 'light as air' again – and again: in the 1981 BBC *Othello* where Bob Hoskins plays Iago (figure 33 (a) and (b)); in Oliver Parker's 1995 film (where, as the lightness of the trifle makes it blossom gorgeously in space, Kenneth Branagh's Iago, out of frame, has pushed his wife face-down, straddled her, and is sodomising her) (figure 34 (a) and (b)); in 2004, on stage, where Antony Sher's Iago finishes in figure 35 what he began in figure 31.

Can we say that, in the hands of (male) actors, Desdemona's hand-kerchief is acquiring (female) behaviour – and a reputation that goes with it? That as the dexterity of the actor dazzles – Sher 'wows' as he makes the handkerchief fly – so the semiotic diversity of the diva is trapped in one,

(a)

(b)

33. (a) and (b) Bob Hoskins, Iago (1981).

(a)

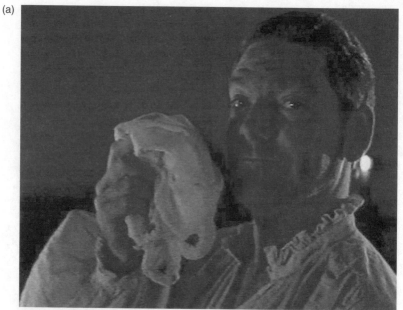

(b)

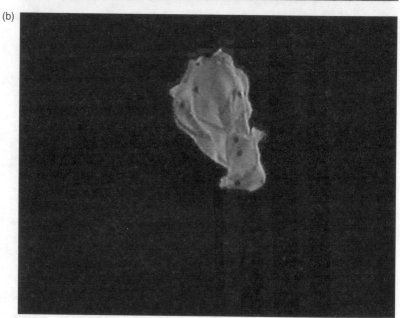

34. (a) and (b) Kenneth Branagh, Iago (1995).

35. Antony Sher, Iago (2004).

over-determined signification, the object arrested to tell one story? And that, as the theatrical still 'takes' this image (the photograph, we remember, constitutes theatre record, theatre history, and what we can remember of 'lost' performance) and gives it to memory as what persists, *Othello* is made, three hundred years on from Thomas Rymer, not just what he mocked, the tragedy of a handkerchief, but the tragedy of a 'trifle', and of women 'light as air'?

Mulling over these questions I move on to two more images – figures 36 and 37 – images not 'of' performance but somehow pretending to be, ostensibly quoting or plagiarizing performance, observing as I go that visual regimes enact coercions, that ways of looking determine ways of thinking, and that what we can make of something depends on what we can see of it. Figure 36 shows the cover of the souvenir programme of the National Theatre's 1997 *Othello*, itself a reproduction of the poster that appeared on hoardings, in the London underground, and along the South Bank advertising the production (that opened in September) directed by Sam Mendes with Simon Russell Beale as Iago. Shot in black and white shading into grey, the photograph that 'says' *Othello* to purchasers of theatre tickets 'is' the handkerchief falling through space. Figure 37 shows the front cover of the 1997 Arden 3 *Othello* – arguably, the most universally recognized edition of Shakespeare on the face of the planet. Another image shot in black, white and grey, this cover photograph surely can't be remembering the National Theatre poster (since both graphics must have been in production at the same time). But it uncannily reproduces it. So: more iconic accident, more mnemonic reserve? On this book cover, the handkerchief delivers instant 'brand recognition', works like a designer label. The floating trifle has landed a job in PR! But as this cover image, simulating a relationship with a performance it seems to be remembering (even as it absents any actor from it), floats free of actual performance, thereby conning interpretation, so the poster image turns out to fake a relationship between advertising and product, between what it appears to be passing off as a production still and the production. The 1997 *Othello* didn't do what it said on the package. Russell Beale's Iago didn't throw the handkerchief.[37]

---

[37] This production did its remembering in other ways. Maureen Beattie (Emilia) remembers her director, Sam Mendes, running upstairs in a break from rehearsals at the National to ask (and receive) permission from Trevor Nunn (the NT's Artistic Director and Mendes's boss) to quote business from his 1989 RSC *Othello*: Nunn put the interval at 3.3.293, after Othello and Desdemona's exit on 'I am very sorry that you are not well.' So her lost handkerchief (and traces of Desdemona) remained fully visible on stage across the interval. Mendes's production remembered Nunn's. Then in 2004, Greg Doran quoted Mendes's quotation – with a difference. He put the

A co-production between the Royal National Theatre and the Salzburg Festival

Othello
by William Shakespeare

NT Royal
National
Theatre

36. Programme cover from the 1997 National Theatre *Othello*. Designer: Michael Mayhew.

So here, on the one hand, the photographic still recruits objects into a false (looking) economy, its product, false memory. On the other, it positions the still itself as an object, setting out on a career as potentially liable to diversion as the handkerchief's. But should these transactions make us anxious? Given the power we invest in objects to remember,

interval later, at the end of 3.3 ('I am your own forever' (line 482)). Earlier, staggering out of Othello's grip around his throat ('Villain, be sure thou prove my love a whore' (line 364), Sher's Iago was all injured merit. 'God buy you, take my office', he shrieked, ripping his ensign's stripes off his uniform and throwing them to the ground (line 380). Those stripes stayed on stage, so it was Iago who was remembered across the interval.

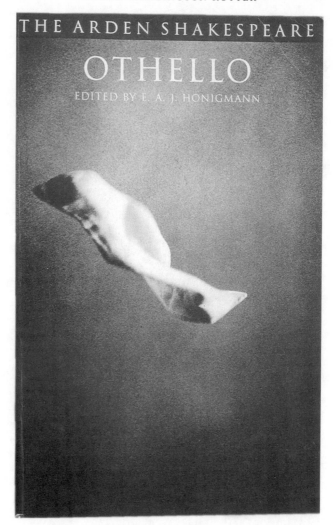

37. The cover of the 1997 Arden edition of *Othello*. Designer: Newell and Sorrell.

should we be responsible for using them to remember accurately, to tell the 'right' stories? And anyway, what are the uses of 'true' memory in the theatre, where *all* we remember is 'false'? This takes me back to the top of this essay – to Declan Donnellan's observations on the creative uses of 'wrong' memory. If I worry about the sexual politics of co-opting the handkerchief to the 'wrong' image, using it to plant false memories that prepare viewers and readers to mis-remember *Othello*, Donnellan reassures me – paradoxically by offering another 'wrong' memory that works to explode my 'anxiety of remembering'. Figure 38 gives the front cover 'pose' on Cheek by Jowl's souvenir *Othello* programme (2004), a white handkerchief clenched (strangled?) in a black fist. This photograph doesn't document performance. (The hand isn't even Othello's (Nonso Anozie).) Nor does it refer to Shakespeare's text. (In the script, Othello doesn't handle the strawberry spotted handkerchief.)[38] Privileging the handkerchief, like the NT poster and the Arden cover, Cheek by Jowl's image makes *Othello* the tragedy of a handkerchief. But unlike them, Cheek by Jowl radically, iconoclastically re-presents the icon. What's in this photograph? I see an image that disturbs knowledge, 'what you know you know'. An image gendered male. An image of violent possession, seizure. (Against the power of that hand, the handkerchief hasn't got a chance.) And an image (as against those others advertising a 'show' of 'trifles') that suggests, as the disclaimer puts it, that 'this play may contain scenes of violence' – and that men may have something to do with them.

Moreover, this photograph shows an object *remembering*. And what it's remembering is backward, to rehearsal, that 'specialist area of translation studies' (as Donnellan calls it) when, beginning *Othello* rehearsals, the director started thinking seriously, sceptically about the handkerchief, wondering why Othello's mother had given her son 'this thing'. As told in its history, an object of love, the handkerchief became for Donnellan a 'symbol of parental abuse – a nasty little passive/aggressive present – that tells him to fantasize about his partner and says "don't expect fidelity in marriage", "expect erotic *infidelity*". Some 'gift' – it poisons her son's marriage. *How dare she?*'[39]

If the photograph is remembering backward, to this history of director's bewilderment and rage, it's likewise remembering forward, to performance. As Cheek by Jowl played it, the handkerchief told a story never, ever before revealed on stage, of its 'real' life – as a sadie-max fetish.

---

[38] Leastwise, not the strawberry handkerchief. An Angus McBean photograph of John Dexter's 1964 National Theatre production shows Laurence Olivier clutching the *other* handkerchief, the one Desdemona produces – 'Here, my lord' (3.4.52) – in response to his 'I have a salt and sullen rheum offends me, / Lend me thy handkerchief' (lines 51–2). While McBean's photographs were often studio set-ups that captured a 'performance' that belonged to a theatre of his own imagination, this one appears to be close to actual performance, as a cross reference to the Stuart Burge film (1965) made of the 1964 production shows. The 'wrong' handkerchief, bracketed with its series of negatives ('not', 'Not?', 'no' (lines 54, 55)), is the object, balled up in Olivier's gesticulating fist, that prompts his story of absence, 'That handkerchief . . . .' About Desdemona's other handkerchief there is much to say – at another time.

[39] In conversation, October 2004.

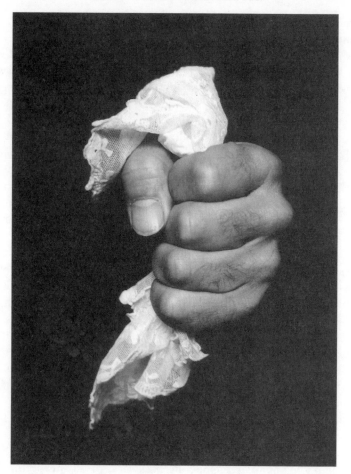

38. Programme cover from the Cheek by Jowl *Othello* (2004). Design: Eureka!

When Donnellan's Bianca, the 'white' woman who travels through the play as Desdemona's symbolic double, walked on stage, spectators saw a fantasy built of latex and leather straight out of *Pulp Fiction*: black hair, red lips, corpse-white skin, skyscraper heels. (Kirsty Besterman's last part for the company had been Cordelia.) As Cassio (Ryan Kiggell) tried to mollify her with promises of a 'convenient time' to 'strike off this score of absence', and absentmindedly offered her the handkerchief to be getting on with, she balked, waspish, suspicious: 'This is some token from a newer friend!' (3.4.176, 178). He answered with a gesture that was, at first, bizarrely incomprehensible, moving away from her, to the wall. There, he

39. Desdemona's handkerchief (1979) – now mine.

braced himself. Then he thrust out his buttocks as if inviting sodomizing – and shuddered with pleasure as, languidly, she approached, dragging the handkerchief through her hands as if teasingly masturbating it, then whipped him while she talked dirty of its provenance, her voice salaciously lubricant: 'To the felt absence now I feel a cause. / Is't come to this? Well, well' (3.4.179–80). He climaxed; shoved the handkerchief down his trousers, wiped his groin – and held out the damp rag to Bianca, to 'have it copied' (line 187). Later she brought it back – and, when he protested, shoved it into his open mouth.

'Memory', writes Roach, 'is a process that depends crucially on forgetting.'[40] Making spectators look, up close, at the sex that Shakespeare's

---

[40] Roach, *Cities of the Dead*, p. 2.

play-text puts somewhere else, out of sight; making them see the hand-kerchief as a sex toy used to play out, for post-adolescent kicks, a deeply clichéd jealousy/punishment scenario, Cheek by Jowl invented for the object a whole new career path that forgot Iago's 'trifle'. And remembered instead a 'thing' of darkness, violence, and pain.

POST SCRIPT

Afterwards, stories return. I'm offered sightings of the RSC's lost prop-erty. One handkerchief (from the 2004 *Othello*) is hanging, I'm told, in Tony Sher's front hall – next to Cyrano's nose. Another turns up at my house, wrapped in purple tissue paper. The note enclosed with it, from Karen Keene, once mistress of the RSC's hire wardrobe, tells me it's from the 1979 *Othello* – so figure 39 shows the handkerchief Bob Peck is holding in figure 30. Or one *like* the one he's holding. For Keene also tells me *three* strawberry handkerchiefs were used in that production. (We get a glimpse of the object as theatre drudge. There have to be 'understudies'. Desdemona's handkerchief takes a beating in the theatre. Might get torn. Might get lost.) Holding it in my hand, I admire the work that's gone in to the handkerchief – women's work – the strawberries embroidered by hand, the lace border sewn on with tiny stitches, an enigmatic design, *alla moresca*, in one corner, stitched white-on-white. I notice that the cloth has been mended. This handkerchief carries the wounds of its working life. But I don't attempt Iago's tricks. I don't try throwing Desdemona's handkerchief into the air. Because I take very seriously the caution from Keene that comes with this gift: 'Be careful where you drop it.'

CHAPTER 8

On the gravy train: Shakespeare, memory and forgetting

Peter Holland

> The act of memory is a physical act and lies at the heart of the art of the theatre. If the theatre were a verb, it would be 'to remember'.[1]

As so often, it is easiest to begin with a story. In the summer of 2002 Harriet Walter played Beatrice in Gregory Doran's production of *Much Ado About Nothing* for the Royal Shakespeare Company in the Royal Shakespeare Theatre at Stratford-upon-Avon. It was on about the fourth occasion that I saw the production that it quickly became clear that it was not her night. She was fairly late appearing on stage in the elaborate sequence that opened the show, an assembling of Leonato's household that carefully defined social relationships and status. At the opening of 2.1, the sequence leading to the revels, she was 'off', the actors' term for missing an entrance completely, leaving the other actors stranded on stage for some seconds before she arrived to pick up the rhythm of the scene. But it was the end of the orchard scene where Beatrice is gulled that created the oddest problem, the one that has continued to intrigue me and gives this chapter its title. Standing alone on stage, drenched by the hose with which Hero had energetically watered her, does not make speaking the complex stanzaic forms Shakespeare gives Beatrice easy:

> What fire is in mine ears? Can this be true?
> Stand I condemned for pride and scorn so much?
> Contempt, farewell; and maiden pride, adieu.
> No glory lives behind the back of such.
>
> (3.1.107–10)

Except that that evening I thought I heard Beatrice say 'No *gravy* lives behind the back of such.' I nudged my wife, our signal to each other that

---

As this chapter was in its very last stages of revision, Lyn Tribble kindly sent me proofs of her excellent article 'Distributing Cognition in the Globe', *Shakespeare Quarterly* 56(2005), 135–55. Our reading and thinking overlap fascinatingly, though I have not altered my piece in the light of hers.

[1] Anne Bogart, *A Director Prepares* (London: Routledge, 2001), p. 22.

there was something about a moment to discuss at the interval, but at the break she was fairly sure she hadn't heard it.

We met Harriet Walter the next day. She raised the topic: 'You were in last night, weren't you? You heard what I said. I knew the word began with *g* and ended in *y* but I couldn't remember it and *gravy* was the only word I could think of.' We did our best to reassure her, pretty convincingly, that I was probably the only one to have noticed. But the problem of her memory has stayed in my memory.

It might of course have been possible to conduct a Freudian analysis of such a slip of the tongue in the manner of 'The Psychopathology of Everyday Life'.[2] Perhaps her lack of control that evening led her to be *rav*ing or to make a *grav*e error, rather than be subject to the 'law' at the heart of *glory*. Or perhaps it was simply that her mind was already running on her dinner after the performance. But her failure of memory became my memory: I remember that moment more powerfully, more immediately than any other in the production, even if, when I choose to or when I am thinking about a scene in the play, other memories from the production will become present, can be conjured back: sets and costumes, moves and blocking, readings that I liked or disliked but which were not, in the sense of the gravy train, accidental errors.

The erasure of *glory*, an error Harriet Walter probably never made in the rest of the run, though the memory of the mistake was equally probably present every time she approached the phrase thereafter, seems part of the process of memory and forgetting, the always vulnerable, always potentially falsified reconstruction of memory that surrounds performance, the exchange between the two which is the subject of this paper in my exploration of memorial construction and reconstruction, the central terms of my argument, but an exchange especially potent in that theatre, a theatre in which the memory of other memories is present with a peculiar intensity for those of us who can trace our long histories of watching productions there but also a theatre in which the act of memory has in one very particular sense been erased. For the Royal Shakespeare Theatre was originally opened under another name, as the Shakespeare Memorial Theatre, the place of cultural memory of or for Shakespeare. The theatre as a site of memory may seem to us an obvious cultural memorializing for Shakespeare and yet the history of the building of the

---

[2] See, for example, chapter 5, 'Slips of the Tongue' in Sigmund Freud, *The Psychopathology of Everyday Life* (The Pelican Freud Library, vol. 5. Harmondsworth, Middlesex: Penguin Books, 1975), pp. 94–152.

theatre in the aftermath of the Shakespeare tercentenary celebrations of 1864 is of a slow move towards the acceptance of a theatre, rather than a statue or other cultural monument, as the right choice for that act of memory. In February 1875 a group of local businessmen agreed that

This is an opportune time for renewing the project which was proposed in 1864 for erecting a suitable Monument to Shakespeare in his native town, and that Monument should take the form of a Memorial Theatre ... [3]

The theatre burned down in 1926 and the new theatre of 1932 was again named the Shakespeare Memorial Theatre, functioning both as a memorial to Shakespeare and, in an odd way, a memorial to its predecessor, still a shell-like presence adjacent to the site. Only in 1961 was the Memorial Theatre itself deleted from the present tense of cultural memory to become the Royal Shakespeare Theatre, the sovereign's approval acting as a cultural substitution for social memory. What had begun as a project of social memory bridged outwards into public memory until it became an act of public forgetting.

As Edward S. Casey defines it in his superb essay 'Public Memory in Place and Time', a kind of supplement to his astonishing book *Remembering: A Phenomenological Study*, social memory is 'memory held in common by those who are affiliated either by kinship ties ... or by engagement in a common project. In other words, it is memory shared by those who are *already* related to each other'.[4] The creation of the Shakespeare Memorial Theatre was then an act of social memory, a stage along – or should it be 'up'? – from Casey's schematic definition of individual memory. The theatre becomes a location of the last of Casey's four divisions of memory, public memory, memory 'out in the open, in the *koinos cosmos* where discussion is possible ... but also where one is exposed and vulnerable'.[5] There are clear interactions between this conceptualization of public memory and the project of Peggy Phelan in *Mourning Sex* where her investigation of 'Performing Public Memories', the subtitle of her brilliant study, includes the analysis of the uncovering, the disinterring of the Rose Theatre, an as it were 'real' Shakespeare

[3] Quoted in Marian J. Pringle, *The Theatres of Stratford-upon-Avon 1875–1992: An Architectural History* (Stratford-upon-Avon: The Stratford-upon-Avon Society, 1994), Stratford-upon-Avon Papers 5, p. 10.

[4] Edward S. Casey, 'Public Memory in Place and Time', in Kendall R. Phillips, ed., *Framing Public Memory* (Tuscaloosa: University of Alabama Press, 2004), pp. 17–44 (p. 21). See also Edward S. Casey, *Remembering: A Phenomenological Study*, 2nd edn, (Bloomington, Indiana: University of Indiana Press, 2000) and his essay on forgetfulness, 'Forgetting Remembered', *Man and World* 25 (1992), 281–311.

[5] 'Public Memory', p. 25.

theatre. A full understanding of the meaning of the naming of the Shakespeare Memorial Theatre would need to intersect complexly with Phelan's excavations, for the finding of the Rose during the archaeological dig on the construction site transformed, in Phelan's words, 'the economic, architectural, future-directed aspiration implied by "construction site" into a place of retrospection, memory, and history'.[6] The building of such a theatre as the SMT, like the finding of the traces of the Rose, is, then, already an act engaged in history, not in a future, an act of memory recovered from forgetting, an attack on cultural obliteration and amnesia. Somewhere here there is a complex negotiation with Paul Ricoeur's vast and ambitious project in his recent book *Memory, History, Forgetting* but it is a negotiation I can only gesture towards and not, here, track.[7]

Located between Casey's concepts of social and public memory, he places a crucial step, 'collective memory', the term which seems to me most to replicate the peculiar characteristics of memory and forgetting that are performed by a theatre audience in relation to the performance they collectively witnessed. Though Casey offers the assumption that collective memory is '*distributed* over a given population or set of places', his description of the group as lacking 'prior identity', as being 'formed spontaneously and involuntarily' through its 'convergent focus on a given topic', seems a necessary precondition of the definition of the theatre audience, 'members of this momentary collectivity', as he calls the group, 'linked solely by the cynosure on which their attention falls'.[8] Even if his version of collective memory is of an attention that 'need not occur at the same time', Casey's term covers exactly the variety of remembering, the range of forgetting, that is fundamentally definitional of that singular collective noun, the noun that masks its own plurality, that is an *audience*.

Yet when he sees this '[c]ollective remembering' as 'unremittingly plural – so plural that group memories do not count', he is constructing a unanimity, a space where 'the singularity of the ... group of co-rememberers is what counts',[9] where, fundamental to my project at this point of examining the interaction of audience and actor and memory and forgetting and Shakespeare and performance, the group of terms whose intersections are the subject for this chapter and indeed this collection, is the necessary acceptance of the impossibility of the singularity

[6] See Peggy Phelan, *Mourning Sex* (London: Routledge, 1997), p. 86 but see also the whole of chapter 4, 'Uncovered Rectums: Disinterring the Rose Theatre', pp. 73–94.

[7] Paul Ricoeur, *Memory, History, Forgetting* (Chicago: University of Chicago Press, 2004), first published in French in 2000 as *La Mémoire, l'histoire, l'oubli*.

[8] Casey, 'Public Memory in Place and Time', pp. 23–4.   [9] Casey, 'Public Memory', p. 24.

of that memory by or for an audience, a singularity always already necessarily different, different because what is heard and seen as well as what is remembered is uncontrollably individual.

In my memory of the actor's forgetfulness, of Walter's substitutive act that creates and burdens the space of this memory, there can only be this act of individual memory that descends from, denies the collective memory of the group that saw that performance. But it is also the case that the moment makes visible the actor's memory, a feature fundamental to performance only through its sustained masking, known only by its absence. We assume the actor remembers; we are troubled only by its temporary visibility. If the actor's memory becomes visible at such a moment of forgetting and replacing, it becomes a local form of trans-mutation in the representation of that broad cultural process at the confluence of memory, performance and substitution that Joseph Roach so magnificently explored as the concept of 'surrogation' in his 1996 study *Cities of the Dead*.[10] But I already need, in order to begin to open out the space I shall want to be exploring, a space in which memory becomes forgetting and yet then reconstructed as memory, to add two further examples of the performance of memory and forgetting, in these both the performance of memory and its antithesis in the performance and by the performance and by me in relation to the performance.

For the experience of performance is also a structuring of memory; leaving the theatre at the end of performance is already to be aware of the excess of forgetfulness, of how much we immediately cannot remember of what has just occurred, of the inadequacy of the attempt to remember as, instead, we create constructs of memory, deliberate attempts to fix the memory of the event. It is not simply that memory is partial and frag-mentary but rather that the degree of the fragmentation, the vast and necessary failure of its partiality, its inability to be impartial, becomes the controlling feature of its creation. Hence there is the insistence with which Simon Forman, our earliest extant extensive reviewer of Shakespeare in performance, in the four reports of productions, three by Shakespeare and one not, that he wrote in his 'Bocke of Plaies' in 1611, writes as it were to and for himself so repeatedly the aggressive command 'Remember', five times in his account of the non-Shakespearean play about Richard II alone. The report becomes a series of instructions to himself to 'Remember therin how ... Also remember how ...

---

[10] Joseph Roach, *Cities of the Dead: Circum-Atlantic Performance* (New York: Columbia University Press, 1996), p. 2.

Remember also ... Remember therin Also howe ... Remember also howe ... ', an aggregation of memories through the conscious act of remembering in the writing of the performance into memory.[11]

So I too remember how, in John Barton's 1981 restaging of his production of *Hamlet* with Michael Pennington at the Aldwych Theatre in London, Hamlet and Horatio sat side-by-side on a bench, audience left, as they toyed with Osric in 5.2. *Hamlet*, the Shakespeare play supremely about memory and remembering, speaks the words 'remember' and 'memory' more often than any other Shakespeare play (thirteen and ten times respectively), together with five occurrences of 'remembrance'. The play's last use of 'remember' occurs in this scene, 'I beseech you, remember' (5.2.105), a line usually a request to Osric to remember that he should put his 'bonnet to his right use; 'tis for the head' (94). But Pennington divided the line, memorably, making 'I beseech you' the request to Osric and then, reaching into the bag he carried with the few objects from his former life that had survived the trip towards England, he pulled something out – what? I don't remember – and showed it to Horatio, asking him to remember its significance, its place in the memory structure of the events performed earlier in the play. The line-reading, as characteristically fresh as so much of Pennington's and Barton's work on the play, also engaged with the production's repeated fascination with memory as theatrical event, marked by the accumulation on the stage of objects, props and pieces of set, that functioned as both a futurity of memory constructed by the production and a memory of the central line of the tradition of performance of this play.[12]

Some years after the performance I asked Pennington about this moment. Initially he did not remember the moment. Then he recalled that he had done this for one or two performances before dropping the idea. The moment of my memory of his Hamlet's memory is accidental, not part of the production of the play as run but a momentary invention, a singularity that becomes forgotten and abandoned as the actor decides not to like what I found I liked enough to remember, value becoming now enshrined in the process of recollection, in the voluntary and involuntary choosing of the memories out of which the production will become constructed. The moment survives only as memory, as the

[11] I use the transcript of 'The Bocke of Plaies' in G. Blakemore Evans and J. J. M. Tobin, eds., *The Riverside Shakespeare*, 2nd edn, (Boston: Houghton Mifflin Company, 1997), pp. 1966–8 (here p. 1967).

[12] The most substantial account of the production, though a limited one, is by Michael L. Greenwald, *Directions by Indirections: John Barton of the Royal Shakespeare Company* (Newark, NJ: University of Delaware Press), pp. 186–97.

recollection of an individual member of the audience, for none of the normal ways in which a performance can be documented can note the event: it will not be in the promptbook, nor in the stage manager's nightly reports, nor in any reviews (themselves, of course, structures of remembering performance, ways of telling readers what the reviewer remembers, finds memorable, wishes them to note as remembered).[13]

The hesitations I have voiced earlier about Casey's formulation of 'collective memory' for its plurality across places and spaces might serve, though, to define the difference between the audience that sees a production on one particular occasion and the audience that sees a production across its entire run. If *Les Misérables* is more or less the same in London or New York or Reykjavik, a series of attempts, as set out in the complex contracts for the show, to reproduce as exactly as practicable the production that Trevor Nunn directed in London, and if a Royal Shakespeare Company production is usually more or less the same in Stratford or in London, we cannot fully mask the variabilities, those memories that cannot be shared by the different collectivities of the different audiences. Even if casting remains constant – and RSC shows are often recast in their move south – the show is never the same two nights running.

Pennington's invention for a brief span of the production's life is a complex statement for the memory of – or do I mean 'by'? – the production. In a case like this the memory is of something invented and then unlearned. Yet, basic to the performance of the scripted play comes the actor's act of memory. Somehow in the process of rehearsal, across the weeks of preparation for performance, actors learn their lines. Their aim is to learn accurately. In the event, they often commit a mistake to memory and then repeat it throughout the run of a production or make a mistake during a performance and then continue with the error. Some actors become remarkably prone to mistakes and the increasing incidence of error is something directors and audiences – and, most vulnerably, other members of the cast – have to decide how to or whether to tolerate. Late in his career, Robert Stephens, whose memory was undoubtedly affected by his alcoholism and generally poor health, played Falstaff in Adrian Noble's production of both parts of *Henry IV* for the RSC in 1991. In the scene where Falstaff gives his own version of the Gadshill robbery, increasing the number of men in buckram suits he fought with at each successive stage of the story-telling, he adds to the, now eleven, men in

---

[13] Michael Pennington does not note the action in his book-length study of the play, *Hamlet: A User's Guide* (London: Nick Hern Books, 1996).

buckram 'three misbegotten knaves in Kendal green' (*1 Henry IV*
2.5.225–6). Every time I saw the production, Stephens turned *Kendal
green* into *Kensal Green*, from a coarse green woollen cloth, originally
made in the town of Kendal in Cumbria in the Lake District in the north
of England, and known as such since the fourteenth century, into the
name of a London suburb, a stop on the Bakerloo line of the London
underground[14] and the location of one of London's biggest cemeteries,
which last may have been the reason it came to Robert Stephens's mind as
an intimation of mortality. What is more, the mistake had become so
ingrained in the performance that Michael Maloney, as Prince Henry,
always responded, a few lines later, 'how couldst thou know these men in
Kensal green' (235–6). The transformation of one place-name into
another is an easy error, especially when the substituted name is more
familiar to someone who lived in London. Not in this case a matter of
forgetting but of remembering, the alteration was carefully remembered
through the run, where frequently, elsewhere in the plays, Stephens
groped for any word that would do when his memory failed.

Professional theatres have long constructed both a space and an
institutionalized role defining the vulnerability of the actors' memory.
OED defines the prompter in its specifically theatrical sense as 'A person
stationed out of sight of the audience, to prompt or assist any actor at a
loss in remembering his part' (2.b). As Alfred Corn noted in his poem
'From the Prompter's Box', this invisibility extends to an effective denial
of the prompter's existence in a conventionalized erasure of the prompter's name: 'No. No, the program never credits Prompter.'[15] Unacknowledged by the audience but identified for the company, the
prompter's presence defined the entire orientation of the stage in the
eighteenth century with, conventionally but not ubiquitously, the side of
the stage on the audience's right and actors' left being known to actors as
'prompt-side', P.S. in the standard abbreviation in promptbooks, and the
opposite side as O.P. (opposite prompt). This spatial definition is also not
part of an audience's experience but, outside the Anglo-American tradition and especially in the structure of European theatres and opera-
houses, the prompter's place is visible even if the individual is not. The
rounded hood at the downstage-centre point of the stage's edge, that
bulge on the line of division between stage and auditorium, is the marker

---

[14] My thanks to my sister Ruth Maxwell for help with the tube-map.
[15] Alfred Corn, 'From The Prompter's Box', *The Nation* 7 June 2004 (www.thenation.com/doc/
20040607/corn).

of the prompter's recognizable concealment. Behind it, in a well below the stage floor, the prompter stands, in opera repeating or mouthing the libretto in the singers' eye-line as they look towards the conductor.[16] Known but in hiding, present but not to be revealed, the European theatre prompter asserts the likelihood of the actors' failure of memory, reminds the audience, through their knowledge of the meaning of this readily apparent physical space on stage, of the fallibility of memory.

In Shakespeare's theatre the prompter or book-holder or book-keeper had functions during a performance that now are the prerogative of the stage manager: cueing entrances and effects, for example. Laurence's Olivier's *Henry V* (1944) shows the prompter, looking rather like Shakespeare, present on stage at audience left, shooing the gentlemen to their onstage stools (never the practice of the Globe), cueing music and entrances as well as following in the book in case an actor should have need of him. The same practice of the visible book-holder has been adopted by Patrick Tucker's Original Shakespeare Company for their performances dependent on actors learning their lines from cue-scripts and with errors of memory and missed cues so common during their unfamiliar mode of work that the prompter is a crucial figure in the audience's perception of their productions. But the prompter at the Globe was offstage, positioned behind the arras or the grating in the stage-doors (depending on whether one agrees with Tiffany Stern or Andrew Gurr and Gabriel Egan),[17] from where the performance could be heard without making this figure who combined stage-management and actors' support seen.

Inadequately learned special speeches might well have needed the prompter's help, since, as John Higgins's *Nomenclature* (1581) defines it, he 'telleth the players their part when they are out and have forgotten'.[18] Benvolio sees the speech that Romeo indicates the masked revellers have ready for their entrance at the Capulet party as something outdated in its prolixity: 'We'll have ... no without-book prologue, faintly spoke / After the prompter, for our entrance' (*Romeo and Juliet* 1.4.4–8). Shakespeare's characters can often be put out of their parts, especially if, like Mote

---

[16] See, for one example among many, the illustrations of the Künstler Theatre in Munich (1907–8) in Richard and Helen Leacroft, *Theatre and Playhouse* (London: Methuen, 1984), pp. 135–6.

[17] Tiffany Stern, 'Behind the Arras: The Prompter's Place in the Shakespearean Theatre', *Theatre Notebook* 55 (2001), 110–18; Andrew Gurr and Gabriel Egan, 'Prompting, Backstage Activity, and the Openings onto the Shakespearean Stage', *Theatre Notebook* 56 (2002), 138–42.

[18] Quoted Stern, 'Behind the Arras', p. 111.

addressing the ladies in *Love's Labour's Lost*, onstage action disturbs the
speaker, however perfectly he has learned his part:

> MOTH. They do not mark me, and that brings me out.
> BEROWNE. Is this your perfectness?
>
> (5.2.173–4)

The early modern prompters and their successors are not seen onstage,
except in a rare example like Frank Bristowe, the prompter to the
Snaggleton circuit of theatres, 'formerly an Officer in the Army', in H. J.
Byron's play *The Prompter's Box* (*c.* 1870), described on his first entrance
as 'an old white-haired man, with bent back, and appearance of age, but
with the remains of a thorough old gentleman'.[19]

But in one area of theatre practice the prompter has needed to have a
particular visibility. Certain non-professional forms of theatre have
assumed that the actors do not need to learn their lines at all and instead
enabled them to rely on a continuous prompt. In 1602, Richard Carew, in
his account of the Cornish 'Guary miracle' plays, noted that 'the players
conne not their parts without books, but are prompted by one called the
Ordinary, who followeth at their back with the booke in his hand, and
telleth them softly what they must pronounce aloud'.[20] It seems at least
probable that the man with stick and book in Jean Fouquet's familiar
image of 'The Martyrdom of Saint Apollonia' and in his less well-known
'The Rape of the Sabine Women' is offering this kind of continuous
prompt. Philip Butterworth has written at length of a modern exemplar
of this figure, the 'maestro' in the *Representación de Moros y Cristianos*
currently performed in the village of Trevelez in Spain, who 'stands
behind the performers, in full view of the audience, and provides them
with all their lines'.[21] In contemporary Mexican soap-operas actors do not
learn their lines at all but are fed lines, moves and emotions by the
prompter through ear-pieces. As an actor reports,

It's easy, because it's one person who speaks, who tells you everything. O.K.
Then they say 'Go, go to the door. Go to the door. Come back, come back,
come back. O Maria I love you. Yeah, me too. Me too. Cry cry cry.'[22]

---

[19] Henry James Byron, *The Prompter's Box. A Story of the Footlights and the Fireside* (n.p., 1870?), p. 6.

[20] Richard Carew, *The Survey of Cornwall* (London, 1602), fol. 71v.

[21] Philip Butterworth, 'Prompting in Full View of the Audience: A Medieval Staging Convention', in
Alan Hindley, ed., *Drama and Community: People and Plays in Medieval Europe* (Medieval Texts
and Cultures of Northern Europe, vol. 1; Turnhout: Brepols Publishers, 1999), pp. 231–47 (p. 234);
see also his 'Book-Carriers: Medieval and Tudor Staging Conventions', *Theatre Notebook* 46
(1992), 15–30.

[22] From Clive James, 'Postcard from Mexico City', Carlton UK TV, 1996, quoted Butterworth,
'Prompting in Full View', p. 245.

In what can be seen as a strange extrapolation of this notion into modern rehearsal practice, Jeremy Whelan has developed the Tape Technique in which actors abandon their books in the rehearsal room and record their roles on tape, then act the scene without speaking while the tape plays, re-record their lines, rehearse again and so on through six iterations, by which time '[you] will probably find that you remember 60 to 90 per cent of the dialogue'.[23]

Unacknowledged though the early modern prompter may have been, later prompters used their unequalled knowledge of their companies to write vitally important theatre histories. John Downes, who became prompter of the Duke's Company in the 1660s, worked in that capacity for the United Company and Betterton's company until he retired in 1706, after which he published *Roscius Anglicanus* (1708), the most substantial and comprehensive single account of Restoration theatre to have appeared. Downes's preface notes his qualifications for the task, lying in his longevity of experience:

The Editor of the ensuing Relation, being long Conversant with the Plays and Actors of the Original Company ... Emboldens him to affirm he is not very Erroneous in his Relation.[24]

William Rufus Chetwood, prompter at the Theatre Royal in the mid eighteenth-century, published a *General History of the Stage* in 1749 and *The British Theatre* in 1750, in both cases using his position as the person who served to correct actors' failures of memory to act as the theatre's public memorialist of its own history. Theatre history can be conceptualized as a form of writing emerging primarily from the prompters' memories, memories which in Downes's case include one spectacular example of an actor's error that may be in part a failure of memory, an error that, if not quite a gravy/glory error, has similar resonances. Noting a performance of *Romeo and Juliet*, Downes reports

Mrs. *Holden* ... enter'd in a *Hurry*, Crying, O my Dear *Count*! She Inadvertently left out, O, in the pronuntiation of the Word *Count*! giving it a Vehement Accent, put the House into such a Laughter, that *London* Bridge at low Water was silence to it.[25]

The error did not drive Mrs Holden from the stage. But the failure of memory or the fear of the failure that that failure would constitute can

---

[23] Jeremy Whelan, *Instant Acting* (Cincinnati: Betterway Books, 1994), p. 18.
[24] John Downes, *Roscius Anglicanus*, ed. Judith Milhous and Robert D. Hume (London: Society for Theatre Research, 1987), p. 2 (=A2r).
[25] Downes, *Roscius Anglicanus*, p. 53.

make even a great actor retire. Charles Macklin, who played Shylock for
nearly fifty years across the eighteenth century and to whom the role must
have been remarkably familiar, played the part yet again in the spring of
1788, at the age of eighty-nine, exhausted after helping to put out a fire
near the theatre the night before. At the end of the scene with Jessica (2.5)
his memory failed and he apologized to the audience for 'a terror of mind
I never in my life felt before; it has totally destroyed my corporeal as well
as mental faculties'.[26] The fear of their memory failing at some point in a
run leads others now to retire from the stage and stick to films and
television where the memory can be short-term and retakes mask the
problems. The fear is central to the process of performing, as Shakespeare
notes at the start of Sonnet 23, 'As an unperfect actor on the stage / Who
with his fear is put besides his part' (1–2). Even in rehearsal, at the point
at which an actor is off-book, needing a prompt, acknowledging publicly
the failure of memory it involves, is painful. As Antony Sher commented,
during the rehearsal process for *Richard III*, 'Each time I have to take a
prompt it feels like a tiny humiliation.'[27]

Actors learn their roles in remarkably different ways. What works for
one person, for example writing out the role long-hand, will not work for
another who needs, for instance, to say the lines aloud to a listener over
and over again or another who learns by rote each time adding one line to
those previously learned. Carol Rutter's chapter explores this further.

Yet what I find most remarkable is the virtual silence in books on actor
training on how to remember the lines. A search through the relevant
section of the library produced not a single passage, not even, as one
might have expected, a number of helpful suggestions for the novice actor
to experiment with. When, for instance, Peter Barkworth, a successful
actor himself, wrote a section in his popular book of hints for actors,
About Acting, on 'Learning the Lines', he urges being off-book before
rehearsals begin but gives no indication how the learning might happen.[28]
Among the many books on my shelves aimed at the budding
Shakespearean actor, only Adrian Brine, in his *A Shakespearian Actor
Prepares*, devotes a section to it, called, predictably, 'How Do You

---

[26] William W. Appleton, *Charles Macklin: An Actor's Life* (Cambridge, Mass.: Harvard University
Press, 1960), p. 226.

[27] Antony Sher, *Year of the King* (London: Chatto and Windus, 1985), p. 130. See also Lois Potter's
excellent article, ' "Nobody's Perfect": Actors' Memories and Shakespeare's Plays of the 1590s',
Shakespeare Survey 42 (Cambridge: Cambridge University Press, 1990), pp. 85–97.

[28] Peter Barkworth, *The Complete About Acting* (London: Methuen Drama, 1991), pp. 17–20.

Remember All Those Lines?'[29] But, after two brief pages on the need for a precise memory and on Elizabethan memory-systems, Brine relies on the assumption that '[t]o commit a passage to memory, it helps to plug into that chamber of the brain where sounds and rhythms are stored – to make contact with the musical part of the memory'.[30] After which he sets off on the familiar clichéd trail of alliteration and Shakespeare's musical harmonies.

In a superb study of the relationship of actors' memories to Shakespeare's writing in the 1590s, published in 1990, Lois Potter commented that '[a]lthough the study of memory is an important branch of psychology, I have been unable to find any work devoted to the specific problems of actors'.[31] But through the early 1990s Helga and Tony Noice published a series of studies, culminating in a book, reporting experimental data on how actors remember lines. Working with professional actors, a mnemonist and control groups of students, and accepting actors' statements to them that they did not use rote learning as their standard process, the Noices documented the use of gist learning, plan recognition systems, and the creation of problem-solving units by the actors.[32] The test subjects proved to learn by elaborating the texts, working through explanatory processes designed to understand the character and the reason for each line, connecting them together through sequencing the explanations. Even though these methods usually result in a lack of verbatim learning among most people, the Noices showed that, for professional actors, the results were unexpectedly accurate. It seemed to them that, even in cases where actors were presented with a segment of text for a comparatively short period, rather than the weeks of investigation that constitute the modern rehearsal process, the analytic processes ingrained in their professional practice led to similar investigations of the text, a

---

[29] Adrian Brine and Michael York, *A Shakespearian Actor Prepares* (Lyme, NH: Smith and Kraus, Inc., 2000), pp. 280–9.

[30] Brine and York, *A Shakespearian Actor*, p. 282.   [31] Potter, '*Nobody's Perfect*', p. 86.

[32] See, for example, Helga Noice, 'The Role of Explanations and Plan Recognition in the Learning of Theatrical Scripts', *Cognitive Science* 15 (1991), 425–60; Helga Noice and Tony Noice, 'The Effects of Segmentation on the Recall of Theatrical Material' *Poetics* 22 (1993), 51–67; and their 'An Example of Role Preparation by a Professional Actor: A Think-Aloud Protocol' *Discourse Processes* 18 (1994), 345–69. Their work is summarized in 'The Mental Processes of Professional Actors as Examined through Self-Report, Experimental Investigation and Think-Aloud Protocol', in Roger J. Kreuz and Mary Sue MacNealy, eds., *Empirical Approaches to Literature and Aesthetics* (Norwood, NJ: Ablex Publishing Corporation, 1996), pp. 361–77. See Tony Noice and Helga Noice, *The Nature of Expertise in Professional Acting: A Cognitive View* (Mahwah, NJ: Lawrence Erlbaum Associates, 1997) – my thanks to Lyn Tribble for pointing me to the monograph. Noice and Noice corroborate, using different materials, my account above of the infrequency of exploration of memory processes in manuals for actor training (*The Nature of Expertise*, pp. 1–8).

serious and in-depth study that, by developing an inwardness in the understanding of the mental processes of the character, resulted in memorization of what that character speaks.

In one experiment they set the actors up against a professional mnemonist who used his own techniques derived ultimately from the long traditions of the *ars memoriae*.[33] The data showed actors basing their memory processes on role interpretation through 'micro-level' analysis. They conclude

Although the actor's strategy is directed towards deriving the deep meaning of the text, the process involves attending to the exact words ... It appears that actors do not memorize their scripts *per se* but use a unique strategy that concentrates on the underlying meaning but nevertheless produces word-for-word retention. At no time did the actors attempt to memorize the words directly, but rather tried to discern why the character would use those particular words to express that particular thought.[34]

As it happens, at least one professional actor, Anne Bancroft, used instead the modes of learning derived from the techniques of the professional mnemonist they studied, Harry Lorayne.[35]

While the Noices' investigation make good sense in relation to modern actors, especially to American actors trained in contemporary modes of actor-theory and working on modern texts, they are of course alien to the work of early-modern actors and to the early-modern practice of memory. Since the work of Frances Yates on *The Art of Memory*, there has been comparatively little work on early-modern mnemotechniques.[36] Instead, the major thrust of research has pushed earlier to medieval systems of memory, through the exhilarating work by Mary Carruthers on the ways in which the emphasis on memory and the structures used to describe it and encourage its practice made use of a series of repeated modellings of the space and processes of memory, primarily the image of the blank tablet waiting for inscription, the placing of memory across a structure such as the hand or a seraph's wing, and the choice of a room or storehouse in the imagination in which the objects to be memorized are

---

[33] Helga Noice and Tony Noice, 'Two Approaches to Learning a Theatrical Script', in Ulric Neisser and Ira E. Hyman, Jr, eds., *Memory Observed: Remembering in Natural Contexts*, 2nd edn, (New York: Worth Publishers, 2000), pp. 444–56.

[34] Noice and Noice 'Two Approaches', p. 454.   [35] Noice and Noice 'Two Approaches', p. 447.

[36] Frances Yates, *The Art of Memory* (London: Routledge and Kegan Paul, 1966). But see, for example, M. T. Jones-Davies, ed., *Mémoire et oubli au temps de la renaissance* (Paris: Honoré Champion, 2002) and William N. West, '"No Endlesse Moniment": Artificial Memory and Memorial Artifact in Early Modern England', in Susannah Radstone and Katharine Hodgkin, eds., *Regimes of Memory* (London: Routledge, 2003), pp. 61–75.

to be placed.[37] Medieval memory systems were not greatly interested in Quintilian's concerns with the *memoria verborum*, that particular branch of the arts of memory concerned with verbal memory, precise remembering of words, a central feature of rhetoric, though one that Quintilian despised if its purpose was simply exact memory.[38]

In Lina Bolzoni's superb work on early-modern memory techniques, *The Gallery of Memory* (in Italian in 1995, translated into English in 2001), the importance of the theatre as a place of memory becomes ever more strongly visible. Through her exploration of the topic we can see the influential place of the theatre as a site of memory in, for instance, Anton Francesco Doni's theatre of fame in the 1560s.[39] We are not a long way here from the function of theatre as the space of memory that Marvin Carlson has recently charted in *The Haunted Stage*, his definition of 'The Theatre as Memory Machine'. The sense in which theatre is intimately bound up with systems of memory is fundamental to theatre; as Herbert Blau states: 'theatre is ... a function of remembrance. Where memory is, theatre is.'[40] The frequency of these early modern memory theatres underscores Frances Yates's mistake of assuming that Robert Fludd's images of memory theatres in his *History of the Two Worlds* (1619) were, in fact, images of the Globe Theatre in London.[41] When Hamlet states his response to the ghost's injunction,

> Remember thee?
> Ay, thou poor ghost, while memory holds a seat
> In this distracted globe
>
> (1.5.95–7),

he is imagining his head as a theatre, the space for a memory-system, while the audience, in response, memorializes his memory in the Globe Theatre in which they sat – or stood. The layered pun is of the mind as a theatre and the theatre as a mind, the mind as a theatre of memory and the theatre as a place where the mind investigates how it remembers.

---

[37] See Mary Carruthers, *The Book of Memory* (Cambridge: Cambridge University Press, 1990) and Mary Carruthers and Jan M. Ziolkowski, eds., *The Medieval Craft of Memory* (Philadelphia: University of Pennsylvania Press, 2002). See also Bruce R. Smith's essay in this volume for other modes of early modern memory.

[38] See Carruthers and Ziolkowski, *Medieval Craft of Memory*, p. 10.

[39] Lina Bolzoni, *The Gallery of Memory* (Toronto: University of Toronto Press, 2001), pp. 196–204.

[40] Quoted in Marvin Carlson, *The Haunted Stage: The Theatre as Memory Machine* (Ann Arbor, MI: The University of Michigan Press, 2001), p. [vii].

[41] For Yates's work in this area see *The Art of Memory*, pp. 320–67, and the extended argument in her *Theatre of the World* (Chicago: University of Chicago Press, 1969).

What actors did in the period to remember may have included such an *ars memoriae*, art of memory, but was especially concerned with finding processes for exact memory. In a system with very limited rehearsal time, a process of individual learning of role from cue-scripts and with actors having virtually no access to the entire text of a scene, it becomes absolutely crucial that the actor is word-perfect accurate with his cues. Give an actor the wrong cue and he would have been unlikely to have known what was happening. The only major modern investigation of actors' recall (conducted in 1986) shows roughly the same thing: the recall is accurately driven by cues.[42] The amateur actor Flute, as Thisbe in *A Midsummer Night's Dream*, learns his part 'cues and all' and speaks it as he has learned it, much to the annoyance of Peter Quince, his equally amateur director (3.1.94). Having been given the roll of paper with his own speeches and the last few words of the preceding speech as a cue, the 'parts' Quince handed out at the end of the casting scene with the injunction 'I am to entreat you, request you, and desire you to con them by tomorrow night' (1.2.92–3), Flute has indeed 'conned [it] with cruel pain' (5.1.80).

Nick Bottom's instructions to the rest of the cast also recognizes the agony of learning: 'Take pains; be perfect' (1.2.101). Actors learned their lines on their own, an activity of study. The aim was indeed to be 'perfect', in the sense the *OED* defines as '[h]aving learnt one's lesson or part thoroughly' (*a*.2.c), with, as one of its earliest examples in this sense, Costard's comment in *Love's Labour's Lost* 'I hope I was perfect. I made a little fault in "great"' (5.2.553–4). Being 'word-perfect', a coupling *OED* dates no earlier than 1894 (word, *n*. 29), involves study. Snug the joiner needs his part as soon as possible, 'for I am slow of study' (1.2.63) which *OED* interprets as the earliest example of the theatrical sense of 'the action of committing to memory one's part in a play' (study, *n*. 6.b).[43] Tiffany Stern, in her work on the history of rehearsal, has found numerous examples in the period of this sense of studying[44] but her later work also shows that revision to plays tended to change the middle of speeches rather than the beginnings and endings, working along part lines

---

[42] See William L. Oliver and K. Anders Ericsson, 'Repertory Actors' Memory for their Parts', *Program of the Eighth Annual Conference of the Cognitive Science Society* (Hillsdale, N.J.: Lawrence Erlbaum Associates, 1986), pp. 399–406.

[43] Compare also the verb form, 'Of an actor: To commit to memory and exercise oneself in the rendering of (a part)' (study *v*. 9.b, with examples from *Twelfth Night*, 1.5.171–2 and *Hamlet* 2.2.542–3). Note also the association of study and pain in Viola's comment 'I took great pains to study it' (*Twelfth Night* 1.5.188).

[44] Tiffany Stern, *Rehearsal from Shakespeare to Sheridan* (Oxford: Clarendon Press, 2000), pp. 61–4.

and ensuring that the cues are left 'intact and so does not force more than one actor to relearn his part'.[45] Like Harriet Walter's transformation of *glory* into *gravy*, the beginning and ending of the speech, like that for a word, is a crucial part of the scene's momentum.

In 1988 Lois Potter surveyed the actors in the English Shakespeare Company's cycle of the histories to ask them about their acts of memory, particularly significant when the actors were playing numerous roles across the sequence. There was one remarkable example of the gravy train:

John Darrell, who had to say 'Good my lord of Lancaster' in one play and 'My Lord of Gloucester' in another, found himself addressing Richard of Gloucester as 'Good my lord of Lanc-, Leicester – Gloucester' ('all famous cheeses', he pointed out).[46]

But it is, inevitably, the major catastrophe that is recalled and the small acts of false memory that are forgotten. In the only substantial study I know of the details of actors' forgetfulness, of their mislearning and misremembering, Laurie Maguire studied six of the BBC Shakespeare television productions, checking the words spoken on the videotapes against the play-text of the performance version that the BBC published. As she comments, 'critics interested in memorial error can collate the BBC text as published with the text as performed'.[47] The time pressures of production meant that scenes could not be endlessly reshot in search of verbal accuracy. As the script editor commented, 'the version that is finally chosen for transmission has to be the best in terms of performance rather than absolute textual correctness'.[48] The six plays produced 598 errors, many tiny changes of quantity or possessives, tense or mood, but many too more substantial ranging from small additions (O yes, truly, then, why, come, ay, O, and other extra-metrical versions of 'umm' and 'er'), to small substitutions ('Well met Hastings!' for 'How now Hastings!') to changes of number (Caesar's 'three and thirty wounds' became 'three and twenty wounds') to garbled transpositions and major omissions.[49]

Maguire's interest in these minute processes of actors' memory was generated by a concern with whether a group of printed versions of early

---

[45] Tiffany Stern, *Making Shakespeare: From Stage to Page* (London: Routledge, 2004), p. 135.

[46] Potter, 'Actors' Memories', p. 94.

[47] Laurie E. Maguire, *Shakespearian Suspect Texts: The 'Bad' Quartos and Their Contexts* (Cambridge: Cambridge University Press, 1996), p. 136.

[48] David Snodin, quoted Maguire, p. 135.

[49] Maguire summarizes her evidence and gives numerous examples on pp. 136–46.

modern plays, including but not limited to the texts once known as the 'bad quartos' of Shakespeare, could indeed be the product of what is called memorial reconstruction, the reconstruction by one or more actors in an Elizabethan theatre company of the whole play from their knowledge of their own parts and their memories of hearing the whole play, a version that could then be sold off to a publisher without the approval of the theatre company which owned the play. Though there was an argument at one stage that such a reconstruction could have been done by someone taking down the play in shorthand or by memorial reconstruction from the audience and though we actually have examples of such playhouse reporters for Spanish drama of the period, there seems little likelihood that what these early modern English texts represent was the product of the phenomenally developed mnemotechniques of an audience member.[50] Instead, memorial reconstruction is seen as a moment when the actor or a small group of actors remember the whole play, not just their own roles, using their memories to make the text anew, to move the text, in particular, from a context of performance to one of print-culture, to make it possible for their own memories of the creation of performance to become others' experiences of the play as read text.

Though there is inevitably a certain amount of scepticism about the process, Betty Shapin showed, in a little-known article published in 1944, that even a modern actor could reconstruct a scene from memory with both a reasonable degree of accuracy and a tendency towards exactly the kinds of errors that the theorists of early modern memorial reconstruction had supposed, concluding that

> The types of variant in the imperfect and authentic texts of *Hamlet*, attributed by Dr Duthie to the faulty memory of a hypothetical reporter making a deduced memorial reconstruction, are identical with the variants in the imperfect and authentic texts of *Witch Hunt*, which are known to be due to the faulty memory of an actual reporter making a deliberate memorial reconstruction.[51]

At one stage it was argued that the First Quarto of *King Lear* was indeed such a text and Duthie based his 1949 edition of the play on exactly this now discredited assumption, hypothesizing that it was 'a memorial reconstruction made by the entire company', perhaps made

---

[50] On the work of a *memorión*, see Jesús Tronch-Pérez's fascinating article, 'Playtext Reporters and *Memoriones*: Suspect Texts in Shakespeare and Spanish Golden Age Drama', in Tom Clayton et al., eds., *Shakespeare and the Mediterranean* (Newark, NJ: University of Delaware Press, 2004), pp. 270–85.

[51] See Betty Shapin, 'An Experiment in Memorial Reconstruction', *Modern Language Review* 39 (1944), 9–17 (p. 17). My thanks to Thomas Pettit for drawing my attention to this article.

King Lear 1.1.108-20 (Folio text)	*King Lear* 1.1.108-20 (Henry's text)
Let it be so. Thy truth then be thy dower;	Let it be so. Thy truth then be thy dower;
For, by the sacred radiance of the sun,	For, by the sacred radiance of the sun,
The mysteries of Hecate and the night,	By the mysteries of Hecate and the night,
By all the operation of the orbs	By all the operation of the orbs
From whom we do exist and cease to be,	By whom we do exist and cease to be,
Here I disclaim all my paternal care,	Here I disclaim all my paternal care,
Propinquity, and property of blood,	Proximity, and property of blood,
And as a stranger to my heart and me	And as a stranger to my heart and me
Hold thee from this for ever.	Hold thee from this for ever.
The barbarous Scythian,	The barbarous Chronos,
Or he that makes his generation messes	Who makes his generation dishes
To gorge his appetite, shall to my bosom	To gorge his appetite, shall to my bosom
Be as well neighboured, pitied, and relieved	Be a friend, neighbour and relative
As thou, my sometime daughter.	As thou, my sometime daughter

40. *King Lear*, 1.1.108-20, Folio text and Henry's text compared.

'during a provincial tour, the company having left the prompt-book (and the author's manuscript also, if the prompt-book was a transcript) in London'.[52]

But I want now to offer a different image of memorial reconstruction of *King Lear*. An actor is rehearsing the first scene. It is a group rehearsal in the early modern sense and, though many of the rest of the company still have scripts in their hands, sheets of text rolled up, something approximating to the roll on which the role is written, he is speaking from memory. The speech is the oath that denies paternity, the terrifying and impossible separation from Cordelia (figure 40). The first few lines are accurate enough. There are two tiny changes: 'The mysteries of Hecate and the night' (1.1.110) has an added extrametrical word, starting the line now with 'By', and 'From whom we do exist' becomes 'By whom we do exist' (112).[53] The two changes increase the rhythmic repetition: so that each of the four lines is more emphatically anaphoric in their syntax: 'by

---

[52] See G. I. Duthie, *Shakespeare's 'King Lear': A Critical Edition* (Oxford: Basil Blackwell, 1949), pp. 73-5.

[53] All the passages quoted from *The King is Alive* are my transcriptions from the DVD version. In a few cases it is difficult to be quite sure about the words spoken but that does not affect my argument at any point.

the sacred radiance ... [By] [t]he mysteries of Hecate ... By all the operations ... [By] whom we do exist' (109–12). This is the kind of change that any actor might make and it is likely that no director, other than perhaps Sir Peter Hall, would bother to pick him up on it.

But then the speech begins to veer a little further from the standard track. 'Propinquity, and property of blood' becomes 'Proximity, and property of blood' (114). The stranger word, which textual scholars would prefer as the *lectio difficilior*, has become a more familiar one, an approximation, a synonym. Is the mistake that of the actor, an accident of false memory, or is it a deliberate one, perhaps an instruction from the director, a choice to use a word easier for a modern audience to understand? Given that the Royal Shakespeare Company changed the title of Philip Massinger's play *Believe As You List* to *Believe What You Want* for their production in 2005, the idea that one might make such small changes for clarification seems reasonable enough and 'proximity' is rhythmically and phonically remarkably proximate to 'propinquity', both four-syllable words with the same vowel-sequence 'o-i-i-i'. The lines start to drift further. 'The barbarous Scythian, / Or he that makes his generation messes' becomes 'The barbarous Chronos / Who makes his generation dishes' (116–17). To some extent, 'dishes' for 'messes' is a synonymous substitution but it misses the messiness of 'messes', even if the sense of apportionment and portion-control is the same. The rhythm of the second line has slipped badly, losing a whole foot, and, though Chronos did chop up his children, only an audience unduly sensitive to the racial slur against Scythians and classically-educated enough to understand the reference to Greek mythology would prefer the change.

From 'Be as well neighboured, pitied, and relieved' to 'Be a friend, neighbour and relative' (119) is pretty catastrophic. Shakespearean verse most often depends for its energy on the force of the verb, especially the noun-turned-verb or as here a participial adjective. 'Be a ... neighbour' is far weaker than 'Be as well neighboured'. There is no source for 'friend' other than the tendency to list and 'relative' while perhaps connected with 'relieved' simply creates a series of possible social relationships where Lear's adjectives have to do with degrees of active social interactions: the fact of behaving as a neighbour, the emotional response of pity, the help to meet human needs through relief.

In rehearsal, these last changes ought to result in an abrupt halt. In performance, though an actor might create this jumble, someone sensitive enough to the rhythms of Shakespearean verse would probably know there was something wrong and check before the next night. But this passage is not taken from such a context. It is, instead, an act of memorial reconstruction or rather, to complicate the issue, the performance of a representation of memorial reconstruction. It comes from Kristian Levring's remarkable film *The King is Alive* (1999). A group of tourists – English, American and French – and their African driver are lost in the desert, stranded at a long-abandoned mine when they have lost their way and their coach's engine has died. There is nothing to do but wait for help while one of the group, the cock-sure survival-savvy Jack, heads off across the desert to the nearest village, some days' walk away, directed there by the old African, Kanana, who is the place's sole inhabitant, whose language only Jack speaks and whose voice is the choric voice-over, retrospective commentary to the film, a rare, possibly unique, example of a voice-over that needs subtitles.

After a few days Henry, an Englishman, is sitting under the shade where Kanana, unmoving, is always seen, looking at the others reacting in various ways to their plight. Henry muses on what he sees: 'Some fantastic striptease act of basic human needs. Is man no more than this? It's good old Lear again.' Charged by the analogy he sets out to write out the play from memory, 'as much as I can remember of it or what I think I can remember', casts the others and begins to rehearse it. When one of the group collapses with heart trouble, he takes over the role of Lear. The rehearsal I have been describing follows this. The changes in the text are not an actor's mistakes, nor the deliberate changes of a director; they are the text as Henry has remembered it. The errors are the effect of the limitations of memory, the impossibility of remembering the play. Henry reconstructs quickly and easily. Though the film deliberately occludes its own time-scale, Henry writes with a fluency and an accuracy that is enviable. This is, after all, not Ray Bradbury's *Fahrenheit 451*, where people resisting the state have trained themselves as mnemonists, aiming to become the human embodiment of a particular book, becoming the means of preserving a novel in a world where all texts are marked for destruction.

In a powerful way, especially given the painfulness of experiencing *King Lear*, the film becomes a commentary on Virgil's famous line in *The Aeneid*: 'forsan et haec olim meminisse iuvabit', 'one day perhaps he will rejoice to have remembered even these things' (line 203). Yet Henry's memory proves finally to be without joy and extremely painful. In the desolate last moments of the film, as the survivors mourn the death of their Cordelia and as the arrival of two truckloads of itinerant African workers brings them not only rescue but also an audience, the remainder of the cast speak fragments of the text, moments that come back to their memories, primarily but not entirely from the play's end, fragments that are reread, reheard in the light of the events of the film's, rather than the play's, tragic climax. Threateningly, the interlocking of the play and the performers, the dual catastrophe, makes *King Lear* both cause and effect of the film's cast's brutality. Yet in the film's narrative there is a strange throwback to a kind of non-Shakespearean text: though its Cordelia dies, its two Lears do not. Early in the film, soon after the project of rehearsal begins, one character asks his wife what happens in the play: 'And you get to play the evil daughter, right?' 'Sure, I get to play the real bitch. You don't have to worry, you know; nobody has to fall in love and everybody gets to die in the end.' But neither statement is true: Henry's lament as Lear over the body of Gina, his Cordelia, is a desolate expression of love; and this is a drama without a mountain of corpses.

For Shakespeareans, the understanding of Henry's memory processes is complicated by two factors. The first is that the director, his co-scriptwriter and most of the crew are Danish. Though he had a Danish scholar's advice, Lars Kaaber, Levring had, as he said, the problem that 'English is not my language and I had to prepare myself very rigorously for this. I had to read a lot.'[54] The second is that, as Levring comments, '[a] lot of the actors have Shakespeare in their roots'.[55] Henry is played by David Bradley and the cast also includes David Calder, Janet McTeer, Lia Williams and Miles Anderson, all well known as Shakespearean actors, some with many years' experience with the Royal Shakespeare Company. Bradley might well be able to write out *King Lear*; the actor, in other words, haunts the character. The kinds of errors that, elsewhere in the film, are made by McTeer and Williams are an almost comic layering of their own knowledge of the play, just as there is the comedy of an actor playing a character unable to act.

Martha Nochimson, whose article on *The King is Alive* seems to be based solely on the film as viewed, identifies Henry as 'an Englishman with a long career behind him as an actor and director'[56] but there is nothing to prove that. We see Henry running the rehearsals and giving the actors tips on how to breathe and how to get into their characters but

---

[54] From an interview with Levring in Richard Kelly, *The Name of This Book is Dogme 95* (London, Faber and Faber, 2000), p. 213. On Dogme 95 I found the following works also helpful: Shari Roman, *Digital Babylon* (Hollywood, CA: IFilm Publishing, 2001); Mette Hjort and Scott MacKenzie, eds., *Purity and Provocation: Dogma 95* (London: BFI Publishing, 2003); Jack Stevenson, *Dogme Uncut* (Santa Monica, CA: Santa Monica Press, 2003).

[55] Stevenson, *Dogme Uncut*.

[56] Martha Nochimson, '*The King Is Alive*', *Film Quarterly* 55.2 (2001), 48–54 (51).

it is the kind of thing I might suggest and I have not directed a play since I was eighteen. Richard Kelly, outlining the film's action as an introduction to an interview with Levring, describes Henry as 'an English scholar now reduced to the chore of script-reading'.[57] Kelly seems to have had access to the filmscript for there is nothing in the film itself – or at least the DVD release version – to identify Henry as an English scholar, though the character does make a living reading scripts: *King Lear* is remembered on the backs of the pages of one of them. Once implanted, the description is dangerously attractive: this feat of memorial reconstruction is not by an actor remembering a play he was in, nor by a director recalling his production, but by a scholar for whom the play is familiar as an object of study, a resource, a lens through which the world can be viewed. It is, as it were, *King Lear* remembered by one of the authors in this volume rather than by a theatre worker.

Of course the play becomes the bleak resource through which this motley group can be examined. But Levring resists the neatness of reading each tourist against a character. If McTeer's Liz is both Goneril and Regan, 'the evil daughter', it is Catherine, the French self-described intellectual who, rejecting the offered role of Cordelia, refuses to be in the play at all, who becomes the poisoning Goneril, making Gina ill by damaging one of the rusted tins of carrots which, comically, is all the cast find to eat. It is David Calder's Charles, the only father in the film, the production's Gloucester, who, after killing Gina, hangs himself, becoming both an iconic image of a dead Cordelia and revealed as the film's true Fool, the role his mousey daughter-in-law is playing. Throughout, then, this both is and is not Lear, the memory both a recall and an impossibility, the play both made memorably present and permanently, appallingly absent.

Throughout the film, the play's language is available for use but also never understood, at least until the final sequence. On the one hand, the character playing Goneril rehearses her kiss of Oswald (4.2.22) over and over again, playing out her seduction of the character playing Oswald repeatedly in an aggressive act towards her husband, the production's Albany and Kent, using the text to mock her '[m]ilk-livered man' (32). On the other, as the observer Kanana comments on the isolation that the rehearsal process identifies, one from another: 'I can say they were afraid but they didn't hold each other. They began to say words. Words made them forget. For a while they went round and said words without talking

[57] Kelly, *The Name of this Book*, p. 209.

to each other. Henry listened ... Together they said words. They still
didn't say them to each other ... I didn't understand a word they said.
Nor did they. I think that Henry understood what they said'.[58] 'Words
made them forget.' If in one sense Kanana means that they used *King
Lear* to make them forget the desperate condition of waiting for rescue, in
another he also means that *King Lear* is also a sign of what they are
forgetting, the Western assumptions of culture from which they are
increasingly separated as the torment continues. Though Henry understands the words he is no more able to intervene and prevent the ending
of their play than any of the others. In this space remembering *King Lear*
is a sign of having forgotten so much else.

There is another layering in the film-making method of *The King is
Alive*. The film is identified as *Dogme #4*, the fourth of the films made
according to the Dogme 95 vow of chastity, the attempt by a group of
Danish film-makers, led by Lars von Trier and Thomas Vinterberg, to
resist the methods of Hollywood. Their films would be shot entirely on
location with no props or sets brought in, with no use of non-diegetic
sound (no music, for instance), by a handheld camera, with no special
lighting or filters and the director must not be credited.[59] The techniques
of *The King is Alive* must then be read against the manifesto (with one or
two fallings-off needing to be acknowledged) and in turn against the
techniques of mainstream movies. But it can also be read against the
Shakespearean theatre, a space of authenticity, a memory of a triumphant
form of theatre-making with which the techniques of twenty-first century
theatre seem in tension and which has come to function for us as a dream
and memory. Making theatre in the desert might in one sense be seen as a
yearning for the Elizabethan stage while the forms of filming, in their
rejection of the inauthentic, are a denial of the metonymic processes that
fundamentally underpin that mode of theatre. If Dogme 95 is an attack
on a form of illusion, it is in this case a memory of a theatre practice that
was always illusionistic, from its casting of males as females to the 'four or
five most vile and ragged foils' which 'much disgrace ... / The name of
Agincourt' (*Henry V* 4.0.49–52).

In Marvin Carlson's formulation of theatre as a haunted space, theatre
practice, like this example of Dogme 95 film-making, is endlessly haunted
by the memory of Shakespeare and of the early modern theatre. I want

---

[58] These comments are taken from three different moments in the film, the ellipses marking the
separate sources.
[59] For the text of the manifesto, see, for instance, Hjort and MacKenzie, *Purity and Provocation*,
pp. 199–200.

finally to turn from *The King is Alive* as a space of the recovered memory of a particular play to a different kind of recovery of a memory of Shakespeare. If theatre is the space in which the cultural memory of Shakespeare is acute in anglophone cultures, then in Germany that memory becomes peculiarly physicalised as weight. As Michael Patterson puts it, 'Shakespeare is felt by the Germans to be *vorbelastet* (weighed down with all that has gone before).'[60] That weight can be articulated, of course, as a set of memories of Shakespeare that have little or nothing to do with an early modern construction of the plays, depending instead on an entire cultural history of appropriation. In the 1970s the German theatre director Peter Stein confronted the problem as the necessary steps in research to take his company, the Schaubühne, towards a production of a Shakespeare play (eventually *As You Like It*, initially unknown). With what can seem almost like a parody of Teutonic thoroughness, the ensemble – actors, directors, assistant directors, dramaturgs – met for two years, from 1971 to 1973, under the guidance of the playwright Botho Strauss, for Shakespeare seminars, reading the plays together, considering the potential of particular plays to be performed by the company, a rather difficult process, given that, as one actor recalled, 'we wanted to choose one suited for the complete casting of our ensemble group, with a fair part for each person, and with no old leading roles – since our ensemble is made up of younger people'.[61]

After a hiatus, the group started working again in 1975, turning from Shakespeare texts to exploring Elizabethan culture and social organization, researching the historical and cultural contexts for Shakespeare, working from extensive reading lists on contemporary writers, science, philosophy, politics, theatrical forms and so on. Each actor learned new skills (playing the lute, singing madrigals) and presented the skills and the research results at weekly meetings. By the end of 1976, five years after the beginnings of the process, and still hesitant about actually producing a Shakespeare play, Stein created a show that presented the results of the research across two long evenings. The production had the English title *Shakespeare's Memory*, a title which enabled a confluence of two senses of memory, expressed in German by two different words: '*Erinnerung* (the thing remembered) and *Gedächtnis* (the faculty of memory)'.[62]

---

[60] Michael Patterson, *Peter Stein* (Cambridge: Cambridge University Press, 1981), p. 123. My account of Stein's work is heavily dependent on Patterson's book and on Peter Lackner's article, 'Stein's Path to Shakespeare', *The Drama Review: TDR* 21.2 (1977), 79–102.

[61] Elke Petri, quoted Lackner, 'Stein's Path', p. 81.   [62] Patterson, *Peter Stein*, p. 125.

The spectacle – and the scale and visual splendour of the events necessitate seeing it as spectacle – contained a vast array of materials, from a selection of folk drama including a mumming play to Elizabeth's Armada speech at Tilbury, from a huge cross-section of an Elizabethan ship to Erasmus's philosophical dialogue 'The Fish Meal' (played while the audience sat and ate a meagre banquet), from sections of Burton's *Anatomy of Melancholy* to parts of Giordano Bruno's *The Feast of Ash Wednesday*. At the end of the second evening the actors performed thirty fragments of Shakespeare plays, mostly soliloquies, on a huge structure created from all the pageant wagons, tables and platforms used throughout, dubbed Shakespeare's island.

Condemned by some reviewers, especially for the poor performance of the Shakespeare extracts which had, after all, been the purpose of the whole mammoth exercise, *Shakespeare's Memory* functioned effectively as the enabling exercise for Stein to move towards a promenade production of *As You Like It* the following year. If on the one hand the recovery and construction of a memory of Shakespeare seemed to be effectively stating that the understanding of the plays depend on our recognition of the otherness of history, something that German appropriation of Shakespeare found deeply problematic in that context of appropriation emblematized by the concept of *unser Shakespeare*, on the other hand the theatricality that defined one aspect of the presentation of these recovered memories that created the show warred with the academicism of other aspects of it so that the excitement of the research and the commitment of the actors to this prolonged process turned into the pride with which the trophies from the library work were displayed. As the reviewer in *Die Zeit* commented, this pride 'is sometimes childish, often an intimidating and precocious showing-off ("look, this is how educated you have to be to understand Shakespeare")'.[63]

From our perspective the problem of Stein's ensemble's scholasticism is exacerbated by the inadequacies of its output precisely as research, for the extent to which these particular accumulations of the materials drawn from a broad European intellectual tradition, often materials unknown in early modern England, could conjoin with the local English vernacular forms of folk-play or historical record is both vulnerable and dubious. As a performance of a representation of the specificities of Shakespeare's imaginative memory, the personal memory of the writer, the contextual sources that generate the writing and hence the possibility of performance

---

[63] Patterson, *Peter Stein*, p. 131.

itself, *Shakespeare's Memory* looks grotesquely inadequate in its definition of the structures that enabled that cultural formation. The materials of *Shakespeare's Memory* were too emphatically defined by an educated and aristocratic world, inadequately responsive to the everyday. As a performance of a representation of a constructed European concept of the context for that creation, it emblematises a particular, local formation of memory, a mark of a German intellectual and theatrical tradition transformed into performance. We can see for instance how the investigation of popular dramatic forms in *Shakespeare's Memory*, something that, by and large, the main line of scholarly research had ignored, engaged with Robert Weimann's study of *Shakespeare and the Popular Tradition in the Theatre*, first published in German in 1967, though not translated into English until 1978.[64]

In one particular way, though, the production of *Shakespeare's Memory* allowed the audience a free play to create its/their particular memories. Set in a vast space, performed in multiple locations with the audience strolling between them, this promenade production made it possible for the audience member continually to redefine his/her relationship to the show, to watch or not to watch, even, in some sections, to ask an actor to repeat material. Somewhere between performance and museum (or museum as performance), *Shakespeare's Memory* redefined the audience's ability to remember. A monstrous representation of the kind of work that a dramaturg does in German theatre institutions, *Shakespeare's Memory* has to be the largest programme-note ever constructed, an accompaniment and preparation for the audience to a Shakespeare production as yet unrehearsed, a kind of proleptic memory of a production yet to be staged.

But *Shakespeare's Memory* also defined what these actors had been able to recall, to turn into Shakespeare's memory, partly, at least, as a function of their fear of forgetting how to play Shakespeare's plays at all. Remembering Shakespeare in this way was a means to approach the fear that Shakespeare generates, the fear of inadequacy in tackling the plays in production but also the fear of forgetting that those productions necessarily engage with, the fear of a text known and yet permanently unknown and unknowable, impossible adequately to remember and memorialize, the inevitability, as it were, of, like Harriet Walter's gravy,

---

[64] Robert Weimann, *Shakespeare und die Tradition des Volkstheaters* (Berlin: Henschelverlag, 1967), trans. as *Shakespeare and the Popular Tradition in the Theatre* (Baltimore: Johns Hopkins University Press, 1978).

beginning and ending in the right place but misremembering everything in between.

Theatre is a space of memory haunted by its own forgetfulness, by what we cannot remember when we leave the theatre, by the actor's memory that is visible only when it fails to work, by the texts that haunt the stage as unperformed and those that haunt through their performance. Nietzsche argues that 'a happy life is possible without remembrance ... but life in any true sense is absolutely impossible without forgetfulness'.[65] In remembering performance we need to acknowledge the necessity but also the intense desirability of being on this gravy train.

---

[65] Quoted Casey, 'Forgetting Remembered', p. 284.

PART IV

Reconstructing Shakespearean performance

CHAPTER 9

Remembering Bergner's Rosalind: As You Like It on film in 1936

Russell Jackson

During cinema's first decades – from the 1900s through the 1950s – films of Shakespeare's plays had a double existence, conceived both as a means of preserving great performances and also of taking interpretation beyond the boundaries imposed by the stage. Although it has long been discarded by the critics and – for the most part – by audiences, Shakespearean films were dominated for a long time by the notion of an individual performance as something owned by an actor and carried by him or her through whatever circumstances might be thrown up by new productions or revivals of a play. Nowadays British actors often joke that a colleague will be 'giving' his or her First Murderer or Waiting Gentlewoman, in an allusion to the not-quite-forgotten days of stock interpretations and customary 'lines' of parts. The more sophisticated theoretical enquiry into the status of the work of art in the age of mechanical reproduction, and the issues associated with 'aura' since Walter Benjamin's seminal essay, are still to a degree circumvented or at least qualified by a desire on the part of audiences to be able to enjoy individual performances – Olivier's Richard III, for example – which have long since ceased to be available 'live'.[1] The uneasy relationship of early cinema with live performance was exemplified by the various devices used to assert the equal status of films with the theatre (prologues, credit sequences introducing 'the players' and so on) and has its more sophisticated equivalent in the framing devices used by some makers of Shakespeare films to establish theatrical performance as a dimension of the originals they seek to convey: Olivier's use of a 'tuning-up' orchestra

---

Note: some material in this chapter also appears in a paper on aspects of Czinner's film of the play and that by Christine Edzard (1992), 'Filming *As You Like It*: A Playful Comedy Becomes a Problem,' given at the French Shakespeare Society's annual conference in 2005 and published in the conference proceedings.

[1] Benjamin's essay, 'The Work of Art in the Age of Mechanical Reproduction', was first published in 1936. For a lively and provocative discussion of the issues surrounding 'live' performance, see Philip Auslander, *Liveness* (London and New York: Routledge, 1999).

and an illustration of the traditional paraphernalia of players at the opening of his 1948 *Hamlet* is a notable instance.

As You Like It, directed by Paul Czinner and released in 1936, shared with other early sound films of Shakespeare plays (and in particular the 1935 Warner Bros. *A Midsummer Night's Dream* and the 1936 MGM *Romeo and Juliet*) the desire to win approval by affording Shakespeare the facilities offered by synchronized sound and the newest techniques of design and cinematography.[2] At the same time – and to a greater degree than either of the American films – it sought to preserve a 'great performance'. The film has not been commercially available in Great Britain or mainland Europe for many years: on videotape and, latterly, on DVD it has been available in the United States but until recently the British Film Institute did not even have a viewable study or exhibition print. It is notable for Laurence Olivier's first foray into Shakespearean film (as Orlando), and for the performances of some Shakespearean stalwarts of the period, including Henry Ainley as Jaques and John Laurie as Oliver, but the film's stock has never been high. In accounts of the history of Shakespearean film it has had few admirers. The most generous and sympathetic is Kenneth Rothwell, who admires the resourceful direction of Czinner and the expert editing by David Lean and is clearly bewitched by Bergner's energetic and quicksilver performance – a reaction which, as we will see, is not dissimilar to that of many reviewers in the 1930s.[3] Nevertheless, Rothwell writes with the benefit of some sixty years' hindsight and the experience of the subsequent career of Shakespeare in the cinema. For its contemporaries, this *As You Like It* was the occasion for reflections on the more fundamental question of whether Shakespeare

[2] *As You Like It*, directed by Paul Czinner was an Inter-Allied Film Producers in collaboration with 20th Century Fox. The 'scenario' was credited to R. J. Cullen, and J. M. Barrie is listed as having 'suggested' the 'treatment' – a word which seems to indicate the general approach, rather than its usual meaning as an early outline draft of the script. Music by William Walton, designs by Lazare Meerson, cinematography by Hal Rosson and Jack Cardiff. Cast: Rosalind, Elisabeth Bergner; Orlando, Laurence Olivier; Oliver, John Laurie; Celia, Sophie Stewart; Exiled Duke, Henry Ainley; Frederick, Felix Aylmer; Jacques, Leon Quartermaine; Le Beau, Austin Trevor; Charles, Lionel Braham; Adam, J. Fisher White; Touchstone, Mackenzie Ward; Corin, Aubrey Mather; Silvius, Richard Ainley; William, Peter Bull; Phebe, Joan White; Audrey, Dorice Fordred. The British premiere was on 3 September 1936.

[3] Kenneth Rothwell, *A History of Shakespeare on Screen: A Century of Film and Television* (2nd edn, Cambridge: Cambridge University Press 2004), pp. 47–50. In Jack J. Jorgens's *Shakespeare on Film* (Bloomington, Indiana: Indiana University Press, 1977) the film is characterized on the first page of the opening chapter as 'charming, decorative, overly mild' and then merits only a couple of passing references in the course of a general account of the techniques of film adaptations. Michael Anderegg has a succinct discussion of the film in his *Cinematic Shakespeare* (Lanham, Maryland: Rowman and Littlefield, 2004), p. 99.

was really suitable for the screen, especially now that synchronized dialogue had imposed new responsibilities on film-makers. The film's epilogue, in which Elisabeth Bergner mutates from Rosalind (in her wedding finery) into Ganymede and back again, engages playfully with the medium's hesitation between going beyond the stage's capabilities and invoking its status. In a similar fashion, Bergner's own interpretation of the role of Rosalind – 'her Rosalind' – is supposed to be one of the film's principal attractions. The extent to which it succeeded in achieving this and the reception it was afforded have significance in the history of the cinema's relation to theatre and of the European theatre itself. The 1936 film is what is left to us of one of the acknowledged 'great performances' of the second decade of the twentieth century, Elisabeth Bergner's Rosalind.

In the London season of 1933–4 Bergner had two great acting successes, one after another. On the West-End stage *Escape Me Never*, adapted from the novel by Margaret Kennedy, opened in December 1933 to great acclaim and ran for 232 performances. Early in the New Year the film *Catherine the Great* had its royal première and proved equally successful. One day a newspaperman buttonholed her as she was leaving the theatre: 'Just one word, Miss Bergner, what does it feel like to wake up in the morning and find yourself the "toast of the town" and "the greatest, the most talked about woman on earth"?' Her reply (as her husband Paul Czinner later told her when he read it in the paper) sounded laughably arrogant: 'I am afraid I don't remember. It happened so long ago.'[4]

Bergner was simply telling the truth. Since the mid-1920s she had been one of the most famous – and idolized – stars of the German-speaking theatre and cinema, and she was lucky to be able to repeat the experience. Being Jewish, she was very lucky indeed that when the Nazis seized power in 1933 she had already established herself in England as a stage and film actress. Soon after her stage-door interview she was to share the experience of so many who found themselves starting all over again after the Nazi seizure of power exiled them from the countries – and the languages – in which they had made their reputation. Her career, though, failed to

---

[4] Elisabeth Bergner, *Bewundert viel und viel gescholten. Elisabeth Bergners unordentliche Erinnerungen* (München: Bertelsmann, 1978), p. 122. Unless otherwise indicated, this is the source for Bergner's statements about her career. She also contributed a concise account of her removal to London to the exhibition catalogue *Theater im Exil, 1933–45* (Berlin: Akademie der Künste, 1973). The title of her 'disorderly' memoirs is from the opening lines of the third act of Goethe's *Faust, Part Two*, in which Helen of Troy announces herself: 'Bewundert viel und viel gescholten, Helena, / Vom Strande komm' ich, wo wir erst gelandet sind...' ('Much admired and much scolded I, Helena, come from the shore where we first landed...').

maintain the astonishing upward curve that had begun in the 1920s. Her performance as Shaw's Saint Joan in the first Berlin production, directed by Max Reinhardt, had been a key element in her phenomenal rise to stardom, but her rendition of the part in English at the Malvern festival in 1938 did not win Shaw's approval or lead to a London production, and the play written for her by J. M. Barrie, *The Boy David*, proved an expensive failure in 1936.[5] After her emigration to the United States at the outbreak of war she and her husband were not able to secure the kind of footing in the film industry they had enjoyed in Germany and Britain. (She later wrote that she thought his insistence on making films only with her had hindered his prospects.) Unlike many of her fellow-exiles she was able to maintain a reasonable level of material comfort, and the couple moved to New York to concentrate their efforts on the theatre. She was a staunch friend and supporter of her compatriots, including Brecht, though the production of his version of *The Duchess of Malfi* in 1946 was a fiasco and failed to provide him with the Broadway success he desired.[6]

In the early 1930s Bergner was still trailing clouds of glory from her sensational career in the German-speaking theatre. It was a time when many artists from mainland Europe were wooed by London theatres and the British film industry: not only actors and musical comedy stars, but also technicians, composers and designers. Actors who had made their reputations in German cinema and theatre – such as Paul Henreid, Oskar Homolka, Fritz Kortner, Lilli Palmer, Conrad Veidt and Anton Wohlbrück – found employment in both media, especially in works where their accent and exoticism were assets.[7] Many had moved across the Channel and the North Sea with the hope of crossing the Atlantic. Before sojourn abroad was turned into exile, many products of the German theatre had established careers in Hollywood. Ernst Lubitsch, Wilhelm Dieterle

---

[5] Bergner's relationship with Shaw was complicated: in 1934 she and Czinner were on the verge of being allowed to film *Saint Joan*, but made the mistake of sending Shaw's draft script to the playwright James Bridie for comment without Shaw's knowledge. See Michael Holroyd, *Bernard Shaw, Vol. 3: The Lure of Fantasy, 1918–1950* (London: Chatto and Windus, 1991), pp. 380–2. Dissatisfaction with the Malvern performance, hastily rehearsed, using Reinhardt's cuts and in imperfect English, cannot have helped.

[6] See John Lyons, *Bertolt Brecht in America* (Princeton: Princeton University Press, 1980), pp. 142–50. The production's misfortunes included a bizarre clash of theatrical cultures when George Rylands was imported from England to take over direction of the play, which was adapted by Brecht and 'translated' from his version by W. H. Auden.

[7] A particularly useful and comprehensive account of the theatrical 'emigration' is Frithjof Trapp et al., eds., *Handbuch des deutschsprachigen Exiltheaters, 1933–1945*, 2 vols. (München: K. G. Saur, 1999). Other notable émigré members of the film world included the scenarist Carl Mayer (*Das Kabinett des Dr. Caligari, Der letzte Mann*) and the producers Erich Pommer and Max Schach – the latter responsible for sixteen films between 1935 and 1938.

and Edgar Ulmer, who had all worked with Max Reinhardt's theatre companies, were already functioning as directors, soon to be joined by Billy (formerly Billie) Wilder and Fritz Lang. Among the theatre directors who worked in London in the 1920s and early 1930s were Max Reinhardt, director of 'high art' spectacle, and Erik Charell, the producer of lavish sentimental extravaganzas: Reinhardt's *The Miracle* was revived in London in 1934, and Charell brought *White Horse Inn* to Drury Lane and later staged *Casanova* at the London Hippodrome.[8]

Much has been written about the effect on the émigrés of the sudden shift from voluntary to enforced residence abroad, and the acute situation of having no home base to retreat to and no secure prospect of regular employment. Those who were used to a seemingly endless series of satisfying roles in the structured world of the state and municipal theatres found themselves in a dismayingly fluid and unpredictable artistic *milieu*. British theatre was dominated by a commercial sector in which there was no equivalent of the 'true' repertory system (with a standing repertoire of plays periodically augmented and adjusted) that prevailed in German-speaking countries, and little of the directors' theatre already flourishing there. Even when foreign artists achieved the relative security of a long run, the very fact that they were expected to play seven or eight times a week was a shock to their system. A 'first wave' of artistic refugees has been identified, consisting of those who arrived in London in or before 1933, including several (among them Bergner) whose already established international status made life easier. A 'second wave' followed after the annexation of Austria in 1938 made it clear that there would be no future for theatre and film workers in the other major centre of their world, Vienna. Bergner's situation was relatively privileged, but nevertheless the extraordinary success story of her life up to the mid-1930s, with its unexpected boost in London in the years before the outbreak of war, was decisively interrupted.

The film of *As You Like It* presented Bergner in the role in which she had confirmed spectacularly what was already a brilliant career in the theatres of Germany and Austria – waking up in 1925 to find herself the toast of several cities. The circumstances under which the film was made reflect the high esteem Bergner enjoyed at the time, and it represents many of the ambitions of the British – and indeed European – film

---

[8] See Tim Bergfelder, 'The Production Designer and the *Gesamtkunstwerk*: German Film Technicians in the British Film Industry of the 1930s', in Andrew Higson, ed., *Dissolving Views: Key Writings in British Cinema* (London: Cassell, 1996), pp. 20–37.

industry in the 1930s. As an imperfect and in many ways tantalising recollection of what was regarded as one of the greatest performances of the principal role in the 1920s, *As You Like It* is also representative of the uneasy relationship between Shakespearean films and their theatrical antecedents. Bergner's Rosalind is an attempt to preserve a performance for posterity and to make it available to a wider audience. In her case, the audience would be wider in the sense that it would extend beyond the German-speaking public. That the film was not received with unqualified enthusiasm has a great deal to do with notions of Shakespeare as a national possession, and also with the perceived problems attached to Bergner's persona and the discourses of femininity that expressed her appeal in this and other roles. What was revelatory and appealing in 1920s Germany spoke less directly to critics and audiences in 1930s England.

Bergner's reputation was established early on as a player of young women in whom a strong element of pathos combined with a degree of impetuous boyishness and skittish high spirits. Among the various character types – the *Fächer* – into which actors in the German theatre were routinely cast, she insisted on being considered as a *Naïve*. (The alternatives included *Salondame* and *Sentimentale* and 'character' actress.)[9] After she became famous the terms in which she was written about consistently emphasize the quality of vulnerability suggested by her short stature and slight physique, together with her large, expressive eyes and fine facial features. Her habitual coiffure – blonde hair with a side parting – resembled Garbo's and was as distinctive as Louise Brooks's shiny black 'helmet'. In some roles – including that of Wedekind's Lulu – Bergner set this vulnerability against a strong suggestion of perverse and passionate sexuality. Siegfried Jacobsohn described her in the title role of Strindberg's *Queen Christina* (Berlin, 1922): 'She has the character's childishness, innocence and carefree nature, and she has teeth, claws and grasp, ferocity, toughness and dash. She has all of these not alongside but in and through one another with an astonishing, entrancing richness of hovering, shimmering, flickering tones. Termagant and girl.'[10] Reviewing the premiere of *Saint Joan* (1924) Jacobsohn identified a similar duality, this time between determination and frailty: 'Shaw describes his Joan: a

---

[9] Bergner, *Bewundert Viel*, p. 23. The context was an interview with a prospective employer. 'I'm a *Naïve*, though – Do you take me for a *Sentimentale*?' Bergner asked indignantly on being offered a line of parts. The response was 'How do you know I'm taking you at all?'

[10] *Die Weltbühne*, December 1922, in Siegfried Jacobsohn, *Jahre der Bühne. Theaterkritische Schriften*, ed. Walter Karsch with the assistance of Gerhart Göhler (Reinbeck bei Hamburg: Rowohlt, 1965), pp. 213–15 (p. 215).

clever, cheeky country girl with extraordinary spiritual power. Bergner is that, and goes beyond it to what the glance of a visionary's eyes and the irresistible power of a voice of steel can make of a child's delicate body.'[11]

Perhaps the single most eloquent and revealing document of Bergner's appeal to at least the men in the audience is provided by Arthur Eloesser's slim hagiographic volume, *Elisabeth Bergner*, published in Berlin in 1927. The author, a critic and dramaturg of some standing, describes Bergner's female following, from teenage girls to fashionable ladies, and the rapt attention he is able to command when, after delivering a lecture at one venue or another, his hosts wine and dine him and surround him with fans eager for a vicarious glimpse of '*die Bergner*.' Eloesser admits that there is a good deal of *Eros* in Bergner's appeal, in a passage that offers almost limitless opportunities for meditating on the male gaze and what it can do for a fellow:

> Bergner is the most charming and complete edition of the femme-enfant, and I hope that it will be a long time before we have read her all the way through. A child that every man wishes to adopt, but in whom he also thinks – not without a special tenderness – of the woman. And Bergner is a witch, who perhaps ought to be burned at the stake in good time like her saint Joan; for she is a ghost, a spirit of the air, a Puck, an Ariel, who unsettles and preoccupies a great, earnest, hard-working city, who confuses the minds and even the senses of people – and not only those of the young and the men.[12]

For *femme-enfant*, then, we should read *femme fatale*. Bergner is troped as a book we read, a child a man might wish to adopt, a woman he fancies and – as she is also a threat to the seriousness of the city – a witch he just might have to burn at the stake. Duality is an inadequate term for such a polysemous, polyandrous being, who goes a few steps beyond Wedekind's Lulu or the messianic virgin/apocalyptic whore figure represented memorably in the two Marias of Fritz Lang's *Metropolis* (1927). It is hardly surprising that the frontispiece to Eloesser's book should show Bergner as Saint Joan, sitting meekly but with her robe arranged to display her shapely legs.

Her Rosalind costume, worn with minor variations (and presumably in successive editions) from 1923 to 1936, invariably consisted of a russet tunic resembling a gym-slip, worn over a soft-collared shirt, tights of the same colour with very short shorts worn over them, and dainty lace-up

[11] *Die Weltbühne*, October 1924: *Jahre der Bühne. Theaterkritische Schriften*, pp. 237–9 (p. 239).
[12] Arthur Eloesser, *Elisabeth Bergner* (Berlin-Charlottenburg: Williams und Co. Verlag, 1927), pp. 79–80.

41. Elisabeth Bergner as Rosalind, photographed in the open air in the late 1920s, from
Arthur Elosser, *Elisabeth Bergner* (Berlin-Charlottenberg, 1927).

ankle boots (see figure 41). Her coiffure remained defiantly girlish (she
hated wigs and when other parts absolutely required them she never wore
them before the first night). Orlando's failure to recognize this Ganymede
as a boy – if not as a princess – could be explained by the elaborateness of

Rosalind's first-act court costume (in the film she wears a high-necked dress, a wimple and one of those elaborate conical head-dresses) and his acceptance that boy-girls are a fact of life. Given the emphasis on physical expression in her performance, the costume's resemblance to a gym-slip or a dancer's practice dress is understandable: as well as being alluringly displayed, her legs are allowed more freedom of movement than even the short skirts of mid-1920s fashion afforded. In the London magazine *Screen Pictorial* (April 1936), a journalist reported from the set of *As You Like It* on a first encounter with Bergner: 'Her hair is straight and soft and golden. Her face is the shape of an almond. Her body is incredibly small, yet exact in proportion; her limbs – in the short jerkin, breeches and tights she wears to disguise Rosalind as the youth, Ganymede – are at once the crazy envy and hopeless obsession of every chorus girl in London.'

One witness can stand for many as representing the effect of her early stage performances in the role. Herbert Ihering describes Bergner at the Lessing-Theater in Berlin in 1923:

I had already seen Elisabeth Bergner as Rosalind in Vienna. Since then her performance has become even richer and freer. Her inspired gift for improvisation, that is often destructive in tightly composed plays, kindled itself to become an incomparable asset with the looser form [of the comedy]. We were delighted as the words flowed through the relaxed body. We were enchanted by the way everything remained in a single stream of creativity. Elisabeth Bergner spun into one another shame and jubilation, boyishness and girlishness. She swayed at the knees, and an emotion was illuminated. She held out her hands tentatively, and a joke was made tangible. Her voice broke, and one experienced the double transformation: from the girl into the boy and from the boy into the girl he was playing. An exhilarating experience.[13]

Like many other critics, Ihering (a demanding judge of acting) was moved by the apparently uninhibited physical expressiveness of Bergner's performances. But not every role Bergner attempted either suited her particular gifts or showed her to her best advantage, and it was important that she should break out of the *gamine* type. A decisive break seemed to come with Nina, in O'Neill's *Strange Interlude*, at the Berlin Künstler-theater in 1929. Felix Hollaender wrote in the *8-Uhr-Abendblatt* that he had 'never seen her play with such completeness, truthfulness, simplicity and grandeur. She has come a long, long way from her Juliet to Nina.'[14] Ihering himself welcomed 'the rebirth of a great artist' with an emphatic,

---

[13] Herbert Ihering, *Berliner Börsen-Courier*, 25 April 1923, in Günther Rühle, ed., *Theater für die Republik im Spiegel der Kritik, 1917–1933*, 2 vols., (2nd edn, Berlin: Henschel Verlag, 1988), p. 503.
[14] Felix Hollaender , *8-Uhr Abendblatt*, 5 November 1929, in Rühle, *Theater*, pp. 984–6.

declaratory response, as though the experience defied normal expectations of grammar: 'Elisabeth Bergner acted. Elisabeth Bergner examined the role. She shaped the lines. She joined up the sentences. Accident and improvisation had disappeared. A form, a realised human being, a gifted artist... Elisabeth Bergner as she was in the best of her first performances.'[15] The performance seemed to confirm her as a versatile and powerful actress. Although in itself the cult of Bergner as *femme-enfant* (like that of Louise Brooks) is a significant document in the history of the culture of the Weimar Republic, in terms of the artist's own career one might have hoped by the end of the 1920s that it would have been a passing phase rather than a permanent definition of her talent.

In the British theatre, though, Bergner had to begin by playing her strongest suit, and the roles of German-speaking repertoire were hardly likely to come her way. It was the 'naïve' role as a boyish girl in *Escape Me Never* that afforded her first great success, and on film as Queen Christina her accent would be an advantage rather than a liability. As the *Times* reviewer of *Escape Me Never* observed, 'What she would do in a piece of which the emotion was cumulative and the form developing, we do not know, but there are chances here to learn much of her and all that is learnt is to her credit' (9 December 1933). A film of *As You Like It* would both preserve her most famous performance, bringing it to a new audience – and perhaps also (though this was of course not mentioned) it might well represent her last appearance as Rosalind. At the age of thirty-nine and after some fourteen years in the role, her performance of innocence was beginning to look a little too experienced. The fact that the film represents a record of a famous and well-established interpretation of the principal role may explain one of its odder qualities: the lack of contact between Rosalind and Orlando. Laurence Olivier seems not to have enjoyed his experience, and he complained that Bergner did not do him the customary courtesy of reading in her lines 'off camera' when appropriate.[16] Rosalind as Ganymede uses a deep voice – Bergner refers in

[15] Ihering, *Berliner Börsen-Courier*, 5 November 1929, in Rühle, *Theater*, pp. 986–7.
[16] On Bergner and Olivier, see John Cottrell, *Laurence Olivier* (London: Weidenfeld and Nicolson, 1975), p. 101–3, and Anthony Holden, *Olivier* (London: Weidenfeld and Nicolson, 1988), p. 95–7. Holden's account reports Bergner's insistence (in an interview with the biographer) that Olivier treated her and her husband condescendingly as foreigners. The actor 'was not charming or friendly to work with'. For her part, Bergner seems to have taken to arriving no earlier than lunchtime, while Olivier was anxious to get back to London to rest before playing in *Romeo and Juliet* in the evening! Neither of the actors refers to the experience in their respective autobiographies. Felix Barker's *The Oliviers* (London: Hamish Hamilton, 1953), evidently written with privileged access to its subjects' personal views and recollections, attributes the failure of Bergner to be present during some of their scenes to 'the ways of the cinema' in which Czinner was

her autobiography to the '*Bierbass*' she could adopt at will – which makes her seem very bossy indeed. When Ganymede is impersonating Rosalind, Bergner's voice is lighter, but the element of putting Orlando in his place still seems to predominate. Armed with a supple branch with a single leaf on the end, which she deploys as if it were an instrument of mild if not quite titillating chastisement, Rosalind/Ganymede/Rosalind is a wistfully stern taskmistress. There's no sign that Orlando finds this anything other than peculiar – he certainly doesn't for a moment find himself fancying the figure before him – and there is no sense of the level of self-conscious complexity that performances and critics have explored in recent years. Bergner as Ganymede may well be have seemed more appealing to the cinema audience than to Orlando. It is they (and Celia) who witness the apogee of her love-sickness, the forward roll she executes to demonstrate how many fathom deep she is in love. Meanwhile Olivier has to act opposite something called 'Bergner's Rosalind' rather than an inter-pretation that might be altered or developed by whatever he does: it is tempting to imagine one detects signs of this in the somewhat distant look that comes into his eyes when he is in shot with her.

In terms of the cinema business of the early 1930s this was a 'prestige film' – that is, it typified the kind of film American and European studios were striving to produce – often at a financial loss – to raise their reputation in a response to the threat of the economic slump to the film (as to other) industry, a process of spending one's way out of recession that Tino Balio has described fully and succinctly: 'A prestige picture is typically a big-budget special based on a presold property, often as not a "classic", and tailored for top stars.'[17] In Great Britain, Alexander Korda had set himself up as a producer of such films, and in Hollywood the major studios each found their own way of producing them: MGM led the way with lavish adaptations of theatrical and literary classics and such multi-star extravaganzas as *Grand Hotel*, and Warner Brothers, having created a niche in earthy but spectacular musicals (*Gold-diggers of 1933*, *42nd Street*), moved into the real prestige with *A Midsummer Night's Dream* (1935) and then – forsaking the unprofitable Shakespeare – the series of historical romances featuring Errol Flynn, of which *The Adventures of Robin Hood* (1938) is probably the finest. RKO made its

experienced. Barker also suggests that Olivier, acutely aware that on film Orlando's mistaking Rosalind for a boy would seem incredible, 'even made Orlando a trifle mad in the vain hope that this might lend a touch of credibility to an impossible situation' (p. 72).

[17] Tino Balio, *Grand Design. Hollywood as a Modern Business Enterprise, 1930–1939* (Berkeley: University of California Press, 1993), p. 179.

own stylish niche with the Astaire–Rogers musicals, in which the designs of Van Nest Polgaze, the gowns of Orry-Kelly and the choreography of Hermes Pan (with Astaire supervising his own and Miss Rogers' numbers) predominated. RKO was the home of the 'BWS' – the Big White Set, seen at its most opulent in the Venice Lido of *Top Hat* and the improbably spacious art deco hotel and cabaret of *The Gay Divorcee*.

Lazare Meerson's sets for *As You Like It*, like those for the Warner Bros. *A Midsummer Night's Dream*, are at once fantastic – James Agate compared the ducal palace to the RKO Big White Set – and realistic.[18] That is, in the interests of fantasy, they are as real-looking in natural detail as the designers can manage. But whereas for Max Reinhardt the Warner Bros. art department, supervised by Anton Grot, provided a forest with many dream-like elements, which conjures up at least a century of graphic art as well as film (Arnold Böcklin as well as Fritz Lang's *Nibelungen* films), the forest built for Czinner at Elstree by Meerson has a determinedly down-to-earth quality, which is then vitiated rather than enhanced by the sense of its artifice. Is this a country of desire, a land of lost content? Not really. Nor, unlike the ominous haunted wood of Reinhardt's *Dream* (a film that represented a summation of thirty years of fairy forests he had created and directed), is this a place where real lions and snakes might lie hidden. In fact it's a reminiscence – albeit on a bigger scale – of many an old-fashioned English Arden from the Victorian and Edwardian tradition that the theatre had already left behind. As the anonymous reviewer from *The Times* put it, invoking the Ideal Homes exhibitions staged at the London indoor arena, the forest 'often looks like a wild garden temporarily assembled at Olympia' (4 September 1936).

Not only is the sense of a numinous, threatening nature absent from the film: unfortunately, Czinner also fails to manage festivity well. In the final sequence, which seems to take place in the grounds of a palace that cannot logically be that of the usurping Duke Frederick, flocks of sheep and a sudden plethora of rustics pour through high wrought-iron gates to join in a rustic revelry that becomes an orgy of unfocused hat-waving and random cheering. A draft script indicates: 'Old gates – hundreds of sheep come through the gate followed by Shepherds among whom is Corin.

---

[18] James Agate, *John o'London's Weekly*, 12 September 1936, reprinted in *Around Cinemas* (London: Home and Van Thal, 1946), pp. 173–7 (p. 173). Agate also suggests comparison with the lavish musical biography *The Great Ziegfeld*, also currently playing. The production designer, Lazare Meerson, was a Russian émigré who had worked extensively in the French film industry – his films included Feyder's *La Kermesse Héroique* (1935) – and had been brought over to London by Alexander Korda.

Peasants follow among the shepherds.'[19] Everyone in the forest wears spick and span clothes – even the well-scrubbed Audrey – and nothing suggests a winter wind at any point. There are no dark places in these woods.

In a perceptive article Samuel Crowl has noted the way in which both this film and Reinhardt and Dieterle's *A Midsummer Night's Dream* render the erotic charge of their central situations harmless and childish, and in the case of *As You Like It* Crowl has identified the involvement of J. M. Barrie as a contributing factor.[20] In the making of Czinner's film Barrie was a distinct presence, but the extent of his influence is debatable. The opening credits announce that 'the treatment' was 'suggested by J. M. Barrie'. He had become obsessed with Bergner after seeing her on stage in *Escape Me Never* and had encouraged her and her husband to pursue the film project.[21] According to Bergner's autobiography he even wrote a prologue, never filmed, which would have featured an animated and speaking bust of Shakespeare, and he was a regular visitor to the set, where the spluttering of his pipe occasioned many retakes. The most tangible result of his obsession was his emergence from self-imposed retirement to write a play for her, *The Boy David*. So far as concerns the film, it seems likely that his contribution was limited to encouragement, and to his appreciation of the boy-girl (*femme-enfant* might have been too *louche* a concept for his conscious mind) disporting him/herself in an idyllic forest. Bergner had become one of his 'lost boys' combined with Peter Pan – whose stage incarnations were traditionally shapely young women – and it was she who brought him out of the deep depressive withdrawal precipitated by the death of the favourite among his adopted sons (see figure 42).[22]

Bergner's exotic accent either charmed or confused (one only has to hear her speak 'the howling of Irish wolves' to discover what was wrong) and some reviewers were in two minds about the reminiscences of the actress's other roles. The *Daily Express* (30 September 1936) declared that Bergner was 'ridiculously miscast' as Rosalind, and found 'a querulous

---

[19] 'Scenario' in Birmingham Shakespeare Library: s313–8Q. (This is in fact a full shooting script.) The collection also includes a box of publicity material, notably the sheets for three full-size colour posters for the British release.

[20] Crowl's article, first published in *Literature/Film Quarterly*, is adapted and incorporated in ch. 5, 'Babes in the Woods: Shakespearean Comedy on Film', of his *Shakespeare Observed: Studies in Performance on Stage and Screen* (Athens, Ohio: Ohio University Press, 1992).

[21] On Bergner's encounter with Barrie, see Peter Scott, *The Eye of the Wind. An Autobiography* (London: Hodder and Stoughton, 1961), ch. 29. Scott, who was Barrie's godson, was responsible for bringing them together.

[22] The standard work on this aspect of Barrie's emotional life remains *J. M. Barrie and the Lost Boys* by Andrew Birkin and Sharon Goode (London: Constable, 1979).

42. *As You Like It*, 1936. Three-Sheet poster for the British release of Paul Czinner's film.

touch and too much coyness to her always exaggerated performance' – a verdict that would have astonished her admirers in the 1920s, but which expresses a response which most of the British reviewers expressed more tactfully. Graham Greene felt that Bergner's 'tear-stained, bewildered pathos' was more appropriate to the constant nymph than to 'the reckless-tongued Rosalind' (*Spectator*, 11 September). Ernest Betts in the *Era* (6 September) thought Rosalind 'a beautiful performance' but noted that this was despite the moments 'when it seems one's mental geography has become a confused mixture of Arden, the Never-Never Land and the Tyrolese haunt of another inescapable Nymph'. This Rosalind was 'a quaint blend of Peter Pan and Wendy'. Barrie's involvement in the film, proclaimed in the publicity as well as in the opening credits, led to some inevitable comparisons. Bergner 'makes of Rosalind a shallow, childlike character, posturing through some dreamlike adventure in the Never-Neverland' (*Morning Post*, 4 September). For the *Daily Telegraph*, which admired her, Bergner had been successful despite her accent and despite the fact that 'her appearance, her mannerisms, her technique . . . are all essentially modern' (7 September). *The Times*, while praising her for speaking the lines 'with clarity and relish', complained that she 'underlined' them excessively, 'as she underlines her conception of the character' (4 September). Sidney Carroll, mentioning that in his capacity as director he had tried to persuade Bergner to play at Regent's Park four years previously, complained in *The Sunday Times* (6 September) that her performance on film was 'too nervous, too restless. It underlines at moments where it should trifle, and throws away thoughts that merit emphasis.' Despite his evident desire to re-direct the performance, Carroll admired its 'brilliant moments', including, as well as 'those flashing smiles, those irresistible wiles, those elfin twists and turns', the somersault itself. But he detected 'too much of Barrie and too little of Shakespeare' in the conception, and found Bergner's antics 'suggestive of some tricksy sprite, springing from a Hebridean isle, not the tall, divinely fair Rosalind in the Forest of Arden'. The *Manchester Guardian* suggested that Bergner was sometimes too elaborate in the way she would 'draw out the lines as if they were threads upon which she was braiding her thoughts,' producing too 'sophisticated' and 'skittish' an effect. 'But she creates a Rosalind who is tender and roguish by turns and more lively than any we have seen' (4 September 1936).

A very few critics noticed (or thought fit to mention) the oddest aspect of Bergner's performance: its sexiness. Carroll referred to Bergner's 'quicksilver changes of sex', but without specific reference to any erotic effect. For the *Leeds Mercury* (26 September) her 'counterfeit boy' had 'always womanly qualities lingering near the surface. And they come to the top in the whimsical ways of which Bergner is mistress.' Given that this was a famous element of her appeal as acknowledged by German critics and admirers, the lack of response may well indicate a cultural difference, an English sense of proper restraint. There are hints in some reviews that the performance's unusual emphases might be interpreted as foreign: *Film Weekly* (12 September) complained of 'a rather Teutonic conception of Rosalind, too mournful when adverse fortune comes, too strident when in happy mood in boy's clothes'. As Stephen M. Buhler observes, 'Bergner's performance, intended to be reassuringly feminine, quickly becomes irritating in the context.' He suggests that Czinner may well have underestimated the British audience's readiness to accept 'gender-bending', given the popularity of Marlene Dietrich and Greta Garbo.[23] (Buhler has a point, but it may be that the genders were more easily bent in the film's own time, and that the over-playing of femininity works with rather than against the effect.) Englishness was also an issue for the *Yorkshire Post*, whose critic clearly associated the role with a brisk girl-guide Englishness and found Bergner 'too elfin, not nearly robust enough to accord with our usual English conception of this enterprising girl who sets off with a doublet and hose to look for her lover in the forest of Arden' (4 September). The sense that (in contrast to some of the British actors) Bergner was not representative of the true, traditional sense of the role was invoked: she was 'rather more waif-like than the authentic Shakespearean text would suggest' (*News Chronicle*, 4 September). In a review headlined 'Shakespearean Heroine – with a Difference', the *Daily Sketch* suggested that the accent of this 'pixie of the forest' 'grace[d] Elizabethan English as piquantly as it does a modern play', but regretted the lack of 'music in her poetry' (4 September). Such expressions as 'waif-like', 'elfin' and 'piquant' intimate a kind of attractiveness that is exotic and slightly (if pleasurably) disturbing. Raymond Mortimer in the *New Statesman and Nation* was more direct about sexuality: 'Miss Bergner's gravest mistake is that she has taken from Rosalind her innocence ... the smile at moments lengthens to a leer; the jerkined girl weighs the luscious Orlando with too greedy and too knowing an eye, and we feel that she will reveal herself a witch and gobble him up. Peter Pan has got mixed up with something out of Strindberg' (12 September 1936).

---

[23] Stephen M. Buhler, *Shakespeare in the Cinema. Ocular Proof* (New York: State University of New York Press, 2002), pp. 131–2.

The film's premiere was furnished with appropriate celebrities: the *Daily Film Renter* (1 September 1936) reported an invitation list including Lilian Baylis (representing the Shakespearean establishment) and such international stars as Marlene Dietrich, Charles Laughton and Edward G. Robinson, with Alexander Korda, Robert Donat and Gracie Fields from the British film industry and – of course – Sir James Barrie. The usherettes would be costumed as Ganymede, the pay box turreted, and the proscenium frame disguised as 'the beautiful Forest of Arden.' A 'gauze covering the whole stage opening [would] depict the meeting of Rosalind as Ganymede with Orlando in the forest'. Outside the cinema 'a huge canvas, 40 feet square, [would] be placed above the canopy at the front of the house'. This was to be 'an oil painting outlined in Neon lighting'. Such dressing of cinemas for grand openings was customary with 'prestige' films – and extended to their initial runs in the provinces: exhibitors received detailed suggestions from distributors along with the 'press book' for a film's release.

Always anxious to gauge a film's intrinsic qualities but responsible for warning exhibitors about its potential as an earner, the columnists of the trade press were respectful in their accounts of Czinner's film but – as might be expected – qualified in their predictions for the box-office. *Kinematograph Weekly* (10 September) concluded that the film 'seldom remain[ed] for long within the province of popular entertainment', with the 'richness and prodigality of the dialogue' as the chief stumbling block: 'To appreciate the film every word must be followed, and the task imposes too great a strain on the masses, the vast majority who insist upon talk being subservient to action, for it to be inevitably box-office.' This was a verdict that would be repeated in the trade press's response to Shakespeare films through the 1930s and 1940s: there was simply too much complicated talk for 'the masses' to take on board.

The review in the *Daily Film Renter* (4 September) suggests the distance between Rosalind as a film role in Britain in 1936 and as a star part on stage in Germany in the 1920s:

It is, of course, Bergner's film throughout, and *within the limits of the part* she acquits herself with distinction, but *the role she plays is hardly worthy of her acknowledged abilities*. This fact, in addition to the fragmentary pattern of the subject as a whole, militates against the subject's popular appeal, but it cannot be denied there are audiences who will appreciate the artistic way in which the piece has been screened.   [My emphases]

Like the *Daily Express* review quoted above, this would have been unthinkable when Bergner was performing Rosalind in the

German-speaking theatre, but places her and the film firmly in the consciousness of the generality of British filmgoers of the 1930s, for whom
Shakespeare was exotic and forbidding enough without the added pecu-
liarities of her personal interpretation and mannerisms. Reporting on the
London opening the American show-business journal *Variety* praised the
film's qualities as a 'sincere and faithful effort' to put Shakespeare's
comedy on screen, and commended Bergner for her success 'within the
limitations of her origin and training' – but the overall result was a movie
that was 'too much lacking in the accepted standards of screen technique
to arouse much enthusiasm among the multitude' (16 September). After
the first preview in the United States, *Variety* responded with respect but
again expressed no optimism about box-office: the story was too static, and
the actress's accent was 'a real hurdler in the instance of speaking Shakespearean lines'. The lack of 'fanfare and flourish' and 'heavy dramatics' in
Czinner's direction was as it should be: 'But that also restricts the picture
pretty much to those who liked the subject in the first place ... It will
never be a knocker-downer to them as don't care' (11 November 1936).

Nor was it. By all accounts the film was unable to recoup the £1.5m of
its negative costs, and it failed to find a market in the United States.[24] In
this respect it shared the fate of the 1935 *A Midsummer Night's Dream* and
the 1936 *Romeo and Juliet*, and seemed to confirm the commercial and
artistic disadvantages of filming Shakespeare's plays. Bergner's own career
continued to falter. After the comparative failure of the *As You Like It*
film, and the honourable defeat of the stage production of *The Boy David*
in 1937, a reviewer of Bergner's next film, the English version of *Der
Träumende Mund*, wrote that 'one cannot say with any certainty whether
Miss Bergner can sustain a role involving depths of passion or peaks of
tragedy. She has a rare command of pathos, which is a very different
matter, but the pathos is that of a stricken child, not of a mature woman'
(*Theatre World*, October 1937). In other words, she had not yet managed
to move beyond the character type in which she had been made her mark,
and which she had been obliged to adopt once again in exile. Bergner's
subsequent film career was disappointing, and she left Britain in the early
months of the Second World War in circumstances that were unfortunate

---

[24] Specific figures for the film's box-office have not been located, but *Harrison's Reports*, a trade
periodical devoted to exhibitors' reports of takings at over 500 venues in the United States, listed it
as 'Poor' (the lowest category) in a summary of the performance of 20th Century Fox products (20
March 1936, p. 45). The same publication, describing the mixed but still unsatisfactory fortunes of
the 1935 *Midsummer Night's Dream*, observed 'It would be wise if the producers refrained from
making pictures out of the plays of Shakespeare' (19 December 1936, p. 204).

for her reputation there: she failed to return after completing location work in Canada for Michael Powell and Emeric Pressburger's film *49th Parallel*, choosing instead to join Czinner in the United States. The film of *As You Like It* remains a tantalizing glimpse of one Bergner's 'signature' roles, a performance adrift from its context in the theatres of Weimar Germany. It was not shown in Germany or Austria under the Nazi regime, and because of its unavailability outside the United States it seems not to have been seen there after 1945. In 2002 a showing was organized at an art-house cinema in Düsseldorf: for all its absurdities, the film still held its audience and when the lights went up some of the older members of the audience were in tears. Bergner had returned to Germany after the war and picked up a career on stage and screen, but this was their first glimpse of her younger self. It may even have been not so much a memory of their own as of their parents' generation.

CHAPTER 10

Shakespeare exposed: outdoor performance and ideology, 1880–1940

Michael Dobson

This chapter seeks to investigate the cultural forces which motivated the rediscovery of open-air Shakespearean performance during the late nineteenth and early twentieth centuries. It's a remarkable enough phenomenon in itself – after all, the absence of a roof to protect the audience is one aspect of the Shakespearean theatre for which no one had ever expressed any nostalgia before this period – but it is of even greater interest, as I hope to show, when seen in the context of the same era's investment in the open-air revival of Greek and Roman drama. It is perhaps worth remembering from the outset that the Elizabethan theatre had itself been understood, even in its own time, as a memory or even survival of the classical dramatic tradition. The Dutch visitor Johannes de Witt, sketching the Swan playhouse in or around 1596, labelled his drawing with the Latin terms appropriate to a Roman auditorium, not only because he habitually wrote in Latin as all good European intellectuals should but, as his commonplace book explains, because he believed that England had preserved a tradition of theatrical architecture unbroken since its years as a province of Rome.

The post-Renaissance return to the open-air performance of Shakespeare has its first stirrings, as with so much else in the modern reception of the plays, with David Garrick. At the climax of the Jubilee in Stratford in August 1769, Garrick intended to bring Shakespeare's imaginary characters onto the streets of Shakespeare's real home town: but his culminating pageant, a procession of Drury Lane actors presenting mobile *tableaux vivants* from the plays, was in the event cancelled due to torrential rain. This event, or non-event, is nowadays mainly remembered, if at all, in the context of Enlightenment bardolatry and Stratford tourism. What I'll be pointing out in what follows, however, is that Garrick's impulse to take Shakespeare's characters outside into the fresh English air is one which for the last century and more has haunted the domestic performance history of the canon to an enormous and unacknowledged extent. What I'll mainly be examining is an under-explored dimension of the English Shakespearean theatre's encounter with modernism – though not with the chrome, urbane, cosmopolitan side of modernism, but with its woody, folksy, nationalist underside.

As a discipline, Shakespearean performance history has throughout its existence suffered in its intellectual prestige from a fatal tendency towards the anecdotal and the parochial, so I'm proposing to get the main self-indulgent personal reminiscence in this chapter out of the way at once. I trace my own interest in the topic of taking Shakespeare outdoors back to a minor incident in the English class war, which in the 1970s was surely being fought nowhere more bitterly than around the environs of Bournemouth. In the early summer of 1977, the state secondary school which I was then attending received, unprecedentedly, a communication from the enormous private boarding school at nearby Canford Magna: would our school be interested in block-booking tickets to see their forthcoming production of *Troilus and Cressida*? If you know Bournemouth, you'll know that local opportunities to see *Troilus and Cressida* have always been pretty scarce; and so it was agreed that, for the first and I think only time, a busload of Bournemouth sixth formers would venture inside the high, broad, impregnable gates of Canford School. Innocent as I then was, I had never set foot inside a private school, and so as the bus began to move up the great driveway of what used to be one of John of Gaunt's larger manor houses I was curious to see how the school's interior might look. But my curiosity in this direction was never to be sated, since a series of signs directed the bus to turn off the drive and traverse acres upon acres of manicured grounds, finally arriving at a temporary car park in a field well away from the school buildings. Nearby was a sort of large indented slope dug into the side of a mound, lined with concrete terraces, like those of a football stadium except curved; and in front of them was an odd structure with a roof, which with sinking heart I could just recognize as a stage. Dressed for a stifling school hall on a summer evening, we interlopers filed apprehensively along a row to huddle together on the hard cold damp terraces, right behind the cast's parents, whose cushions, blankets, waxed Barbour jackets and thermos flasks, veterans of who knew how many point-to-points and gymkhanas, proclaimed that they'd known all along that this was to be an outdoor production. During the first half of the performance, I reflected that we were at least marginally better off than the curlèd darlings on stage, whose only protection against the chill evening wind was provided by a selection of vaguely toga-like garments, which I wouldn't have chosen to wear even indoors and in decent privacy.

But during the second I revised this view, since it began to rain, with just the same slow, monotonous, seemingly endless insistence which Canford's brightest and best brought to the speaking of Shakespeare's dramatic verse. The question which formed itself in my mind with similar insistence, and which this chapter is really devoted to answering, was as follows: why? Why, in the English climate, long after the invention of the comfortable roofed proper theatre, would anyone choose to stage Shakespeare's plays in the open air?

When I say 'anyone', I should add, I really mean 'almost everyone'. In 2004 I carried out the exercise of marking a map of England and Wales with red dots indicating all the venues where outdoor performances of Shakespeare were taking place during June, July and August, and even the most cursory mining of publicity brochures and what's-on websites soon gave both countries the appearance of sufferers from terminal measles. I had to mark approaching three hundred red dots, and it was soon clear that it would have been impossible during those months to get further than twenty miles from an outdoor Shakespeare venue without fleeing to the moorlands of Scotland. The theatrical organizations involved ranged from large professionial set-ups like the New Shakespeare Company, based in central London, down to amateur groups as small as The Villagers, near Gosport in Hampshire, who endearingly describe themselves on their website as 'a group of friends who accidentally put on a Shakespeare play every July'. Some of my dots represented other such indigenous local productions; others represented only a visit of a night or a week from one of a number of restlessly vigorous small touring companies, such as Illyria or Chapter House, both of whom specialize in performing in the grounds of country houses and castles. But others marked the sites of entire seasons of outdoor Shakespeare, some at multiple venues (as in the case of the Cambridge Shakespeare Festival). It is very possible, in fact, that the number of performances of Shakespeare given outdoors in England every year exceeds the number given indoors – a statistic which would have appeared the more visibly remarkable had I shaded my map in different colours so as to indicate not only the whererabouts of these performances but the average summer rainfall in their respective areas.

Something more is demonstrated by the scale of all this, surely, than a disinterested national preference for difficult acoustics and uncomfortable seating. The phenomenon of English outdoor Shakespeare clearly meets ideological needs more pressing than any desire for a comfortable or even dry night at the theatre, and I hope to expose at least some of them over

43. The Open-Air Theatre, Regent's Park, *c.* 1933. Reproduced from Winifred Isaac, *Ben Greet and the Old Vic: A Biography of Sir Philip Ben Greet.*

the remainder of this chapter. I will do so primarily through uncovering the histories and pre-histories of two open-air Shakespearean theatres, both of them established in 1932 – the same year in which the Royal Shakespeare Theatre opened in Stratford, outnumbered by these roofless contemporaries. One of them is the best-known professional outdoor theatre in England, the Open-Air Theatre in Regent's Park, in London (see figure 43). Here, in the modern auditorium which has now replaced the original deckchairs, the New Shakespeare Company play every summer to audiences of up to 1,800 per performance. Their professed motto, which appears in most of their programmes, is a quotation from *A Midsummer Night's Dream*, 'This green plot shall be our stage', and they are the true heirs, as I'll show, to a small late-Victorian and Edwardian touring company, Ben Greet's Woodland Players, whose playbills and programmes invariably bore the slogan 'Under the Greenwood Tree'. The venue with which I'll be concluding, by contrast, is altogether less sylvan, but it is nonetheless the best-known amateur theatre in the country, outdoors or in. It offers just as long a season every summer – seventeen weeks – but its season consists primarily of Shakespearean productions rehearsed elsewhere, which compete for a range of prizes. On a map it is to be found at the extreme bottom left of the English mainland: it is, of

44 The Minack Theatre in 1932.

course, the very temple of English non-professional Shakespeare, Minack (see figure 44). This theatre is hewn into a precipitous Cornish cliffside close to Land's End: it boasts the Atlantic itself as its stage's backdrop, and is aptly and apocalyptically described by one commentator as 'England's first and last theatre'.[1] It was established, and indeed largely constructed, by one Rowena Cade, a figure who is depicted by the theatre's official mythology, in characteristically English fashion, as a pragmatic amateur who simply made the whole project up as she went along without any ideas being involved at all. If I achieve nothing else in this chapter, I should like to re-identify Minack not just as a monument to Cade's sheer willpower, but as one outcome of the powerful inter-section of three apparently contradictory tendencies in early twentieth-century culture: Hellenism, naturalism and nationalism.

As my account of the range of the summer's *al fresco* productions may have already suggested, English outdoor Shakespeare is a phenomenon which traverses the categories of professional and amateur, and, less obviously, it also has mixed loyalties to mainstream, academic and fringe theatre. The production which initiated the Shakespearean theatre's

[1] Denys Val Baker, *The Minack Theatre* (Penzance: G. Ronald, 1960), p. 24.

rediscovery of the great outdoors, perhaps surprisingly, was very consciously an avant-garde one: the *As You Like It* staged in woodlands at Coombe Warren in Surrey in summer 1884, repeated in 1885. This was the first effort by a group called the Pastoral Players, who were essentially the theatre club of the Aesthetic Movement: one of their moving spirits, indeed, was Oscar Wilde, who described the costume worn by Phoebe as 'a sort of panegyric on a pansy'.[2] This comment's emphasis on the look and dress of the production is appropriate, since its prime *raison d'être* was the temporary emancipation of its designer, E.W. Godwin, from the tinselly constraints of the West End. This emancipation, paradoxically, was achieved through a retreat to the economic mode of amateur drama that had been dominant a century earlier: the venture was sustained by aristocratic patronage, its audiences including the Prince of Wales himself, and though many of the cast were hired professionals the role of Orlando was played by the Aesthetic hostess Lady Archibald Campbell. Godwin enjoyed absolute artistic control over every detail of the play's mise-en-scène, to an extent impossible in the commercial theatre, and, while professional theatre critics commented approvingly on the production's realism, the aesthetes themselves waxed lyrical about the exquisite and complete coordination of its colour scheme.[3]

The fact that this show, a landmark in the emergence of the modern director, took place outdoors was partly dictated by a painterly preference for seeing colours by natural light; but it also chimed happily with Godwin's sustained interest in the classical theatre and indeed the classical past more generally. As well as providing lavish Alma-Tadema-style designs for West End plays on classical themes (such as John Todhunter's *Helena in Troas*, for which he built an imitation Greek auditorium inside Hengler's Circus in 1886), he published extensive essays on classical dress, including a whole series on the costumes that ought to be used in productions of those Shakespeare plays with ancient Greek settings, such as *Troilus and Cressida* and *A Midsummer Night's Dream*.[4] Godwin's twin interests, in a single artist's complete control of the theatrical event and in ancient drama, would become more visibly central to theatrical modernism in the next generation, most obviously in the work of his illegitimate son by Ellen Terry, Edward Gordon Craig, whose 1911 manifesto

[2] *The Dramatic Review*, 6 June 1885, p. 297. Quoted in John Stokes, *Resistible Theatres: Enterprise and Experiment in the Late Nineteenth Century* (London: Elek, 1972), 48.
[3] Stokes, *Resistible theatres*, pp. 47 – 50.
[4] Godwin published these in *The Architect* in 1875: see Michael Walsh, 'Craig and the Greeks', in *Drama Forum*: www.cssd.ac.uk/dramforum/journal/craig2/html.

for a drama school (in *The Art of the Theatre: Second Dialogue*) would famously demand both masks and 'two theatres, one open-air, one indoors'.[5] But meanwhile a neo-classical revival of unroofed theatre was in the air already, and not just among the more intellectually advanced. It isn't merely coincidental that the revival of English outdoor theatre should have taken place during the heroic age of classical archaeology, from Schliemann's work at Hissarlik (Troy) (1871–90) to Arthur Evans's at Knossos (1899–1935). The pursuit of reforms to the classics syllabi at Oxford and Cambridge, downplaying philology in favour of a broader attempt to reconstruct ancient cultures, had finally persuaded the university authorities to relax a Victorian ban on student performances, and in 1880 English undergraduate drama had its rebirth, in the form of an all-male production of Euripides's *Agamemnon* at Balliol College, Oxford, in the original Greek, starring a young Frank Benson as Clytemnestra. Three years later, Girton College, Cambridge staged an all-female production of Sophocles's *Electra*, and in 1887 the newly established Oxford University Dramatic Society staged a lavish *Alcestis*, for which they simply bought the leftover auditorium, set and costumes which Godwin had designed for Todhunter's *Helena in Troas* the previous year.[6]

It was abundantly clear from the outset that any elite school interested in continuing to produce Oxford and Cambridge classicists needed to stay abreast of all this: Eton, Harrow and Winchester, for example, all paid for visiting performances of the 1880 *Agamemnon*, and in 1882 the headmaster of Bradfield College in Berkshire, Herbert Branston Gray, invited Benson to stage an *Alcestis* there.[7] All these shows took place indoors, but Gray, supported by an energetic young classics master called Lepper, was determined to give Bradfield a pre-eminence in educational revivals of Greek drama which it has never lost. Armed with the measurements of the auditorium at Epidauros, Lepper set teams of schoolboys to work with shovels in an abandoned chalk pit in the school grounds, and they duly proved that clean-limbed sons of the Empire could be fit successors to the conquering heroes of antiquity. By 1890 the first purpose-built unroofed theatre to be constructed in England since the Renaissance was complete. An expression, and indeed a product, of

---

[5] Quoted in Michael Walsh, 'Craig and the Greeks'.

[6] The best-known relic of this Victorian and Edwardian boom in academic Greek drama nowadays, incidentally, is probably Ralph Vaughan Williams's overture to Aristophanes's *The Wasps*, commissioned for a Cambridge student production in 1910.

[7] See Fiona MacIntosh and Edith Hall, *Greek Tragedy and the British Theatre* (Oxford: Oxford University Press, 2005), ch. 15, 'Page versus Stage: Greek tragedy, the academy, and the popular theatre', *passim*. I am very grateful to Dr MacIntosh for access to this study in manuscript.

the same muscular Hellenism which in 1896 would inform the first modern Olympic Games, this theatre is still in use: it has now been the venue for a triennial performance of a Greek play in the original for a century and a quarter.[8] Other schools and colleges followed suit, and have continued to do so; Canford, for example, built its own Greek theatre during the 1920s, while Bryanston dug theirs to mark the Festival of Britain in 1951. (Even as recently as 1964 the designers of the most futuristic educational building of the post-war period, the all-new St Catherine's College in Oxford, felt obliged to include a small Greek theatre in its grounds.) Nor was all this confined to England: the most famous emulator of Bradfield's example was William Randolph Hearst, who did his bit to keep the University of California at Berkeley at the forefront of classical studies by paying for the construction of the famous Greek theatre on their campus in 1903. Oddly, though all the English examples I've mentioned have regularly been used for this purpose at different times, it is the Hearst Greek Theatre which enjoys the distinction of being the first of these neoclassical auditoriums to have served as a venue for English outdoor Shakespeare. Within a year of its completion, it played host to productions of *As You Like It* and *Hamlet* mounted by the English actor-manager Philip Barling Ben Greet.

Ben Greet was the single most important popularizer of outdoor Shakespeare, and he continues to exert an enormous if largely unrecognized influence on the forms of Shakespearean performance favoured by amateurs, by nature-lovers and by Shakespeare's Globe on Bankside. As one obituarist put it on his death in 1936, much of Greet's career was devoted to the proposition that 'under the greenwood tree or some semblance of it [Shakespeare's] pastoral plays should be best enjoyed'.[9] Whether or not Greet saw the aesthetes' *As You Like It* at Coombe in 1884–5, he certainly heard about it and recognized its commercial potential: within a year of the Pastoral Players' final performance of the play, the first batch of Greet's copycat Woodland Players were on the road with their own outdoor *As You Like It*. Greet had a knack, indeed, for bringing together elements from the academic, avant-garde and even

---

[8] I am grateful to Lepper's son, Charles Lepper, for showing me this auditorium in the summer of 2004. As if to demonstrate the connections between this classical revival and Shakespeare, Lepper junior, who practically grew up in the Bradfield theatre, went on to become a Shakespearean actor, later understudying Claudio in Peter Brook's famous Stratford *Much Ado About Nothing* in 1950.

[9] *New York Times*, 19 May 1936.

religious stage (he had extensive contacts at Oberammergau)[10] and making them saleably mainstream. ('Mr Greet occupies a unique position in the dramatic world', commented one admiring journalist in 1908. 'He is anything but a literary and impractical 'crank', but a highly successful actor and director and a man of affairs.')[11] As the same obituarist also recognized, his productions borrowed extensively from contemporary classicism ('Greet's open-air theatre recalls the Greek', he said), not least in the shape of their improvised auditoriums. As one expert remarked when recommending Greet's methods to amateur dramatic societies in 1919,

in purely pastoral locations, the ideal [open-air theatre] is that which most closely approximates to the form of the Greek amphitheatres, a curving hillside with a level playing-space at the bottom and a screen of trees behind the actors.[12]

Where Greet couldn't find adequate trees in situ, incidentally, he simply filled out the existing vegetation using his own potted shrubs. His productions were Hellenic too in some of their costuming: the Athenian nobles in his many productions of *A Midsummer Night's Dream* always wore antique robes and tunics, just as Godwin would have recommended (even though, as Greet solemnly pointed out, 'The wearing of Greek and Roman draperies is an art and must be very carefully rehearsed.').[13] His shows conflated the classical and the Shakespearean in other ways too: prescribing acting style in a note to his edition of *Dream*, Greet makes the unlikely observation that 'This comedy is after the Greek style: repose and limited movement and gesture were always observed.'[14]

But Greet's shows managed to borrow from native antiquarianism too, selling the 'authenticity' of seeing Shakespeare performed in the open air. Greet collaborated with William Poel during the 1880s and 1890s, notably on the latter's revival of the morality play *Everyman*, and though he was himself no doctrinaire neo-Tudor he recognized the practical advantages of playing without elaborate and expensive sets. His acting editions of Shakespeare plays list three main ways of mounting them, apparently in descending order of preference: '(a) in the open air, (b) with a simple but artistic setting [in the Elizabethan manner], and (c) with all the pomp and

---

[10] Greet even gave public lectures about the Oberammergau passion plays, for example at the London School of Economics on 3 October 1930 (New York Public Library for the Performing Arts: Greet scrapbooks, MWEZ 10,007).

[11] *Toledo Daily Blade*, 18 April 1908.

[12] Roy Mitchell, *Shakespeare for Community Players* (Toronto and London: J. M. Dent and Sons Ltd, 1919), p. 57.

[13] *The Ben Greet Shakespeare for Young Readers and Amateur Players: A Midsummer Night's Dream* (Garden City, NY: Doubleday, Page and Co., 1912), p. 108.

[14] Greet, *Dream*, p. 46.

circumstance of the modern public's requirements'.[15] The blocking and business which the editions recommend is described as identically suitable for (a) and for (b) – so that the Woodland Players' productions seem mainly to have offered a more accessible, outdoor version of what Poel's English Stage Society tried to offer in hired halls, a definitely Elizabethan Shakespeare rescued from scenic elaboration.[16] His obituarist took this point too: 'For Ben Greet the play was the thing, not the scenery. In that respect he was one with Shakespeare.'[17] The sense that acting Shakespeare outside provides direct access to the one true original method, indeed, has remained a recurrent motif: in 1934, for example, when the Richmond Shakespeare Society was established specifically to mount Greet-like outdoor productions beside the Thames, an enthusiastic local journalist observed that

> if the society's interpretation of *Much Ado About Nothing* [with special Elizabethan dances] is to be taken as a foretaste of what we may expect in the future, then Richmond will be one of the few places where Shakespeare's works may be seen as they were intended to be seen – and heard.[18]

Just as important as Greet's claims to authenticity, though, was the Woodland Players' skill at profiting from one of the same widespread attitudes that had enabled the Greek plays to happen at Bradfield: a sense that outdoor performances of educationally valuable old plays could be exempted from all normal moral prohibitions against live drama.[19] There was something innately healthy about seeing Shakespeare's plays

---

[15] Greet, *Dream*, p. 3.

[16] Greet was, however, willing to compromise in some respects: only the mechanicals in his productions of *A Midsummer Night's Dream* wore tights, and he would often employ a small local orchestra to play the Mendelssohn incidental music ('If music be used in this play it is difficult to find anything so appropriate as that of Mendelssohn' Greet, *Dream*, p. 22, and *passim*).

[17] With their neo-Elizabethan rusticity, Greet's outdoor productions deliberately appealed to a growing sense that Shakespeare belonged to Old England more importantly than to the West End: the Woodland Players' advertisements for their 1887 performances at Barrett's Park in Henley-in-Arden excitedly promised '*As You Like It* performed *for the first time* in Shakespeare's native Forest of Arden'.

[18] Richmond Shakespeare Society archive: unmarked press cutting, album 1.

[19] Compare the bracing tone of the programme note to one of Greet's American productions of *A Midsummer Night's Dream*, 1925:

> Open-air plays have been universally recognized as being at once unique, delightful and educational. They have been given at nearly every university and college in this country as well as in England. Surely a movement which has resulted in the revival of 'A Midsummer Night's Dream', one of the most glorious plays ever written, is worthy of public goodwill and support . . . No other play lends itself better for outdoor performance. OUR TRUE INTENT IS ALL FOR YOUR DELIGHT.
> (Preserved in the personal scrapbook of Ruth Vivian, a former leading light of the Smith College Dramatic Society who toured in Greet's company throughout the 1920s: New York Public Library for the Performing Arts, MWEZ n.c.18,835.)

performed on a lawn rather than in surroundings of red plush, something which breathed the same bracing, invigorating air as amateur sport, and this was discreetly reinforced by the cuts Greet silently made to the plays' texts. What Greet had profitably recognized was that thanks to the recent development of electric lighting[20] (and electric amplification) he could now offer lucrative evening performances of Shakespeare not only without the expense of booking an indoor theatre but to audiences who might otherwise have refused to enter one. Throughout the 1880s and 1890s his Woodland Players took what Greet called Shakespeare's 'pastoral plays' (mainly *As You Like It, A Midsummer Night's Dream, Twelfth Night, The Tempest,* and *Much Ado About Nothing*) to a variety of hitherto unexploited venues all over Britain, thereby rescuing the Bard from the seedy taint of the West End. As one spectator put it, Greet restored Shakespeare to his proper rural innocence: 'when the play was done and the audience dispersed over the soft grass, with the night sky above, spangled with stars, the lovely evening they had spent was unspoilt at the end by the glare of gaslight and shouts for cabs'.[21] The Woodland Players' itineraries included annual visits to the gardens of King's College, Cambridge and Worcester College, Oxford; performances in the grounds of public schools such as Rugby; and visits to respectable municipal gardens, at Cheltenham and even Bournemouth,[22] and in 1901 to a site then belonging to the Royal Botanical Society at the top of the Inner Circle in Regent's Park. Very much in the spirit of their era, they also gave numerous performances at polite patrician garden parties, for which the Woodland Players advertised themselves as 'The Latest Novelty and most charming entertainment', and at which Greet would arrange for well-placed local amateurs to give musical performances between the acts. If the play was *A Midsummer Night's Dream,* he would also arrange for local children to join the cast as supernumerary fairies (ideally, he specified, twenty-four of them – who might between them bring as many as forty-eight parents into the audience).[23] As this practice may suggest, the

---

[20] See e.g. the surviving playbill from a Greet production in Hartford, Connecticut, 16 May 1908: 'In the evening the grove will be lighted with apparatus brought by the Ben Greet Players and especially designed for such occasions' (NYPLPA, Woodland Players scrapbook, MWEZ 23,659).

[21] Winifred Isaac, *Ben Greet and the Old Vic* (London, 1963), 216.

[22] See the interview with Greet in *The Bournemouth Graphic,* 25 September 1902, in which he boasts of having brought theatre to the town over a period of 'fifteen or sixteen years'. Pressed on the subject by the journalist's first question, Greet tactfully insisted that Bournemouth, so far from being boring, had 'many splendid facilities'. (A subsequent touring Shakespearean actor-manager, Anthony Quayle, would describe the town in the 1980s as 'the graveyard of the English theatre'.)

[23] Greet, *Dream,* p. 58.

Woodland Players deliberately offered morally safe family entertainment, convening an enormous and hitherto largely untapped middlebrow audience for live Shakespeare. Indeed when Greet published some of his bowdlerized acting texts in 1912 he called them *The Ben Greet Shakespeare for Young Readers and Amateur Players*, and each volume bears a preface which concludes with a reassuringly improving exhortation: 'inwardly digest your Bible and outwardly demonstrate your Shakespeare: you will then start in life pretty well equipped'.[24]

The Woodland Players, however, weren't Greet's only company, and he didn't exclusively work outdoors: in fact by 1903 he was hopelessly overstretched and in severe financial difficulties, so he did what English Shakespeareans invariably do when they want a little respect, proper working conditions and a reasonable income: he went to America. One of his official envelopes from the pre-war years, sent from the Woodland Players' Broadway office in 1914 (presumably in pursuit of yet another booking on yet another massive transcontinental tour of colleges and parks) proudly records what must nowadays, alas, seem the most unlikely of all the venues to which the Woodland Players took their outdoor Shakespeare: the lawn of the White House, where the company performed before President Roosevelt on 14 November 1908 (see figure 45).[25] With the outbreak of the First World War, however, Greet returned to England, where he joined Lilian Baylis in the management of the Old Vic, and though he continued to mount US tours he spent most of the 1920s running what would now be called the Old Vic's educational outreach department, setting up special matinee performances for schools in cavernous East End music halls.[26] (It was this work which resulted in his knighthood, and in the naming of Greet Street in Southwark.) He spent the last five years of his life, however, back in his signature mode. In 1932 the Royal Botanical Society's lease expired on Greet's favourite slope in Regent's Park and a younger actor-manager, Robert Atkins, could hardly not involve Greet when he set out to established the Open-Air Theatre as a permanent summer venue for the performance of Shakespeare.[27] Quaintly designated 'Master of the Greensward' (figure 46), Greet was employed as a consultant, a player of minor roles and a speaker

---

[24] Greet, *Dream*, p. viii.
[25] See e.g. Montrose J. Moses, 'Pastoral Players', in *The Theatre*, December 1908.
[26] See e.g. *The London Graphic*, 11 December 1920.
[27] See J. C. Trewin, 'Robert Atkins and the Open Air Theatre, Regent's Park', in *Robert Atkins: An Unfinished Autobiography*, ed. George Rowell (London: Society for Theatre Research, 1994), pp. 113–19.

45 The Ben Greet Woodland Players performing for President Roosevelt on the White House lawn, 14 November 1908. This quartet of photographs, with the central portrait of Greet, was reproduced on his American office stationery: this is in fact an envelope (postmarked 18 November 1914, and addressed to one Dr E. L. Stephens of the Southwestern Louisiana Industrial Institute, probably in pursuit of a tour date), and it has emblazoned across its obverse (on the flap) the words 'The Ben Greet Woodland Players / From the Offices of L. M. Goodstadt / Thirteen Twenty-Eight Broadway, New York City'.

46 Ben Greet as Master of the Greensward at the Regent's Park Open-Air Theatre, *c.* 1934. Reproduced from Winifred Isaac, *Ben Greet and the Old Vic: A Biography of Sir Philip Ben Greet*.

of impromptu prologues, presiding genially over what his biographer terms 'the result of the pioneer work to which he had devoted the best part of his life – the presentation of Shakespeare's plays out of doors in natural and neutral surroundings'. The theatre, though now vastly remodelled and extended, still mainly performs what Greet labelled the 'pastoral plays', with *A Midsummer Night's Dream* in its repertory in two seasons out of every three: and like the Woodland Players the New Shakespeare Company tend to play to audiences who rarely see Shakespeare performed anywhere else. Typical Regent's Park regulars can't imagine a summer that doesn't at some point include a family picnic at yet another *Dream*, but wouldn't touch Cheek by Jowl with a bargepole, much as many families in American cities religiously go to see *The Nutcracker* every Christmas but wouldn't even consider seeing any other ballet at any other time of the year.

The choice of repertory made by Greet's Woodland Players for their outdoor tours, subsequently followed by Atkins and his successors at Regent's Park, is every bit as striking as the Pastoral Players' choice of *As You Like It* for their performances at Coombe Woods. Despite these productions' affinities with stylized, unfamiliar modes of performance, whether borrowed from the Greeks or from the Elizabethans, their producers seem nonetheless to have understood outdoor performance primarily as the perfect consummation of Victorian and Edwardian naturalism. Even better than a wood near Athens consisting of extremely lifelike simulations of trees, apparently, is one consisting of real trees, and even better than having real tame rabbits on an indoor stage, *à la* Beerbohm Tree, is having real wild ones on an outdoor. Similarly, the perfect solution to staging a play which includes both ancient Greek aristocrats and English rustics appears to be performing it in a Greek auditorium which is in an English park, a strategy of which Peter Quince, with his anxious insistence that his players will need real moonlight and a real wall in order to enact 'Pyramus and Thisbe', would surely have approved. Greet would even sometimes state on posters for *Much Ado About Nothing* that 'the Church scene is omitted as not suitable for representation out of doors'[28] (what would *Much Ado About Nothing* be like without the church scene?): it is as though outdoor performance was felt to be especially suitable for audiences completely lacking in imagination, but only so long as the plays involved depicted events all of which might have happened on wet grass.

This underlying adherence to naturalism becomes most spectacularly visible around *The Tempest*, which Greet had claimed could only be performed adequately 'out of doors amidst the enchantment of nature', since it needed 'the idea of infinite space above and the mystery of the magic island beneath'.[29] In 1932, the same year that the picturesque open-air theatre at Regent's Park was inaugurated with a trial production of *Twelfth Night*, a positively sublime counterpart opened in distant Cornwall, with a production of the play for which it had been purpose-built (figure 47). Here at Minack was something the West End had never managed to provide even in the heyday of the proto-cinematic special effect, *The Tempest* with a real sea – and, more often than not, a real tempest. Indeed the most famous of all Minack anecdotes concerns one fogbound matinee of this inaugural production, during which a two-masted barque actually ran aground on the rocks immediately behind the stage, among the waves ninety feet below – so that this historic show became a *Tempest* with a real shipwreck too. (Certainly Minack has Regent's Park beaten hands down if what you want from open-air Shakespeare is sheer physical risk: a noticeboard welcomes spectators with the words 'THE MINACK THEATRE IS BUILT INTO THE CLIFFSIDE. AS A

---

[28] Isaac, *Ben Greet*, p. 218.   [29] Isaac, *Ben Greet*, pp. 66–7.

47 *The Tempest* at Minack, August 1932.

RESULT THE WHOLE SITE IS POTENTIALLY HAZARDOUS. PLEASE
TAKE PARTICULAR CARE OF YOUR OWN SAFETY AND THAT OF ANY
CHILDREN FOR WHOM YOU ARE REPONSIBLE. KEEP TO THE STEPS AND
PATHS AT ALL TIMES.')[30] But despite its perils and inconveniences, or
perhaps because of them, Minack remains one of the most striking of
modern Shakespearean theatres, and I want to close by looking a little
more rigorously at its early history and its intellectual affiliations than
have other commentators to date.

Accounts of Minack inevitably focus on its founder and indeed principal architect and builder, Dorothy Rowena Cade (1893–1983), marvel-
ling at how unlikely it should have been that this provincial spinster,
already thirty-eight when she built Minack, should have become such a
major figure in English outdoor Shakespeare. The souvenir booklet sold

[30] Not that others haven't tried to outdo it in this respect. Inheriting Brownsea Island in Poole
Harbour in 1962, the National Trust determined to publicize its opening to the public by setting
up the still-running Brownsea Open-Air Theatre to stage *The Tempest* on it to mark Shakespeare's
four-hundredth birthday in 1964 – a venture requiring the entire cast and audience to be ferried
across a major shipping lane and stranded on the island for the duration of the performance.

by the organization that now runs the theatre, The Minack Trust, stresses that Cade's only experience of practical involvement in the theatre prior to her arrival in Cornwall in her thirties was the title role in a domestic production of *Alice in Wonderland* when she was eight, and it gives the impression that she drifted into dramatic activity in a wholly improvisatory manner, completely out of touch with any major currents in artistic thought. In fact Cade had a great deal in common with E.W. Godwin, in that she was primarily a designer, and Minack, in the best modernist tradition, began as very much a designer's theatre (in its early seasons it even boasted some very fine modernist programme and poster designs by the artist Hilda Quick). Cade's greatest technical skills were in costume design, and she first became involved in local amateur dramatics in 1929, when she manufactured the clothes and props for an outdoor production of *A Midsummer Night's Dream* at nearby Crean. As surviving photographs of this show's 1930 revival reveal (figures 48 and 49), this was every bit as visually coordinated a piece of work as anything the Pastoral Players ever staged, and every bit as full of child-fairies as Ben Greet might have wished: look in particular at how the curls at the top of the disaffected fairies' hats match the curl on Titania's headgear. Cade's surviving costume drawing for Demetrius, moreover, preserved at the theatre's museum, not only gives him Greek dress, in the approved manner, but also a Greek spelling, 'Demetrios'. But Cade had something in common with Lady Archibald Campbell too, namely that she was a hostess. Cade's granite house on the cliffs near Porthcurno had already been the venue for a range of social and artistic activities before this, and after the success of the 1929–30 *Dream* Cade decided in effect to use amateur theatricals as its crowning social stunt. She more or less co-opted the company who had staged *A Midsummer Night's Dream* (essentially the works amateur dramatic society of the area's chief employer of educated technicians, the Eastern Telegraph Company, now part of Cable and Wireless) by buying the headland at the bottom of her garden for £100 specifically in order to turn it into an irresistibly spectacular venue for a follow-up production of *The Tempest*. Working over the winter of 1931–2, the cliffs' native granite discreetly supplemented with concrete, Cade enabled Minack House to preside over the most talked-about auditorium in the county. (At the same time she completely altered the nature of the society she had only recently joined by hiring professionals from London to direct and to play leading roles.) It is hard not to see these manoeuvres as in part the expression of a Lucia-like social and artistic ambition: Fowey might have had Arthur Quiller-Couch and Daphne Du Maurier,

48 *A Midsummer Night's Dream* at Crean (1929, revived in 1930), with costumes by Rowena Cade. Note the disaffected pixies.

49 Bottom and Titania in *A Midsummer Night's Dream* at Crean (1929, revived in 1930), with costumes by Rowena Cade.

St Ives all those potters and painters, but now, in artistic circles west of Penzance, Cade's word would be law.

Both the determination with which Cade pursued her theatrical project, and its intellectual and ideological bases, are helpfully clarified when one learns of her educational background. As the theatre's booklet fails to point out, the young Cade had in the early 1900s attended Cheltenham Ladies' College. Cheltenham had been moulded by its greatest principal, Dorothea Beale (founder both of Girton in Cambridge and of St Hilda's in Oxford), specifically to produce women worthy to take their share in the management of Britain's imperial destiny. Its students were once described as 'The League of Empire Loyalists in gymslips', and to this day their most marked common trait is an invincible conviction of their own moral fitness to govern the world. During Cade's time at Cheltenham the school was very much in the forefront of the revival of classical drama: school and house plays included 'Scenes from Homer' (tableaux with dialogue, depicting the lives of Andromache, Nausicaa and Penelope), as well as Robert Bridges's neoclassical verse play *Achilles on Scyros*: and among many lavish outdoor pageants staged for successive Founder's Days there was a moralized, backbone-stiffening 'Pageant of Ancient Empires'. There was also a school trip to see an Oxford student production of Aristophanes's *The Frogs*, and, as the school's official history boasts, 'Free graceful expression was encouraged in various ways. The College was one of the first schools to use the Dalcroze system of Eurhythmics.'[31] Nor could Cade have complained of any lack of exposure to Shakespeare, indoors or out: there were visiting performances by Frank Benson's troupe and by the local branch of the British Empire Shakespeare Society; the girls of one house performed appropriate scenes from *Richard II* in the College garden; and there was also a visit from Rosamund Mayne Young's company with a Greet-style outdoor production of *Twelfth Night* (which was, incidentally, the second play to be performed at Minack, in 1933).[32] It is in this context that one has to look at the auditorium at Minack, as the product of someone who had always seen outdoor Shakespeare in a classical context: fittingly, one spectator, looking at the theatre she had built, remarked that 'one can only think of Rowena Cade as one of the Olympians',[33] and one early performer there

[31] A. K. Clarke, *A History of the Cheltenham Ladies College, 1853–1953* (London: Faber and Faber, 1954), pp. 134–5.
[32] E-mail from Rachel Roberts, school archivist, 18 October 2004.
[33] Averil Demuth, *The Minack Open-Air Theatre: A Symposium* (Newton Abbot: David and Charles, 1968), p. 14.

observed that 'There is a Greek or Elizabethan simplicity about it.'[34] As another commentator put it, accurately if bathetically conflating the theatre's major influences, 'Whether it be [at] the Minack, or Epidaurus, or the Regent's Park Theatre in London, the play's the thing.'[35] Appropriately to this combination of the classical and the Shakespearean, Minack's most ambitious pre-war production was an epic *Antony and Cleopatra* in 1937, directed by Neil Porter from the Old Vic, a pageant of ancient empires indeed: Cade's notes as costume mistress record the purchase of no fewer than 100 pairs of sandals from Woolworth's in Penzance. Tellingly, the script of the Stewart Granger film shot at Minack in 1944, *Love Story*, set against the backdrop of a production of *The Tempest*, unblushingly refers to Cade's auditorium as 'the old Roman amphitheatre up on the cliff'.

So Minack is a direct heir to Bradfield and to Ben Greet, a stage where classicism and Elizabethan antiquarianism can be reconciled with naturalism, as a suitable venue for literal-minded *Tempest*s and gestures off out to sea towards Actium. But sitting on its terraces at the end of August 2004, waiting to see a gannet-haunted *Midsummer Night's Dream*, having spent much of the wettest English summer on record researching outdoor Shakespeare, the question I had first asked at Canford remained: why do Shakespeare outdoors at all? The answer, surely, has less to do with what outdoor performance at such locations does aesthetically for the plays than with what the plays do ideologically for the locations. At a time when the British Empire had proved that the national literature was eminently and perhaps worryingly exportable – as, for example, more and more Folios left England for new homes in the United States – the English needed to identify Shakespeare with the homeland itself by whatever means were available. In an 1885 essay called 'The Open Air', for example, the patriotic Richard Jefferies tried to invoke Shakespeare as a sort of male English Ceres, his texts merely a literary version of the fertile native landscape:

What part is there of the English year which has not been sung by the poets? all of whom are full of its loveliness; and our greatest of all, Shakespeare, carries, as it were, armfuls of violets, and scatters roses and golden wheat across his pages, which are simply fields written with human life.[36]

---

[34] Tim Cribb, in Demuth, *The Minack*, p. 67.   [35] Demuth, *The Minack*, p. 23.
[36] Jefferies, 'Outside London', from *The Open Air* (1885), in S. J. Looker, ed., *Jefferies' England* (London: Constable, 1937), p. 327.

The trouble with this formulation is that national landscape and national literary culture seem to be rivals: indeed Jefferies goes on to claim that 'The lover of nature has the highest art in his soul.' Surely more convincing and efficacious than this solitary, introspective vision would be a collective ritual by which the inseparable bond between national poet and national landscape could actually be celebrated in the flesh? In 1769 Garrick had tried to enact such a thing in the streets of Stratford: but it was the Pastoral Players' *As You Like It*, performed in the same year that Jefferies's essay was first published, which had succeeded in finding a better alternative, as many subsequent comments make clear. In 1919, for example, Roy Mitchell's *Shakespeare for Community Players* recommended outdoor productions for their 'native quality', on the grounds that if an amateur actor-manager sets up his theatre somewhere suitable in the open air, 'Instead of having to say "This is coopered up to look as much as possible like Arden", he finds himself saying, "This *is* Arden."'[37] In fact, everywhere one looks under the surface of English outdoor Shakespeare one finds the desire to sit in an English field and say 'This *is* Arden.' Compare the glee with which L. Du Garde Peach, celebrating the proliferation of village amateur dramatic societies in 1939, reports that 'today it is no unusual thing, somewhere in the quiet English countryside, to hear Sylvius apostrophizing his Phoebe or Orlando his Rosalind and, on looking over the hedge, to find a shepherd, script in hand, conning his part'.[38] Or compare Aidan Clarke, even closer to the perilous boundary between English whimsy and English mysticism, on the Richmond Shakespeare Society's 1935 *Midsummer Night's Dream*, which for him simply released the innate, mutually reinforcing Englishness and Shakespeareanness of its Thameside location:

As I walked in, I saw a group of green fairies sitting in a corner of the field. Within the gates, in leafy dells and winding mossy ways, were lightly clad nymphs, creatures of the garden and the wood, nimble dancing forms, majestic personages crowned and garlanded. I felt that the figures I beheld were always there, but [for whatever reason...] I had failed to see the rightful regular residents of Richmond's Terrace Gardens. From the moment in which I saw my first fairy, onwards in the dusk, and all through the night, what men now call reality became a dream; and the older dream, Shakespeare's dream, all men's dream, the great old dream of Merrie England...became the reality. The river god claimed our allegiance and the garden deities our never quite forgotten

---

[37] Mitchell, *Community Players*, p. 57.
[38] L. Du Garde Peach, 'Village Drama', in Patrick Carleton, ed., *The Amateur Stage* (London: Geoffrey Bles, 1939), p. 155.

ancient love . . . The fairies sang, and blessed the Terrace Gardens . . . The Bard of Avon will find no better stage than this green plot beside the silver Thames. His servants, and our friends, the Richmond Shakespeare Society, have done much towards the recovery of Merry England – for keeps.[39]

The development of electric light and electric amplification, para-doxically, seems to have freed up the moderns to be unabashedly nostalgic for an imagined pre-industrial, artisan England with an artisan Shakespeare as its embodiment and voice.

It is surely just such a desire as Clarke's to secure a forever lost, forever threatened Merry England by playing Shakespeare all over it which informs this entire period's vogue for outdoor production. And only this, I think, can account for the fitness which devotees continue to find in the location of Minack as 'England's first and last theatre': looking out over the Western Approaches, it seems designed to guarantee that should a second Spanish Armada sail up the Channel, the first thing its look-outs would see would be an amateur production of *A Midsummer Night's Dream* or *The Tempest*. In fact that 1932 opening production might have been expressly designed to solicit the comment which it indeed widely received: 'Well might this be Prospero's island.'[40] Minack labels all of the British mainland as Shakespeare's, in a posture at once of beckoning lighthouse and of defensive sentinel. It is appropriate, I think, that soon after the end of the 1939 summer season Minack was requisitioned by the Ministry of Defence and fitted with a gun emplacement. It's a reminder, perhaps, that England wasn't the only European country to have spent the 1930s engaged in healthy outdoor pursuits by which strength might be achieved through joy, building neo-classical concrete auditoriums, staging imperial pageants and celebrating in the same breath an authentically native culture and an identification with the imagined Apollos of ancient Athens. Twee and even philistine as the legacy of modern outdoor Shakespeare may remain, perhaps it is just as well that in England, as the likes of Ben Greet and Robert Atkins never tired of demonstrating, the only ancient Athenian anyone could really see themselves identifying with was that tireless star of open-air rehearsals, Bottom the Weaver.

[39] RSS archive, *Richmond and Twickenham Times*, (11?) May 1935.   [40] Demuth, *The Minack*, p. 26.

PART V

Performance memory: technologies and the museum

CHAPTER 11

Fond records: remembering theatre in the digital age

W. B. Worthen

We have become immigrants of subjectivity.

(Pierre Lévy, *Collective Intelligence*)[1]

I was speaking recently to a PhD student, one of those students who dramatize the changing world that is, inevitably, inhabited differently by students than by their 'teachers'. Jane McGonigal is writing a dissertation on the drama of immersive and pervasive gaming. These are not the textual MUDs nor the graphically displayed online games – war games, the Sims – in which players all over the world log in and play with and against other unseen, widely dispersed, yet somehow not quite unknown players.[2] Instead, McGonigal is interested in games most directly comparable to 'smart mobs', those dynamic groups that first reached public consciousness during the Seattle World Trade Organization protests in 1999, using cellphones and wifi laptops to give the 'mob' a greater degree of coherence, intelligence and agency.[3] In the kind of game that McGonigal is archiving and analysing, participants use digital technologies not to play on the screen but to play in that other scene, that world before the screen. While you might think such games are like a digital treasure hunt – go to the hotspot, get the clue – what makes these games fascinating is their dynamic character, the extent to which the game is interminable and boundless. You get a strange email, go to a website, find

---

[1] Pierre Lévy, *Collective Intelligence: Mankind's Emerging World in Cyberspace*, trans. Robert Bononno (Cambridge, MA: Perseus Books, 1997), p. xiii.

[2] Jane McGonigal's dissertation, 'The American Avant-Game: Networked Play and Performance at the Turn of the 21st Century', is being written under the auspices of the PhD program in Performance Studies, University of California, Berkeley. For more information on her research, see <http://www.avantgame.com>. A MUD, for Multi-User Domain or Multi-User Dungeon, is an interactive online chatroom, in which players – usually representing themselves as online avatars or characters – perform in a textually mediated playing space.

[3] See Howard Rheingold, *Smart Mob: The Next Social Revolution* (Cambridge, MA: Basic Books, 2002), for a lively study of the mobile telephone as 'a kind of remote control for people's lives' (p. 194).

some information about an event downtown; on the way, you get an SMS on your cellphone, directing you to a different location, telling you to look for the security guard and get the information. How do you respond? Go to the original site? To the new one? Hang up the phone? What information? If you can't tell where the game begins and ends, if you can't tell whether you're in the game, maybe you're in the game. This is a long way from the Creative Anachronists jousting in city parks, from Dungeons and Dragons roleplaying, from theme parks and fantasy vacations. As Sherry Turkle put it a decade ago, 'Today's children are growing up in the computer culture; all the rest of us are at best its naturalized citizens.'[4]

So, I'm in my office talking to Jane about her dissertation (and yes, this is in the 'old style', as Winnie puts it, we're talking F2F, IRL) when she lets slip, 'You know, I don't really have to remember things, since anything I really need to know is online.'[5] In one sense, of course, it's not true: you do need to remember your name, where you live, how to use an ATM, your password. Yet there's a crucial truth here too. As William J. Mitchell puts it,

I don't do much mental arithmetic any more; calculators and computers take care of that. I don't rack my brain for half-remembered facts; I look them up on the Web. I routinely exist in the condition that J. C. R. Licklider presciently identified, way back in 1960, as 'man–computer symbiosis' – except that Lick-lider, Doug Engelbart, Ivan Sutherland, and other pioneers of interactive computing mostly had dialogue with desktop workstations in mind, whereas I now interact with sensate, intelligent, interconnected devices scattered throughout my environment. And increasingly I just don't think of this as computer interaction.[6]

McGonigal and Mitchell suggest something that has become pervasive, whether in the register of utopian enthusiasm or paranoid terror, today: a sense not so much that digital technologies are new tools for us to use – even the notion that they are 'tools' may be just 'a reassuring viewpoint to those concerned about runaway technology' – but that the relationship

---

[4] Sherry Turkle, *Life on the Screen: Identity in the Age of the Internet* (New York: Touchstone, 1997), p. 78.
[5] Some of the naturalized citizens may not recognize the lingo of texting here: F2F='face to face'; IRL='in real life.'
[6] William J. Mitchell, *Me++: The Cyborg Self and the Networked City* (Cambridge, MA: MIT Press, 2003), p. 34.

between user and used has always been a cybernetic feedback loop.[7]
'As human beings become increasingly intertwined with the technology
and with each other via the technology, old distinctions between
what is specifically human and specifically technological become more
complex.'[8]

Digital technology is not the first technology to change human lifeways
in ways that may – under certain social, economic and geographical
conditions, at least – alter the practices of human being in ways that
appear to alter the content of being human. And in many ways what
digital technology does best is to raise the question of whether change is
change in kind or merely in degree. You probably can no longer submit a
concordance as a PhD dissertation in English literature. Technology here
enables us to do something more easily without really changing the
nature of the work; perhaps it also dramatizes the conceptual impover-
ishment of work that was nonetheless once extremely difficult to do. On
the other hand, while it may be possible to do all the calculations needed
to drive a space capsule to the moon without a computer, it is not
possible to do so quickly enough actually to get the job done. The speed
of the computer and the principle of timesharing compress processes to
the extent that simultaneity and sequence become indistinguishable.[9]
Pierre Lévy has made an analogous point about writing itself, distin-
guishing not between mechanical or analog and digital technologies but
instead between a single instance of this transformation and the consequences of the digital revolution more generally, which has mapped a
variety of representational practices and the platforms that sustain them
to a single binary code. While 'the ontological status or aesthetic properties of a printed text' generated from digital technologies – and this is as
true of printed books as it is of texts generated from your laptop and
printed on an ink-jet printer – 'are no different than those of a text
prepared with the tools that were available in the nineteenth century', if
we instead 'consider the set of all the texts' – which, of course, now
include still and moving visual imagery, sound, even scent and tactile
recordings – 'that the reader can display *automatically* by interacting with
the computer through a digital matrix, we enter a new universe for the
creation and reading of signs'. The challenge of the 'cultural fecundity' of
digital technology is, as Lévy sees it, to understand its new 'means of

---

[7] Malcolm McCullough, *Abstracting Craft: The Practiced Digital Hand* (Cambridge, MA: MIT Press, 1996), p. 78.
[8] Turkle, *Life on the Screen*, p. 21.   [9] See Mitchell, *Me++*, p. 13.

potentializing information', particularly 'the appearance of new genres associated with interactivity'.[10]

Digital technology, and digital culture are predicated on the principles of information theory (the *abstraction* of information from its material conveyance, the *selection* of the message from a field of transmission, the *dissociation* of information from 'meaning'): this sense of the medium of representation – *information* – enables binary code as the means of transmission, and like all systems of encoding necessarily bears its own ideological freight. I'm going to have to bracket the impact of information theory on the shaping of dramatic information for now, but it's important to recognize that as digital technologies are actualized in new and surprising ways, they extend and elaborate our engagement with 'information', as well as our appetite for it to be pervasively available in easily accessible, image-rich, highly portable formats. For N. Katherine Hayles, '*Virtuality is the cultural perception that material objects are interpenetrated by information patterns*', and it is the pervasiveness of the virtual, particularly the sense that information 'is increasingly perceived as interpenetrating material forms' that Hayles sees as definitive of 'the posthuman'.[11] Whether we are vivified by medical implants or feel a shred of panic or relief when the cellphone is off network, it's clear that digital culture has altered the ways we understand and enact 'the human', and so may alter 'the human' as well. The 'instruments of liberation from … the idiocy of unconnected life – the narrowly constrained existence imposed by limits of locality, time, memory, and processing power' are also, of course, instruments of marketing, surveillance and of social transformation in ways we are just beginning to recognize.[12] Are we liberated from the vulnerability of isolation, or becoming 'less self-reliant than ever, not because we are less independent, but because we are so much more connected'?[13] How does this sense of connectivity, of the interminable flow of information, conversation, connection, relate to a different archive, the archive of human actions, the archive of performance, the archive of drama?

Shakespearean drama is an unusually interesting site for such questioning. Although the progressive academic community was more or less

[10] Pierre Lévy, *Becoming Virtual: Reality in the Digital Age*, trans. Robert Bononno (New York: Plenum, 1998), pp. 53–4.
[11] N. Katherine Hayles, *How We Became Posthuman: Virtual Bodies in Cybernetics, Literature, and Informatics* (Chicago: University of Chicago Press, 1999), pp. 14–15, 19.
[12] Mitchell, *Me++*, p. 208.
[13] Mark Federman, McLuhan Program in Culture and Technology, University of Toronto, quoted in Ken Belson, 'Saved, and Enslaved, by the Cell', *New York Times* (10 October 2004): 4:12.

scandalized by Harold Bloom's officious *Shakespeare: The Invention of the Human*, the sense that drama provides a kind of repository, the software (so to speak) by which an early modern sense of 'humanity' might be (re)animated is widespread, and for good reason, even if we might wonder if we still have the hardware to run the program.[14] Whether we think Shakespeare's characters are 'characters' or not, whether we think the things they represent are 'people' or not, and whether we think those representations are fundamentally like us or not is perhaps beside the question: we would have no interest in Shakespeare, no interest in any non-contemporary *drama*, perhaps not even in the residual practices of live *theatre*, if we did not believe they spoke or could be made to speak about some recognizable slice (white, male, northern, European, whatever) of human experience in some way. It is precisely this sensibility that stands at the centre of the typical controversies that swirl around Shakespeare, including Bloom's effort to locate Shakespeare at the origin of (Western) humanity, and so of a conservative sense of the humanities.

I want to ask how contemporary Shakespeare dramatizes the impact of new technologies on the performance of 'humanity' – or 'humanities' – it may bring into view. To do so, I'll be looking today principally at films that gesture directly toward the impact of digital technologies on a conception of the drama. Michael Almereyda's *Hamlet*, for instance, with its obsessive, slightly anachronistic investment in *recording* experience, is surely 'poised', as Courtney Lehmann remarks, 'on the verge of a new technology of expression'.[15] Almereyda's film situates the play at the intersection of several technologies of dramatic performance, 'remediating' the drama (in Peter S. Donaldson's suggestive phrase) as writing, film and digital media, while notably dropping theatre from the mix.[16] And while Hamlet's camera – a Fisher-Price PXL 2000 toy camera, marketed for a year or so in the late 1980s – was almost instantly obsolete, it now has a small yet significant following among aficionados and video artists, including Sadie Benning and Michael Almereyda. Moreover, its visible presence and consequence in the film's action is a palpable part of the film's canny display and interrogation of recording technologies, reframing McGonigal's aside about the transformation

---

[14] Harold Bloom, *Shakespeare: The Invention of the Human* (New York: Riverhead, 1998).

[15] Courtney Lehmann, *Shakespeare Remains: Theater to Film, Early Modern to Postmodern* (Ithaca: Cornell University Press, 2002), p. 96.

[16] My thanks to Peter S. Donaldson for providing me with an advance copy of this superb essay, 'Hamlet among the Pixelvisionaries: Video Art, Authenticity, and "Wisdom" in Michael Almereyda's *Hamlet*', in Diana Henderson, ed., *Concise Companion to Shakespeare on Screen* (Oxford: Blackwell, 2006), pp. 216–37.

of human capacities by the technologies we use to realize them. How does the film's transformation of 'drama' resonate with the transformations of digital culture?[17] In her rich and provocative reading of the 'technologies of memory' in the film, Katherine Rowe points to the 'polychronic' nature of technologies, their insertion in a rhetoric that is simultaneously progressive and nostalgic. Almereyda's *Hamlet* responds to the ways 'Shakespeare's own plays allegorize their relation to media that were both new and old at the time of their earliest performance' – though it's notable that both Rowe and Almereyda take the *book* as the sole instance of this technology, to the exclusion of the *stage*.[18] Ethan Hawke and Julia Stiles are deeply coloured by the affective and vestimentary codes of contemporary cyberpunk. Yet while Hamlet and

---

[17] Hamlet uses a Pixelvision camera, the PXL 2000 made by the toymaker Fisher-Price as a way to introduce children to home video; the camera was introduced in late 1987 and withdrawn in 1989. Its distinctive look and somewhat hazy images, the screen shading into black toward the edges of the frame, is a function of its remarkable technological specifications. Designed to record both sound and images on chromium-oxide audio cassette tapes (the camera ran the tapes at high speed, a 90-minute tape produced five minutes of video), some cameras also came with a hand-held viewer that could be adapted to battery power (as Hamlet has evidently done in the film). Built to record in very low light, the camera refreshes the screen at half the rate of a standard NTSC video camera (as Michael O'Reilly explains, 'Standard NTSC video is 30 fps [frames per second], 2 fields per frame, for a screen refresh rate of 60 times per second. This [the PXL-2000] only refreshes the screen 15 times per second'); it accomplishes this feat by gathering a significantly narrower data stream, providing roughly 100 lines of resolution to the standard NTSC camera's 500. O'Reilly explains that the PXL-2000 achieves its characteristic ghostly shimmering through the sub-pixel 'dithering' that occurs between the pixels (this is akin to the effect that sometimes occurs when film, with its greater resolution, is transferred to videotape). While we might regard this 'dithering' as a negative feature of the PXL-2000, 'this dithering has a counter-intuitive effect. It is the same effect that anti-aliasing has on fonts on a computer screen. The fonts look best (and are perceived to be sharper or of higher quality) when there is a small amount of blurring that takes place, instead of seeing the jagged edge of each pixel that makes up the letter... Events and imaging of a sub-pixel nature are of paramount importance to making video look less like video and as a by-product more like film.' This 'sub-pixellist viewpoint', combined with the camera's unusually wide depth-of-field are perhaps responsible for the camera's typical use, both by Hawke's Hamlet, and by directors like Benning and Almereyda: all those extreme low-light closeups of Ophelia, the face-in-the-camera confessional. For a useful summary of the camera and its popularity, see Michael O'Reilly, 'Pixelvision', <http://www.michaeloreilly.com/pixelpage.html> accessed 10 November 2004. See also 'The Pixelvision Home Page', <http://elvis.rowan.edu/~cassidy/pixel/> accessed 10 November 2004, and 'Dead Medium: The Fisher-Price Pixelvision', Dead Media Project, Working Notes 35:7, <http://www.deadmedia.org/notes/35/357.html> accessed 10 November 2004. For a useful summary of the camera's development and use by video artists, see Donaldson, 'Hamlet among the Pixelvisionaries'.

[18] Katherine Rowe's superb article, '"Remember Me": Technologies of Memory in Michael Almereyda's *Hamlet*', in *Shakespeare, the Movie, II: Popularizing the Plays on Film, TV, Video, and DVD*, ed. Richard Burt and Lynda Boose (London: Routledge, 2003), pp. 37–55, brilliantly sets Almereyda's 'polychronic' representation of digital media alongside an inquiry into alternative memory technologies, notably writing and the printed book; I quote here from p. 39. While I hope it's clear that my effort here is to locate the *digital* as a specific elaboration of technology in the film, I am deeply indebted to this fine article.

Ophelia look hip enough to have gone to Seattle the year before (or the year after: the shooting script was completed in 1998 and the film was released in 2000),[19] the film's visible evocation of *digital* technology is more or less confined to Hamlet's editing suite: though we glimpse a cellphone once, and Hamlet travels with a laptop, there's nary a PDA in sight, and Claudius's power to make the sequential appear simultaneous is hedged by the fact that he, like everyone else in the film, seems to have discovered neither email nor the internet.[20]

In his preface to the screenplay, Michael Almereyda notes that 'nearly every scene in the script features a photograph, a TV monitor, an electronic recording device of some kind'.[21] Almereyda points to the presence of 'electronic recording' as his principal innovation in the world of *Hamlet*, but rather than a fully digitized cyberculture, his *Hamlet* reflects the 'polychronic' world of technological change, in which various modes of representation jostle uncertainly against one another and seem to offer competing ways of enacting, extending and even preserving human action. The technologies of reproduction are scattered in witty, incisive ways throughout *Hamlet* and, at the risk of tedium, I'd like to catalogue them.[22] The film opens with Hamlet's video diary, combining images of Hawke's Hamlet with cartoons and film footage of stealth bombers in the Bosnian war. We see Hamlet digitally recording Claudius's opening speech – a news-conference, lots of flashbulbs and microphones – on his hand-held PXL 2000 Pixelvision camera and monitor. Claudius's 'so much for him' is delivered ripping a copy of *USA Today* – and its cover photo of Fortinbras – in half. Ophelia attempts to meet Hamlet by drawing a picture of the outdoor fountain (3:30? she writes, before Laertes and Polonius intercept her message). We first see the Ghost shut in an elevator on a security monitor, and later see the 'fishmonger' scene through the security camera's lens. Ophelia takes both 35mm and Polaroid photographs, and we see her taking pictures (during Polonius's advice to Laertes) and developing them in the darkroom while she waits

---

[19] Michael Almereyda, 'A Note on the Adaptation', *William Shakespeare's Hamlet, Adapted by Michael Almereyda* (London: Faber and Faber, 2000), p. xvi.

[20] Rowe notes that both Baz Luhrmann and Almereyda 'layer technologies in a way that regularly feels anachronistic, altering the viewer's sense of distance from the modern *mise-en-scène* and from the Shakespearean text', including the absurd, yet 'dramatically necessary' fact that Claudius sends his murderous message to England in the form of a floppy disk rather than via email; the 'just-in-time-delivery economy of the web is wholly absent from the film' ('Remember Me', p. 45).

[21] Michael Almereyda, 'Preface', *William Shakespeare's Hamlet, Adapted by Michael Almereyda* (London: Faber and Faber, 2000), p. x.

[22] I refer to the DVD reissue of the film: Michael Almereyda, dir., *Hamlet* (Miramax, 2000), DVD Buena Vista, n.d.

for Hamlet; she scatters the Polaroids as her herbs and flowers – 'here's rosemary' – during the mad scenes. The television is on in the background – showing something exploding and burning – during Hamlet's scene with the Ghost, and Claudius watches Bill Clinton on the TV in his limo during the prayer scene. Hamlet seems to be contemplating the 'To be, or not to be' soliloquy (3.1.58) by watching the Vietnamese monk Thich Nhat Hanh discussing 'being' and 'interbeing' on television, considers it again while recording himself putting a gun to his temple and in his mouth, and finally – famously – delivers it walking down the 'action' aisles of a Blockbuster store, shadowed by *Crow II* playing on the monitors behind him.[23] Claudius communicates with Rosencrantz and Guildenstern mainly by telephone, using a speaker-phone in his bedroom, a cordless phone and a car-phone (remember them?); on the move as they are, they take his instructions on their mobile. Hamlet uses a payphone in the basement of the Elsinore Hotel to remind Gertrude to avoid the bloat king's reechy kisses while he lugs the guts away. Polonius wires Ophelia with a microphone for her meeting with Hamlet (and brings her a Happy Birthday Mylar balloon). After Hamlet discovers the trick and Ophelia flees, she hears his calumny on her answering machine. Hamlet's *Mousetrap* is a 'film/video', composed of digitized animation and selections from ersatz home movies, silent films, advertising and a porn film. Hamlet lifts the floppy disk that Rosencrantz and Guildenstern are to deliver to the king of England and edits it on his laptop on the jet to Heathrow (on the plane he also sees the news of Fortinbras – 'how all occasions' – and plays with some postcards). Hamlet sends a fax to Claudius to announce that he's returned to Denmark and Claudius faxes Hamlet to invite him to duel Laertes. The duel itself is judged electronically and, as Hamlet dies we see a grainy, black-and-white Pixelvision replay of various images of the film, intercut with 'live' image of Hamlet's eye. Robert McNeill delivers a pastiche of Fortinbras's and the Player King's lines from a television newsdesk to conclude the action, and the film ends with these lines scrolling on the teleprompter. We do, by the way, see Hamlet in a coffee shop, *writing* – that is, using a hand-held pen to inscribe the poem to his celestial soul's idol in a notebook – and we even see a theatre once: Hamlet, who has hijacked Claudius's limo and is about to shoot him when Claudius laments 'words without thoughts never to heaven go', stops the car and flies down the street, in front of the

---

[23] References are to *William Shakespeare: The Complete Works*, ed. Stanley Wells and Gary Taylor *et al.* (Oxford: Clarendon Press, 1986).

Broadway marquee for Julie Taymor's stage reanimation of the Disney (animated) film, *The Lion King*.[24] Needless to say, the theatre is closed.

The scattering of 'technology' in the film frames its central conceit, that Hamlet uses video recording and digital editing throughout the film as a means of reflection; it's the way several of his soliloquies are delivered and the means of the film's opening and closing. As Sherry Turkle put it in 1995, 'People explicitly turn to computers for experiences that they hope will change their ways of thinking or will affect their social and emotional lives.'[25] Turkle's book is oddly synchronized, now, for us, with *Hamlet*, documenting a moment in emerging technology that has quickly passed from view, though its attendant anxieties may well remain with us. Almereyda's *Hamlet* is surely on the brink of digital culture but only on the brink: the film has, today, an oddly archaic feel, not merely because Hamlet should be able to afford – and could have afforded even in 1998 – better equipment, but because of the mysterious absence of other technologies, notably wireless communication. Hamlet's choice of the PXL 2000 identifies him with a 1990s indie avant-garde (that includes art-filmmakers like Sadie Benning and films like Almereyda's *Another Girl, Another Planet* and *Nadja*) interested in exploring the visual effects of a residual (or even obsolete) avatar of an emerging technology, digital filmmaking. That is, while the film's use of recording seems to strike a tech-forward stance, *Hamlet* seems to deploy a kind of Shakespearean anachronism – video cameras but no email – to mark the impact of technological change on its sense of dramatic possibility; after all, the most astonishing innovation of the PXL 2000 is that it makes video recordings, with sound, on *audio cassette tapes*. (Perhaps one of the liabilities of instant communications will be the death of drama – cm bk 2 vrna. J ok, L.) Rather than regarding Almereyda's film as already belated at the moment it was made, we might regard it from a slightly different angle, as at once documenting and exploring digital technology's effect on the drama's representation of the 'human' at the moment of its first impact.

The 'rogue and peasant slave' soliloquy deftly allegorizes both the film's position on the horizon of technology and its sense of the place of drama in technological culture. In the written play, presumably in

---

[24] Providing a rich list of Almereyda's quotations from other Hamlet films, Elsie Walker identifies the marquee from its 'best musical of the year' tag, noting that *The Lion King* also derives from *Hamlet*; Elsie Walker, 'A "Harsh World" of Soundbite Shakespeare: Michael Almereyda's *Hamlet* (2000)', *EnterText* 1.2 (June 2001), p. 324.

[25] Turkle, *Life on the Screen*, p. 26.

Shakespeare's theatre, and surely in most theatrical productions since, Hamlet's confrontation with the actor is a means of developing a complex network of reflections. It's a bookish speech that Hamlet misremembers and then recalls again, smacking not so much of dramatic speech in 1600 as of the emphatic, Marlovian diction of a decade before. O'ersized with coagulate gore, eyes like carbuncles, as a figure of mechanical and inhuman revenge, Pyrrhus seems ambivalent at best as a model for Hamlet's task; the actor's performance, too, seems at once to galvanize Hamlet into comparable extroversion ('Who calls me villain') and to embarrass him with the unseemly promiscuity of performance ('Why, what an ass am I') (see *Hamlet* 2.2.551–607). And yet, for all the hesitations enforced by language and its enactment, by the playwright's and the actor's ways and means, Hamlet catches his image in the glass of acting: playing's the thing.

Unlike the many film *Hamlet*s that dispense with all (Olivier) or most (Zeffirelli keeps only a few lines from the soliloquy) of this scene, Almereyda's *Hamlet* retains Hamlet's soliloquy and frames the encounter with the Player as a moment in which both Hamlet and *Hamlet* imagine themselves. The camera, constantly cutting back and forth between Hamlet's face and the images on his computer screen and video monitor, defines 'reflection' in an internalized, psychological register, an aspect of the scene underscored (as it is often in *Hamlet* and throughout Shakespeare film) by having Hamlet's speech presented as voice-over, interior monologue replacing the act of speaking. But while Shakespeare's Hamlet faces and faces down a living actor, Almereyda's Hamlet faces an image, an actor-in-character, an image that's almost purely image, the actor absorbed as 'movie star' icon : James Dean. We might think that the film image provides Hamlet with a somewhat simpler choice – in effect, asking him to contemplate the 'character' rather than its performance, as though Pyrrhus could be staged without the simultaneously affecting, alienating histrionic aggression of the live actor. But if a stage Hamlet always confronts 'character' in the register of enactment, Hawke's Hamlet confronts 'character' in the register of the image, laminated to the outsized absence of the star. While the Player, in a sense, brings the dead language of Pyrrhus to life, enforcing its horror through the grotesque process of taking it on, Hawke's Player – James Dean – registers the pastness of his drama in the register *of* the past. We cannot see James Dean with anything other than nostalgia: like Buddy Holly or J. F. K., the image of James Dean inescapably evokes a nostalgia for what didn't come into being as action, at least as much as for what did.

Almereyda's allegory of the place of drama in the technologies of contemporary performance opens with this confrontation: Hamlet's encounter with the Player is played to the music of nostalgia, sustained not merely by the image of the young, dead star, but by the softly elegiac frame that black-and-white film – like photography – draws around the past. Roland Barthes associates photography with the theatre through the 'singular intermediary' of death; insofar as Barthes claims 'the original relation of the theater and the cult of the Dead' ('to make oneself up was to designate oneself as a body simultaneously living and dead'), so 'Photography is a kind of primitive theater, a kind of *Tableau Vivant*, a figuration of the motionless and made-up face beneath which we see the dead.'[26] While Shakespeare's stagey Player is a precursor to the lambent image of James Dean, the stage and the photograph articulate the living and the dead with a difference: Shakespeare's Hamlet is harrowed by the ways the absent ghosts of Pyrrhus and Hecuba possess the actor's presence; Hawke's player is always already gone. In the film, we first see Hamlet on his bed, watching Dean simultaneously on a TV monitor over his bed and on his PXL 2000 handheld; the screen fills with Dean, but when the camera pulls back, we are now behind Hamlet's head (see figure 50). He is sitting at his desk, computer screen to the left, various photo-postcard portraits of the dead in the centre (manufactured images of the Droeshout Shakespeare, Nietzsche and Mayakovsky now, and later we see Che Guevara), TV monitor with Dean to the right. Except now, Dean has been replaced by a very different image, John Gielgud as Hamlet – in a velvety romantic-Renaissance 'period' slashed doublet – speaking to Yorick's skull, from Gielgud's 1944–5 production at the Haymarket, a clip taken from Humphrey Jennings's elegant wartime propaganda film, *A Diary for Timothy*.[27] It's a canny image. Silently imaging Gielgud as Hamlet, Hawke's screen summons the memory of silent film (which will soon play a crucial part in Hamlet's *Mousetrap* film/video), deftly incorporating and displacing the theatrical tradition into the film archive, recalling the moment of its transformation, the moment of the theatre's demise as the definitive technology of the drama, the moment of the

[26] Roland Barthes, *Camera Lucida: Reflections on Photography*, trans. Richard Howard (New York: Hill and Wang, 1981), pp. 31–2.

[27] I'm grateful to Peter Holland for confirming the identification of John Gielgud, and especially to Luke McKernan of the British Universities Film and Video Council for drawing me to Jennings and *A Diary for Timothy*, and for several other invaluable pointers. I am also thankful to Olwen Terriss, formerly of the British Film Institute film and television archives, who also assisted me in efforts to identify elements of Hamlet's film archive. See *A Diary for Timothy*, dir. Humphrey Jennings, written by E. M. Forster (Crown Film Unit, 1944–5), DVD Image Entertainment, 2002.

50 Hamlet's desk. From *Hamlet*, directed by Michael Almereyda (2000)

invention of 'liveness' by the possibility of recorded performance. Theater and live acting still exist, of course; they can even be preserved, in a way, by film. Capturing a silent Gielgud marks the moment when acting could only be understood in relation to other living actions. The moment of the invention of 'liveness' by recording is, paradoxically, the moment of the death of 'liveness', the moment of theatre's passing into the realm of residual technology. As Philip Auslander puts it, 'historically, the live is actually an effect of mediatization'. Yet while Auslander suggests that 'the historical relationship of liveness and mediatization must be seen as a relation of dependence and imbrication rather than opposition', Almereyda's film tends to suggest that this imbrication should be understood as part of the uneven, halting succession of technologies.[28]

But of course Gielgud was not a silent star: what we remember Gielgud for is that voice, the audible echo of a nearly bygone theatricality. First educated at Lady Benson's Acting School, and the great nephew of Ellen Terry, Gielgud self-consciously stood as a fulcrum between the rhetorical

---

[28] Philip Auslander, *Liveness: Performance in a Mediatized Culture* (London: Routledge, 1999), pp. 51, 53.

traditions of the nineteenth-century stage and the economic realities of twentieth-century acting. A splendid Hamlet, a landmark Lear, alternating Romeo and Mercutio with Laurence Olivier, grooming younger actors (Richard Burton) and directors (Peter Brook), teaming with Ralph Richardson in the definitive performance of modern roles (Spooner and Hirst in Harold Pinter's *No Man's Land*), Gielgud's formative role in the modern London stage is, of course, complemented by his extensive career in film (Hitchcock's *The Secret Agent*, 1936) and television (Edward Ryder in *Brideshead Revisited*, 1981), culminating in the role that Peter Greenaway assigns him in *Prospero's Books*, ventriloquizing Shakespeare-as-Prospero, writing/reading/narrating the entire text of *The Tempest*, grounding the play's substantial life in *that voice*. Almereyda's film invokes Gielgud as an icon of the dramatic theatre, only to displace liveness as an element of Shakespearean drama.

Gielgud's career outlines the transformation of theatre by the technologies of recorded performance, and this technological narrative is enacted by Almereyda's camera work in Hamlet's confrontation with the Player. The camera begins behind Hamlet's left shoulder; we can see both screens, the screen of the computer (yellow digital flower, short film clips of a man and woman, eventually kissing) and Gielgud to the right. But as the camera dollies around behind Hamlet's head, we lose sight of Gielgud and, crossing over the postcards, attend to the computer screen. In his fascinating account of the 'craft' of digital design, Malcolm McCullough remarks that 'Where a photographic print requires little more work to make many identical images, a computer image requires little more work to make many, no two of which are exactly alike... So where the mass-produced photograph was the characteristic metaphor of the modern, today the digitally generated image, in its place, has become the effective metaphor of the postmodern.'[29] In Almereyda's *Hamlet*, theatre is displaced first into film, where it remains only as a memorial trace, the recollection of a different mode of production, attention and action (the *Hamlet* scene Gielgud is playing – itself an isolated clip of wartime London 'bearing up' in Jennings's film – is itself cut from Almereyda's film: this is our only glimpse of poor Yorick's iconic skull). The transformation of the modern to the postmodern is read as a transformation in the technologies of production and performance – theatre, photography, film, digital image capture – perhaps leading us to wonder about the place of drama in the 'culture of simulation'.[30]

[29] McCullough, *Abstracting Craft*, p. 47.   [30] Turkle, *Life on the Screen*, p. 61.

As Walter Benjamin recognized some time ago, film transfers the site of performance from the auratic presence of the live actor to the work of the camera, which at once 'need not respect the performance as an integral whole'. Citing Pirandello's prescient sense that the film actor's 'body loses its corporeality, it evaporates, it is deprived of reality', Benjamin notes that in the 'Age of Mechanical Reproduction', the audience's identification in the process of performance is not through the actor but through the work of the camera.[31] Acting is auratic, continuous, occupying the temporal and material duration of unique human bodies. Film acting is a consequence of the camera and the editor: shot out of sequence from a range of angles and perspectives and then edited into a narrative series, film depends on the sequentiality of projection (frame to frame, 24 per second) to lend still photographs the appearance of human animation. But Hamlet's film is poised on the brink of a further transformation, as mechanical reproducibility gives way to the process of digital reproduction.

Digital editing transforms images into data that can be manipulated in a much wider range of ways, ways finally disconnected from the scale of human time, perspective, or sequence. As we lose sight – for good, it turns out – of both Dean and Gielgud, our attention is focused on the editing screen, as Hamlet manipulates the icons on the screen to begin editing his film. Almereyda emphasizes the emerging functions of digital technology as a metaphor for human consciousness, rapidly cutting now not between the computer and television screens, but from the computer screen to a close up of Hamlet's eyes, sustaining the now commonplace sense that the computer, its strategies of archiving and displaying 'information', has fully displaced both the stage (the theatre of the mind) and 'the book and volume of [the] brain' (1.5.103) as the most dynamic contemporary model of human thought. And as Hamlet conceives catching the 'conscience of the King', the screen goes black; the next image is the video box, *The Mouse Trap*, 'A Film/Video by Hamlet', which turns out to be in Claudius's hand.

Shakespeare's *Hamlet* might be said to oscillate between the technologies of writing and acting: the Player brings a palpably literary text to histrionic 'life', and Hamlet vows to 'wipe away all trivial fond records' (1.5.99) in order to take on the Ghost's summons to action. In an important sense, though (as Hamlet's *revision* of Claudius's letter on his

---

[31] Walter Benjamin, 'The Work of Art in the Age of Mechanical Reproduction', in *Illuminations*, ed. and introd. Hannah Arendt, trans. Harry Zohn (New York: Schocken, 1985), pp. 228–9.

laptop suggests), the mastering art of Almereyda's film is not writing, nor acting, nor even filming: it's *editing*. Much as Hamlet's encounter with the Player resonates throughout the play's meditation on acting and action, Almereyda's allegory of technological change opens from Hamlet's scene of editorial composition. When test audiences thought the Shakespearean plot (begin with the sidekicks seeing the Ghost, bring in the stars in the second scene) 'felt flat', Almereyda's way of fashioning a more 'urgent start' for the film was to sit down with Ethan Hawke, get the 'pixel camera' and work 'out a new introduction, a video diary excerpt from one of our favourite speeches' – the 'what a piece of work is a man' speech (2.2.305–10) – that had been dropped from the film.[32] Opening the film with narration drawn from later in the play delivered from the TV monitor, *Hamlet* enacts Almereyda's sense of the play as hypertext, 'favourite' bits sequenced into a fundamentally visual structure of representation, susceptible not only to being interlinked in various nonlinear ways, but of being combined readily with other dataforms: a cartoon Godzilla, a stealth bomber, explosions. In the opening scene, Almereyda's camera also shows the sign of Hamlet's editorial agency, the mousehand working along the bottom of the frame. As anyone using word-processing, an Ipod or a digital camera knows, the fundamental changes in digital music and imaging technology have only partly to do with the expanded accessibility and portability of recorded 'information', text, downloaded music, photographs or moving images. After all, ever since print's power of duplication released the manuscript book from its lectern chain, books and images have been portable; what digital technology has enabled is an exponential increase in the ease and power with which we can rework this data, transform it into something else. Re-colour your photographs, burn a remix for a party, animate your web page, download your girlfriend or boyfriend (or at least their photos) into your cellphone: everyone's an editor. But while digital editing surely expands Benjamin's sense that modern technologies of reproduction – print and film – have begun to erase the distinction between 'author and public' ('At any moment the reader is ready to turn into a writer'), it also alters the relations of production definitive of mechanical reproducibility. Mechanical technology is a technology of *reproduction*: a single text, image, sound can be copied to a stable medium that enables exact duplication and massive dissemination (it is 'modern man's legitimate

---

[32] Michael Almereyda, 'Director's Notes', *William Shakespeare's Hamlet, Adapted by Michael Almereyda* (London: Faber and Faber, 2000), p. 135.

claim to being reproduced', and reproducing himself, that 'the capitalistic exploitation of the film denies', preferring instead to 'spur the interest of the masses through illusion-promoting spectacles and dubious speculations'.[33] Digital technology is a technology of *transformation*: rather than copying text, image or sound to distinct stable media, it transforms them into a common electronic code. Because this code, regardless of what it encodes, is stored the same way, these different dataforms are susceptible to being combined, exchanged, realized in ways that depart significantly from the form of their initial recording (select a menu, change the font; punch a button, animate the text; click the mouse, wrap it around Mick Jagger singing; click it again, and maybe those are *your* lips). As films like *Forrest Gump* and journalistic controversies about the editing of digital photographs – is cropping a mechanical photograph the same thing as digitally editing an object or person out of the image? – have shown, in its ability to render data as 'information', *digital reproduction* is a kind of oxymoron. Although digital technology certainly enables reproducibility – driving printing presses and other mechanical devices – what the encoding of expression as electronic bits and bytes enables is the ready alteration of modes of expression, and with it consequent (and still unexplored) changes in the subjects that engage that expression.

For this reason, it's important to see the impact of digital technology not merely in its networking and connective functions (which are largely absent in the film – who uses fax when an email attachment will do?); Almereyda's *Hamlet* trains our attention on editing as a critical and creative practice, where the subject frames and encounters his own reflection. Almereyda/Hamlet's editing implies a continuity between the personal archive and the public visual record (though as Donaldson points out, to play PXL-2000 images on anything other than camera's small monitor requires the user to reconfigure the camera to use videotape rather than the audiotape for which it was manufactured; in this sense, Pixelvision is perhaps more innately suited to the 'psychologically regressive' mode of personal confession that connects Hawke's Hamlet with the early films of Kyle Cassidy and Sadie Benning).[34] At the same time, though, the process of reproducing that archive in the personal register of the home computer suggests a different relation to experience, evoked by the seamless suture of the digital editing suite. If Almereyda registers an anxiety about emerging technology, it may well arise in the asymmetry between Hamlet's film and his own, for Almereyda's film

[33] Benjamin, 'Work of Art', p. 232. [34] Donaldson, 'Hamlet among the Pixelvisionaries'.

pulls back from the technological implications that Hamlet seems to explore. Although Almereyda includes some arty tricks (the dim image of Sam Shepard's ghost we see haunting the final scenes with Horatio and Marcella at Hamlet's apartment; the Ghost disappearing into the Pepsi machine), his film seems in fact to eschew the kind of abrupt transformation of archive and image that draws Hamlet to the screen. For all its allusion to other *Hamlet*s, Almereyda's film is straightforward in its visual narrative, using none of the morphing, stop-action, or animation effects we've come to expect even in relatively realistic films.

That is, while Almereyda's film emphasizes the presence of recording technologies in the world of *Hamlet*, it seems less certain of the consequences of those technologies: while Hamlet's editing seems to mark the passing of both theatre and conventional film, Almereyda's film remains understandably committed to cinema. This asymmetry is perhaps most clearly marked by Hamlet's film, *The Mousetrap: A Tragedy*. As Katherine Rowe notes, 'Unredacted, uncited, unrehearsed films do not have a robust existence', and by transforming his trick from theatre to 'film/video', Hamlet not only participates in the strategies of technological surveillance more characteristic of 2000 than 1600, but situates his production in a different relation to the cultural archive.[35] Rowe argues that 'The found footage in *The Mousetrap* works differently from Hamlet's home videos, stitching together fragments of familiar imagery in a way that evokes a variety of earlier forms associated with the cinematic experiences of visual presence'; while the film 'generates strong individual and collective responses', though, home video technologies 'are now so individuated that we really have no idea if we can go around handing our version of the past to someone else – as Ophelia does her photographs – and expect it to be legible'. In this sense the / of Hamlet's 'film/video' marks more than a moment of generic indecision. Rowe argues that 'video allows us to receive and process content in intimate ways. Yet cinema provides the cognitive grammar that organizes that content in socially legible terms and produces it as shared knowledge'.[36] Hamlet's 'film/video' means at once to stake its claim to the socially legible forms of cinematic representation, but to do so through the means of digital editing – the process that has made the making of videos (well, DVDs) like Hamlet's a widespread possibility.[37]

[35] Rowe, 'Remember Me' p. 39.　　[36] Rowe, 'Remember Me' p. 52.

[37] It might be noted in this sense that what I take to be crucial about Hamlet's *Mousetrap* is not its 'home movie' character but the fact that as personal video it has been digitally edited; it's also important to recognize that even the 'home movie' elements in Hamlet's film are in fact archival.

Using similar graphic design for *The Mousetrap* and *Hamlet*, Almereyda invites us to see the two films articulating a kind of metafilmic
commentary. In Shakespeare's play, the play-within-the-play is bracketed
from *Hamlet* in stylistic terms: the static character of its action, its moral
simplicity, the outmoded formality of its language are all set against the
more complex, multiple, fluid and ambiguous forms of Shakespeare's
play. Yet Hamlet's film/video stands in a different temporal relation to
Almereyda's film than *The Murder of Gonzago* does to *Hamlet*. While *The
Mousetrap* is projected from a videotape, we have not seen Hamlet
messing around with tape: the film has been copied to video from
Hamlet's digital editing suite (surely the quality of the film would be
better if he'd had a DVD burner). Packaged in its artful video-cassette
sleeve, *The Mousetrap* seems less like a 'home video' than like an art film:
despite the 'amateurish' quality of its herky-jerky editing, Hamlet's 'film/
video' positions itself not as part of an artistically and ethically stable
'past', but as a work poised at the tipping point between video art and a
coming technology, the digital film.[38]

In this sense, the film/video articulates the intersection of recording
and reproducing technologies, and so of different eras, genres, socialities
of visual-recording representation: although it's something of a low-tech
product, it nonetheless foregrounds the impact of digital representation.
The film opens and is punctuated by the digitally animated rose,
blooming and dying; the image is strikingly generic, the kind of imagery
that comes packaged with the editing suite. Hamlet's 'childhood' is
represented by two equally generic 'home movies' – file footage that
seems to represent the 'home movie' rather than being actual home-movie
film – drawn apparently from two different eras. In the first – perhaps
taken from advertising – a 1950s family sits happily before a large boxy
television, dominating the lower right corner of the screen; in the second,
we see a family in what appears to be an earlier scene, perhaps the 1940s –
the patterned furniture, wallpaper, hooked rug, mother sewing, no TV in
sight – and watch as the father follows the little boy to the bedroom,
down a long, Olivier-like hallway. Time passes, signalled by a retro-cool
animated globe reminiscent of sci-fi films (the Jetsons are back on

---

[38] Donaldson provides a superb reading of the way that Almereyda's original decision to incorporate
video art – by having Hamlet's 'To be or not to be' soliloquy take place *both* in the Whitney
Museum's Bill Viola retrospective *and* in the Blockbuster store – was pre-empted by production
problems; as Donaldson suggests, the dialogue between Hamlet and Viola's 'Slowly Turning
Narrative' would have included an additional 'remediating' element in the film by situating
Shakespeare in relation to the 'potentially powerful presence of video as fine art'. See 'Hamlet
among the Pixelvisionaries'.

television selling dishwasher detergent, to say nothing of the 1950s-to-1970s imagery of The Gap, Old Navy, Target, and Yahoo!). The film then attends to the poisoning, first registered in silent film, and then in a manifestly retro-animation of the work of poison; to me this is reminiscent of the *Rocky and Bullwinkle* style, though it also recalls Terry Gilliam. If Hamlet's film recalls the theatre at all, it's that moment when theatre was preserved in the rhetoric of silent film: we see various silents of men dying in stagey excess, a Cleopatra-like queen, closing finally on a king crowning himself, the moment that frightens Claudius with false fire. And there's the porn film.

What's striking about Hamlet's film is at once its archival character, and its manifest emphasis on editing, the extent to which, to tell the contemporary story, Hamlet resorts not only to the technology of the digital suite but to its inherent modality, reducing all information to 'information', data bits that are indistinguishable and susceptible to being reconfigured in a range of signifying environments. In this sense, Hamlet's film foretells a sense of the subject (the sense we see at the end of the film when Hamlet's 'live' experience in the film is replayed as pixellated 'memory') sustained throughout the film. At the same time, though, it's important to see how this use of film/video is not all that characteristic of Almereyda's film, which – while digitally edited – doesn't really use the full range of digital effects: colour saturation, slow and fast motion, stop action, warping of perspective and, of course, animation. Elsie Walker is certainly right to note both Almereyda's rich and ironic texture of allusion to earlier Shakespeare films, and she points to the 'fragmentary style and rapid rhythm of the film, the disjointed editing and eclectic musical choices which draw attention to its construction, the way many of the key speeches are interrupted and/or separated from their bodily sources, the cacophony of surround-sound, and the dominance of advertising signs (visual and verbal)' seems to interrupt and finally displace the more leisurely contemplation of Shakespeare's text.[39] Yet while Almereyda's *Hamlet* is rapidly paced, expunging the signs of the stage and erasing the theatre's techniques for foregrounding the duration of *speaking* as the sign of the subject, replacing them with the now-conventional voice-over that rekeys temporality in the visual register of changing camera shots, the visual style of Almereyda's film is relatively conventional, even in the ways it absorbs Hamlet's video-diaries to the register of the soliloquy. Almereyda's film is the residual of which Hamlet's is the emergent, and

---

[39] Walker, 'Harsh World', p. 333.

this asymmetry marks the film's brinksmanship: Almereyda really isn't part of Hamlet's culture.

What would it mean to see Shakespearean drama as Hamlet does? We can get a glimpse of this sense of the drama, of editing replacing acting as the vehicle of the drama, from a different film: Baz Luhrmann's *William Shakespeare's Romeo + Juliet*.[40] Much has been written about Luhrmann's investment in the culture of the image in this film, yet, like Almereyda's *Hamlet*, Luhrmann's film tends not to foreground its digital character: yes, filming in Vera Cruz was cut short by a hurricane that destroyed the set of the beach scenes, and led to some quite evidently digitalized clouds blowing by (and sometimes apparently moving into the wind); the giant Christ statue that stands in the roundabout was matted into the film (though the giant Virgin atop the church is, in fact, part of the building). But *Romeo + Juliet* is no *Matrix*. Where we see the impact of digital technology is in the conception of the film's action: in the editing. Whereas the 'digital' is confined to Hamlet's screen in Almereyda's film, it seems to provide the condition of Luhrmann's imagination, and of the world of Verona Beach that his film projects. The film's editor, Jill Bilcock notes that the scoring of the stupendous opening scene not only owes its conception to Sergio Leone westerns but its sound as well. Shown sitting at her editing suite, Bilcock reports that they went to a video store, bought 'one of those spaghetti westerns and stole the music off it and chopped it up'. In the 'Commentary' version of the film, Luhrmann, screenwriter Craig Pearce, cinematographer Donald McAlpine, and production designer Catherine Martin lament Bilcock's absence from the recording session, particularly since the opening scene was 'totally constructed and written by Jill'.[41]

Romeo + Juliet opens with the prologue delivered by the TV-encased anchorwoman, and introduces its 'credits' of the dramatis personae through a fast-paced series of cuts incorporating digital zooms of helicopter shots from above the city (which attend to the matted-in logos of the Montague and Capulet towers) into still and motion shots of the *dramatis personae* (shots drawn, we will discover, from later in the film), newspaper headlines, the family trees, and the text of the prologue itself,

---

[40] *William Shakespeare's Romeo + Juliet*, dir. Baz Luhrmann, DVD Twentieth Century Fox Home Entertainment, 2002.

[41] *William Shakespeare's Romeo + Juliet*, 'The Editor', 'Commentary'. Digital technology here is now formative in all elements of filmmaking. Interviewed for the DVD, Kim Barrett the costume designer notes the ways that costume designing today depends on digital editing, in which the actors are composed into costume renderings.

'a pair of star cross'd lovers'. For all its echoes of Westerns and Woo (Tybalt's twofisted-falling-sideways shooting), the opening gas-station scene draws its energy and conception at once from its echoes of Sergio Leone and from the pace of its editing, which contributes to the film's evocation of the globalized – and colonial – economy of digital culture. While there are no hanging-in-the-air *Matrix* or *Crouching Tiger, Hidden Dragon* effects, the opening scene shifts scale and perspective incessantly in ways rendered possible and available through digital editing. The scene is brilliantly fast-paced; by my count, no single camera shot is held longer than five seconds, and most are between one and three seconds: the longest shot of the scene is the final, lingering, slow-motion shot of the gas station erupting in flames. Changing perspective (distant shot, instant move to close up, as on Abra), and changing position (Capulet car, door, boot), the energy of the scene arises from the crisp editing, editing that emphatically treats the image as 'information' in the technical, 'information-theory' sense: stasis is mere noise, entropy; change in the signal creates the possibility for information to be transmitted. Some of the 'Western' elements had, in fact, to be edited in: Bilcock notes that the producers were concerned that the gunfight seemed to show no bullets hitting anything, and so she had to edit in the various shots of the bullets spraying around, hitting the oilcan and sending the metal sign spinning. But the story is also told through the recollection of simpler technologies, particularly the 'wipe' dissolves, in which one scene (the shot of the Montague boys driving down the highway in their car) is replaced as a new scene (the gas station) is 'dragged' across the screen. If we feel that we're back in the 1960s *Batman* series, it's no surprise: the 'swoosh' sound and blurred screen used to establish a change in location and focus (as when we zoom to Capulet at his desk) emphasizes the comic-book quality of the film's opening scene by framing it in the register of comic-book TV.

Much more than Almereyda's film, *Romeo + Juliet* dramatizes the dramatic consequences of digital editing, the consequences of *The Mousetrap*. Transforming imagery into information enables its editing to transpire differently, not only foregrounding the way that earlier styles of action, of gestural embodiment and representation can be replayed as pastiche, but articulating a very different sense of the nature of film communication. From its earliest days, film has been fascinated by its ability to reframe the real, drawing audiences to films of locomotives passing and hijinks with a water hose. But film also has the ability to render the real by rendering what's invisible to the human eye visible, interpretable: Muybridge's studies of motion anticipate the ways in which not only the speed of film but its ability to take a range of perspectives reshapes the viewer's understanding of the construction of the world. At the same time, and again from its moment of inception, film has also been fascinated by the possibility of staging alternative worlds, of forcing the viewer into possible perspectives on the merely imaginary and impossible perspectives on the real. Digital film and digital editing are, in this sense, another place where that question of the impact of new technology comes into view: are the kinds of vision that digital editing enables a merely incremental change in the practice of film or a wholesale transformation in the framing of the visible? It's not merely that digitalization enables the stop-action manipulation of imagery, hanging Keanu Reeves in the air, or the insertion of digital effects (dodging the bullets as the air parts around them): transforming the image into data, it enables the image to be broken down and reassembled in different contexts, with different sequence, in ways that enable new ways of imagining the world. As the use of imaging technology in medicine suggests, what the computer enables us to do is to see what cannot be seen or at least to imagine that we are seeing it.

Remembering theatre, we might recall one of the animating gestures of modern theatricality, the sense that the image enacts its most powerful, coercive work when it conceals, displaces or denies its means of production. Sherry Turkle has anatomized a stunning transformation in the ideology of computer culture in the final decades of the last millennium, poised in the late 1980s between the 'traditional modernist expectation that one could take a technology, open the hood and see inside' and the Macintosh graphical user interface, which transformed (and so popularized) computer use: rather than needing to know a programming language that engaged more or less directly with the programming technology 'under the hood', the graphic user interface enabled users to stay on the surface, manipulate images that could then drive the computer's functional applications.[42] 'Thus, by the late 1980s, the culture of personal computing found itself becoming practically two cultures. There was IBM reductionism vs. Macintosh simulation and surface: an icon of the modernist technological utopia vs. an icon of post-modern reverie.' Indeed, the triumph of the Macintosh surface has led, as Turkle argues, to an explicitly ideological transformation in our understanding of the meaning and purpose of 'transparency'.

---

[42] Turkle, *Life on the Screen*, p. 35.

In 1980, most computer users who spoke of transparency were referring to a transparency analogous to that of traditional machines, an ability to 'open the hood' and poke around. But when, in the mid-1980s, users of the Macintosh began to talk about transparency, they were talking about seeing their documents and programs represented by attractive and easy-to-interpret icons. They were referring to having things work without needing to look into the inner workings of the computer. This was, somewhat paradoxically, a kind of transparency enabled by complexity and opacity. By the end of the decade, the word 'transparency' had taken on its Macintosh meaning in both computer talk and colloquial language. In a culture of simulation, when people say that something is transparent, they mean that they can easily see how to make it work. They don't necessarily mean that they know why it is working in terms of any underlying process.[43]

Almereyda's Hamlet uses a version of Microsoft Windows, which once required a DOS command to load, but which now emulates the superficial character of the Macintosh 'desktop'. Although Hamlet's *Mousetrap* jumps abruptly from digital imagery to cell animation to film imagery, Hamlet's editing tends – in ways more or less analogous to the more foregrounded use of digital animation in *The Matrix* and of digital editing in *Romeo + Juliet* – to subordinate editorial intervention to narrative coherence (it's perhaps notable in this regard that neither Hamlet nor Almereyda provide a full list of credits to the films that are cited; they're just drawn, like much else in the emerging world of digital property, from the archival ether, 'file footage'). Hamlet deploys Brecht's favorite filmic device, the montage that spoke to him most vividly about technology's ability to disembed images from the machinery of ideological seduction. For Brecht, the 'discovery' enabled by epic theatre can be 'accomplished by means of the interruption of sequences', an interruption that 'here has not the character of a stimulant but an organizing function'; recognizing that montage is often deployed as a merely stimulating 'modish procedure', Brecht nonetheless models the theatrical *gestus* on 'the method of montage decisive in radio and film', which should compel the spectator 'to adopt an attitude vis-à-vis the process, the actor vis-à-vis his [*sic*] role'.[44] At the same time, Hamlet's editing, in principle and perhaps as enabled by GUI technologies, tends not to open the principle of his own montage to view. Like the machinery of epic theatre, perhaps

[43] Turkle, *Life on the Screen*, p. 42.
[44] Walter Benjamin, 'The Author as Producer', *Reflections: Essays, Aphorisms, Autobiographical Writings*. trans. Edmund Jephcott (New York: Schocken, 1978), p. 235.

montage has been finally absorbed to narcotic aesthetics not of the conventional stage but of the invisible rhetoric of the digital screen.

'During long periods of history, the mode of human sense perception changes with humanity's entire mode of existence.' As Walter Benjamin suggests, 'The manner in which human sense perception is organized, the medium in which it is accomplished, is determined not only by nature but by historical' – and technological – 'circumstances as well'.[45] When Jan Kott, in 'Hamlet of the Midcentury', remarked that '*Hamlet* is like a sponge. Unless it is produced in a stylized or antiquarian fashion, it immediately absorbs all the problems of our time', he had a specific, mediagenic Hamlet in mind: 'I prefer the youth, deeply involved in politics, rid of illusions, sarcastic, passionate and brutal. A young rebel who has about him something of the charm of James Dean.'[46] Separated from us, now, by a half century, Dean has emerged as the icon less of political rebellion than of bitter ennui, an irritable, disengaged, undirected angst trapped within regimented 1950s America; fittingly enough – and nothing marks the distance from Dean to Hawke so clearly – the Cracow Hamlet of 'late autumn, 1956, read only newspapers', and the Warsaw Hamlet of the following year could be visualized 'in black sweater and blue jeans. The book he is holding is not by Montaigne, but by Sartre, Camus or Kafka.'[47] Our understanding of ourselves, and how dramatic action represents us, speaks to and for us, is necessarily changed by the media 'in which it is accomplished': much as we have come to understand the impact of the technological transformation separating Hamlet's Player from James Dean, we're just beginning to recognize the impact of the transformation separating Dean from, say, Baz Luhrmann. Like other forms of literature and performance, drama provides 'equipment for living', but I think we now have to understand the drama alongside all that other equipment beeping and buzzing, clicking and flickering, transmitting and receiving about, around, and inside us, among 'information' signals that transgress even the most intimate thresholds of that minimal subject of the drama: the human.

---

[45] Benjamin, 'Work of Art', p. 222.
[46] Jan Kott, 'Hamlet of the Midcentury', *Shakespeare Our Contemporary*, trans. Boleslaw Taborski (New York: W. W. Norton, 1974), pp. 64, 62.
[47] Kott, 'Hamlet of the Midcentury', pp. 68, 69.

CHAPTER 12

The Shakespeare revolution will not be televised: staging the media apparatus

Robert Shaughnessy

I

On the evening of 7 September 2003, the minority digital arts channel BBC Four claimed a historic first in the history of British televised Shakespeare: a live broadcast of *Richard II* from Shakespeare's Globe on London's South Bank. Occupying nearly four hours of a late summer evening, the broadcast bucked the postmodern cinematic trend of the post-millennial small-screen Shakespeares (as represented the same year by ITV1's police-procedural *Othello* and Channel 4's refugee *Twelfth Night*), offering a nakedly theatrical engagement with the play and the performance event. Staged as an 'original practices' production as part of the Globe's 2003 Season of Regime Change, *Richard II* was an example of the kind of floridly anti-demotic, sumptuously costumed Shakespeare that has not been seen since the end of the BBC Time-Life Television Shakespeare in the mid-1980s: swathed in the vibrant fabrics of the Italian high fashions of the fourteenth century, performed by an all-male cast led by Mark Rylance playing Richard with a humorous self-awareness which milked the player-king trope for all it was worth, this was Shakespeare's history as period high camp. The sense of theatricality was amplified for the home viewer by the fact that the coverage of the performance, replicating the Globe's participatory, crowd-pleasing ethos, visibly foregrounded the show's setting and conditions of reception. Shot chiefly from the front, the production unavoidably incorporated the presence of a quietly appreciative theatre audience, dutifully chuckling and applauding at strategic moments. The viewing audiences' responses were framed and regulated by a range of support mechanisms, including pre-show and interval interviews and commentaries (with talking-head expertise provided by Michael Wood, Zöe Wanamaker and Corin Redgrave, vox pops among the audience),[1] and

---

[1] Wood was a familiar figure to British TV audiences as the presenter of the four-part mini-series *In Search of Shakespeare* in 2003; Zoe Wanamaker is another well-known British television face as well

305

a documentary sequence tracking the work of preparation and rehearsal and briefly outlining the Globe's history (a further level of framing and commentary was supplied in interactive digital form, in the shape of scrolling text offering actors' bios, plot synopsis and textual commentary).[2]

Live Shakespeare (and live theatre generally) on television was less of an innovation than the instigators of this production believed: the first British television Shakespeares (beginning with 1937 with an eleven-minute extract from *As You Like It*)[3] were routinely performed and transmitted in this manner, and live transmissions of West End theatre performances remained a feature of BBC arts scheduling into the 1960s (the residual theatricality of much televised Shakespeare up until the 1980s is a related issue which has been well documented).[4] Still, there was on this occasion a palpable sense in the commentary that the reversion to a modus operandi that has long been standard for other forms of cultural broadcasting (opera in particular) was not only innovatory but laden with potential risks. This was voiced in the opening spiel, delivered to shaky hand-held camera by the broadcast's frontman, the BBC's political editor Andrew Marr (a familiar media face whose presence seemed calculated to enhance the show's cross-over appeal as 'political' drama, and who at one point, perhaps thinking of Joseph Fiennes and Gwyneth Paltrow in *Shakespeare in Love*, referred to the Globe as 'Shakespeare's big O'):

Never before have we tried to bring you live, uncut theatre performance of Shakespeare ... If it rains, then you, along with the actors, may have to struggle a little bit; if somebody breaks a leg, or forgets their lines, or if one of the groundlings starts to pelt them with rotten fruit, then we won't be panning away for a studio discussion. So it's all a bit of a risk. I hope you think it's worth it.

---

as daughter of the theatre's founder; and as son of Michael Redgrave whose poetic player-king provides the ultimate template for Rylance, and brother of Vanessa, who had played Prospero at the Globe in 2000, Redgrave was a natural choice.

[2] It appears to have originally been the plan to afford viewers the option of selecting camera angles during the broadcast (as announced on the BBC website 22 August 2003), but this was not in the event carried through: the BBC's research into the viewing habits of the BBC Four audience ('which tends to be between 30 and 55 years old'), according to the show's interactive editor, Kate Bradshaw, indicated that they 'would want the red-button app simply to provide them with more information about the play' (quoted in 'BBC Four to Air ITV-Enabled Version of Shakespeare's "Richard II"', *Tracy Swedlow's itvt newsletter*, Issue 5.16 Part 3, 1 September 2003, www.itvt.com, accessed 22 July 2004).

[3] See Kenneth Rothwell, *A History of Shakespeare on Screen: A Century of Film and Television* (Cambridge: Cambridge University Press, 1999), pp. 95–124.

[4] See for example the views collected in J.C. Bulman and H.R. Coursen, eds., *Shakespeare on Television: An Anthology of Essays and Reviews* (Hanover and London: University Press of New England, 1988).

What is telling here is not the rather tired and predicable litany of clichés, caricatures and warmed-up folklore about performance and its audiences but that, however flippantly it is phrased, there is both unease and anxiety about (and perhaps latent hostility towards) live theatre itself. Human and natural contingencies that are the accepted currency of almost every other form of live television (including news broadcasting, coverage of sports, politics and music, and reality TV) are here magnified into lurid threats of breakdown and sabotage. The scene of theatrical performance is a raw, gaffe-strewn zone, something like outtake TV in its scope for unexpected comedy, humiliation, pain and failure. The sedate, sump-tuous and incident-free performance that followed was to prove this anxiety to be groundless (and it was evidently judged enough of a success for the experiment to be repeated almost exactly a year later, in a broadcast of the Globe's *Measure for Measure*).[5] Nonetheless, the suspi-cion that theatre is a potential embarrassment that just might not live up to the claims being made for it registers not only the occupational hazards of live broadcasting but also a sense of the marginal status of theatre within television-saturated culture. The BBC Four broadcast of the Globe *Richard II* brought theatre and television into unusually close alignment, provoking the kind of generalized and generic worries about the former's ability to behave itself on the latter's terms, but the professed investments of this theatre in particularly intense kinds of interactivity, intimacy and spontaneous encounter intensified the impression that there was more to this live broadcast than the fact of temporal immediacy. During the pre-show discussions and the interval, in keeping with familiar Globe rhetoric, audience members struggle to articulate the feeling of being 'part of' the performance, of 'having a relationship with' actors who for their part talk of the unique 'buzz' that comes from working in the space. The difficulty is that these crucial constituents of the Globe experience are only retrievable as testimony and anecdote: for the TV viewer, the mysterious bond between actors and spectators has to be taken on trust, since the ever-visible audience is an inert and inscrutable presence throughout. Rather than inducting the viewer into the essential Globe experience, the experiment of live broadcasting simply reinforces the sus-picion that one must be missing something, rendering a performance more static and ponderous than even the most 'theatrical' of the BBC Television Shakespeares.

---

[5] Broadcast on BBC Four on 4 September 2004.

Although the broadcast was apparently as much of a departure for the Globe as for the BBC, an accommodation between modern media culture and a theatrical enterprise widely canvassed as a pre-technological alternative to it, it might also be seen as a logical extension of its already highly developed systems of performance documentation and dissemination. The Globe is pioneering and distinctive in the extent to which it is a *mediated* theatrical project; widely circulated as image, as an online resource open to exploration and inspection in uniquely close detail, the stage and the building that houses it offer a potent combination of the material and the virtual, making it the haunt of the scholar, the pilgrim, the tourist and the internet surfer. Conceived during the pre-internet age as an attempt to memorialize and activate Shakespearean performance values of presence, experiential encounter and environmental context, the Globe now sits at the centre of a state-of-the-art international network of digitized resources and access routes, including educational outreach, online learning support, virtual tours and videoconferencing. These both publicize its core activities and, more problematically, substitute for and even displace them: why go to the Globe when it's as easy and more cost-effective to arrange for the Globe to come to you? The ironies are obvious enough: if the 'authentic' Globe experience is, ostensibly, based on actually being there, the organization's pragmatic accommodations with the local, national and global education markets reveal a less fundamentalist logic; many of the activities sponsored by Globe Education derive their authority from both the physical structure and scholarly infrastructure, while not necessarily having to take place in or even near the official centre. And if this diaspora of mediatized encounters with the Globe experience derives its authority from the actual practice on site, the validation process works the other way also: performances there, while apparently eschewing both modern theatrical technology and modern media, are in actuality dependent upon, conditioned and deeply informed by them. W. B. Worthen has demonstrated how, in terms of its physical structure, the restored historicity of the Globe is only authentic up to the point which modern theatre economics, fire regulations and sanitary requirements will allow, that its 'regimes of ... performativity' are 'evocative of a wide range of contemporary performance' and that 'touristical, recreational, historical, everyday-life, and theatrical genres of behaviour all frame its occasion of Shakespearean drama'.[6] Worthen also

---

[6] W. B. Worthen, *Shakespeare and the Force of Modern Performance* (Cambridge: Cambridge University Press, 2003), p. 103.

employs the occasion of the 2000 Globe *Hamlet* to pose the question of whether the characteristic self-awareness that was particularly evident in this production might be less stage-centred and more screen-related than those involved might recognize or want to admit, in that it was 'traced not so much by metatheatrical self-consciousness as by the habits of newer, modern genres of performative history'. Concerned to locate the Globe both in relation to the 'mediated metonymies' of theme-park experience (p. 110) and within a more general cultural context in which 'theatre is no longer ... our master trope for interrogating acting, action, performance' (p. 113), Worthen indicates that its insistent privileging of liveness as a crucial component of authenticity is an anachronistic and defensively nostalgic gesture which, however unwittingly, eradicates the complexities and the multiple allegiances of its performance practice.

The argument here parallels the case made by Philip Auslander (whom Worthen cites), who has argued that 'the live is actually an effect of mediatization, not the other way round', and that the displacement of the theatrical by the mediatized as the general paradigm of performance has meant the live arts have struggled to sustain their cultural position and sense of purpose: in general, he concludes, the 'response of live performance to the oppression and economic superiority of mediatized forms has been to become as much like them as possible', and 'evidence of the incursion of mediatization into the live event is available across the spectrum of performance genres'.[7] In the Globe's case, practitioners frequently refer to the theatre's unique ethic of liveness, spontaneity and encounter by referring to what it can do that the screen media cannot; it is represented, typically, by Mark Rylance's distinction between 'presentation' and 'play': 'cinema and television ... are in essence mediums of "presentation". They cannot respond to their audiences'; whereas at the Globe, for the performer 'involving and responding to an audience', 'playing is all'.[8] As Auslander remarks, the distinctiveness and unique value of live theatre is often defined (perhaps can only be defined) in terms of its presumed antagonist: 'the only way of imputing specificity to the experience of live performance in the current cultural climate is by reference to the dominant experience of mediatization'.[9] Even at the Globe, the quality of the live encounter can be contextualized as

---

[7] Philip Auslander, *Liveness: Performance in a Mediatized Culture* (London and New York: Routledge, 1999), p. 51, p. 7.

[8] Mark Rylance, 'Playing the Globe: Artistic Policy and Practice', in *Shakespeare's Globe Rebuilt*, ed. J. R. Mulryne and Margaret Shewring, (Cambridge: Cambridge University Press, 1997), p. 171.

[9] Auslander, *Liveness*, p. 6.

media-derivative; as Lois Potter, reviewing the 2000 season suggests: 'the media self-consciousness of our age makes it easier for us to understand characters who perform with one eye on their audience, and this is one reason the metatheatrical humor of the Globe works so well.'[10]

The problems inherent in attempting to distinguish live Shakespearean theatre from the media culture in which it is implicated, a habit which is tied up with what Walter Benjamin would describe as an enduring faith in the unique, irreproducible and auratic quality of theatre as an art-form,[11] are conspicuous in the case of Shakespeare's Globe because the nature of the enterprise forces them into visibility, but the difficulty is not a new one. In the more polemical modes of twentieth-century Shakespeare performance criticism, the sense that live Shakespeare deserves to be valued, defended and promoted against the encroachment of mass media forms, has been strong, and consistent. In 1906 the late Victorian revivalist Sidney Lee bemoaned 'the unintellectual playgoer' who has 'little or no imagination to exercise', and is therefore content with 'speciously beautiful ... realism of that primal type, which satisfies the predilections of the groundling, and reduces drama to the level of the cinematograph';[12] three quarters of a century later, little seems to have changed for the chronicler of the 'Shakespeare revolution', J. L. Styan, who, writing in 1976, invokes a Shakespearean dramaturgy which calls 'for the audience to be alert and hyperconscious', involved in a ' "participatory" art, unlike the "consumer" art of the modern passive media like film and television'.[13] Performance criticism frequently works in terms of a set of oppositions which can be variously refined to differentiate theatre from cinema and television, as well as the illusionist from the non-illusionist stage: between the genuinely popular and the spuriously populist, simple and complex art, distance and immediacy, imagination and meretricious spectacle, active and passive consumption, bodily presence and alienated spectatorship, communal and individuated audiences, human craft and commodity culture, the unique and unrepeatable event and the mass-produced artifact. As Auslander argues, the grounds upon which these means of characterizing the live and the mediatized allegedly rest are less stable and more interchangeable than they appear: the essentialized status of the live is a discursive effect, only recognized

[10] Lois Potter, 'This Distracted Globe', *Shakespeare Quarterly* 52 (2001), 124–32 (p. 132).
[11] Walter Benjamin, 'The Work of Art in the Age of Mechanical Reproduction', *Illuminations*, ed. Hannah Arendt and trans. Harry Zohn (New York: Harcourt, Brace and World, 1968), pp. 219–54.
[12] Sidney Lee, *Shakespeare and the Modern Stage* (London: John Murray, 1906), p. 23.
[13] J. L. Styan, *Perspectives on Shakespeare in Performance* (New York: Peter Lang, 2000), p. 25.

through its binary, and only really valued once it seems under threat: 'prior to the advent of those technologies (e.g. sound recording and motion pictures) there was no such thing as "live" performance, for that category has meaning only in relation to an opposing possibility' (p. 51). Moreover, both the live and the mediatized, as categories, often take on each other's characteristics: 'like live performance, electronic and photographic media can be described meaningfully as partaking of the ontology of disappearance ascribed to live performance, and they can also be used to provide an experience of evanescence' (p. 51); the theatre, as I shall discuss below, increasingly models itself on television and film. Even as it insists upon the practical and theoretical separation of theatre and the screen media, performance criticism has repeatedly turned to the culturally dominant forms as a means of characterising theatrical performance, sometimes where one would least expect it. Styan's denunciation of the 'passive media' is immediately followed by an account of a Shakespearean theatre which revels in 'sudden switches of mood from tragedy to comedy and back again; abrupt changes of style from the realistic to soaring ritualism', and the 'surprising change of location or a leap in time';[14] this sounds remarkably close to a filmic aesthetic of montage; more generally, performance criticism's concern with speed, fluidity and flexibility of action and location echoes the spatial and temporal imperatives of cinema.[15]

The habit of comparing early-modern drama with modern film in order to make the former seem more familiar, accessible or comprehensible can work in a number of ways, but the readiness of the analogy is an indication of how far the cultural dominance of the newer medium retrospectively shapes our perception of the old, prompting us to actively re-imagine the theatrical *as* cinematic. Shakespearean drama's anticipation of cinema is defined by its scenic and temporal flexibility, but also by its ability to shift between the everyday, the epic and he fantastic. Such a Shakespeare need not necessarily be continuity-edited; as one of the more adventurous practitioners to have worked in both media, Peter Brook, suggests. Writing in *The Empty Space* in 1968 of the 'cinematic structure' of plays 'written to be performed continuously' in 'alternating short scenes'[16] Brook advances a fairly routine view, but in interview given two

[14] Styan, *Perspectives*, p. 25.
[15] For a particularly original and provocative rethinking of Shakespearean dramaturgy as proto-cinematic, see Courtney Lehmann, *Shakespeare Remains: Theater to Film, Early Modern to Postmodern* (Ithaca and London: Cornell University press, 2002), p. 90.
[16] Peter Brook, *The Empty Space* (Harmondsworth: Penguin, 1968), p. 96.

years earlier he talks in more avant-garde terms of Shakespeare's drama as 'pop collage', of the 'post-Godard techniques' he wished to see in Shakespearean film, and of 'the free theatre-free cinema that the original Elizabethan Shakespeare must have been'; he speculates upon a filmed Shakespeare played simultaneously on three screens, which would have 'exactly the possibilities of the Brechtian stage and an Elizabethan one'.[17] Brook's proposals for a Shakespearean counter-cinema are considerably more radical than anything yet attempted in the cinematic mainstream (perhaps Peter Greenaway's *Prospero's Books* comes closest to achieving the kind of multiple articulation that Brook evokes, although both Godard and Brecht are visible in Brook's *King Lear*); more importantly, the advocacy of a vocabulary of exchange and collision between media technologies, forms and vocabularies anticipates the format of post-modern performance. The director widely thought of as Brook's successor, Robert Lepage, who has been even more adept at manoeuvring between film and the stage, has similarly advocated that whereas theatre and film currently 'tend to clash', their future lies in their potential to 'meet and merge' – a future indicated by his 1997 mixed-media collage *Elsinore*, a solo piece shaped by 'TV influences ... flashbacks, jump-cuts and zapping', which also made use of 'flash-forward, intercutting, cross-fade, image flow, multiple imaging' while underscored 'with a cinematic sound design which combines melodramatic flourish, postmodern pastiche and New Age ambience.'[18] Apparently as far from Globe-style authenticity as it is possible to get, the show nonetheless laid claim to a kind of fundamental textual authority that Globe purists might acknowledge, and which could be harnessed through media technology: 'The text's musicality is an essential element of Shakespeare's writing. In the first folio edition of *Hamlet*, there are many sound cues, telling us which syllables to accentuate and how to balance the iambic pentameter.' Working with 'a machine that recognises different types of pronounced syllables and that associates a particular musical sound with each one', Lepage sought, in his words, to '"X-ray" the text', revealing its 'musicality' and forcing the actor 'to speak the text in a non-natural way, almost to sing it.' Far from operating in a void of free-form postmodern

---

[17] Quoted in Geoffrey Reeves, 'Finding Shakespeare on Film: From an Interview with Peter Brook', *TDR* 11, 1 (1966), pp. 118–21.

[18] Andy Lavender, *Hamlet in Pieces: Shakespeare Reworked by Peter Brook, Robert Lepage, Robert Wilson* (London: Nick Hern Books, 2001), p. 146, p. 143.

relativism, 'preserving the meaning of the play becomes a very important part of the process.'[19]

II

The instances discussed so far may be taken to indicate that what Auslander defines as a 'media-derived epistemology' has played a larger part in modern theories of historical and contemporary Shakespearean performance than has been generally recognized; the argument could certainly be extended to incorporate 'approaches to performance and characterization, and the mobility and meanings of those within a particular cultural context' (p. 33).[20] Since the 1980s, especially, the theatre's debts to cinema have been much in evidence, mainly in the form of the prevailing postmodern referentiality that loads stage productions with citations of the Shakespearean film canon (Olivier and Branagh for *Henry V*, Kurosawa for *Macbeth* and *King Lear*, Luhrmann for *Romeo and Juliet*), references to the work of auteurs such as Hitchcock, Truffaut and Welles or to the well-known works of popular cinema (ranging from *The Wizard of Oz* to *Star Wars*), and pastiche or quotation of generic visual styles: film noir (*Hamlet, Macbeth*), cyberpunk (the histories), Bollywood fantasy (the late romances).[21] In 1984 the director-designer team that was to define the template for the Stratford style of much of the 1980s and 1990s, Adrian Noble and Bob Crowley, spoke of the Kenneth Branagh *Henry V* as like working on a film scenario; this was remarkably prescient, in view of Branagh's reworking of the production on film five years later. In this instance, the theatrical source was unacknowledged. The same period has seen the major companies increasing the number of transfers of stage productions to television and film, beginning with the RSC's *Nicholas Nickelby* in 1981–2, and including, for the same company, Noble's *A Midsummer Night's Dream* (first staged in 1994; released on film two years later), Trevor Nunn's *Othello*, and the Gregory Doran

---

[19] Quoted in Rémy Charest, *Robert Lepage: Connecting Flights*, trans. Wanda Romer Taylor (London: Methuen, 1997), pp. 127, 174–5.

[20] One case-study would be John Barton's *Playing Shakespeare* series for Channel 4, first broadcast in 1984, in which the disciplined energies of small-scale, intensively tutored studio performance seem perfectly attuned to (for which read: are naturalized to) the small screen. The studio Shakespeare movement that began in the mid-1970s itself provides an exemplary instance of a theatrical form replicating televisual rhetoric in its adherence to immediacy and intimacy, and to the aesthetics of the close-up.

[21] For an overview of the cinematization of the RSC's work during the 1980s, see Robert Shaughnessy, 'The Last Post: *Henry V*, War Culture and the Postmodern Shakespeare', *Theatre Survey* 39, 1 (1998), 41–62.

Macbeth of 1999; as well as Richard Loncraine's adaptation of Richard Eyre's Royal National Theatre *Richard III* (1990; 1996) and Trevor Nunn's *The Merchant of Venice* (2001); and, for the English Shakespeare Company, the video version of the *Wars of the Roses* cycle (1989). Despite Terry Hands's confident declaration as Artistic Director of the RSC in 1988 that the future of the company lay in modelling itself on Ingmar Bergman's Royal Drottningholm Theatre in Stockholm, combining theatre-making with film production ('I believe in the 1980s a major theatre company should be making films'),[22] the British Shakespearean theatre's relation to actual film-making has remained largely aspirational, while with few exceptions, the screen versions have sought to preserve rather than transcend or even significantly refashion the productions' stage origins.[23]

In this respect, at least, despite its self-positioning within the media landscape, British Shakespearean theatrical culture continues to resist, or at least qualify, the dominance of the mediatized. It is at this point that the experience of recent and contemporary Shakespearean performance seems to part company with Auslander's account of a general perfor-mance culture which routinely 'incorporates mediatization such that the live event itself is a product of media technologies', so that 'in the theatre, as at the stadium, you are often watching television even when attending a live event, and audiences now expect live performances to resemble mediatized ones' (pp. 24–5). As the foregoing discussion has attempted to demonstrate, this may ring true at the level of media epistemology and general visual style, but in a more literal sense it is hardly representative at all of most current Shakespearean performance.

Certainly, when compared to the standard practices of the large-scale contemporary popular performance, the stages of the Royal Shakespeare Theatre and the Globe appear technologically destitute – and proudly so. The compact hands-free, wireless headset, sprouting like a cyborg extension from the performer's face, has migrated from the call centre and

---

[22] Quoted in John Vidal, 'The selection of the fittest', *Guardian*, 7 April 1988.

[23] The relationship between stage production and screen record can work in a number of ways of course: sometimes a television transfer can work by making manifest the latent cinematic or televisual aspects of the original show. Such was the case with the 1968 BBC TV record of the 1963 RSC *Wars of the Roses*: although the touchstone figures at the time were Brecht, Artaud and Beckett, the screen version, while very much a 'straight' record of the production, reveals the equally significant traces of Italian neo-realism, as well as of the art-cinema auteurs who, Samuel Crowl contends, inspired 'the spare, sparse, monochromatic set and costume designs', which were 'derived ... from the influence of the great black-and-white films of Bergman, Welles, and Renoir' (*Shakespeare Observed: Studies in Performance on Stage and Screen* (Athens, OH: Ohio University Press, 1992), p. 159).

pop concert to the West End musical, so that the amplified voice is coming to seem more 'natural' than the unmediated; video projection and digitally generated scenography has become increasingly sophisticated, recently culminating, on the London stage, in the virtual world of the Trevor Nunn–Andrew Lloyd-Webber extravaganza, *The Woman in White*, which opened in 2004. However familiar media devices have become in other performance contexts, they remain relatively rare in Shakespearean theatre (as, for the most part, in most 'serious' drama), and they are rarely unobtrusive in application. Two examples from the 1997 RSC season: firstly, Ron Daniels's production of *Henry V*, which began with the image of war as media memory, as Henry watched newsreel footage of the First World War; and which staged the threats at Harfleur through a tannoy, the relay neutralising Henry's charm diminishing his humanity, as 'reproduction seem[ed] to flatten out the sound into a merciless coldness'.[24] Second, Michael Boyd's Swan production of *The Spanish Tragedy* had the voice of Revenge amplified, distorted and distributed around the theatre, thereby locating the figure in the realm of the non-human. The Swan's 2001 *King John* found a solution to the problem of Prince Arthur's death-plunge, treated as an accidental fall from the upper balcony: as timber splintered and a dummy crashed to the floor, bathos was instantly converted to a strangely resonant, prophetic pathos, as Arthur's amplified final words squeezed through an echo-chamber and the stage was flooded with a blue wash:

> O me! My uncle's spirit is in these stones.
> Heaven take my soul, and England keep my bones!
> (4.3.9–10)

In such instances, the mediatized voice somehow marks the end or the limits of the human: a child's whisper, already a memory, rippling through history.

In general, onstage video or cinema screens in Shakespearean production are deployed in overtly 'political' plays or in plays which can be actually made to seem political through the introduction of the technology. A recent example of this in Britain can be seen in the RSC's 2004 touring production of *Julius Caesar*, in which the stage crew carry 'video cameras that transpose public speeches to a screen behind an empty stage';[25] the first major instance that I have been able to trace on the

---

[24] Robert Smallwood 'Shakespeare Performances in England', *Shakespeare Survey 51* (Cambridge: Cambridge University Press, 1998), p. 238
[25] Benedict Nightingale, *The Times*, 22 October 2004.

English stage was in the 1983 RSC production of the same play, which was directed by Ron Daniels. Sponsored by Link Electronics, the production was an early, limited experiment in multi-media Shakespeare, its most conspicuous feature a large flat video screen which was flown in for the forum scenes, upon which were projected larger-than-life black-and-white live relays of Caesar's final speech and assassination and Brutus's and Mark Antony's set-piece addresses. Reminiscent of 'a large Bakelite TV set from a Fifties Ideal Home exhibition', according to the *Guardian's* Michael Billington,[26] this was highly noticeable as a retro-chic artefact in its own right, as part of a mise en scène informed by the principle of anachronistic eclecticism, simultaneously period-style Roman, Ruritanian and cheesily futuristic, in a manner which, as a number of reviewers observed, crossed the MGM epic with *Star Wars*. Occupying a dominant upstage position that in the first scene was dominated by a huge, Big Brother-style image of Caesar (with 1984 just round the corner, the Orwellian aspect of the telescreen was another frame of reference), and that would in the later scenes be filled with ripped flags and netting, the screen served a fairly straightforward function in the world of the production as an instrument of propaganda and manifestation of the state-sponsored politicization of the media (and mediatization of politics). This was not enough to impress the critics, who for the most part considered that the presence of the TV screen was easily, and all too obviously, readable as an attempt to impose contemporary relevance (in a similar vein, the production programme also paraded a range of soundbites solicited from contemporary politicians and political commentators on the ethics of the conspirators' coup d'état). It was generally felt that the juxtaposition of the actor and his screen double distracted and divided the attention ('I was never decided which of the two I was supposed to look at', complained the *Daily Telegraph's* John Barber),[27] but, more interestingly, the variety of interpretations that were offered as to what the device was supposed to be doing and what it actually achieved suggest a more complex and unpredictable set of relations between the live and the mediatized, even in this rather literal-minded instance. One of the key effects of multiplication of points of view and modes of spectatorship was to unsettle the spectator's sense of where the 'real' focus was: while most reviewers emphasized their determination to stay properly attentive to the theatrical scene, Giles Gordon of the *Spectator* admitted that the

[26] Michael Billington, *Guardian*, 31 March 1983.
[27] John Barber, *Daily Telegraph*, 31 March 1983.

inevitable lure of the screen means that 'the eye is drawn to events enacted there in two dimensions rather than to the same, but actual, events on stage'.[28] Although for Gordon this allegorizes the passive voyeurism and disempowerment of the citizen-spectator in contemporary culture – noting the reactions of the Senate to Caesar's demise, he remarks, 'I suspect they'd have found the murder more real, seeing it on the box' – it also suggests the capacity of even a 'technically rather shaky' monochrome televisual image, in which 'faces are clear in close-up' but 'decidedly fuzzy in mid-shot' (*Guardian*) to undermine its live source and drain it of affect and significance. On the one hand, the staged event is readable as the place of the true and the real, and the screen the medium which distorts, simplifies and tells lies ('the actual scene', as John Barber put it, versus 'a bad movie version'); on the other, the television image reveals in close-up the reality of character and motive, as when 'Mark Antony, played by David Schofield, appears to us as apparently totally sincere and overcome with grief in his great speech, yet behind him on the screen, we see only the calculating eyes of a politician seeing how well he is orchestrating a mob.'[29] What the reviewers also noticed was that, like a parasite invading the body of its host, the media apparatus was clearly dictating the terms of the staged event: the positioning of the cameras meant that blocking and movement has to be restricted 'so that Caesar seems pinned centre stage during the assassination in case he gets off camera' (*Guardian*).

All things considered, it is not surprising that the telescreen was abandoned later in the run; it was a sign of how loosely integrated into the show the device was that when the production transferred to London the following year, it was generally considered the better for the omission.[30] However, it did receive one particularly positive, and polemical, endorsement, from the *Morning Star* reviewer, the terms of which identify the politics of the production with an inherently suspicious attitude towards the media: 'Daniels registers the telling contemporary parallels between Shakespeare's most political play and our own media-manipulated "democracy" by having us see on a giant TV screen the talking heads that glibly front the political realities taking place on stage.'[31] Only weeks before Margaret Thatcher coasted to her landslide second election victory, it might have seemed difficult to conceive of the

---

[28] Giles Gordon, *Spectator*, 16 April 1983.   [29] Judith Cook, *Scotsman*, 31 March 1983.

[30] One irony that emerged in the course of research for this chapter is that the videotape that is included in the production records of this show (held at the Shakespeare Centre Library) was made relatively late in the season, so that there is no video record of the use of the video.

[31] Gordon Parsons, *Morning Star*, 4 April 1983.

official media (and at this stage, when Britain only had access to two major television networks, this was the only kind there was) as anything other than collusive with state repression or corporate exploitation; within this political framework, television is already theatrically marked as dangerous and duplicitous, especially when it is at its most persuasive. There is a nationalistic dimension too: for many British spectators, mediatization implies Americanization, with all of the suspicions that that arouses. The idea of media manipulation was also germane to the English Shakespeare Company's 1980s *Wars of the Roses* cycle, which reached its culmination, at the end of *Richard III*, with, as Barbara Hodgdon documents, 'three monitors, suspended to form a framing triangle', which 'come alive with Richmond's face in close-up'; thus 'the commodified image of the ruler ... replicated three times ... constitutes the new order's uninterrupted, unitary discourse about itself'.[32] This was heavily reminiscent of the press-opportunity photo-finish of Bogdanov's 1986 *Romeo and Juliet* at Stratford, and to very similar purpose: the public show of reconciliation revealed as scripted and stage-managed, patently insincere, media moment. In *Richard III*, as Bogdanov and Pennington recalled, the sudden revelation of modern media machinery at the end of a sequence of heavily armoured battle scenes spectacularly confirmed that the cycle had finally arrived in the contemporary world: 'the armour and the video were the only real props and without them the production – indeed the whole cycle – had no climax'.[33] Signalling the establishment of a new political style rooted in image manipulation as much as force of arms, the activation of the screens heralded a Fukuyaman end of the kind of history that, in the *Wars of the Roses* cycle, had seen chain-mail jostling with combat fatigues, and pikes facing pistols. That was then, this is now.

These examples of cameras and screens have tended to feature in live Shakespeare performance as a practical strategy, creating a semblance of studio-performance-scale detail and intimacy via the close-up, as a way of suggesting ready-made relevance, and also as a way of framing moments and events as opportunist, untrustworthy, somehow unreal and fake. But it can also have the unintended consequence of undermining and displacing the live performance itself. In a particularly notorious instance, Peter Sellars's Goodman Theatre production of *The Merchant of Venice*, which visited London as part of the Everybody's Shakespeare

---

[32] Barbara Hodgdon, *The End Crowns All: Closure and Contradiction in Shakespeare's History* (Princeton: Princeton University Press, 1991), pp. 125–6.

[33] Michael Bogdanov and Michael Pennington, *The English Shakespeare Company: The Story of 'The Wars of the Roses', 1986–1989* (London: Nick Hern Books, 1990), p. 115.

international festival in November 1994, fifteen large television screens placed onstage and round the auditorium relayed live action as well as connecting the play (spuriously, many critics felt) with the recent riots in Los Angeles via news footage. The results were divisive: whereas Peter Holland felt that it merely exposed actors who 'seemed far more comfortable when acting to camera than on the spaces of the Barbican stage',[34] W. B. Worthen proposed that the microphones and videos effected a 'technological dispersion of stage "character"' which drew the show 'into dialogue with the ways other media – particularly television – represent modern subjects, and so into conflict with ... the live enactment of (realistic, psychological "character")'.[35] But whether one regards this kind of insistent, fractious mediatization as misguided and redundant or purposefully deconstructive, Sellars's tactics point to a more pervasive issue: it is not just that the overpowering imperatives of the media system means that the incorporation of its technologies of support, selection and amplification tends to diminish or interrogate the capacity of the live to function normally in its own terms; it is that its workings tend to call into question what those terms actually are.

We can see this happening even in a recent production which, according to most of its reviewers, was one of the most thoughtful and successful attempts yet to integrate film and video technology into live Shakespeare performance: the 2003 production of *Henry V*, directed by Nicholas Hytner with Adrian Lester in the lead, on the Olivier stage of the National Theatre. From the outset, this was promoted as an assertively, even aggressively, contemporary production; in rehearsal during the months leading up to the American-led invasion of Iraq, the pre-publicity heavily hinted at the current resonances: 'a charismatic leader in the flush of youth commits his troops to war. The risks are huge; the cause debatable; and bloodshed certain.' In the context of Hytner's first season as Trevor Nunn's successor as Artistic Director of the organization, in which he determined to use the National as a platform for the vigorous interrogation of contemporary nationhood and national identities, it was no surprise to anyone that this was an anachronism-free, fully modern-dress production (unlike the fairly recent RSC productions of 1994 and 1997, which had broadened the range of visual reference to the First and Second World Wars), which cheerfully underlined the

[34] Peter Holland, *English Shakespeares: Shakespeare on the English Stage in the 1990s* (Cambridge: Cambridge University Press, 1997), pp. 258–9.
[35] W. B. Worthen, *Shakespeare and the Authority of Performance* (Cambridge: Cambridge University Press, 1997), p. 84.

contemporary relevance which the Globe's simultaneous 'season of
regime change' only hinted at: the political manoeuvrings of the first
scenes were conducted by party apparatchiks in New Labour-style sharp
suits around a conference table piled high with laptops and leather-bound
document folders, and well-stocked with bottles of mineral water, the
final negotiations in an anonymous luxury hotel furnished by Louis XIV;
the battle scenes between were played on a bare stage populated by
heavily-armed troops in bulky, wired-up combat fatigues that made them
look like khaki astronauts; guns were fired, explosions were heard, and
jeeps would drive on and off. The Archbishop of Canterbury, thankfully,
did not present the Salic Law exposition in Power Point, but the parallels
between this tortuous legitimation of a decision that had already been
made and the Blair government's so-called 'dodgy dossier' of evidence
against Saddam Hussein were there for the spotting (as were those
between Henry's religiosity and that of George Bush and Tony Blair);
Chorus, played with breathless, entirely non-ironic ferocity by power-
suited Penny Downie, was a combination of party spin-doctor and
embedded war correspondent. The Eastcheap gang sported crew-cuts,
England football shirts and carrier bags stuffed with cans of lager, and
Pistol (Jude Akuwudike) was a dreadlocked Rastafarian who was shared
one of the production's best moments in his encounter with the disguised
Henry, who, when challenged, named himself as 'Harry Leroy'.

The Luhrmannesque contemporary setting was, for the current English
Shakespearean theatre, hardly front-page news, but it was contained in
this instance within a highly developed and self-conscious media framework, which emphasised how far the conduct of Henry's war, and the
lessons that were to be drawn from it, were tied up with its management
and manipulation as broadcast material. The first two scenes played in
front of a floor-to-flies backdrop of blank screens which, as the action
shifted to Eastcheap in 2.1 came to life with a huge talking-head of
Canterbury in full Salic Law flow, rapidly zapped away by Nym in favour
of live snooker. At the end of the scene it screened a home (or rather pub)
video of a dreadlocked Henry and Falstaff (Desmond Barrit, who had
played the role for the RSC in 2000, and who thus planted within the
production memories of that company's *This England* cycle), a lo-fi
reworking of the flashback sequence in Branagh's *Henry V* film whose
shaky camerawork and murky sound suggested an unsteady operator at
the end of a marathon boozing session. It was a reminder not only of the
connections that Henry had severed with a world of hustling and classless
camaraderie, but also, for a brief moment, of how technologies of sight

and sound might work within a different kind of culture of memory to the official one. For the most part, though, the instruments of the media remained in this production in institutional hands. Naturally, Henry was accompanied on his campaign by a tame news corps: caught on film at the gates of Harfleur (3.3), Henry ordered the cameras to stop rolling so that he could issue his threats of rape and infanticide off record; the next scene opened with Alice and Catharine glumly watching a newscast of the town's capitulation – little wonder, here, that the Princess suddenly realised that it made very good sense to learn English, fast. In another crucial off-camera moment, Henry's order for the killing of the French prisoners (brought on in canvas hoods that recalled news pictures of captured Iraqi soldiers) was followed by a mass shooting. The culminating example of this production's exploration of the interplay between warfare, propaganda and news media manipulation was the video insert that bridged the transition from the fourth to the fifth acts: artfully pastiching the commemorative documentary video collection that was put together by CNN after the first Gulf War (*Desert Storm: The War Begins* and *Desert Storm: The Victory*), this offered a sanitized montage of 'greatest hits' moments from Henry's campaign, complete with 24-hour news-style running captions and soundbites ('10,000 French Dead'; 'A Royal Fellowship of Death', '29 English Dead') backed with a tongue-in-cheek, blandly optimistic, vernacular techno version of 'Deo Gratias', concluding with the simple slogan 'Victory' superimposed upon a fluttering Union Jack.

Entirely appropriately, this *Henry V* was the second Royal National Theatre production to go live as part of the online resource Stagework, which features the *Battle of Agincourt* video, the pub movie and Lester's Blair-style prime ministerial broadcast, as well as excerpts of the Breach and Harfleur scenes (the fact that this forms part of the larger government-sponsored Cultureonline initiative is an indication that the production's stance towards the current Gulf War was sufficiently neutral or well-camouflaged so as not to cause offence). If there is a satisfyingly circular aspect to this remediatization of a media-conscious stage show, the quasi-documentary style of the material disseminated online also confirmed its claims to both theatrical authority and political cogency rested upon televisual verisimilitude; 'even the rifles', the website announced, 'were the same as those currently in use by the British army'. In a context in which the materiality of props and costumes is in itself an index of truth, the repackaging of warfare as mainstream, patriotic infotainment was simply another variant of a preoccupation with the relationship between the 'reality' and 'rhetoric' of conflict that has been central to the play's modern stage and screen history. Throughout the production, live stage action represents the real, the media imagery the fantasy. Once again, however, the capacity of the mediatized image to set its own standards, to impose both its own production values and its compelling rhetoric of the real, not only undermined the show's theatrical aspirations, but also muddied the distinctions that it might have been intended to sustain. It was not just that the realist mise-en-scène of boardrooms and battlefields was in any case assembled from a repertoire of cinematic, televisual and news images (most memorably, when Henry held a gun to Bardolph's head in 3.6, the production consciously evoked one of the iconic images of the Vietnam war), but that alongside altogether larger, slicker, musically scored counterpart up on the screen it could not help looking compromised, insubstantial and derivative. So polished and eloquent was the CNN sequence as a digest of the production's concerns that the rest of it began to seem strangely amateurish and redundant; as electrically driven jeeps trundled on and off stage with all the throbbing power of golf buggies, and small arms fire crackled over the tannoy system as if on television, I for one increasingly wondered why this production was trying so hard to achieve reality effects much more readily achievable on the screen. Indeed, the Breach sequence in particular, shot with handheld steadicams in the mode of embedded reportage, looks far more impressive online than I remember it being onstage.

III

The instances I have discussed up to this point provide examples of how mediatization can function within Shakespearean performance as a self-consciously 'public' political discourse, in the sense that live or recorded relay seems to define a moment, an event, a gesture or a spoken utterance *as* public and political, while at the same time creating at least the suspicion of bad faith. I wish to turn now to a different category of use of media vocabularies and technologies, and one that can be positioned in relation to a rather different strand of cross-media experimentation in performance. In the substantial body of work which is based in the performance art tradition rather than drama and theatre (as represented, for example, by the work of Marina Abramović, Bruce Nauman and Vito Acconci), the deployment of mixed media has been a staple of practice since the 1960s, when the new availability of relatively inexpensive and portable video equipment allowed artists to work with moving images outside the industry or broadcast context, at the kind of intimate scale that encouraged them to think less in terms of scenic enhancement or documentary embellishment than of the non-mimetic potential of the medium, as well as of possibilities of interplay between performance-making, the documentation of routine actions, the realms of dream and fantasy, and everyday life. Since the 1980s these concerns and techniques have been familiar within the theatre-based performance avant-garde; so much so that the video monitor has become as predictable a component of experimental performance as the look-behind-you routine in Christmas pantomime. The relationship between the live and the mediated components of a show may be one of straightforward live relay or duplication; it may also be ironic, cryptic, disjunctive or contradictory or discomfitingly personal. If this seems far closer to the kind of multi-levelled stage and screen Shakespeare envisaged by Peter Brook than the examples I have discussed so far, it also, I want to suggest, works within a model of practice through which, in allowing for the layering of reality, memory, dream and fantasy, in its capacity to entertain simultaneously multiple and contradictory perspectives, types of speech and modes of address, and in its critical, playful approach to the making and unmaking of stage persons, it offers new ways of thinking about the performance of early modern texts in the twenty-first century.

Examples of this kind of mediatized stage Shakespeare, at least within the documented mainstream, are unsurprisingly rare, although a point of departure is provided by what Dennis Kennedy has documented as 'one of the most startling Shakespearean representations of the century',[36] Hansgünter Heyme's provocatively bizarre *Hamlet* at the Cologne Municipal Theatre in 1979, in which a narrow strip of forestage was commandeered by a single camera which relayed close-ups of the cast to eighteen floor-mounted monitors, in particular of a Hamlet who was evidently a keen student of 1970s video art, in that he was 'reduced largely to gestures and to a wondering preoccupation with his own body, which he studied in poses and grimaces in front of the video camera'.[37] If there was a connection here between the solipsism of an artform in which 'by watching themselves create art with their bodies in a "mirror", whether actual or in the form of a video image', artists 'made images of their

---

[36] Dennis Kennedy, *Looking at Shakespeare: A Visual History of Twentieth-Century Performance* (Cambridge: Cambridge University Press, 1993), p. 275.
[37] Wilhelm Hortmann, 'Shakespeare in the Federal German Republic', *Shakespeare Quarterly* 31 (1980), p. 411.

bodies the art itself[38] and the culture of introspection associated with *Hamlet*, it was one which has been sustained through a number of more recent theatrical treatments of the play which have explored film and video's potential both to explore the tropes of doubling and role play and to externalise its hero's interiority. Lepage's *Elsinore* has already been mentioned: integrating live relay and video projection into the sliding and spinning mechanisms of an endlessly mobile set, this collaged and abbreviated version was orchestrated to enable the actor-director, supported by a silent body double and a cast of phantom doppelgängers, to play all of the parts, culminating in a duel between Lepage's Hamlet and his Laertes seen from the viewpoint of their rapiers. For the British critics, at least, the technical brilliance was not enough to compensate either for what they saw as Lepage's shortcomings as an actor or for the lack of emotional depth.[39] *Elsinore* was seen in the National Theatre's Lyttelton auditorium in January 1997; in May of the same year a rather better-received attempt to think the play cinematically opened at Stratford, in the main-house production directed by Matthew Warchus with Alex Jennings in the lead. This was a production stacked with cinematic references: set in a moody, chiaroscuro void somewhere between 1920s Expressionism, film noir and the Tarantino-style gangster movie, it started with a wedding party for Claudius and Gertrude styled as 'a gaudy purple disco' which was immediately reminiscent of both Luhrmann's Capulet ball and *The Godfather*; Jennings's prince 'at times like a cross between [Jack] Nicholson's Joker and [Mick] Jagger's Jumpin' Jack Flash', who 'mimics Groucho Marx for some of Hamlet's one-liners' and 'looks like Stan Laurel', and 'gives us "to be" with a gun to his temple, echoing the psychomania of Mel Gibson', and hence simultaneously citing both *Lethal Weapon* and Gibson's *Hamlet*.[40] Warchus also drastically cut the text to filmic proportions, chiefly by eradicating the political frame of reference so that the tragedy was purely psychological and domestic. Both the opening scene and the final arrival of Fortinbras were excised; in place of the former, the image was of Hamlet, suited in black,

---

[38] Klaus Biesenbach, 'Video Acts', in *Video Acts: Single Channel Works from the Collections of Pamela and Richard Kramlich and the New Art Trust* (London: Institute of Contemporary Arts, 2003), no pagination.

[39] For detailed accounts, see Lavender, *Hamlet in Pieces*, pp. 93–149; Nigel Wheale, 'Culture Clustering, Gender Crossing: *Hamlet* Meets Globalization in Robert Lepage's *Elsinore*', in *Shakespeare and his Contemporaries in Performance*, ed. Edward J. Esche (Aldershot: Ashgate, 2000), pp. 121–36

[40] Andrew Billen, *Observer*, 11 May 1997; Steve Grant, *Time Out*, 14 May 1997; Billen, *Observer*; Robert Gore-Langton, *Daily Express*, 15 May 1997.

standing centre stage pouring ashes from an urn while grainy, silent monochrome images of a young boy, his father and a dog playing in the snow were projected on a screen behind him, and Claudius was heard giving his first speech ('Though yet of Hamlet our dear brother's death / The memory be green' (1.2.1–2)) over the PA system (the footage was seen again at the end, this time with Horatio, in voice-over, evoking the play's 'carnal, bloody, and unnatural acts' (5.2.335)). 'Presumably', wrote one of the production's more thoughtful critics, 'this narrative suture of parental loss with childhood memory would enable viewers' identification with Hamlet';[41] it certainly seemed calculated both to invest Jennings's Hamlet with lost-boy pathos and to supply a psychological core to his exuberant multiple role-playing. But I am also interested in the relation between the stage action and the screen material as a kind of media allegory: not only does the embedding of film within theatre invert the customary relationship between the two within a film-dominated Shakespearean performance culture, it also treats the space of the moving image within performance as the realm of ghosts. In the context of a bracingly secular production which had Old Hamlet making his first meeting with Hamlet wearing a smoking jacket, before drifting off 'like a guest in search of some breakfast',[42] the flickering, speechless monochrome images of father and son evoked memory as early cinema and early cinema as memory; it is yesterday's technology that renders the ghost as truly spectral, that poignantly marks the passage of time, and that registers both the experience of loss and the obsessive work of repetition and recovery. The filmic prologue and epilogue were partnered by the presentation of *The Mousetrap* as a shadow play projected onto a makeshift screen fashioned, tellingly, from a bedsheet: played before a court transfixed in the dark, and taking its visual cues from Victorian melodrama, the penny-dreadful silent screen, Javanese puppet plays and *The Cabinet of Dr Caligari*, the inset play was a cinematic palimpsest, voiced with the clipped, cut-glass clarity of that the era of classic British cinema that produced Olivier's *Hamlet* and Lean's *Brief Encounter*. At the sequence's climax, Jennings slipped behind the screen, merging with shadows that frantically multiplied and dispersed, while the ripples spread outwards from the furious, futile blows that Claudius landed on the screen.

---

[41] Cynthia Marshall, 'Sight and Sound: Two Models of Subjectivity on the British Stage', *Shakespeare Quarterly* 51 (2000), 353–61 (p. 355).
[42] Robert Butler, *Independent on Sunday*, 11 May 1997.

Jennings was armed with a camera as well as a pistol in this production, and proved to be more confident in his manipulation of the former than of the latter; in Steven Pimlott's 2000 RSC production, Sam West went one better with handheld video; now, of course, thanks to Ethan Hawke in Michael Almereyda's film of the same year, the old idea of Hamlet-as-actor-manager has been thoroughly upstaged by Hamlet as video diarist and cineaste. Such instances of use suggest that the small-scale, personal use of media technology might offer qualified scope for some kind of resistance, or at least personal self-definition, in a world which is otherwise corrupt, repressive and ultimately destructive. In my final example, Simon McBurney's production of *Measure for Measure* in the Royal National Theatre's Olivier auditorium in 2004, the media apparatus was quite clearly an indispensable instrument of social discipline and control; but it also showed the potential of the screen as a means of exploring, in complex, provocative and richly imaged ways, the relations between live and screened bodies, and between the spaces of representation, imagination and desire. Cinematically shaped and paced as an interval-less two-and-a-quarter hours, and accompanied by what was described as a 'continuous, cinematic orchestral score',[43] the show sported arthouse movie references, suggesting the murky milieu of Orson Welles's *The Third Man*, the combination of authoritarianism and sexual decadence found in the films of Fellini and Pasolini (prompted, in particular, by David Troughton's powerfully domineering, crop-headed Duke as Il Duce), as well as direct contemporary allusions, such as the prisoners' penitentiary orange (Guantánamo Bay-style) jumpsuits, the suited, shaded and ear-piece-wearing secret servicemen that prowled the stage during the final scene, and the video image of President George W. Bush that flashed up for the 'sanctimonious pirate' who erased 'Thou shalt not steal' from his table of Ten Commandments (1.2.8–10). Mentioned by almost all of the reviewers as an index of the show's topicality, this was an isolated moment of direct political satire; it was actually rather untypical of the production's use of sound and screen technologies. Far from being supplementary to the live action, as a number of critics proposed, the cameras and microphones in this production defined the coordinates of its mediatized public and political space: banks of monitors positioned upstage left and downstage right marked the corners of a performative arena zoned as a disciplinary grid, a place in which the mechanisms of surveillance, interrogation and incarceration were synchronized and

---

[43] Oliver Jones, *What's On*, 2 June 2004.

interdependent. Leaping to life in the transition to the brothel at the end of 1.1 with looped images of cheap porn intercut with shots of a smirking Bush, the screens relayed the subsequent scenes of interrogation and trial in live close-up, with the camera and the microphone operating as the conduit through which public utterances can be entertained and, in a rather Foucauldian sense, as the technology of power/knowledge through which the law conducts – and legitimates – its operations.

The use of head-and-shoulders shots to subject the accusers, the petitioners and the accused to close-up scrutiny, the appropriate register of testimony and judicial inquiry, displayed the detail of studio-scale acting within the open space of the Olivier stage, but this did not mean that the overall performance style was realist in the televisual sense. As a Complicite co-production with the RNT, the show demonstrated the trademark physical articulacy of McBurney's work, wherein the performer's body is as much the vehicle of narrative and sceneographic component as it is the locus of character and in which the improvisational fluidity of image and mise-en-scène conveys the fragility of the boundaries between presence, the present tense and memory, and between reality, fantasy and dreams. Only the second Complicite production of a Shakespeare play in a company history of twenty-one years that includes devised pieces (*More Bigger Snacks Now* and *Anything for a Quiet Life*), adaptations of prose works (*The Three Lives of Lucy Cabrol*, *The Street of Crocodiles*, *The Elephant Vanishes*), play productions (*The Visit*, *The Winter's Tale*, *The Caucasian Chalk Circle*, *The Chairs*), and musical collaborations (*The Noise of Time*, *Strange Poetry*), *Measure for Measure* appealed to McBurney, engineer and choreographer of what he characterizes as 'collisions' between bodies, texts, spaces and objects, as a text which engages with the chaos which, 'as we know, is full of patterns. Fractal patterns ... [that] tell us about the inherent value of living in a world that springs beyond our control. The only thing that matters in face of the unknowable is how we accept it and live with it.'[44] At the heart of the play, as McBurney sees it, is the insistent, recalcitrant body itself, the body which 'has its own rules, its own patterns, rarely coinciding with what the mind has already decided';[45] the body which both reveals meanings and sabotages attempts to impose them. And this was a production in which exuberant physical virtuosity registered the tensions

---

[44] Simon McBurney, 'The Body has its Own Rules', from the NT/Complicite Programme for *Measure for Measure*, 2004.

[45] McBurney, 'The Body'.

between desire and repression, authority and criminality, and in which basic indices of character and motive were visibly, viscerally manifest both as physical needs and as strategies of denial: Isabella, prostrate with her sister-votarists in a cruciform quartet, yet insisting upon 'a more strict restraint / Upon the sisterhood' (1.4.4–5), and then unconsciously kneading her breast during her first interview with Angelo; Angelo himself, a tortured puritan in rimless spectacles, twisting his limbs in knots of self-denial as he clung to his swivel chair, discovering with horror an unbidden erection after the second interview ('What's this? Is this her fault or mine' (2.2.167)) and then cutting his arms with a well-used razor blade in a vain bid to cauterize desire; Pompey, the pimp turned jailor, wrestling with the rigor-mortised corpse of Ragozine in a sequence of exquisitely sick gross-out comedy; Elbow, initially a funny-accented Keystone Cop, who, like one of Dario Fo's maniac caribinieri, turns into a baton-wielding psychopath; and the Duke, whose strategically placed limp chillingly disappears in the final scene along with his friar's habit and his wafer-thin aura of benevolence, to reveal the bullish physiognomy of an autocrat. In the final moments, his marriage 'proposal' is the cue for the discovery of an upstage bedchamber, luxuriously furnished in the style loved by fascists everywhere; pointing towards it in a manner that recognises no resistance and brooks no argument, he coldly informed Isabella that 'What's yours *is mine*' (5.1.536).

Ironically enough, but entirely appropriately, a show which made extensive and sophisticated use of media technology has not yet been transposed to either the small or the silver screen; but this was a privilege afforded the other production of *Measure for Measure* that was seen on the South Bank in the summer of 2004. Broadcast live from Shakespeare's Globe on BBC Four on 4 September, the Globe's production was the National's antithesis: light-hearted, period-authentic, pantomime cross-dressed, its Duke, in the shape of Mark Rylance, an amiable bumbler; for current generations of students, and for future theatre historians, this, rather than McBurney's dark, erotic, exhilarating vision, will be the *Measure for Measure* of 2004 that will survive as something that looks like performance, rather than as story, image, trace and memory. The revolution, it seems, will not be televised.

CHAPTER 13

Memory, performance and the idea of the museum

Dennis Kennedy

We should therefore accept the paradox that, in order really to forget an event, we must first summon up the strength to remember it properly.

(Slavoj Žižek)[1]

Memory, entwined so much in human life and our awareness of death, is one of the most prevalent concerns of observers of culture. However we think of memory – as historical, psychological or pathological – it must enter on some level and at some time into serious considerations of our relationship to the planet, to each other and to ourselves. The operations of memory in the self and in the world remain in part a mystery, though a mystery with a vast amount of scientific and cultural explication attached. As Susan Crane notes,

The mental process of memory takes on corporeal form in the brain, but this physical form is invisible to the naked eye: memory becomes sensible and visual through imaginative recollection and representation ... Memory is an act of 'thinking of things in their absence' ...[2]

When we turn to art production, memory's call is particularly insistent, since art is inevitably caught in the bend that lies between time and attempts to stop it: who are these coming to the sacrifice? For Keats, those still travellers on his dislocated Grecian urn were beautiful because their frozen gestures complicated memory's place in the nature of art. In performance the tension between time and memory becomes acute. Performance is one of memory's greatest tests, precisely because performance does not elude time, because it decays before our eyes, and thus in the moment of its accomplishment escapes into memory. Its remnants

---

[1] Slavoj Žižek, *Welcome to the Desert of the Real!: Five Essays on September 11 and Related Dates* (London: Verso, 2002), p. 22.

[2] Susan A. Crane, introduction to *Museums and Memory*, ed. Crane (Stanford: Stanford University Press, 2000), pp. 1–2; the quotation within the quotation is from Mary Warnock, *Memory* (London, 1987), p. 12.

and residues are the stuff of our histories, whether the positivist archaeology of Andrew Gurr or the performative genealogy of Joseph Roach.
Performance is the opposite of memory and yet is memory's basic material.
It may even be true that performance is unthinkable without memory.[3] It is
not a coincidence that the great dramatist of memory, Samuel Beckett,
wrote an early essay on the great novelist of memory, Marcel Proust.

Memory is significant to the producers of theatre in less philosophical
ways, from the playwright's memory to the actors' memory of lines, from
the work of the prompter to inherited stage business and Stanislavsky's
'emotion memory'. But here I am interested in a topic not much talked
about, how performance is remembered by spectators.

THE RUSE OF HISTORY

In considerations of Shakespeare since the seventeenth century a tension
has existed between the book and the body, the text and actor, the silence
of reading versus the publicity of performing. The monumentalizing
aspect of remembering Shakespeare, the cultural significance of the
English national poet and world icon, usually likes the book. The book is
memory materialized, solidified, made historical and referable, while
performance always escapes it, leaving behind its remembered shadow.
But who is doing the remembering? Do we talk about a spectator's
memory, which is the self, or about cultural memory, which is the other
disguised as the self? I must begin by making distinctions regarding the
memorializing impulse, and I call briefly on two cultural historians.

First, Michel Foucault, whose well-known essay on heterotopias draws
a line between the accumulative and the transitory analysis of time.
Unlike utopias, which by definition are no places, heterotopias are real
places in the world which attempt through material means to represent or
propose a utopian vision. When they are linked to 'slices of time' they are
of two types. The first are 'heterotopias of indefinitely accumulating time,
for example museums and libraries', which since the rise of modernity
have become places 'in which time never stops building up and topping
its own summit'. Museums and libraries are based on the nineteenth-
century utopian dream of enclosing 'all epochs, all forms' within one

---

[3] See Antonia Rodríguez Gago, 'The Embodiment of Memory (and Forgetting) in Beckett's Late
Women's Plays', *Drawing on Beckett: Portraits, Performances, and Cultural Contexts*, ed. Linda Ben-
Zvi (Tel Aviv: Assaph Books, 2003), p. 115. On the general issue of memory and performance, see
Marvin Carlson, *The Haunted Stage: The Theatre as Memory Machine* (Ann Arbor: University of
Michigan Press, 2001).

place 'that is itself outside of time and inaccessible to its ravages'. In direct opposition are heterotopias linked 'to time in its most fleeting, transitory, precarious aspect, to time in the mode of the festival', such as fairgrounds and vacation villages, places which exist specifically to enclose the 'absolutely temporal'.[4] It is clear that performances normally participate in this second type of heterotopia.

Next, Michel de Certeau, whose essay on the history of psychoanalysis summarizes the opposing ways that memory operates in psychoanalysis and historiography. He reminds us that psychoanalysis is based on Freud's most central discovery, 'the return of the repressed'. Through this 'mechanism', as Freud calls it, memory is central to consciousness. If the past, in the form of something which took place during a significant or traumatic event, is repressed, 'it *returns* in the present from which it was excluded, but does so surreptitiously'. This 'detour-return' is for Freud the inescapable way that memory controls the present. Accordingly, memory is the basis of the talking cure: the psychoanalyst guides the patient towards exposing repressed memory and uncovering its significance. We should note that one of Freud's favourite examples comes from *Hamlet*: the son, as a child with Oedipal desires unconsciously wishing to remove the father as rival claimant to the mother's affection, is faced as an adult with the old man's actual elimination. The suppressed then arrives in apparitional state to awaken consciousness. As Certeau puts it, 'Hamlet's father returns after his murder, but in the form of a phantom, in another scene, and it is only then that he becomes the law his son obeys.' The detour-return in Shakespeare's drama is the working model for memory's rule. For Freud the process is 'uncanny', in that the present tries to expel the past but 'the dead haunt the living', the past 're-bites', secretly and repeatedly. History is 'cannibalistic', and memory

becomes the arena of conflict between two contradictory operations: forgetting, which is not something passive, a loss, but an action directed against the past; and the mnemic trace, the return of what was forgotten, in other words, an action by a past that is now forced to disguise itself. More generally speaking, any autonomous order is founded upon what it eliminates; it produces a 'residue' condemned to be forgotten. But what was excluded re-infiltrates the place of its origin ... and, behind the back of the owner (the *ego*), or over its objections, it inscribes there the law of the other.[5]

---

[4] Michel Foucault, 'Texts/Contexts: Of Other Spaces', trans. Jay Miskowiec, *Diacritics* 16.1 (Spring 1986), 22–7, and often reprinted.

[5] Michel de Certeau, 'Psychoanalysis and its History', *Heterologies: Discourse on the Other*, trans. Brian Massumi (Manchester: Manchester University Press, 1986), pp. 3–4. As his translator notes,

Despite our efforts the repressed past invades the present, returning as a ghost of itself to occupy the region of the mind it had been exiled from, the personal counterpart to what Hegel called 'the ruse of history'.

In contradiction to the discourse of psychoanalysis, the historical method 'is based on a clean break between the past and the present'. The past and present are two distinct domains: the present is the place where the work of writing history takes place, relying on the 'apparatus of *inquiry* and interpretation'; while the past is understood as 'set off in time', incapable of direct cognition. As Certeau continues,

Psychoanalysis and historiography thus have two different ways of distributing the *space of memory*. They conceive of the relation between the past and the present differently. Psychoanalysis recognizes the past *in* the present; historiography places them one *beside* the other. (p. 4)

By implication, then, the self apprehends its accumulated recollection as a partial refutation of time, while the historian (whose own self is theoretically placed aside for the sake of the work) insists on the absolute distinction between past and present.

It is a bit surprising that Certeau would see historiography as so conclusively separate from the present. It is now well acknowledged that 'history in reality refers to present needs and present situations wherein those [past] events vibrate', as Croce wrote in 1938.[6] E. H. Carr and Hayden White have elaborated the ways that the writing of history is itself part of history and thus always an elision of the past and present. Yet despite Certeau's overstatement, it will be useful to consider how the discourse of psychoanalysis operates in a different cognitive field than historiography.

FESTIVALS AND MEMORY

The revival of the ancient festival was one of the most persistent aspirations of theatrical modernism. A number of thinkers and artists from the mid-nineteenth century on saw in early festivals what they thought modernity had lost, a deep relationship between performance and the life of the spirit. Especially in the festivals of Greece, they saw an engagement of ordinary time with extraordinary or divine time, so that the ancient festival, by definition a special place, also represented a flight

---

Certeau's phrase for 're-bites' is *il re-mord*, meaning 'it bites again' but playing on words suggesting that it repeats death or brings back the dead (*il remort*) as well as suggesting 'remorse' (*le remords*).

[6] Benedetto Croce, *History as the Story of Liberty*, trans. S. Sprigge (London: Allen and Unwin, 1941; original Italian publication 1938).

from chronological instance. The modern epoch, ruled by the Taylorian stopwatch, stood in direct opposition to the formulas of pre-modern performance: the Dionysia and the Olympiad were wrapped in a fervent longing for the primitive, a hope of escaping the mundane, a substitution of art for religion. In the most influential early instance, Richard Wagner sought to activate his dream of the relationship of the German past to the German present by creating a festival in Bayreuth that would re-order the space of memory. The psychological and the historical would merge. The spectator would be overwhelmed (the self encased in private emotion) but also be taught valuable lessons (the self in relation to the other of history). The 1876 Festspielhaus suggested through a semi-circular auditorium the union of its spectators with each other and with the *Ring* cycle, which progresses with melancholic longing.

In Foucault's terms, Wagner's festival was (and is) a heterotopia of the second type, a location for performance that seeks to revisit a moment of past significance by abrogating time. But it was a high-art festival rather than an anarchic folk event, so that it also called upon the first type, the heterotopia of accumulation of the library or museum, since it evoked a sedimented past and demanded the spectator bring significant cultural capital to the show. Since Wagner endorsed nineteenth-century theatrical historicism, he also created a memory image on stage imbued with an unquestioned belief in the value of archeological reconstruction. The first theatre in history to be dedicated to the work of a single person, who happened to be its founder, the Bayreuth Festival endorsed the contemporary as what Nietzsche would call the eternally recurring.

Not so its immediate imitator, the Shakespeare Memorial Theatre in Stratford, which opened on Bard-day three years later in 1879, the first theatre in history dedicated to a single playwright. Bearing his memory in its name, this time the festival concept was already dominated by the idea of accumulating time, since the purpose of the SMT was to cherish Shakespeare as the English national poet and to celebrate his birth with a few provincial productions whose quality was less significant than the fact of their performance. Other European festivals before the Second World War included the Salzburg Festival, founded in 1920 by the director Max Reinhardt and the composer Richard Strauss, and the Glyndebourne Festival Opera in Sussex, founded in 1934 and managed by the Viennese impresario Rudolf Bing until 1947. Both sought to package for a growing summer audience the exhilaration of place with a concentrated experience of music and theatre. Whatever their original intentions, they became havens for the upper and aspiring classes, with high ticket prices, high social cachet, and a repertory of high art. All my examples were organized along German or Austrian models, part of the *hochkulturbetrieb* or 'high culture business'.

The significant rise of festivals occurred after the war. In the summer of 1947, with much of Europe still in ruins, both the Edinburgh and the Avignon festivals were established specifically to assist in cultural reconstruction. Bing, one of the founders of the Edinburgh Festival and its first director, brought the same conservative attitude to high culture he had displayed at Glyndebourne and would continue at the Metropolitan Opera in New York, which he managed from 1950 until 1972. The purpose of the Edinburgh Festival was to use the arts to recover from the austerities of the war by producing music and drama that evoked the glories of European civilization. In France, the actor and director Jean Vilar was committed to a much more progressive view of art than Bing, yet he established the Avignon Festival specifically to re-invoke liberal European culture considered to be under threat, first by the Nazi invasion and then by postwar spiritual exhaustion.[7] The Avignon Festival was to be a scheme for the maintenance of memory, an act of aesthetic preservation, the cultural equivalent of the Marshall Plan, which had been outlined by General George Marshall two months before, in June 1947 (in a ten-minute speech at the Harvard commencement – he was receiving an honorary degree along with Robert Oppenheimer, General Omar Bradley and T. S. Eliot).

Shakespeare was seen as central to the festival project. Both Bing and Vilar opened their festivals with *Richard II*, and Vilar's production, staged outdoors in front of the massive walls of the Papal Palace, played at Avignon every year until 1953. The festival idea spread widely under Vilar's influence and his lead in staging Shakespeare plays in ancient surroundings was followed in Italy as well.[8] Cultural reconstruction seemed to lend itself to the idea of the festival, a celebration of the amount of recovery already accomplished; the ancient ruins spoke of a romantic continuity with the past.

Surprisingly even the Shakespeare Memorial Theatre caught the fever and immediately after the war hired as artistic director Barry Jackson, the

---

[7] See Jean Vilar, *Le Théâtre, service public et autres textes*, ed. Armande Delcampe (Paris: Gallimard, 1975), p. 468 and *passim*.

[8] For example, Giorgio Strehler opened the Piccolo Teatro in Milan in 1948 with *Richard II*; Luchino Visconti directed *As You Like It* that same year in Rome, designed by Salvador Dalí; in the summer of 1949 Visconti staged *Troilus and Cressida* in the Boboli Gardens in Florence, designed by Franco Zeffirelli.

founder of the Birmingham Rep, to pump some life into its moribund annual festival; Jackson's first season brought in the young upstarts Peter Brook and Paul Scofield to shake things up. Jackson soon tired of the low budgets and retrograde attitudes of Stratford, but his tenure laid the groundwork for the arrival of Peter Hall and the creation of the Royal Shakespeare Company in 1960. Meanwhile the most important architectural development of postwar Shakespeare had occurred, the founding of the Canadian Stratford Shakespeare Festival in 1953 in a small railway town in Ontario, led by Tyrone Guthrie. The open-plan auditorium was heavily influenced by Bayreuth.

Why did festival institutions turn to Shakespeare as a standard? For a number of thinkers and cultural producers after the war, high art represented continuity with a more ordered, less threatening world. A play like *Richard II* with its dependence on artifice and ceremony amid cold-blooded politics, engaged precisely what seemed to have been threatened or lost, a sense that some human endeavours moved outside of time. Shakespeare was crucial to that conveniently invokable memory. I have argued elsewhere that the vast increase in public subsidy for Shakespeare and other classic performance in the following decades, on both sides of the Iron Curtain, was part of a general Cold War competition for aesthetic superiority, a kind of cultural arms race.[9] Here it is only necessary to note that this increase did occur on a large scale, that it brought Shakespeare to greater worldwide prominence, and that much of the advance in his reputation was the result of festival performance.

The location of major arts festivals and their calendar limitations meant that the bulk of audience members must travel to reach them, a circumstance that still applies today, though the journeys are almost always much easier than in 1947. This encourages a sense of pilgrimage to a sacred locale – something that Wagner understood implicitly – but it also means that their spectators are by definition cultural tourists. Tourism, the world's largest industry, has become almost ubiquitous. Over a decade ago Urry and Lash claimed that we live in the age of the 'end of tourism': travel has so infiltrated contemporary life that there is no divide between living and moving. Tourism is no longer just an industry but a way of being.[10]

[9] Dennis Kennedy, 'Shakespeare and the Cold War', *Four Hundred Years of Shakespeare in Europe*, ed. Ton Hoenselaars and Angel-Luis Pujante (University of Delaware Press, 2003).

[10] Scott Lash and John Urry, *Economies of Signs and Space* (London: Sage, 1994), p. 257; thanks to Karen Fricker whose 'Tourism, the Festival Marketplace and Robert Lepage's *The Seven Streams of the River Ota*' is relevant, in *Contemporary Theatre Review* 13.4 (2003), 79–93. This section depends in part on my 'Shakespeare and Cultural Tourism', *Theatre Journal* 50 (May 1998), 175–88. See also James Clifford, *Routes: Travel and Translation in the Late Twentieth Century*, which argues that

Tourism is about incident yet tourists, like wild-game hunters, want to bring trophies home to touch: the memory of their experiences is often commodified. Some aspects of tourism deliberately set out to create memories. Just as family snapshots prompt remembrance of things past, imagined and actual, so souvenirs serve as aides memoires of travel. But the literal souvenir, as Susan Stewart notes, by definition destroys its context and becomes a fetish that can never be more than partial, displaying 'the romance of the contraband'. We do not require souvenirs 'of events that are repeatable' but rather of those 'events whose materiality has escaped us'; thus the souvenir is 'a kind of failed magic'.[11] Most travellers now understand this. In a travel-saturated world, a model of the leaning tower of Pisa is no longer an innocent souvenir but a joke that signifies the tourist's self-awareness. It is kitsch, ironic and knowing. One of the most notable characteristics of postmodern tourism, or 'post-tourism', is avoidance of literal souvenirs and, in substitution, the conversion of experience into lateral material goods: tourists to Paris buy not models of the Eiffel Tower but fashionable clothes and shoes, marking the visit with purchases that back home enable a subtle display of where they have been. Photos and videos of famous or exotic places are of no value unless they include the traveller in the shot, the pictures not only reminiscent cues but material demonstrations that *I was there*.

The accumulation of touristic goods constitutes a personal heterotopia, the archive that materializes memory and that theoretically has no end point apart from the gatherer's death. Though based in individual consciousness and taste predilections, such archives, when they become extensive, often make their way into public museums and theatre collections, where they lose the personal attributes of the collector and stand alone as objective documents. Here we come face-to-face with the great paradox of performance and memory; in Certeau's terms, the tension between the discourses of psychoanalysis and history. If tourism, festivals and all performance are marked by temporal limits, how do we carry back the traces? We can overlay the past on the present (which is the psychology of the self) and we can materialize the past with photos, souvenir programmes, and the detritus of the gift shop (which moves beyond personal consciousness to archive a history). In terms of desire I suppose that the second is meant to prompt the first. Lots of shopping is available

that travel and the state of being between cultures most characterized the period and its anthropological study (Cambridge, Mass.: Harvard University Press, 1997).

[11] Susan Stewart, *On Longing: Narratives of the Miniature, the Gigantic, the Souvenir, the Collection* (Baltimore: Johns Hopkins University Press, 1984), pp. 135, 151.

to memorialize Shakespeare, and has been since the eighteenth century. At the Shakespeare Birthplace in Stratford you can buy Shakespeare watches, earrings, mugs, teapots, ceramic models of Tudor houses, even Desdemona's handkerchief, embroidered with magic in the web of it – which surely ought to come with a health warning.

The inadequacy of all methods of sustaining performance experience does not stop the attempt. In the words of Peggy Phelan, psychoanalysis shows that 'the experience of loss is one of the central repetitions of subjectivity'.[12] Why then do we wish to preserve incident? Because we can be so moved by performance that we do not want to release it? Because we want to share experience after the fact? It is its impermanence that makes performance distinctive and exciting, yet we often wish to staunch its loss. There an ineffable sadness at the heart of touring, and at the heart of spectating, the sadness of not owning the event, the melancholy of its disappearance into memory, a kind of death.

THE HOUSE OF MEMORY

In the pragmatist view of experience, the knower and the known act on each other, subject and object intermingling. Just as the spectacle does not exist without the spectator, so spectation is complete only at the moment of the spectacle. As Pierre Bourdieu put it in a different context, 'The body is in the social world but the social world is also in the body.'[13] All spectation, even when accomplished in a cohesive group, ultimately occurs in individual consciousness – we share the signal but not its reception. Thus any attempt to codify the memory of performance through historiographic methods, accumulating documents and arguing on the basis of evidence, necessarily exists outside the cognition of the spectators. In this sense performance analysis and history are always partial and forms of fiction, just as biography is: the imposition of a perception that is external to individual perception. Thus the job of performance history is to understand and give meaning to the event through social and aesthetic analysis, not to be the sum of the audience's experiences.

Esse est percipi, Berkeley famously wrote, and Beckett agreed: to be is to be perceived. We like to think we live in a shared world, not a

---

[12] Peggy Phelan, *Mourning Sex: Performing Public Memories* (London: Routledge, 1997), p. 5.
[13] Pierre Bourdieu, *In Other Words: Essays Towards a Reflexive Sociology*, trans. Matthew Adamson (Cambridge: Polity, 1990), p. 3.

solipsistic universe of nearly silent imaginings like Beckett's Hamm or Krapp or May. We seek agreed perception, tribal recollection, the discourse of consent. We solicit the perception of others: theatre is a space where the gathered may not know the other but can know that the other is proximate, perceivable, sharing memory.

This is the desire for collective knowledge, a common imaginary, cultural memory. What is cultural memory? It is not actual memory, not individual consciousness. It is a metaphor, a historical and social construct, a way of phrasing our desire for mutual experience. Of course tribes and nations and ethnicities build cultures on collective myths and common premises, even if the premises are contested. But such sharing does not mean that every member of the group holds in psychological memory all the important matters that make up group memory; if that were so there would be no need for cultural memory. Cultural memory is another fiction, forged by the centres of power and the careful distribution of knowledge, reinforced by repetition, education, and methods of information dissemination – through the ideological state apparatus, the media, cultural hegemony or 'necessary illusions'. Cultural memory is the narrative we accede to. The literary canon is one realization of cultural memory, supposedly created through general understanding but activated by powerful political forces. Theatrical repertory is also a canon, an agreed or imposed set of organized displays on our stages; it is not a chaotic archive but an ordered, certified pact with the past, an official memory.

The validity of cultural memory is tested most clearly in the idea of the museum. There are various types of museums – it is estimated there may be as many as 100,000 in the world today – and they can frame the works inside them in various ways, but generally speaking they 'masquerade the constructedness of the museum frame as "natural" historical truth or consensus'. As a result, according to the editors of a recent volume called *Grasping the World*, 'Most museumgoers are not prepared (educated) to analyze both the framework and its contents', because museums have traditionally presented themselves as transparent reliquaries of historical or artistic truth. But museums achieve this appearance only by careful staging, so that their contents are read in a particular light. Thus museums are performances, 'pedagogical and political in nature – whose practitioners are centrally invested in the activity of making the visible legible'.[14]

[14] Donald Preziosi and Claire Farago, 'What are Museums For?', general introduction to their edited volume *Grasping the World: the Idea of the Museum* (Aldershot: Ashgate, 2004), p. 2.

As Stephen Bann notes,[15] modes of organizing material in museums for two centuries have been polarized between 'two broad scenographic practices'. The first uses chronological or stylistic progression, whereby objects are arranged along a temporal axis, from the beginning of a period to its end, rooms following each other by centuries, so that the experience of viewing replicates the passage of time and divides the material into demarcated spaces. This corresponds to Certeau's historiographical approach to memory, where the relationship between the past and the present is one of absolute succession. The second scenographic practice arranges objects from a place, historical moment or school in such a way as to create the dramatic effect of the dining hall or bedchamber of a great house, surrounding the viewer with an illusion of being in the past. This impression in the spectator corresponds to the psychoanalytic approach to memory, imbricating or overlaying the past on the present. Thus we can say that 'the museum, as a house of memory, contained within itself what became distinct practices such as history and psychoanalysis'.[16]

But if museums are a kind of performance, so performance can be a kind of museum, as I implied earlier, especially with regard to Shakespeare. To be precise it is not the performance which has literal museum characteristics but rather the desire to remember it and align it with other performances which leads to cataloguing, critical memory and the tendency to decorporialize the event. We are only too aware that memory is unreliable, that it fades with time, that it distorts experiences and thus distorts our pasts, and can even be falsely implanted. Memory inevitably foregrounds the individual; as in my dreams, I am the constant protagonist of remembered events. So I am also the constant protagonist of my remembered spectation. Do I remember performances accurately? Is there an objective standard for remembering? If I am moved by a performance, will that affect my memory? Will my notes reflect my psychological experience as a spectator or will they already be part of history writing, an invented narrative? Is there a distance between my personal memory and my professional memory?

One set of answers lies in memory research. In the most relevant situation, a clear relationship has been established between emotion and memory. Generally speaking, emotion at the time of an event tends to intensify memory. A recent summary concludes 'there is no question that

---

[15] Stephen Bann, *The Clothing of Clio: A Study of the Representation of History in Nineteenth-Century Britain and France* (Cambridge: Cambridge University Press, 1984), pp. 77–92.

[16] Preziosi and Farago, 'What are Museums For?', pp. 15–16, 19.

emotional memories tend to be quite vivid'; in some studies a correlation
between vividness and emotionality has been shown to be as high as 0.90
for fearful events, 0.89 for sad events, and 0.71 for happy events. Further,
emotional events tend to be mulled over, amounting to 'memory
rehearsal', fixing the incident strongly into consciousness. Yet some vivid
memories of emotional events are completely inaccurate; there is no
consistent relationship between emotion and memorial accuracy.
Observers of an emotional incident (a car crash, for example) can recount
events in great detail, yet video recordings of the incident often reveal
those memories to be seriously inaccurate. (Think of the conflicting
reports of the John F. Kennedy assassination.)

Part of this phenomenon is explained by what neurological studies call
'flashbulb memory', the tendency to remember a powerful instant as if it
had been lit by a flash, and then to fill in the blanks with an invented set
of narrative connectives, the way we might try to make narrative sense of
our dreams. As early as 1959 'the Easterbrook Hypothesis', based on
animal studies, concluded that during an emotional event *arousal causes a
narrowing of attention*, so that an aroused organism becomes less sensitive
to information at the "periphery" of an event'. Extrapolating this to
humans is problematic, but some invitation to do so is provided by a
pattern observed among crime victims known as the *weapon focus effect*:
'witnesses to crimes often seem to "lock" their attention onto the
criminal's weapon and seem oblivious to much else in the scene'. They
will remember the gun or the knife vividly but have poor memory for
other details, including what the criminal looked like.[17]

From this I conclude four related things about performance memory.
One, I am always the protagonist of recollection; though my companions
and other spectators may be in my mind, their experiences are irrelevant
unless they intruded at the time upon my experience. Two, the more the
performance moved or excited me, the less likely my memory of it is
completely accurate; this is especially true of foundational performances
I witnessed as a young man which impressed me deeply, where memory
rehearsal has been frequent. Three, my heightened or flashbulb memory
of specific details may well have caused me to create a context for those
moments that is independent of what actually occurred. Four, 'playing
back' my memory of performance is itself a type of dream performance
and thus doubly subject to the predicaments of accuracy.

[17] Daniel Reisberg and Friderike Heuer, 'Memory for Emotional Events', in *Memory and Emotion*,
    ed. Daniel Reisberg and Paula Hertel (Oxford: Oxford University Press, 2004), pp. 4–5, 7.

Memory and performance are complicated by the prevalence of mechanical and electronic recording, but the complications are often not what they seem. Film and video documentation of performance that we once witnessed live offers the chance to re-examine details, to correct memorial mistakes, and through replay of specific moments to analyse incidental or subtle effects that we may not have noticed in the original performance. For students and historians such recordings often stand in for presentations not seen in the flesh. But it is well recognized in theatre and performance studies that film and video are always partial witnesses, recording only what the camera can see or the operator has chosen to see, denying the force and atmosphere of live performance: they are transformatively false to what they appear to document.[18] Recordings are evidence of live events but must be used with methodological care. Shakespeare productions made as films are a different matter, but we must make a crucial distinction between viewing as an ordinary spectator, the movie running from beginning to end, and using the DVD version for teaching or research, where start and stop, replay and slomo, and frame-by-frame viewing alter the experience substantially. Watching Branagh's *Hamlet* as a movie in a public cinema – if you have the stamina – is psychologically and phenomenologically similar to watching a live theatre performance; from the standpoint of memory the only significant difference is that we can look at it again. The opportunity for complete review is of great importance to the historian of film and performance, but is not very significant a spectator on a night out, who is left with the problem of memory.

FORGETTING *HAMLET*

Is it possible to imagine a world without *Hamlet?* The most famous play in our solar system has been part of Western thought for four hundred years, and now has a reasonable hold on some Asian and African cultures as well. It is a simple matter for journalist-critics, especially London critics, to compare one production or one actor to the last or one from forty years ago. Ironically the play is manifestly about forgetting. From the Ghost's echoing charges to his son – 'remember me!', 'do not forget!'– to the Gravedigger's memento mori, from Hamlet's refusal to remember his love letters to Ophelia to Fortinbras's claim of 'some rights of memory

---

[18] See, for example, Marco de Marinis, ' "A Faithful Betrayal of Performance": Notes on the use of Video in Theatre', *New Theatre Quarterly* 1 (1985), 383–9.

in this kingdom', the tragedy is worried about the failure of memory, its unreliability, the final forgetfulness of death. And for Freud, as we have seen, the play enacts the terrors of the detour-return, bringing the discarded past into the present, overlaying the forgotten on the remembered, re-biting the protagonist with his unsolicited history. 'There's rosemary, that's for remembrance': if Freud had been a homeopath, that could have been his remedy for sufferers of repressed memory. Tincture of rosemary, opheliate of oblivion.

I would like to forget *Hamlet*, the endless quotations, the burden of references, the three texts, 'memorial reconstruction', the stories not completed, the phantom presences endlessly returning: a consummation devoutly to be wished. But as my starting paradox from Žižek puts it, if we really want to forget something 'we must first summon up the strength to remember it properly'. Is it possible to remember properly a text and performances that have been so stitched into my memory that they have become part of me? When I think of *Hamlet* can I ever think of the play or only my incorporation of it? I carry into each new production a jumble of reminiscences: of my first reading almost half a century ago, of many prior performances, my study of its textual, critical and stage history, its location within Western culture, high and low, what I have written and thought about it. I am not a spectator, I am a museum of *Hamlet*.

But even a naive or first-time spectator, a young person seeing the films with Mel Gibson or Ethan Hawke, is likely aware of some of the historical burden. Though the drama may be about forgetting, or trying to forget, its eminence constantly invites considerations of personal and cultural memory: at *Hamlet* we are all guilty cultural creatures sitting at a play.

Perhaps that is why it achieved added significance after the Second World War. In Britain and America the play continued to be seen in the romantic tradition, but things were different further east where issues of historical memory came spectacularly forward.[19] I think of Nikolai Okhlopkov's 'Iron Curtain' *Hamlet* in Moscow in 1954, remembering the Stalinist years of deliberate forgetting. Or the version by Yuri Lyubimov, playing for nine years from 1971, which presented a world of forgetfulness, a massive knitted curtain sweeping everybody into unmarked graves. Or the 'electronic' *Hamlet* by Hansgünter Heyme in Cologne in 1979, in which characters videoed one another as if to prove their existences; at the end Ophelia, dressed as a racing driver, played Fortinbras, as if no one

---

[19] These productions are treated in detail in my *Looking at Shakespeare: A Visual History of Twentieth-Century Performance*, 2nd edn (Cambridge: Cambridge University Press, 2001).

could quite remember the plot. More important still was Heiner Müller's seven-and-a-half hour amalgamation of *Hamlet* and his own by-product play *Hamletmaschine* in East Berlin in 1990; during rehearsals the Berlin Wall came down, the state collapsed, the Cold War ended, the grand Soviet experiment replaced by the consumerism of postmodernity. We are forgetting everything, the production said, okay, let's forget everything.

In 1989 the Museum of Jurassic Technology was established in Culver City in Los Angeles by David Wilson, a special effects man in Hollywood and a visionary collector. Two years later he opened the Delani/Sonnabend Halls as a permanent exhibition, devoted to Geoffrey Sonnabend, 'neurophysiologist and memory researcher', whose three-volume work called *Obliscence: Theories of Forgetting and the Problem of Matter* was published by Northwestern University Press in 1946. Sonnabend, according to the summary leaflet on sale at the museum, 'departed from all previous memory research with the premise that memory is an illusion'. Forgetting, he held, was 'the inevitable outcome of all experience':

We, amnesiacs all, condemned to live in an eternally fleeting present, have created the most elaborate of human constructions, memory, to buffer ourselves against the intolerable knowledge of the irreversible passage of time and the irretrievability of its moments and events.[20]

While Sonnabend did not 'deny that the experience of memory existed', his work claimed that 'what we experience as memories are in fact confabulations, artificial constructions of our own design built around sterile particles of retained experience which we attempt to make live again by infusions of imagination'. Through a series of displays and diagrams, the exhibit creates a sense of Sonnabend's life and work, detailing his 'Model of Obliscence' in which the 'Cone of Obliscence' transgresses the 'Plane of Experience': first experience, then memory, then forgetting (see figure 51). Angels and ministers of grace defend us.

The theory of obliscence has a firm connection to the experience of performance, prompting visitors to learn more about Sonnabend and his relationship to Madalena Delani, 'a singer of art songs and operatic material' with a short-term memory problem, who influenced his thought. There is only one difficulty: no matter how large the library, you

[20] I rely in part on Susan Crane's 'Curious Cabinets and Imaginary Museums', in Crane, *Museums and Memory*, pp. 60–80, where the Sonnabend leaflet is reprinted entire on pp. 81–90; these quotations from p. 85. Its text is also available on the Museum of Jurassic Technology's website www.mjt.org (last accessed June 2005).

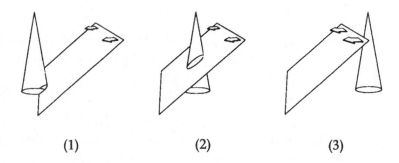

(1)   (2)   (3)

(1) being involved in an experience
(2) remembering an experience
(3) having forgotten an experience.

51 Sonnabend's 'Model of Obliscence' showing the three stages of experience.

will not find a copy of *Obliscence* in it. The book, Sonnabend, Delani and the theory have never existed except in the Museum of Jurassic Technology. Even the word 'obliscence' is an invention, though it has obvious cognates that give it credibility. The exhibition is a sophisticated – I almost said hoax, but that's not right, it is no more a hoax than *Hamlet*. A gallery of curiosities, rewarding as well as mysterious, it is a memory space which draws in its viewers by silently exposing the constructedness of museums and the nature of their performances. From this standpoint traditional museums might be considered hoaxes, since they customarily hide their historiographic and theoretical principles behind the mist of transcendent art. By exhibiting with a straight face a teasing fabrication, the Museum of Jurassic Technology calls cultural memory into question and leaves us with a sense of displacement long after a visit. The exhibit suggests that memory, both personal and professional, is a desperate grappling with time and incident which inevitably alters the value of experience. In effect the exhibit asks that we not forget it, but what is it we will remember?

Is remembering *Hamlet* inevitably false to the encounter of the spectacle? By chronicling Shakespeare performance do we investigate and question cultural value or merely notate the changes that time begets? Is performance history a security against forgetting or a forlorn bell tolling us back to our sad selves? Does history supplant personal memory? Is cultural memory inevitably false to the self? I do not have the answers, but I can summarize what I see as the problems. First, the friction between official or emergent cultural memory and a spectator's personal memory is irresolvable; when the historical encounters the psychological, or the accumulated stability of the archive encounters the fleeting instance of performance, we become uneasily aware of the predicament of time in art. Second, the materializing of personal memory through objects and souvenirs, while understandable as an attempt to recapture past incident, generates further anxiety about the value of experience which escapes capture. And last, recall itself, a private performance of the past in the way that museums are public performances of the past, is subject to so many fallibilities that it might as well be a species of forgetting. We cannot forget *Hamlet* but what is it we will remember?

I fear that Geoffrey Sonnabend has been presiding over this essay, underlining my hesitations about the use of psychology and psychoanalysis in performance history. I have been writing about the spectator for more than a decade but have engaged with the sociological, political and economic rather than the psychological, where I am manifestly tentative. Psychoanalysis was founded on the idea that recollection of repressed trauma, guided and enforced by the doctor, is healing and liberating. But away from the couch Freudian and Lacanian explanations of behaviour seem to me to place too much stress on infancy, not enough on social milieu or the exercise of will. A memory-based psychoanalytic approach can work therapeutically but feels simplistic when applied to spectators who operate both as individuals and as groups. Even Certeau's brilliant understanding of Freud seems a bit soft to me, unwilling to engage with ideology and political power as Foucault did. Despite its importance to the subject, we know very little about the psychology of the spectator; or, to be more accurate, what I know tends to be about myself. Like that repressed ghost scenting the morning air, I have used up my time without providing the kind of evidence that leads to an unmistakable conclusion. 'Adieu, adieu, adieu! remember me', that haunting spectre says, but what is it we will remember?

Afterword

Stephen Orgel

In my youth, we went to the theatre all the time. My father invested in plays and I was taken to some historic opening nights – *Death of a Salesman*, *Guys and Dolls* – though most of the openings I was taken to were followed very shortly by closings. I was also taken to whatever Shakespeare came along – New York Shakespeare in the mid and late 1940s was resolutely unadventurous: ceremonial, declamatory, poetic and arty. It is my impression that I saw Maurice Evans over and over in *Richard II*, though it was probably twice at most. Margaret Webster's *Tempest*, when I was thirteen, I recall dimly now as filmy and 'magical'; in the history of the American stage it is chiefly notable for its Caliban, the powerful black actor Canada Lee, of whom I have no recollection at all. I do remember the Ariel, the ballerina Vera Zorina, whose wispy pirouettes contributed a sense of airy nothingness to the play – a sense reinforced by Webster's replacing Prospero's epilogue with his 'Our revels now are ended' speech. I saw Katherine Cornell's *Antony and Cleopatra* in the same year – the definitively middle-aged Antony was Godfrey Tearle, who looked alternately like Franklin D. Roosevelt and my father, and played the role accordingly. The production is considered significant today, to judge from the numerous citations of it on the web, because Charlton Heston made his Broadway debut in it, 'in a minor role' or 'in a number of roles', depending on which website you believe. This probably is, in fact, all that is worth saying about it: almost sixty years later I can still feel the incredible tedium of that evening. It is true that at school we had a good deal of fun doing *A Midsummer Night's Dream*, for some reason twice in three years – doubtless it was thought to be the only safe Shakespeare. I was Bottom the first time, Snout the second (Snout was more my speed, and I can still recite Wall's speech). But primarily, Shakespeare was boring.

In 1950, however, when I was sixteen, *As You Like It* opened on Broadway, directed by Michael Benthall of the Old Vic, and with

346

Katherine Hepburn as Rosalind – or actually, mostly as Ganymede. I went, over and over. Margaret Marshall, reviewing the performance in *The Nation*, found Hepburn completely miscast, a 'tense, modern, self-conscious, rather spoiled young woman, speaking in a tremolo-ridden voice under some quite unmotivated strain' (4 February 1950, p. 20); but for me she was wonderful, breezy and poised, and the production was light and lively and full of music – it was the first Shakespeare I had ever seen that was really fun. But none of that was what kept me coming back. I kept coming back for Orlando, William Prince, primarily a stage actor with a modest film career (most notably as Christian in Jose Ferrer's great 1950 *Cyrano de Bergerac*), who finally settled into a long run of soap-opera roles. I was to see him again as the lead in *I Am a Camera* a couple of years later, when I was in college, but about that performance I recall almost nothing. His Orlando, however, was a profound experience for me, and I can still see him in the role with complete clarity.

William Prince was tall, handsome, easygoing and ironic, and his Orlando wore white tights. When I was growing up – indeed, until I was about forty – it was customary to say about gay teenagers that they were confused about their sexuality; but in my case, and I imagine in most cases, this was entirely incorrect. I had been perfectly well aware for several years that my sexual interest was exclusively in men, but I was also keenly aware that it ought not to be – the more keenly, as the son of a Freudian analyst, who considered my condition both a case of arrested development and as much his fault as mine (he was quite clear about my being at fault); the fault, he insisted, was correctable and needed correction. This was the only source of confusion about the matter; and I was to spend years trying manfully, so to speak, to refashion myself into my father's image, so unpromisingly represented by the leaden Antony of Godfrey Tearle. But William Prince in white tights should have served me as irrefutable evidence that my father was wrong. Orlando dazzled me the moment he appeared; when he turned his back he smote me to the heart, and I knew there was nothing I wanted out of life more than the world of possibilities those white tights concealed and revealed.

Such moments come as revelations – irrecoverable ones, alas. They are also of the essence of theatre. An account of the lecherous component of audience response would surely be worth writing. Theatre has a long history of eliciting lust as a way of exciting audiences, though it is a history that has yet to be produced. Attacks on the stage by Tertullian, Stephen Gosson, William Prynne are easy to dismiss because they imply that lechery is all theatre is about; but a less totalizing argument – that there is a sexual component to all theatre – would surely be unexceptionable: why else are stars attractive? We are quite comfortable pointing to the sexual component in the development of transvestite parts for women on the Restoration stage, whereby men could see them in tights, and modern theatre from burlesque to the Ziegfeld Follies fulfilled every negative criterion of classic antitheatrical polemics; but such histories are unproblematic for us because the lechery they acknowledge is 'normative', i.e., heterosexual. Starting in the late 1960s, however, theatre began undressing men, not in the equivalent of male burlesque houses, whatever these might be, but on the legitimate stage and often in classic plays; and this is a development that criticism has found much more difficult to accommodate. Reviewers have generally been hostile to it, ascribing it merely to a desire to shock, but such a claim is surely only a cover for admitting that it is genuinely exciting, and not only for the gay men in the audience – hence directors keep doing it.

My touchstone for the nude Shakespeare was John Barton's *Troilus and Cressida*, a 1968 RSC production that moved to the Aldwych in London in 1969, where I saw it. Most reviewers noted, with varying degrees of outrage and embarrassment, Alan Howard's waspishly effeminate Achilles, his overtly sexual relationship with Patroclus and the insertion of a homosexual orgy scene quite uncalled for by the text; but only an unnamed reporter for the *Manchester Evening News* alerted potential audiences to what was, for me, the most blatantly sexual element in the production, the fact that, as he put it, 'The opposing armies fight in near nudity' (24.6.69). The nudity was indeed *very* near, and, for the men, universal: Michael Williams, the superb Troilus, was especially memorable in only a tiny cache-sexe (Harold Hobson, in one of the few favourable reviews, noted 'the extreme beauty of Michael Williams's Troilus' (Sunday Times 17.8.69)), but even the middle-aged Ulysses and elderly Nestor appeared (unfortunately, to my still youthfully unforgiving eyes) in scarcely more. As for 'normative' lechery, Helen Mirren's Cressida was, at one point, undressed, or rather unwrapped from a bedsheet as she twirled across the stage away from Troilus; but the final moment of revelation coincided exactly with her arrival at the wings and disappearance offstage – for exclusively heterosexual voyeurs, the play was a tease.

John Barton's idea here must have been to develop a whole new dimension of transgressiveness in this very transgressive play, but that cannot be the whole story. The actors had beautiful costumes, and out of their costumes most of them were more beautiful still – it was an

impressively lithe and well-built cast, and for anyone who was not genuinely shocked or homophobic, the production was visually stunning.
Dressed and undressed, it was certainly the most beautiful *Troilus and
Cressida* I have ever seen, and it assumed that the norm of beauty was
male – indeed, the role of Helen, the most beautiful woman in history,
was cut. It also assumed, for the men in the audience, a degree of universal homosexual desire, and it is difficult to imagine that this was not
the source of much of the critical outrage it generated. If you admitted
that you liked it, what were you admitting?

All history is memory, and the history of theatre, which we patronize
for our pleasure, is a history of desire. If theatre holds the mirror up to
nature, it can only reveal how much in nature is sexual – Hamlet reveals it
himself, proposing, as 'The Mousetrap' begins, to lie in Ophelia's lap.
The exciting in theatre is never very far from the shocking but even
indignation is a form of wonder. It is a commonplace that we find in
Shakespeare what we wish to find – but how could it be otherwise? As a
dramatic canon endlessly repeated in endless refigurations, Shakespeare
has offered audiences an infinite range of pleasure, proving uniquely
responsive to changing tastes and thus occupying a uniquely poly-
morphous place in that history. Shakespearean drama has increasingly
constituted, over the centuries, a cultural memory, serving as the theatre
where we acknowledge, fashion and perform the desire essential to the
creation of our selves.

Index